PRAISE FOR *THE DEVIL'S HAND*

"Take my word for it, James Reece is one rowdy motherf***er. Get ready!"

—Chris Pratt, all around great guy and star of "The Terminal List" on Amazon Prime

"Carr delivers engrossing backstory, incorporates current events seamlessly, and never flinches from breathless depictions of violence."

—*Publishers Weekly*

"Carr continues to draw on his own experiences as a SEAL to give the story a level of realism that writers who've not actually served sometimes have a hard time achieving."

—*Booklist*

"*The Terminal List* is widely regarded as one of the best debut thrillers of all-time, and rightfully so, but *The Devil's Hand* is even better, and should go down as one of the best books in the genre, period."

—The Real Book Spy

"An action thriller extraordinaire that is not to be missed."

—*Providence Journal*

PRAISE FOR *IN THE BLOOD*

"Gripping . . . fast-paced . . . fans will get their money's worth."

—*Publishers Weekly*

"Quality plot, well-developed characters, and not too over-the-top. Add James Reece to your list that includes Harvath (Brad Thor), Reacher (Lee Child), Bob Lee Swagger (Stephen Hunter), et al."

—Men Reading Books

"Hands down, *In the Blood* is the best book I've read this year. I've said from the beginning that covering Carr is what I'd imagine it would have been like to discover Vince Flynn at the beginning of his career . . . Carr deserves to be mentioned alongside all-time greats like Flynn, Thor, Clancy, and Silva . . ."

—The Real Book Spy

"*In the Blood* is Carr's best book to date and demonstrates a mastery of the genre—it rightly belongs in the constellation of Clancy, Thor, Morrell, and Flynn."

—Townhall.com

PRAISE FOR *SAVAGE SON*

"A great book . . . its f*cking riveting!"

—Joe Rogan

"A rare gut-punch writer, full of grit and insight, who we will be happily reading for years to come."

—Gregg Hurwitz, *New York Times* bestselling author of the Orphan X series

"Absolutely fantastic! *Savage Son* is savagely good, and puts Jack Carr at the very top of the thriller genre."

—Marc Cameron, *New York Times* bestselling author

"A badass, high velocity round of reading! The three parts of this masterfully crafted experience says it all—THE TRAP, THE STALK, THE KILL."

—Clint Emerson, former Navy SEAL and *New York Times* bestselling author of *100 Deadly Skills* and *The Right Kind of Crazy*

"Carr writes both from the gut and a seemingly infinite reservoir of knowledge in the methods of human combat. Loved it!"

—Chris Hauty, *LA Times* bestselling author of *New York Times* Editors' Choice *Deep State*

"Jack Carr triples down with *Savage Son*. From the book's gut-wrenching opening to its sleep-stealing conclusion, Jack's homage to *The Most Dangerous Game* delivers the goods and then some."

—Don Bentley, author of *Without Sanction*

"A masterfully told, heart-thumping tale of modern conflict."

—Lt. Col. Oliver North, USMC (Ret.), *New York Times* bestselling author of *The Rifleman* and *Under Fire*

"*Savage Son* is amazing! This is the kind of book every author wished he could write . . . mind-blowingly good!"

—Simon Gervais, former RCMP counterterrorism officer and bestselling author of *Hunt Them Down*

"Accurate, intense, and raw, *Savage Son* taps into our most primal of instincts. Jack Carr draws you into this predatory pursuit like no other because he's lived it!"

—John Barklow, hunter, navy diver, special operations cold weather survival instructor, and Sitka Gear Big Game product manager

"If you like a fresh approach to action with authentic details and a believable main character, these books are for you. I'm a fan."

—David Morrell, *New York Times* bestselling author of *First Blood*, *The Brotherhood of the Rose*, and *Murder as a Fine Art*

"Jack Carr is back and at the top of his game in *Savage Son*, a heart-pounding, sleep-robbing, edge-of-your-seat thriller."

—Joshua Hood, 82nd Airborne veteran and author of Robert Ludlum's *The Treadstone Resurrection*

"Whether you are a hunter of four-legged game or of man, *Savage Son* will stoke the inner fire of your soul. Jack Carr's attention to detail and experience from the battlefield to the backcountry draw the reader into the field to experience the art of war through the eyes of a man who has lived it."

—Cole Kramer, Kodiak Island Brown bear guide and outfitter

PRAISE FOR *TRUE BELIEVER*

"This is seriously good. I mean—seriously."

—Lee Child, #1 *New York Times* bestselling author of *Past Tense*

"A powerful, thoughtful, realistic, at times terrifying thriller that I could not put down. A terrific addition to the genre, Jack Carr and his alter-ego protagonist, James Reece, continue to blow me away."

—Mark Greaney, #1 *New York Times* bestselling author of *Mission Critical*

"Jack Carr creates an incredibly vivid, emotional, action-packed tapestry of carnage and death."

—Justen Charters, Black Rifle Coffee Company, *Coffee or Die Magazine*

"Packs a punch. Carr's second effort is a well-crafted thriller with timely reflections on the increasingly complicated world of international terrorism."

—*Kirkus Reviews*

PRAISE FOR *THE TERMINAL LIST*

"Double the trouble, twice the action, and quadruple the enjoyment. Careful while reading this one, it could leave a mark."

—Steve Berry, #1 *New York Times* bestselling author of *The Lost Order*

"Absolutely awesome! So powerful, so pulse-pounding, so well-written—rarely do you read a debut novel this damn good."

—Brad Thor, #1 *New York Times* bestselling author of *Spymaster*

"Told with a deft hand and a keen eye for detail, *The Terminal List* . . . is explosive and riveting."

—Kevin Maurer, co-author of the #1 bestselling *No Easy Day* and *American Radical*

"Like a bullet from Jack Carr's custom-built sniper rifle, the story arrives on target with devastating impact. Trust me, you won't be able to put this one down!"

—Mark Owen, *New York Times* bestselling author of *No Easy Day* and *No Hero*

"Crackerjack plotting, vivid characters both in and out of uniform, and a relentless pace to a worthy finish. It's a great start!"

—Stephen Hunter, #1 *New York Times* bestselling author of *G-Man*

"An extremely unique thriller! Absolutely intense!"

—Chuck Norris

"Bravo! Jack Carr is the real deal!"

—Sean Parnell, *New York Times* bestselling author of *Outlaw Platoon*

"Not since Stephen Hunter have we seen an author who so accurately captures the essence of the gun–Jack Carr is a shooter."

—Clint Smith, founder of Thunder Ranch Shooting School

"Jack Carr's *The Terminal List* is a page-turning thriller you won't be able to put down. The detail-focused writing, personal characters, and heart-pounding plot line will keep you coming back for more. An absolute must read!"

—Katie Pavlich, *New York Times* bestselling author, *Fox News* contributor

"Any fan of the novels by Brad Thor and the late Vince Flynn will realize that Jack Carr will soon be joining their ranks."

—*The Washington Times*

ALSO BY JACK CARR

In the Blood

Savage Son

True Believer

The Terminal List

THE DEVIL'S HAND

A THRILLER

JACK CARR

EMILY BESTLER BOOKS

ATRIA

NEW YORK LONDON TORONTO SYDNEY NEW DELHI

For Doctor Robert Bray, Major, United States Air Force, for reasons that remain classified,

and

for the sentinels out there tonight, holding the line for us all.

EMILY BESTLER BOOKS

ATRIA

An Imprint of Simon & Schuster, Inc.
1230 Avenue of the Americas
New York, NY 10020

First Emily Bestler Books/Atria paperback edition February 2023

EMILY BESTLER BOOKS / ATRIA PAPERBACKS and colophon are trademarks of Simon & Schuster, Inc.

For information about special discounts for bulk purchases, please contact Simon & Schuster Special Sales at 1-866-506-1949 or business@simonandschuster.com.

The Simon & Schuster Speakers Bureau can bring authors to your live event. For more information, or to book an event, contact the Simon & Schuster Speakers Bureau at 1-866-248-3049 or visit our website at www.simonspeakers.com.

Interior design by Erika R. Genova

Manufactured in the United States of America

9 10

Library of Congress Cataloging-in-Publication Data has been applied for.

ISBN 978-1-9821-2374-1
ISBN 978-1-9821-8462-9 (pbk)
ISBN 978-1-9821-2376-5 (ebook)

Buried within the 9,723-word text of Executive Order 12333, United States Intelligence Activities, is this sentence in Part 2, Paragraph 13:

2.11 Prohibition on Assassination. No person employed by or acting on behalf of the United States Government shall engage in or conspire to engage in assassination.

Seven days after 9/11, Congress passed a 275-word resolution titled the 2001 Authorization for the Use of Military Force. This document granted the president of the United States the authority to bring individuals and countries involved in the attack to justice. Twenty years later, it remains the sole legal basis for the continuing War on Terror.

. . . to kill the Americans and their allies—civilians and military—is an individual duty for every Muslim who can do it in any country in which it is possible to do it . . .

—AL-QAEDA *FATWĀ*, 1998

Im ba l'hargekha, hashkem l'hargo
If someone comes to kill you, rise up and kill him first.

—TALMUDIC EDICT

PREFACE

ON THE MORNING OF September 11, 2001, nineteen men boarded four planes at Logan, Newark, and Dulles International Airports. All aircraft were bound for the West Coast. The flights were selected because they had the requisite fuel required for transcontinental flights.

Two hours later, the United States would be at war, a war that continues today.

This narrative is not about the events of that September morning. Rather, it is a reflection on the knowledge our adversaries acquired from our response to terrorism in the Middle East and Europe from 1979 through the first half of 2001 and what they have gleaned in the two decades following the seminal attack that changed the course of history.

This is a novel of asymmetric warfare.

I have long wondered what the enemy has learned watching us on the field of battle for what is now twenty years of sustained combat. What lessons have they learned and how have they altered their tactics and strategies to incorporate those lessons? If I were the enemy, what would I have learned?

These are questions I pondered while in uniform and continue to contemplate as an author. Our adversaries have observed us at the poker table for twenty years while having the benefit of seeing our cards. They have studied our tactics and seen our technologies evolve; they've observed our shifting goals and objectives. They have taken notes as we fought in Afghanistan, Iraq, Syria, and other flashpoints around the globe. Our response to a pandemic and the civil unrest plaguing our cities at a time when domestic political ideologies seem irreconcilable has not gone unnoticed. They see a country divided. Have they accounted for that division in their battle plans?

It has been almost twenty years since that September morning. Our enemy has been patient. They have been watching, learning, and adapting. Russia, China, North Korea, Iran, terrorist groups, and super-empowered individuals have been waiting, identifying gaps in our defenses and refining plots that exploit our weaknesses. It is my sincere hope that the operation you read about in the following pages is not currently being planned by a foreign intelligence service. We would be wise to remember that the Athenian historian Thucydides in the Melian Dialogue of his *History of the Peloponnesian War* characterizes *hope* as *danger's comforter.* In modern military and intelligence parlance, the ancient Greek general's text translates as *hope is not a course of action.* While this is true, hope is oftentimes all one has in times of despair. The lesson is one as old as time: Be prepared.

There is arguably no military text as influential as *The Art of War.* The Chinese military strategist and philosopher Sun Tzu knew that "the supreme art of war is to subdue the enemy without fighting." In an asymmetric confrontation, this is of extreme importance for the foe that does not possess a nuclear arsenal. How then would they defeat a superpower? "All warfare is based on deception." The teachings of the Warring States–period general are not foreign concepts to our adversaries—adversaries who play the long game. With those two idioms in mind, if your mission was to destroy a modern empire, what would you do?

This is also a book on the ethics, morality, and legality of targeted assassinations, what the Israelis call *Chissulim*, or eliminations, as an instrument of state power. Is there a difference between using a Reaper

UAV to take out an enemy combatant with an AGM-114 Hellfire or GBU-38 JDAM from fifty thousand feet and sending a 180-grain .300 Winchester Magnum through that same terrorist's brain stem from a thousand yards out? How does the enemy view those different methods of killing? Has the increasing reliance on UAVs to deliver death remotely had the intended effect? Has it saved American lives, or has it recruited more of what Dr. David Kilcullen calls "accidental guerrillas" to the cause?

On September 11, 2001, there were certain groups who stood shoulder to shoulder watching the twin towers fall on television, men with certain skills, men whose only mission in life was to be prepared for war. It is not openly discussed, but within this fraternity there were those who had but one thought: *God, I wish I was on one of those planes.* They are called to the fight: protectors, warriors, guardians. They are out there tonight. They are hunting. If the war returns to the home front, you want one of these sentinels standing by your side, armed and ready.

Prior to 9/11 these men would have chosen airline seats by the windows. Based on the data from previous hijackings, they knew this allowed them to be harder to physically strike in an initial violent takeover of the plane's cabin when terrorists needed to make examples of certain passengers to keep the others in line. Window seats bought them time to observe and plan a course of action. 9/11 shifted the hijacking paradigm. Following that Tuesday morning, those same guardians began selecting seats in the aisle so they could react to a threat instantly. They appear no different than anyone else, unless you know what to look for, unless you are one of them.

Researching this novel was an intensely emotional experience: listening to the calls from those on the hijacked aircraft to their loved ones on the ground, reading about those who perished, trapped in collapsing buildings, some electing to jump to their deaths rather than be burned alive.

I encourage everyone to visit the 9/11 memorial in lower Manhattan. Take your time. Heed its lessons.

As we move past the twentieth anniversary of the attacks and into our third decade of continuous warfare, do we have a clear vision of how this conflict ends? Or has our short-war strategy applied to a long-term conflict condemned our children and grandchildren to fight the sons and grandsons of the men who planned the deadliest terrorist attack in history? Do we still not understand the nature of the conflict in which we are engaged?

I fear we may all know the answer.

Jack Carr
Park City, Utah
September 11, 2020

CHRONOLOGY OF EVENTS

1953: CIA-Sponsored Iranian Coup d'état
1979: Iranian Revolution
1979: Iran Hostage Crisis Begins
1980: Operation Eagle Claw
1980: Iran–Iraq War Begins
1981: Iran Hostage Crisis Ends
1983: United States Embassy Bombing, Beirut, Lebanon
1983: U.S. Marine Barracks Bombing, Beirut, Lebanon
1983: United States Embassy Bombing, Kuwait City, Kuwait
1984: CIA Beirut Station Chief William F. Buckley Kidnapping
1984: United States Embassy Annex Bombing, Beirut, Lebanon
1985: TWA Flight 847 Hijacking
1985: Iran-Contra Affair Begins
1985: *Achille Lauro* Hijacking
1985: CIA Beirut Station Chief William Buckley Executed
1987: Iran-Contra Affair Ends
1987: Operation Earnest Will Begins
1988: Lieutenant Colonel William Higgins Kidnapping, Lebanon
1988: USS *Vincennes* Shoots Down Iran Air Flight 655
1988: Iran–Iraq War Ends
1988: Operation Earnest Will Ends

1988: Pan Am Flight 103 Bombing

1990: Lieutenant Colonel William Higgins Executed, Lebanon

1990: Iraq Invasion of Kuwait

1990: Operation Desert Shield

1991: Operation Desert Storm

1993: World Trade Center Bombing

1996: Khobar Towers Bombing

1998: United States East Africa Embassy Bombings

2000: USS *Cole* Bombing

2001: Ahmad Shah Massoud Assassinated

2001: September 11 Terrorist Attacks

2001: United States Invasion of Afghanistan

2003: United States Invasion of Iraq

2006: Abu Musab al-Zarqawi Killed

2008: Imad Mughniyeh Killed

2011: Osama bin Laden Killed

2020: Qasem Soleimani Killed

2021: Twentieth Anniversary of the September 11 Terrorist Attacks

What's past is prologue.

—William Shakespeare

THE DEVIL'S HAND

PROLOGUE

FOR THOSE NOT INVOLVED in the operation, the day that changed the world started no differently than any other. For a select few, there had been a slight variation to their routines. Aliyah Hajjar was one of those few.

For the past year, Aliyah had been employed by JetClean Industries, a commercial janitorial service specializing in aviation, cleaning planes between flights at Boston's Logan International Airport. She spent her days working her way up and down the aisles with the rest of her cleaning crew, picking trash out of seat back pockets, restocking the lavatories with toilet paper, disinfecting the galleys, and arranging the seat belts.

Aliyah did not mind the work. It gave her time away from her home where she could talk with the other Muslim women assigned to her rotation. It was also time away from her husband.

He had never struck her when they lived in Hamburg. The beatings had started once they moved to the United States after receiving their five-year business visas from the embassy in Berlin. At first, Aliyah thought it was because she had failed to bear him children. Now she knew differently.

She had not understood why the man who had studied to be an accountant in Germany was busing tables and cleaning the kitchen at a Moroccan restaurant outside Cambridge. Their meager take-home pay barely managed to cover the rent and put food on the table of their small Watertown apartment. The first time she pressed him on the subject, he slapped her across the face. Even now the memory of the sting, compounded by shock, caused her eyes to water. When she attempted to turn and run, he grabbed her by the throat and threw her onto their secondhand couch that reeked of mildew, squeezing the life from her as he screamed that she was not to question him again.

Later that night, there had been a knock at the door. Her husband had pointed to the bedroom and told her to stay there until he came to get her. Pressing her ear to the doorjamb, she strained to hear the short, hushed conversation. She recognized her native tongue but could not make out the words. She then put herself to bed and pretended to sleep. The next day, after work, she searched the small apartment and found an unfamiliar suitcase in the broom closet by the entrance. It was filled with cash. She tried to put it back exactly as she had found it.

That night he beat her again. This time, it took a few days for the swelling to go down. When she did return to Logan International, the hijab hid the marks, her bloodshot eyes all that were visible between the black slits.

From then on, she never touched an unfamiliar suitcase, backpack, or bag found in the apartment. She knew it was *hawala*, the ancient system of money transfer originating along the Silk Road. It allowed for the movement of funds around the world without the digital trail left by banks and wire transfers. *Hawalaladars* usually took a percentage of the transfer for their trouble, yet Aliyah noticed no perceivable change in their finances. As a Muslim woman with a strict Islamic upbringing, she was barred from knowing the specifics of their financial situation. She just knew the couch was moldy and her husband took no steps to replace it.

Two weeks ago, she'd returned home from work a little earlier than normal. She had not been feeling well for a few days. As she fished the keys from her purse, she fumbled and dropped them in the stairwell. Had the man coming down stopped to pick them up, smiled, and wished her a good day, she would have thought nothing of it. Instead he passed by without acknowledgment, his foot stepping within an inch of the keys. He was slightly older than she was, though not by much, and was unremarkable, except for one notable feature: It was his eyes that haunted her. *Empty.* Even though it was the height of the summer heat, she felt a chill. Perhaps she really was coming down with something.

No, she thought. *I've seen him somewhere before. Hamburg? Cairo? Somewhere.*

As she pushed the cleaning cart onto the plane docked at gate B32, she wondered if the man with the empty eyes was involved with this evening's mission.

Her husband had called in sick to the restaurant, which Aliyah thought was odd because he was clearly not ill. Yet she accepted it as she did so many other things in her life; the violence had taught her it was best to not ask questions. Then he told her; Allah had chosen her for an important task. Now she understood. She understood why they had applied for business visas in Germany, why her husband had taken this menial job in the United States, why they prayed only at home and did not frequent the mosque, and why she had been forced to apply for the minimum-wage job cleaning airplanes.

The Boeing 767 was scheduled for a morning long-haul flight to Los Angeles. It needed to be cleaned the night before so it would be ready to go the following day.

She adjusted her hijab and knelt, using the blade from her box cutter to scrape gum from the deck. *Disgusting.* She and the other janitors on her crew had been taught to use the short steel edge to remove bubble gum from the underside of seats and from the floor of the aircraft they were entrusted to clean. It was standard industry practice.

What wasn't standard industry practice was what she did next.

She had intentionally maneuvered into a position in first class where she could track the positions of her colleagues. Two were picking their way through the seat backs of the main cabin, filling garbage bags with refuse from the last flight of the day. One was sanitizing the aft lavatory. A supervisor was perched mid-cabin overseeing their work while marking "complete" boxes on a checklist.

Pretending to notice something across the aisle, she moved to the second row and knelt. When she stood back up, box cutters were taped to the underside of seats 2A and 2B.

• • •

As their chauffeured Town Car slowly worked though the morning New York City traffic, Alec Christensen heard the familiar Nokia tone chiming from the new phone in his messenger bag. He fished it out by the third stanza. Tilting the device toward his fiancée in the seat next to him, he smiled, showing off the new caller ID feature.

"You are on that thing too much," she scolded. "It's going to give you a tumor."

"Hey, Dad," Alec said, after hitting the large talk button with his thumb and bringing it to his ear. "Just about there. Oh, really? That's too bad. Okay. Then I'll meet you at the Rainbow Room. Yep. Eight thirty. I'll let her know. See you then."

"What'd he say?" Jen asked.

"He had to move our breakfast to Midtown. A meeting at the office came up, so he can't make it down. He said to send his *deepest regrets*," Alec said, switching to the mid-Atlantic accent so heavy in his father's voice.

"You sound like Julia Child."

"Oh, come on, that was at least a good William F. Buckley. Want to try and swing breakfast with us?"

Jen looked at her watch.

"Well, my boss *is* coming in late today. He's dropping his son off for the first day of kindergarten. Even so, I'd better not. I don't think I'd make it back in time. Are you going to tell him without me?" Jen said, switching topics.

"What do you think?" Alec asked as his thumbs went to work on the small keypad.

"Why don't you just call? This new texting thing is just too weird. I don't see it catching on. And besides, you're missing this beautiful day. Not a cloud in the sky."

"These tech guys like it, and it's actually pretty efficient once you get the hang of it. See, you just have to scroll though these letters until you find the one you want. Just letting the team know I'm on schedule to meet them at eleven at the property on Eighth."

"Think your company is going to buy the building?"

"Probably just lease part of it for now, but you never know. This bubble is going to burst, Jen. It's not going to be pretty, but the companies that survive are going to emerge stronger and gain a huge amount of market share."

"I love it when you talk dirty to me," Jen said, sliding across the backseat of the Lincoln, closer to the man she planned to share her life with.

It would have been faster to take the subway into lower Manhattan, but when Alec was in town his father always provided a car service. Jen suspected it came from protecting his only child. It broke her heart that Alec had no memories of his mother who passed away before he could even crawl.

"How long do you think the meeting will take?" she asked.

"Probably a couple hours. I want to go for a run when it's over so I can think it through. It's a big deal for the company and I want to make sure we are doing the right thing."

"How you run in this city, I'll never understand."

"I grew up doing it, so it's totally normal."

"Well, you be careful. I worry about you running around these streets. It's dangerous."

"Well, it's not as safe as doing sprints on campus at Maloney Field, I'll give you that. But, trust me, I'm a professional."

They had met as undergrads at Stanford but were now two years removed from Cardinal Red. Alex had played lacrosse and liked having had the advantage of growing up in the East when it came to a sport still catching on across the country on the left coast. When he met Jen, he instantly loved everything about her. After graduation, he had elected to join a small struggling Silicon Valley start-up founded by fellow Stanford alums and was taking payment in stock options like almost everyone else. Unlike everyone else, he had a trust fund that kept him from living off ramen noodles.

Jen had been offered a fantastic opportunity at Cantor Fitzgerald and was just beginning her third year as an investment banker. She was planning to apply to Harvard Business School and start classes next fall, a move Alec's father fully supported in the hopes it would lure his son back to the Atlantic seaboard. They had been engaged for the past two months. Alec had wanted to wait to tell his dad in person. He was sensitive to the fact that the man who raised him had done so alone, the love of his life succumbing to cancer so early in their young lives. His father had never remarried. Alec had planned to tell him that morning at Windows on the World with Jen by his side.

"You know what?" Jen asked, before answering her own question. "It's better this way. You two boys have your special moment together, and then I'll let him spoil me at dinner."

"Where do you want to go? I'm sure he'll ask."

"It's Tuesday, so how about the Pool Room?"

"Dad is more of a Grill Room guy, but for you I'm sure he'll make an exception. Are you sure I should tell him without you?"

She put her hand under Alec's chin and twisted his head away from his "texting" so she could look into his eyes.

"I'm positive."

• • •

"Hey, Dad!"

"Right on time, lad," his dad said, looking at his Patek Philippe.

"I still set mine five minutes ahead just like you taught me," Alec said, pointing to his left wrist. "That way I can be five minutes late and still be on time."

"That wasn't really the point, son. The point is to be early. It's disrespectful to be late. Shows you don't treasure our most valuable asset . . ."

"Time," Alec said, completing the sentence he'd heard from his dad so often over the years.

"That's right."

"See, I do listen."

"Mr. Christensen," the maître d' interjected politely. "Your table is ready."

"Thank you, Charles."

They were seated by the giant windows of the iconic New York restaurant. The Empire State Building dominated the view south toward Soho, Greenwich Village, and the twin towers of the World Trade Center. Lady Liberty was even visible in the distance on such a clear day from sixty-five floors up. Alec smiled, picturing Jen grabbing a bite in the lobby of her building. Maybe she had gone ahead with breakfast at Windows on the World by herself before heading to her desk and was looking uptown toward him right at this very moment.

Dobson Christensen was dressed impeccably in a dark three-piece suit, not a single gray hair out of place. His tailor did an outstanding job of disguising the fact that he was not in the best of shape. Like many of his generation, exercise consisted of walking the links at Maidstone and the occasional trek afield at Clove Valley Rod and Gun Club, both of which consisted of equal parts business and pleasure.

Alec's usual Sandhill Road attire of khakis and a blue button-down had been accented with a dark blue blazer and tie. He dressed more formally in New York out of habit, having grown up dining with his father in places that would not approve of the more casual uniforms that were the norm in Palo Alto.

His father placed a white napkin in his lap with great ceremony as a waiter set down a French press. The senior Christensen was a regular.

"For you, sir?"

"I'll have the same, please," Alec said.

"So, tell me about the future of the Internet," Dobson said. "And don't leave out the parts about where I should invest other people's money."

Dobson Christensen was a bit of an anomaly. While most with money and means had sheltered in place in the world of academia to avoid the Vietnam War, Dobson had taken a different path. He'd dropped out of Princeton and volunteered for the Marine Corps. Years later he'd say he did it to just "get it over with," but Alec knew better. Behind the suit, polished shoes, and country club exterior was a fiercely patriotic man who could have volunteered for stateside National Guard duty or qualified for a student deferment but instead was drawn to the fight. He found himself as a door gunner on a Huey gunship, which was shot down on its first mission before he could even fire a shot. The pilot and copilot were killed, but Lance Corporal Christensen survived with a broken back, pelvis, hip, and femur. He spent the rest of his Marine Corps experience recovering, first in Okinawa and then at Walter Reed. His cane and limp were a constant reminder, and when asked about it, he would say that his Purple Heart was a VC marksmanship medal. He liked to joke that he spent more time in boot camp than in Vietnam.

The waiter returned and handed menus to both men. Dobson

put his aside, saying, "I'll have the forestière omelet and a side of your thickest bacon." He wasn't one for wasting that most valuable of assets.

"Ah, I'll have . . ." Alec said, scanning his choices, "the . . ."

A sound he could only associate with a freight train barreling by at full speed shook the room. Stunned patrons gripped their tables, bracing themselves for what some thought was an earthquake even though their left brains were telling them that couldn't be true.

Alec looked to his father, whose eyes were focused southeast. Alec followed his father's gaze and stood, pressing his hands and face to the glass. He watched the plane descend from across the Hudson into the city between the buildings. Veering toward its target, it disappeared into the North Tower of the World Trade Center.

Fire, smoke, carnage, death. *Jen.*

Alec sprinted for the elevator.

"Come on!" he shouted. He glanced at the stairwell and contemplated the option but forced himself to wait, knowing the elevator would still be the fastest way down.

Most people were glued to the windows, watching the smoke rising from the North Tower, so when the elevator doors opened, Alec was alone.

Please, God, let her live. Let her be in the lobby. Just let her live!

Fighting back the bile in his throat, he pressed his eyes shut, willing the elevator to descend faster.

Where did that plane hit?

He knew Cantor Fitzgerald occupied floors 101 to 105 and that Windows on the World was perched atop the North Tower.

Come on! Come on!

The doors parted and Alec launched himself through a group of businessmen unaware of the disaster unfolding just a few miles south. He hit the street at a full sprint. Turning toward the subway, he stopped and looked at the steps leading down, then back toward the dark smoke invading the blue sky over his beloved city. He made his decision.

He ran.

Sprinting toward the smoke and the flames, he dodged those not yet aware that the world had changed. Heart pumping, lungs burning, his legs propelled him forward, tearing through intersections oblivious to the honking horns and the cursing of those he knocked over in his mission.

Sirens, he'd always remember the sirens.

As the mortally wounded building loomed larger, he pushed past people stumbling in the opposite direction, some in a panic, others in a daze. He began to charge by police officers and firefighters yelling at him to turn around. He then heard the screaming engines of what he would later learn was United Airlines Flight 175 as it homed in from the south. He felt the impact in his soul.

Two planes. He had to get to Jen. *Dear God, let her be all right.*

He thrust himself forward, closer to the broken glass and twisted metal, toward the jet fuel burning its way through the steel heart of the structure. He ran toward the dead and dying. He ran toward bodies plummeting from the sky. He ran toward Jen. He ran toward Hell.

• • •

"Sit," her husband commanded.

Aliyah sat, the stale smell of the couch on which he'd first choked her filling her nostrils.

They had already completed *fijr,* their morning prayers, he in the main room and Aliyah in the bedroom. Islam forbids men and women from practicing the second of the five pillars of Islam together.

She'd performed *wudu* with water from the bathroom sink as he did so from the kitchen, ritually washing the body: mouth, nostrils, hands, arms, head, and feet. Though not purified water as prescribed in the Quran, they were on enemy soil and Allah would forgive them this one indiscretion. Instead of adhering to *salah* that morning, she had sat on the bed and looked through the small, dirty window listening to her husband recite Quranic verses in Arabic. They spoke Farsi in the home but true adherents to Islam prayed in the language of the Prophet. She entered the main room only after she heard him finish and turn on the small television.

They watched CNN in silence.

When the first plane hit, she remembered. She remembered Mohammed Haydar Zammar from the al-Quds mosque during their time in Germany. She remembered his hatred of America. She remembered his incessant talking. She remembered the hard floor and paint peeling from the walls of the women's prayer room. And she remembered the man with the empty eyes. Though his picture would not be plastered across television screens around the world for a few days, she remembered where she had first met the man in the stairwell. She remembered him sitting down with her husband in their Hamburg apartment. He was soft-spoken, almost aloof, paying her no attention. She had made them tea. They had talked about planes. His name was Mohamed Atta.

"We have triumphed over our unjust enemy," her husband said, without taking his eyes from the screen.

"Praise be to Allah for this victory," she replied dutifully.

"This," he said, pointing to the billowing clouds of smoke coming from what, until that moment, had been a symbol of America's economic might to the rest of the world. "This is only the beginning."

PART ONE
ORIGINS

"One of the most striking proofs of the personal existence of Satan . . . is found in the fact, that he has so influenced the minds of multitudes in reference to his existence and doings, as to make them believe that he does not exist."

—WILLIAM RAMSEY

CHAPTER 1

CIA Applicant Processing Unit
Dulles Discovery Building
Chantilly, Virginia
Present Day

"IS YOUR FIRST NAME James?"

"Yes," Reece replied.

"Have you ever lied to get out of trouble?"

Reece paused.

"Yes."

"Do you intend to answer these questions truthfully?"

Another pause.

"Yes."

"Is today Wednesday?"

"Yes."

"Have you ever committed a crime for which you were not caught?"

"Yes?"

"Are we in Virginia?"

"Yes."

"Have you ever committed murder?"

"Ah . . ."

"Just yes or no, please."

"No."

Reece saw the polygrapher make a note.

"Are you a United States citizen?"

"Yes."

Through his peripheral vision, Reece saw the polygrapher make another notation and adjust a setting on his laptop.

Great.

"Have you ever been part of a group that has wanted to overthrow the United States government?"

Reece sat in the nondescript room of what would have been a normal office park anywhere else in America. This one was located in Chantilly, Virginia, and was owned by a front company created by the CIA. Reece was halfway through day one of his three-day CIA processing evaluation. Even with his past experience and relationship with the Agency he still had to pass the medical and psychological screening tests to officially join the ranks of Ground Branch. Bureaucracy was, after all, bureaucracy.

"Let's try this again," "John" said in a tone meant to convey exasperation. "Be sure to answer yes or no honestly. And remain completely still. Keep your eyes focused on one point on the wall in front of you or we will have to start all over."

Reece felt his pulse quicken. He'd been on the receiving end of an interrogation before, and then, just as now, he wanted nothing more than to tear his interrogator's throat out. He'd completed a form in the waiting area, answering the exact questions he was currently being asked. He'd even gone over them with his "examiner" before being hooked up to the machine.

"Have you ever been part of a group that has wanted to overthrow the United States government?" the polygraph examiner asked a second time.

"No."

"Have you ever been in the employment of a foreign intelligence service?"

Reece tried to reframe the question in his mind. Instead, a memory intruded; Ivan Zharkov standing in the snow outside his dacha in Siberia, the flames from the downed Mi8 helicopter smoldering behind him, the dead bodies of his security detail strewn about the ground around him, a security detail Reece had killed.

Are you offering to spy for me, Mr. Reece?

"No," Reece responded.

The polygraph examiner made another note.

A blood pressure cuff squeezed Reece's left arm, two rubber air-filled tubes called pneumographs encircled his chest and stomach to record his breathing, and galvanometers had been placed on the first and third fingers of his right hand to measure sweat secretions. His chair was fitted with a sensor pad, thanks to Ana Montes, a senior Cuban analyst at the Defense Intelligence Agency who had been recruited by Cuban intelligence while in graduate school at Johns Hopkins. From 1985 until her arrest on espionage charges in 2001, she routinely passed classified information to Havana that was then transferred to the Soviets. Later, that information was sold to China, North Korea, Venezuela, and Iran. Her Cuban handlers had trained her to manipulate her polygraph by contracting her sphincter muscles, which is why Reece now sat on a sensor. He was also in socks, his feet resting on two individual pads. All movements would be recorded by the polygraph.

The room was small, but not claustrophobically so, about twice the size of a single patient room at a doctor's office. Reece thought it was possible the off-white walls had faded to their current hue by absorbing the fear that permeated the space on an almost daily basis. There was a camera visible in the upper left-hand corner, but Reece was sure the CIA had concealed a few others so as not to miss a single eye twitch or muscle movement. Though he stared at a blank wall, a mirror had been installed just off-center, two-way of course, for observation. The room was bare of any additional distractions other than the small table to his left where the polygrapher sat with his computer. It was unquestionably designed to make CIA candidates as uncomfortable as possible.

"Have you ever committed a crime for which you were not caught?"

Visions of his dead wife and daughter caused his heart rate to increase. Reece swallowed as he remembered watching the silver Mercedes G550 SUV crest the rise on the mountain road outside Jackson through the magnification of his Nightforce NXS 2.5-10x32mm scope, just before pressing the trigger to send a Barnes Triple Shock .300 Winchester Magnum through the brain stem of Marcus Boykin, the first person Reece had eliminated on his quest to avenge his family and SEAL Troop.

"Mr. Reece?" his examiner asked.

"What?"

"We have to get through these questions. Have you ever committed a crime for which you were not caught?"

Reece felt the working end of his Winkler/Sayoc Tomahawk catch in the bone and brain matter of Imam Hammadi Izmail Masood's crushed skull before twisting it out and going to work on the gristle of the terrorist's neck muscles. Reece had freed the head from the terrorist's body so he could impale it on the spiked fence of the mosque as a warning to the others that death was coming for them all.

"No," Reece lied.

"Have you visited antipolygraph.org to prepare for this examination?"

"Yes."

This answer visibly perturbed the examiner.

"Are you sitting down?"

"Yes."

"Have you ever committed murder?"

"I thought we covered that."

"Just yes-or-no answers."

Again, Reece's mind accessed memories he'd never be able to repress. He remembered hitting send on the cell phone that detonated the suicide vest on political fundraiser Mike Tedesco, turning him and SEAL Admiral Gerald Pilsner into human mist.

He remembered shoving the HK pistol into Josh Holder's mouth, feeling teeth breaking around the long suppressor before the .45-caliber bullet blew the back of the Defense Criminal Investigative Service man's head off.

"No."

"Have you ever plotted to overthrow the U.S. government?"

Reece thought of the EFP, Explosively Formed Penetrator, he'd built. It was an instrument of terror overseas, but Reece had used the tactics and techniques of the enemy on home soil. He'd become an insurgent. The IED sent a slug of molten copper through the armored Suburban of Congressman J. D. Hartley in SoHo, eviscerating the conspirator and bringing the reality of war to the home front. Reece saw the look of abject horror in Secretary of Defense Loraine Hartley's eyes as he shot her twice in the chest and once in the head in her Fishers Island mansion.

"No."

"Is the wall white?"

"Sort of."

"Once again, just yes or no."

"Yes."

"Have you ever been involved in the torture of enemy combatants?"

The odor of vomit and piss from the floor of Saul Agnon's hotel room keyed the memory of the attorney's waterboarding and untimely death via a concoction of illicit drugs Reece had acquired to make the murder seem like a drug overdose, giving Reece the time he needed to eliminate his remaining targets.

Reece saw the horror in Captain Howard's eyes as he eviscerated the JAG officer with the sinister curved blade of the HFB karambit. As his guts slipped through his fingers and spilled onto the soft jungle floor, Howard frantically attempted to shove them back inside. Reece skewered them to a tree and forced the lawyer to walk around the trunk, his entrails escaping from his stomach until he collapsed at its base to be eaten alive by the creatures of the swamp.

Reece thought of passing the vodka to General Quism Yedid in Athens, a glass spiked with a Novichok liquid-soluble precursor.

And he remembered filling the 60cc syringe with capsaicin to inject into Dimitry Mashkov to elicit information that led to the location of Oliver Grey.

"No," Reece said.

"Have you used illegal drugs you have not mentioned previously?"

Reece shut his eyes, remembering the drugs his Troop had been given prior to their last deployment. Those PTSD beta-blockers had sinister side effects, side effects that a group of military, political, and private sector conspirators needed to cover up an ambush in Afghanistan and the murder of Reece's family in their Coronado home.

"No."

"Did you intentionally falsify information on your application or security paperwork?"

"No."

"Have you ever stolen anything from your previous place of employment?"

Reece remembered rolling the dolly down the hallway to his Troop's weapons locker in the SEAL Team Seven armory and loading it with rifles, NODs, AT-4s, LAW rockets, a machine gun, claymores, and C-4 to load out for his mission of vengeance. He'd liberated it all before the admiral and his JAG had suspended his security clearance.

"No."

"Have you ever stolen anything worth over five hundred U.S. dollars?"

"No," Reece said, unsuccessfully attempting to block the vision of himself loading the stolen ordnance into the back of his Land Cruiser.

"Do you have any undisclosed relationships with foreign nationals?"

The faces of Ivan Zharkov, Marco del Toro, and Mohammed Farooq flashed through his mind.

"No."

"Have you ever kept a war trophy?"

Reece paused.

"No."

"Have you ever sold government property?"

"No."

"Have you, or do you know anyone who brought back enemy weapons from overseas?"

"No."

"Is there anything in your background that would disqualify you from getting this job?"

Reece remembered his best friend and former teammate, Ben Edwards, holding up the detonator attached to strands of det cord wrapped around investigative journalist Katie Buranek's neck, her head battered and bruised, tears streaming, bandana securing her mouth. Ben had watched in utter disbelief as Reece killed financier Steve Horn and the secretary of defense before centering his M4 on the CIA assassin's face and pressing the trigger, eliminating the final target on his terminal list.

"Mr. Reece?"

"No. Nothing."

"John" removed his glasses and rubbed the bridge of his nose with his thumb and forefinger. He then made a production of turning off the computer, though Reece knew quite well that it continued to monitor his vitals and that the audio and visual recording devices in the room were still running. He wondered who was watching through the two-way glass.

"Mr. Reece, this is not going well."

"Really? I'm shocked."

"You must take this seriously. I have to tell you, almost every answer you've given indicated deception on the polygraph, even your name."

"Well, I've used a couple aliases."

"We covered this, Mr. Reece. Just any names not denoted on your employment questionnaire."

"It's been a busy couple of years, *John*."

"Let me converse with my supervisors. I'll be right back."

"John" left Reece alone in the room, still tethered to the computer and still under surveillance.

Reece looked at the camera in the corner and shook his head.

Fuckers.

Reece knew the polygraph was largely theater. Yes, the machine measured blood pressure, breathing, sweat secretions, and muscle movements, but there was a reason that results of a "lie detector" test were inadmissible in every court in the civilized world. Its value was in making the candidate *think* it could detect deception. It was an expensive prop, one that had gotten more than one candidate over the years to admit to crimes that they would almost certainly have gotten away with otherwise.

Reece had visited the antipolygraph.org site years ago as part of a battlefield interrogation course he'd attended in the SEAL Teams. It was the approved "tactical questioning" course of instruction, meant to provide left and right limits to operators in the field who might not have the luxury of having a BIT, or Battlefield Interrogation Team, attached to their unit. The techniques taught at the approved interrogation school were more akin to how a detective would interview the suspect of a crime in the United States. Reece wouldn't learn the darker arts of interrogation until he was detailed to a CIA covert action unit in Iraq at the height of the war. There he would learn techniques that had come in handy over the years, techniques that were not part of a manual and were not searchable via Google.

Reece shut his eyes.

Calm down, Reece. This is all part of the game, a game you need to win.

Remember why you are here; you made a promise to Freddy Strain's widow.

"I'll find who did this, Joanie. I'll find everyone responsible."

The triggerman was still breathing: Nizar Kattan, a Syrian sniper Reece had vowed to put in the ground. An assassin Reece needed the CIA's robust intelligence capabilities to locate.

There was also the letter. A letter and a safe-deposit box key from his father. A letter from the grave.

Later, Reece. Just get through the day.

Reece's day had started early that morning with a blood draw. He had given a urine sample and completed his vision and hearing tests. He had an appointment at medical the following day to complete his physical. He'd taken the 567-question MMPI-2 psychological test, which he'd found both amusing and irritating. He would have to sit down with an Agency psychologist on his third day. Reece knew the MMPI was designed to uncover psychological issues that might be disqualifying to a candidate applying for employment with the Central Intelligence Agency. It was administered to uncover repressed aggression, psychoticism, alcoholism, anxiety, marital distress, fears, depression, anger, cynicism, low self-esteem, defensiveness, antisocial behavior, schizophrenia, and paranoia.

Paranoia.

Reece noticed that day two contained a long block of "free time" in his printed schedule. He knew this was a placeholder to "retake" the polygraph. Enough SEALs had gone through CIA processing over the years that it was anything but secret. Day three was set aside for an office visit with Victor Rodriguez, director of what was now called the Special Activities Center. The SAC ran the paramilitary wing of the Agency. Vic had tried to recruit him for Ground Branch at their very first meeting when Reece had landed on the USS *Kearsarge* in the Adriatic Sea after he and

Freddy Strain had taken out Amin Nawaz, the terrorist known as Europe's Osama bin Laden. Reece had agreed to finish the job he'd started at the behest of the United States government to track down and turn or kill a former CIA asset he'd worked with and befriended in Baghdad. That mission had led to Freddy's death from a sniper's bullet in Odessa.

His relationship with Katie had taken a bit of a hit when he'd disappeared into the Siberian tundra for six months, tracking the CIA traitor responsible for the death of Reece's father, a legendary Vietnam-era SEAL and Cold War CIA case officer. Reece glanced at the Rolex Submariner on his wrist, a watch that his father had purchased at the PX in Saigon, a watch that had been slipped from his dead hand in a back ally in Buenos Aires. Reece had taken it back from the man responsible before sending him to the afterlife with seven hundred grams of RDX from a Russian claymore.

The polygraph examiner had been gone for ten minutes.

Was he really meeting with a supervisor? No chance. They were just making him sweat. It was all part of the interrogation playbook: convincing unwitting subjects to admit to disqualifying crimes and thereby putting a feather in the cap of the polygrapher who "caught" them. They were especially fond of "catching" and disqualifying those with special operations backgrounds.

Katie had been supportive of Reece's decision to accept a provisional contract with the CIA. She had been with him from the start of the nightmare and helped uncover the conspiracy that led to the ambush of his SEAL Team in the mountains of the Hindu Kush and the slaying of his young daughter and pregnant wife. She'd waited and wondered when he disappeared off the coast of Fishers Island, New York, after saving her life, and she'd been by his side as he recovered from brain surgery at Walter Reed Army Medical Center. Their relationship had taken a romantic turn in the mountains of Montana before they'd been targeted on home soil by a Russian mafia hit team at the direction of Oliver Grey. She'd been through a lot, and even though she had been less than happy when he went off the grid in Russia, she understood. Reece was on a mission, one that was not yet complete.

Reece heard the door mechanism click and turned his head to see the director of the CIA's Special Activities Center enter the room.

"Jesus, Reece, can't you do anything the easy way?" Victor Rodriguez asked.

Vic was second-generation Agency. He was a former Army Special Forces officer whose father had led a squad in Brigade 2506, the CIA-trained group of Cuban exiles that had attempted the 1961 overthrow of Fidel Castro in what would become known as the Bay of Pigs.

Vic had worked his way up through the ranks and had started recruiting Reece when he'd headed the Special Operations Group, the paramilitary side of what was up until 2016 called the Special Activities Division. He still preferred the older nomenclature. He was now responsible for SOG and the Political Action Group, two entities whose work was, more often than not, connected. The dark side of the Agency was in his blood. He'd grown up under the ever-looming specter of Bahía de Cochinos and had vowed to never again allow a failure at the nexus of intelligence and covert action. Victor Rodriguez was responsible for the third arm of U.S. foreign policy; when diplomacy and overt military pressure or intervention failed or was not possible for political reasons, the Special Activities Center was the *Tertia Optio*: the third option.

Vic had convinced Reece to sign on as a contractor and had put on the full-court press when Reece returned from Russia. He wanted the former frogman on board as a SOG paramilitary operations officer. In a late-night phone call a month earlier, Reece had agreed. This three-day screening was part of the process. If Reece passed, he would get an EOD, or Enter On Duty, date and then begin his training at the Farm.

"Can you just tell the twerp to finish up so we can get through this?"

"It doesn't work like that. We discussed the poly, Reece. You need to pass just like everyone else. How hard is it? Medical, dental, piss in a cup, answer some questions. You have a presidential pardon, so even if you are technically lying on the exam you are actually telling the truth."

"Doesn't mean I have to like it."

"No, but you have to do it. Isn't that even some SEAL saying?"

"*You don't have to like it, you just have to do it*," Reece confirmed.

"Good. Just do it. You are being given a lot of leeway because of what you and Freddy did to save the former president. And even though it's not officially recognized or condoned, there are rumors swirling about you taking out Oliver Grey. The Agency, and the counter-intel folks in particular, do not take kindly to turncoats in our midst. They missed Nicholson, Ames, and Grey. It's rumored you gave Grey the sentence most of the Agency wishes on traitors."

"I'm answering these as best I can, Vic."

"They're just counter-intel and lifestyle poly questions. You know the drill; your examiner will tell you to come back tomorrow. Play nice and let's get you to the Farm."

"Understood. Just tell 'John' to stop pissing me off."

"Play nice," Vic repeated before turning to exit the polygraph room. "And please don't throw him through the two-way mirror. Those things are more expensive than you think."

When "John" returned, Reece lowered his heart rate the way he would before taking a long-range sniper shot. He focused on Katie's smile and answered with the correct yes and no answers. It wasn't every day you got to beat a lie detector test.

Passing the polygraph meant Nizar Kattan was one step closer to death.

• • •

Two days later Vic sifted through Reece's test results. No drugs in his system, no sexually transmitted diseases, vison and hearing well above Agency standards. It was the polygraph and MMPI test that concerned him. The MMPI had resulted in paranoid and aggressive personality traits, which was not totally unexpected considering what Reece had been through over the past three years. Vic shifted his focus from the Multiphasic Personality Inventory to the polygraph.

IS YOUR FIRST NAME JAMES? FALSE POSITIVE

HAVE YOU EVER LIED TO GET OUT OF TROUBLE? TRUTHFUL CONCLUSIVE

DO YOU INTEND TO ANSWER THESE QUESTIONS TRUTHFULLY? DECEPTION INDICATED

IS TODAY WEDNESDAY? TRUTHFUL CONCLUSIVE

HAVE YOU EVER COMMITTED A CRIME FOR WHICH YOU WERE NOT CAUGHT? TRUTHFUL CONCLUSIVE

ARE WE IN VIRGINIA? TRUTHFUL CONCLUSIVE

HAVE YOU EVER COMMITTED MURDER? DECEPTION INDICATED

ARE YOU A UNITED STATES CITIZEN? TRUTHFUL CONCLUSIVE

HAVE YOU EVER BEEN PART OF A GROUP THAT HAS WANTED TO OVERTHROW THE UNITED STATES GOVERNMENT? DECEPTION INDICATED

HAVE YOU EVER BEEN IN THE EMPLOYMENT OF A FOREIGN INTELLIGENCE SERVICE? TRUTHFUL CONCLUSIVE

HAVE YOU VISITED ANTIPOLYGRAPH.ORG TO PREPARE FOR THIS EXAMINATION? TRUTHFUL CONCLUSIVE

ARE YOU SITTING DOWN? TRUTHFUL CONCLUSIVE

HAVE YOU EVER COMMITTED MURDER? DECEPTION INDICATED

HAVE YOU EVER PLOTTED TO OVERTHROW THE U.S. GOVERNMENT? DECEPTION INDICATED

IS THE WALL WHITE? TRUTHFUL CONCLUSIVE

HAVE YOU EVER BEEN INVOLVED IN THE TORTURE OF ENEMY COMBATANTS? DECEPTION INDICATED

HAVE YOU USED ILLEGAL DRUGS YOU HAVE NOT MENTIONED PREVIOUSLY? DECEPTION INDICATED

DID YOU INTENTIONALLY FALSIFY INFORMATION ON YOUR APPLICATION OR

SECURITY PAPERWORK? DECEPTION INDICATED
HAVE YOU EVER STOLEN ANYTHING FROM YOUR PREVIOUS PLACE OF EMPLOYMENT? DECEPTION INDICATED
HAVE YOU EVER STOLEN ANYTHING WORTH OVER FIVE HUNDRED U.S. DOLLARS? DECEPTION INDICATED
DO YOU HAVE ANY UNDISCLOSED RELATIONSHIPS WITH FOREIGN NATIONALS? DECEPTION INDICATED
HAVE YOU EVER KEPT A WAR TROPHY? TRUTHFUL CONCLUSIVE
HAVE YOU EVER SOLD GOVERNMENT PROPERTY? TRUTHFUL CONCLUSIVE
HAVE YOU, OR DO YOU KNOW ANYONE WHO BROUGHT BACK ENEMY WEAPONS FROM OVERSEAS? DECEPTION INDICATED
IS THERE ANYTHING IN YOUR BACKGROUND THAT WOULD DISQUALIFY YOU FROM GETTING THIS JOB? DECEPTION INDICATED
FINAL POLYGRAPH TEST RESULTS: INCONCLUSIVE

Vic closed the file and looked at the faded black-and-white framed photograph on the wall of his office. The men wore World War II–era "duck hunter" patterned camouflage uniforms and carried an assortment of small arms, including a Johnson M1941 held by Vic's father.

Never again, Vic thought.

On the front cover of the file he signed his name over his director's signature block and checked a box marked APPROVED.

CHAPTER 2

Angola, Africa

ANGOLA HAD NOT BEEN particularly good to Ismail Tehrani.

He was getting impatient.

It had been six years since he had left Lebanon to become one of the eight million diaspora—Lebanese citizens living beyond the borders. Unique to this group was that they vastly outnumbered their countrymen who stayed behind and continued to endure the chaos the past forty years had brought to the small republic on the Mediterranean Sea.

He missed his native country, but he was on a mission. He had been personally recruited by al-Sayyid Hassan. Well, not directly, but an order from an emissary of the secretary general of Hezbollah was as good as an edict from God; it was said that Hassan Nasrallah was a direct descendant of the prophet Muhammad. Who was Ismail Tehrani to turn down an opportunity to serve Allah at the bidding of the man who had pushed the Israeli dogs from southern Lebanon?

Ismail was only a child when the Israeli rockets and artillery had rained down on the Shiite slums of South Beirut. Hunkered in a corner of their one-room apartment with his mother and cousins, they'd lost electricity almost immediately yet did not risk lighting a candle. His mother had covered him with a thick blanket; the sound of the incoming bombardment and subsequent explosions were endured in darkness. The devastation he witnessed the following morning when he ventured outside cemented his resolve; he would defend his homeland from the invaders.

The war that saw more than four thousand Katyusha rockets fired into Israel and the destruction of critical infrastructure in Lebanon from Israeli warplanes did more than polarize the Arab world. It provided Hezbollah's Jihad Council with an army of young recruits willing to die for the cause. When his father returned from working in Africa to protect his family at the onset of the July War, Ismail remembered him saying that the president of the United States called the Israeli actions part of his "War on Terror" and that his Congress even voted in support of the Israeli onslaught. To Ismail and his family, it was nothing more than American-funded genocide.

Ismail's first taste of combat would surprisingly not be against the Israelis, as he so hoped, but instead against fellow Muslims in Syria, albeit *takfiris.* His brigade commander had explained that Hezbollah could not allow Syria to collapse and come under the control of the United States and Israel. Allah needed his warriors to be strong. Syria could not fall, especially in a Zionist plot to overthrow Bashar al-Assad. Most of Hezbollah's weapons passed through Syria from Iran, and that conduit needed to remain open. It was their lifeblood. He'd heard whisperings that Nasrallah wanted to take territory and open another front against Israel in the Golan Heights. Ismail was in full support, parroting the slogans beaten into them by their instructors as they marched during indoctrination, and then in their more formal training in the west Bekaa Valley: "Death to Israel, Death to America, Eradicate the Jews."

Fighting in the Syrian town of al-Qusayr, Ismail found combat a confusing mix of screaming, shooting, and mayhem. He generally pointed his weapon in the same direction as those in his brigade. He shot when they shot and ran when they ran. A friend he'd known since birth stepped on a land mine. They had not even stopped to pick up the pieces. Another warrior of God had taken a bullet to the face in mid-sentence as he stood to order his militia forward, leaving Ismail covered in chunks of bone and brain. Ismail had fought; he had not faltered. He drew strength from the passage written above their yellow and green flag depicting a fist clenching a rifle similar to the one in Ismail's hands:

fa-inna ḥizbu llāh hum alğālibūn
Then surely the party of God are they that shall be triumphant.

Hezbollah won the day.

Ismail had heard whispers of Unit 910, Hezbollah's external security apparatus responsible for targeting Israeli assets abroad, but had never dared ask about or even speak of them. It was rumored they were also responsible for the assassination of the Lebanese prime minister, though Hezbollah denied the allegation and shifted blame to Israel.

When they pulled him from his unit, it was not so much an ask as it was an order. Ismail had been given a task, one that required him to receive additional training by the IRGC Quds Force in Iran.

The Quds Force is an elite paramilitary unit responsible for external operations specializing in the use of proxy forces unattributable to Iran. The West would brand them terrorists regardless of their targets. Born of the 1979 Iranian revolution, they were accountable only to the Ayatollah himself. Their intelligence apparatus taught Ismail how to assess and recruit assets, identify facilitators, set up safe houses, conduct reconnaissance and surveillance, and transfer information via a clandestine communications network back to Hezbollah.

And they taught him to build truck bombs.

The Party of God wanted Ismail in Angola. Though Hezbollah had worldwide reach through its network of diaspora, they were underrepresented in this southwestern African country, where the corrupt government had outlawed Islam, no doubt at the behest of the Jews. Mosques had been burned and Muslims persecuted. Hezbollah needed a trusted agent in the area to gather information for the Jihad Council. Israel's embassy in the capitol city of Luanda was a target, and Nasrallah wanted to know just how soft an objective it was. Finally, Ismail Tehrani would strike a blow against the Zionist aggressors.

Though a step up from the horrors of al-Qusayr, Angola was a country in transition. After a decade and a half of struggle in a war of liberation against the Portuguese colonists and a follow-on quarter century of civil war, the nation and its people were no strangers to conflict. Those years of strife had conditioned the new ruling class to exercise extreme measures to keep the populace in check. Disappearances of those critical of the Angolan government were commonplace. Torture, gang rape, and public executions were utilized as a means of controlling the populace. *This was Africa.*

Ismail was in the capital when, after thirty-eight years in power, President José Eduardo dos Santos finally stepped down. He had amassed a multibillion-dollar fortune in a country where the average person lives on two dollars a day. For the quasi-dictator of one of the most corrupt regimes in all of Africa, the ability to make $32 billion in oil revenue disappear through a worldwide money-laundering network had been a highly profitable skill.

His King's College–educated daughter had risen to prominence and become Africa's first female billionaire as head of the nationalized Angolan state oil company. It certainly paid to take stakes in companies exploiting the Angolan people and their natural resources. Ismail had read of similar actions by the family of an American vice president; corruption and greed were not ailments relegated solely to the jungles of the developing world.

The northern Angolan province of Cabinda is separated from the rest of the country by a sixty-kilometer strip where the Democratic Republic of the Congo intrudes into what is de jure, though disputed, Angolan territory. Though lumber, cocoa, coffee, and rubber plantations occupy much of the lush landscape, Angola's most lucrative export is oil. It was into "the Kuwait of Africa" that Ismail followed in his father's footsteps. The mass exodus caused by more than half a century of war had created a labor vacuum. At the direction of Unit 910, Ismail applied for and was hired by an asset of the diaspora working at Petróleo Brasileiro S. A. Petrobras, the Brazilian Petroleum Corporation, a company with major stakes in Angolan oil and natural gas production. His job was to escort labor from Luanda in the south to Cabinda in the north, a position that allowed him ample opportunity to surveil the Israeli embassy.

Ismail was discouraged when his intelligence reports did not lead to immediate kinetic action. When in Luanda he prayed to Allah, not in a mosque but in a cramped apartment that smelled of sewage. He passed his information through the imam, who reported back to the council. He dreamed that one day the Jihad assembly would order him to carry out an attack on the Jews, just as his brothers had hit their embassies in Buenos Aires and London before Ismail was even born. Ismail had taken note when his fellow warriors martyred themselves in Bulgaria, though he intended on killing more than six Israeli tourists. He wanted to drive a truck bomb right into the lobby of the Israeli embassy. His death would one day be honored on a monument like the one his trainers had shown him in Behesht-e-Zahra cemetery in Tehran. That attack had meant something. Less than a year after the 1983 Beirut bombings, the infidels had retreated from Lebanon. The martyrs had struck a blow for Allah and sent the Americans scurrying home.

With each passing year, Ismail's hope of a glorious attack on the Jews in Angola dwindled. His recruitment by Unit 910 had been a great honor, but at times he felt abandoned in the squalid African subcontinent, once again the little boy covered with a blanket.

When the assignment came to Ismail, it was not the one he expected. It did not entail acquiring the components to build a truck bomb for a spectacular attack for which he had been trained. It was a rather straightforward task, but one did not question orders from a descendant of the Prophet.

One evening after prayers the imam had given Ismail a package and verbally passed along his orders. Ismail was told the virus would only infect the Jews. Even so, there was a special pill for him to swallow that would ensure his safety. On his next trip north, he was to spray what looked like an asthma inhaler randomly in the marketplace of a local village. Hezbollah had information that the Israelis were secretly at work converting diamond mine workers to Judaism, all the while using the gems to fund their campaign of worldwide domination. Ismail expected nothing less of the Jews.

Three days later, he was en route to Cabinda with a new group of workers in one of the planes that Petrobras used to transport people to and from Luanda. The following afternoon he visited a marketplace just east of the city, a market that supplied workers for the Jews. He purchased a bracelet from a woman selling jewelry off a blanket of purple and orange and ate a meal of *chikwanga* and *catatos* from a vendor; he'd grown quite fond of the fried caterpillar dish; its spicy mixture of insects, onions, peppers, and tomatoes reminded him of the prawns from the coast of Lebanon.

Ismail depressed the asthma inhaler as he moved through the crowded bazaar at ten different places, just as he'd been instructed. Though he trusted his imam and the Hezbollah secretary general, he still took the special immunity pill: no sense in taking chances. He wanted to be sure he was healthy enough to destroy the Israeli embassy when the time was right.

Within thirty-six hours the local clinic in Cabinda began to admit patients exhibiting flu-like vomiting, hemorrhaging in the eyes, and bloody noses very similar to the hemorrhagic outbreaks that had occurred in the Democratic Republic of Congo just to the east in 2014 and 2016. The same clinic had experience with a rare episode in 2005 that killed thirty-nine children in a northern Angolan village.

The next day, dozens of infected villagers began flooding the clinic, prompting a notification to the World Health Organization. Having experience in this part of the world where hemorrhagic outbreaks were not out of the ordinary, this one was quickly contained. The doctors and nurses in equatorial Africa were well versed in hemorrhagic virus protocols. Personal protective equipment was mandated, bleach was used to disinfect all surfaces and equipment, and blood samples were sent to the Pasteur Institute in Dakar, Senegal, for further study. Though the index case was never identified, the data indicated that this was a small, contained outbreak in a crowded, hot market, probably originating with the meat handlers. It was catalogued as yet another in a long string of mysterious hemorrhagic viruses that plagued the Dark Continent.

Bodies of the dead were collected and burned in a mass crematorium, as was standard practice to destroy a fast-moving infection like Ebola. If there was a positive attribute of hemorrhagic viruses, it was that they burned themselves out quickly, often killing the host agent before they could spread the infection via blood or saliva. Thankfully, there had never been a recorded case of hemorrhagic virus spreading via respiratory pathways like the flu or a common cold.

The following day, Ismail returned to the capital, depressing his inhaler in the departure area of Quatro de Fevereiro International Airport, as per his instructions, before returning to his small apartment in time for evening prayers.

Less than twenty-four hours after the release, he took a taxi to Multiperfil Hospital, thinking he had food poisoning, maybe from his meal in Cabinda.

Ismail was dead the next day.

Three weeks later his name would be listed among 457 others in a World Health Organization report that was then forwarded to the Centers for Disease Control, or CDC. The report indicated the WHO had successfully contained another Ebola outbreak in Angola. Data like that was important to the continued financial support from the United States.

The name Ismail Tehrani would not spike on any intelligence agency radars, even if someone had run it through a national intelligence database in Israel or the United States.

His body was thrown into a pit, doused with gasoline, and set aflame, just another casualty of hemorrhagic fever, an infectious disease not uncommon in equatorial Africa.

CHAPTER 3

National Biodefense Analysis and Countermeasures Center
Fort Detrick, Maryland

COLONEL TOM GARRETT STUCK his head through the office door and nodded to Major Courtney Burke, who was on the phone with her husband. She held up a finger and mouthed, "One minute."

"Yep, I'll be home in about four hours. Need me to pick up dinner? Chinese? Sounds great. Love you, too."

"And how is everything on the home front?" Garrett asked his colleague.

"All is well. Peter is selling homes and juggling the kids, and I'm about to enter a place that doesn't officially exist," she said, pushing back her chair and logging out of her computer. "How is Haley?"

"She's still saving the world at the CDC."

"Does it ever strike you as odd that you are here weaponizing viruses that could destroy the world while she is working on immunizations and antidotes for those same viruses?"

"Every day."

"Why don't you go first today? I'll finish this up," she said, pointing to some papers on her desk. "Meet you there in a minute."

Colonel Garrett reached the end of the hallway, slid his ID card through a reader, and punched in a four-digit code. The door was marked BIO CONTAINMENT LEVEL 4. Only seven facilities in the United States were approved for Bio Level Four contagious disease study, and the National Biodefense Analysis and Countermeasures Center in Fort Detrick, Maryland, was one of them. Created in the wake of the 2001 anthrax attacks, its official charter was to perform research on pathogens for which no vaccine or treatment exists in order to better understand the threat of bioterrorism. Unofficially, they had another mission.

Unlike popular Hollywood movies, television shows, and novels, one did not first enter into bio-containment level one, then two, then three, and then finally four. That looked good on camera to up the suspense as an actor steadily worked his or her way toward the deadly viruses within. In reality, the very few doctors cleared to work with the lethal pathogens bypassed levels one, two, and three. Their TS/SCI clearances had an additional designation, a SAP or Special Access Program, allowing them access to the inner sanctum of U.S. contagious disease research. Fewer still had access to another room, one that only a select number of specialists and officials knew existed. That "additional room" was where the colonel was going today.

He looked up at a camera above the door.

Before a security guard at a remote location unlocked the door, he verified the code and card, and visually compared the colonel's face to his official photo on file as the facial recognition software confirmed he had approved access.

Garrett entered what looked like a small locker room in any gym in America. The only difference was that instead of smelling like body odor, Old Spice, and sweaty socks, this one smelled like bleach. He maneuvered around a short steel bench and swung open the door to one of the lockers that lined the wall. He removed his clothes and hung them neatly in the locker, which sealed and locked when he closed it. He then moved to the next door. It had felt odd going through the process the first time, knowing that he was being watched on video and that every move he made was being recorded. Now, after fifteen years, it was just another day at the office.

Standing naked in front of the next entry point, he heard the familiar whoosh of the air lock as the door opened. He stepped into a room of stainless steel. He felt and heard the door seal behind him. Moving to the center of the room, he raised his arms. Similar to a car wash, warm soapy liquid rained from the ceiling and walls, coating his exposed body. He closed his eyes and focused his mind on what the next two hours had in store. The soapy spray shifted to distilled water before the blowers came on to dry him. Putting on UV goggles, he nodded to let the controller know he was ready. An unknown finger touched a button, bathing the room in UV light that would not damage skin but would kill any foreign contaminants. The entire process took only three minutes. It wasn't as important on the way in as it was on the way out. The exit process would take three times as long to ensure the death that lived behind the walls did not see the light of day.

The UV light shut off and Garrett heard the air locks open to allow him access to the next room. He went through the process the same way a normal person would make their coffee each morning, with no variation. However, with coffee, if you forgot the cream or ran out of sweetener, you wouldn't release a contagion upon an unsuspecting public, killing untold millions of your fellow countrymen.

Still naked and monitored on video, he entered the small room and removed a disposable "bunny suit" from a stainless-steel hook. He stepped into it and glanced at the incineration drawer where he would deposit it on the way out. He put a hair net on his head before taking the rubber bio-protective suit from another hook and sealing himself inside. Lastly, he attached the helmet and tethered himself to a power and air cord that would keep him alive beyond the next set of doors.

Looking up at the camera, he gave a thumbs-up. He again felt the air lock engage as the next set of doors opened into an anteroom, where he reattached his tether to ensure the suit was powered and air was flowing. The doors closed behind him, leaving him sealed in a room designed to prevent any contaminants from escaping. He picked up a metal clipboard and Fisher space pen to go over the day's test while he waited for Major Burke to pass through the sterilization process and join him. There were no separate considerations given to male and female medical professionals working with infectious diseases. Perhaps the military was more progressive than it was given credit for.

One door away was bio-containment level four. The world's deadliest pathogens were mere feet away behind a brightly labeled set of airlocked stainless-steel doors. Colonel Garrett knew he was still on video and was acutely aware that everything in front of him beyond the doors was also recorded for security reasons and for purposes both procedural and historical. In bio-containment level four the most lethal diseases known to man were studied and tested as scientists created antibodies that might one day save the human race. That was not where he was going today.

Colonel Garrett and Major Burke had another mission.

The door behind him opened and Garrett watched as his partner connected her tether to power and air. Ensuring she was good to go, she flashed a thumbs-up at the camera and the doors sealed shut behind her.

The two soldiers moved to a wall to their left, a wall that looked just like the others in the facility, only this one had two alphanumeric keypads attached on opposite sides. The colonel moved to the one on the left. They were far enough away from each other so that one person could not possibly reach both at the same time. He looked at Courtney and they both entered seven-digit access codes. If they did not both enter their codes within ten seconds of one another the doors would automatically lock down until credentials could be reverified. Then supervisors up the chain of command, both military and civilian, would be required to reapprove access. A green light blinked, and the doctors looked into a small keyhole camera that they knew was using a laser to biometrically scan their faces. Only after they were approved by the system did a remote security guard grant them access.

The wall parted and they walked into a world fewer than a hundred people in all of government knew existed, re-tethering to their life support system as the heavy steel doors shut behind them.

While level four bio-containment was filled with fancy electron microscopes and had ample space for multiple scientists, this room was surprisingly small. Colonel Garrett hadn't met a doctor yet who didn't feel claustrophobic during their first experience. It wasn't necessarily the confined space or the oppressive feel of the rubber suit; rather, it was knowing what secrets the room concealed. Only two such facilities had been constructed, and the United States government disavowed any knowledge of their existence. President Nixon had signed the Biological Weapons Convention in 1972. It went into effect on March 26, 1975, and outlawed the development, stockpiling, retention, and production of biological agents and toxins for hostile purposes, making what took place in Maryland a violation of international law. Technically speaking the two doctors were about to commit a war crime.

Instead of stainless-steel tables and file cabinets, or expensive microscopes and computers, this room resembled a spacious closet. Unlike bio-containment level four, no video or audio recording devices documented the sensitive research and development that took place in this highly restricted section of the facility. The room was designed to withstand a magnitude nine earthquake and remain intact if hit with the equivalent of ten tons of TNT. It was equipped with a triple power backup system in case of a power outage, one of them coming from a separate section of the power grid built to withstand an electromagnetic pulse from the sun or a nuclear device. If all three failed, or if the six-foot-thick walls were breached from the outside, it was designed to self-incinerate, killing everyone and, more important, every *thing* inside. The cabinets and freezer were constructed of vinyl and plastic composites, which made them more conducive to burning and melting in the three-thousand degree heat if that emergency mechanism were triggered.

Its official designation, for those select few read into the program, was the Dark Room. Unofficially, by those who ventured inside, it was called the Bat Cave, not after the caped crusader of comic book lore, but for the caves of Zaire where the dreaded Ebola virus had spawned in the spoor of bat guano. Behind the doors of the Bat Cave were where the contagious diseases of bio-containment level four were weaponized for offensive warfare.

How could so much death fit inside such a small room?

Even with all the security protocols set up to restrict access and knowledge of its true purpose, there was another way inside.

The pedigreed baboon had started life at the Southwest National Primate Research Center in San Antonio, Texas, before being transported to his current home in Maryland. More specifically a custom breed *Papio anubis Papio hamadryas,* he belonged to a colony established in 1972 for this precise purpose. The colony had been genetically bred for medical research and was ideally suited for bioweapon sensitivity testing. The center's selective breeding and environmental manipulations resulted in the animals' having a genetic structure similar to that of humans.

The baboon had been sedated in a separate, yet attached, animal research facility. It was now entombed behind a thick Plexiglas barrier. Using the robotic arm, Colonel Garrett opened the freezer and removed a small vial. With practiced efficiency he extracted a sample and injected it into the test subject while Major Burke took notes.

Their research involved infecting a series of animals with a new monoclonal cocktail as part of a dose exposure curve experiment. The biomedical researchers were in search of sublethal viral doses of a biological agent that put the United States government in violation of international law. Today's experiment confirmed that the dose was lethal.

After it was done, an automated tray removed the primate from view and sealed him inside what was essentially a crematorium. When the doors eventually opened again, not even ashes would remain. The tray was then sprayed down with a solution of chemicals before being dried with a blower and exposed to fifteen minutes of intense UV light. It was as if the primate had never existed.

Their work complete, the two doctors then prepared to exit the classified structure. They would pass through the four air locks, remove their rubber bio-protective suits, incinerate their "bunny suits," then receive the naked spray-down and UV light treatment before their lockers would be opened and they could put their clothes back on.

Once again under audio and video surveillance, they would reemerge to join the land of the living, both making it home in time for dinner with their families, leaving the secrets of the Bat Cave safely behind.

CHAPTER 4

The White House
Washington, D.C.

PRESIDENT ALEC CHRISTENSEN STOOD behind his desk in the Oval Office, looking down on the Rose Garden through windows of ballistic glass that framed one of the most recognizable rooms in the world. He was flanked by the national flag to his left and the flag of the president of the United States to his right. He ran his left thumb across a ring that hung on a chain hidden beneath his button-down Oxford dress shirt. It was the ring he had never been able to slide onto Jen's finger. It reminded him of death and kept him focused on his mission.

It had been almost a year since his election night victory, when state after state came in for the popular war hero during a time of economic and racial tension that threated to rip the country apart. The talking heads and pollsters had been ecstatic as their projections came to fruition, especially after the brutal beating they had taken years earlier when they'd confidently projected at 100 percent the odds of victory for the Democratic ticket over someone they dismissed as a reality TV star with no chance of becoming president. They'd lost a substantial amount of credibility that night and were hoping to gain some of that trust back by making the right calls this time around.

By all indications, the new president had shown no overt interest in politics until he recovered from the wounds he sustained in Afghanistan. To the media establishment and a populace looking for a bright light on the political scene, he was a savior. He came from money, went to all the right schools, and had focused his efforts on a small Silicon Valley start-up a few years before 9/11. In campaign speeches, he didn't lead with the story that had catapulted him into the public consciousness, as he didn't want to be seen as taking advantage of Jen's memory, but then, he didn't need to. The media did that job for him: his fiancée killed on 9/11, the future president running into the burning building in an attempt to save her, the smoke inhalation, being carried out unconscious by a firefighter, a firefighter who then rushed back into the North Tower only to be buried in the rubble; the young entrepreneur working in the debris for days alongside firefighters, police officers, first responders, and citizen volunteers until collapsing from exhaustion. A journalist captured a photograph of him that would become emblematic of America's response to the attacks: covered in the gray dust of the day, not wandering in a daze as were so many others, but sleeves rolled up, crowbar in hand, eyes fiercely set, prying a slab of concrete in the desperate search for survivors, in a desperate search for Jen.

When the *New York Times* identified him as the son of a prominent Manhattan financier and reported that his fiancée was missing in the rubble, they ran it with the headline "The Spirit of New York." He applied to Army Officer Candidate School from his hospital bed a week later. What followed was basic training at Fort Benning, Georgia, then Ranger School, and then his first assignment with the storied Tenth Mountain Division at Fort Drum, New York, before deploying to Afghanistan. After thirteen months of sustained combat in a valley that would see some of the toughest battles of the War on Terror, he'd been wounded by an IED in an ambush while on a mounted patrol to a nearby village. He'd pulled himself from his burning HMMWV, the screams of his dying turret gunner muffled by a ringing in his ears, a ringing that remained an ever-present eulogy to those who never made it home. He was halfway to cover when he realized he was dragging the lifeless torso of his driver, whose body from the waist down was still strapped in the vehicle. First Lieutenant Christensen had taken a 7.62x39mm round to his left hand as he made it to a rock by the side of what passed for a dirt road. Instead of rendering aid to his wounds, he called in artillery from their forward operating base and coordinated CASEVAC for the wounded. He ignored his own injuries and led a flanking element to counter the insurgents raining death down from elevated positions, the same positions he knew were probably used to attack and subsequently defeat the British and Soviets before him.

Alec had returned home and written a bestselling book. His narrative did not chronicle his experience in Afghanistan as would be expected. Instead he profiled six families, juxtaposing fathers and sons, the fathers having volunteered for Vietnam and the sons having volunteered after 9/11. The only mention of his own service came from the preface, where he framed the stories to come. Titled *You'll Be a Man, My Son*, from the famous Kipling poem "If," many hailed it as worthy of the Pulitzer Prize until he threw his hat in the political ring, at which point opponents then derided it as a well-thought-out publicity stunt to raise his public profile in a deliberate attempt to draw comparisons to John F. Kennedy's *Profiles in Courage*.

When he decided to enter politics as a Democrat, the party elites were ecstatic to have a combat-tested veteran in their ranks at a time when they needed credibility on the foreign policy front. He became a darling of the liberal media, with answers that came across as compassionate, yet firm, even when his stance took a more libertarian position. Comparisons to JFK were in the talking points from a media establishment still enamored with the myth that was Camelot. That was all part of Alec's plan.

Running for California's 25th Congressional District, he won a narrow victory in a self-funded campaign. While his opponent said he was buying the election, Alec pointed to her ties to special interest groups, in particular her support of the pharmaceutical industry's "pain clinics," which were nothing more than opioid pill mills, ruining lives in a deliberate campaign to addict, decimating entire communities while enriching corporate leadership, lobbyists, and the politicians who made it all possible. As a primary reason for much-needed change, Alec's campaign highlighted the amount of wealth the incumbent had accumulated over the course of her twenty-six years in Congress, much of it coming from the highly unpopular opioid industry. It didn't hurt that he polled very well with females of both parties. In a district that was almost split down the middle politically, it was said that Republican housewives made the difference. It's hard to compete with the story of running into a burning building after the woman you love, especially when it's true.

Alec studied the life and political career of the legendary John Dingell of Michigan. As a liberal Democrat from the rust belt, Congressman Dingell would become the longest-serving member of the House of Representatives in congressional history, while holding strong to his steadfast belief in the individual, fundamental right to self-defense. He clearly articulated how the firearm transcended the changing political whims of his party. His sixty years of government service were proof to Alec that those positions were consistent with a progressive agenda and could still win elections in California. It didn't hurt to have millions of new gun owners who had changed their positions on private gun ownership as they watched their cities descend into chaos the summer of the presidential election. They didn't want to abandon their party, nor did they want to rally behind a movement with a rallying cry of defund the police. Alec offered a strong alternative.

He was an early adopter and one of the first to harness the power of social media. As with most technical innovations, the establishment was slow to adapt; Alec was not. His days in Silicon Valley, along with his time in combat, taught him that adapting faster than your enemy led to victory. He built his platforms using the best digital designers and tailored his message to a more libertarian-leaning youth segment of the voter bloc. Decriminalizing certain drugs on one side, staunchly supporting the Second Amendment on the other, while championing the environment and a sustainable heath care plan, all falling under the umbrella of freedom, resonated.

Later there would be those who would accuse his friends in that early tech start-up of manipulating social media algorithms to get one of their own into the White House. Was that true? Even Alec didn't know for certain. What most people saw was a young, vibrant, wealthy, handsome candidate with a background tailor-made for politics. He fit the fairy tale.

Though many in his own party despised his success, the elites also saw him as a future presidential candidate. There was even talk of a presidential run early on, especially after he took the stage as a newly minted congressman at the 2008 Democratic convention in opposition to the war in Iraq. They had wanted to trot out a respected, young antiwar face of the party as a way to solidify the youth vote during a time when support for the wars in Iraq and Afghanistan was at an all-time low. As always, Alec was thoughtful in his remarks, well informed on geopolitics, and most important, *likable*, causing many commentators to wonder aloud why the Democratic Party wasn't running him, at least as a VP pick.

Alec was patient. He learned how Washington worked. He cultivated the relationships that would allow him to operate effectively in the swamp while remaining popular in California, a state he would have to win in a presidential bid. He laid the groundwork, continued to build his social platforms and harness their power. No longer was he dependent on the "kingmakers" of the legacy media establishment. Their power was waning, but they were too self-absorbed to notice. He built his own platforms in the new media and focused his messaging on those who digested their news via their smartphones and made their decisions largely based on influencers. He started a podcast before most people even knew what they were. Legacy print and cable media scoffed at him, but by the time he announced his campaign for the 2020 presidential election his podcast reach dwarfed the ratings of those in conventional media, the same media that continued to make cynical comments night after night from their soundstages in New York, D.C., and Atlanta. He could talk directly to the people and continue to build his base through engaging content and considerate conversations. He dominated the new media space in a way the rest of the Democratic field could only dream about. He studied the data, capitalized on relationships with influencers to co-opt segments of their audiences, and built a voting bloc powerful enough to sway an election.

That power made the party elite nervous. He was not under their control and therefore was unpredictable, but they also saw him as a way back into 1600 Pennsylvania Avenue. Both Alec and the party leadership knew he would have to go farther left for his vice presidential pick to balance the ticket, a chance to keep power for a sixteen-year run. If they wanted to fundamentally transform the country, they were going to have to support the popular congressman. His vice presidential pick from Florida's 9th District made him the first president in U.S. history to win with a female on the ticket. The fact that she was an Army JAG Corps veteran and of Cuban descent brought in the electoral votes from one of the more hotly contested battleground states in recent history. That she remained a major in the National Guard and "outranked" the new commander in chief, who had been medically retired as a first lieutenant due to his combat injuries, was a source of ample comedic material for the late-night talk shows. Even the women of *The View* could not stop themselves from fawning all over them both. It kept Alec center stage and made him relatable.

As the most eligible bachelor in D.C., he was a staple on the covers of magazines at supermarket checkout lines. In a world where a reality show about finding love trumped ratings across the board, he was a star. He enjoyed female company, but it always became clear after a few months that they would never be his top priority. Truth be told, his attention was on a ghost, one that was never far away.

Alec turned from the window and looked down at the Resolute Desk, which had been a part of the room since Queen Victoria had presented it to President Rutherford B. Hayes in 1880. It was built from wood recovered from the HMS *Resolute*, a British ship that was abandoned after becoming trapped in the ice while on an arctic expedition in 1854. An American whaler recovered the ship two years later and returned it to the United Kingdom. President Christensen looked at it as a symbol of hope and resolve. Just shy of one hundred years after fighting the war for independence, the former colonial rulers gifted a desk made from one of their naval vessels to the leader of the country that defeated them. After contentious beginnings and the war that birthed a nation, the two countries had become the staunchest of allies.

He rarely walked into the Oval Office without thinking of the iconic photo of JFK working at that very desk with John Jr. peeking out through the kneehole panel at his feet, a photo that would not be published until after the assassination in Dallas.

President Christensen took a breath and looked at the four files on his desk. They had been delivered by his national security advisor that morning. Three of them were the reason for the journey he'd taken over the past twenty years.

The president is the only person in all of government who has unfettered access to the nation's most closely guarded secrets. Everyone else is read into and out of special access programs based on "need to know." Information is compartmentalized for reasons of national security. The real trick is knowing what to ask for and where to look. The young president was searching for something specific.

Alec had not made his request immediately upon taking office. He had already waited two decades. He could wait a few more months. The new president needed to learn, research, and plan; he needed to lead. He had inherited a country still reeling from the economic repercussions of an almost complete shutdown in response to a virus that had originated halfway around the world. The follow-on civil unrest had devastated the nation. Those wounds were slowly healing, in large part due to Alec's leadership.

He'd had access to some of the documents included in the files when he was in Congress, but there were two new files that he was particularly interested in today.

The commander in chief pressed his knuckles into the oak timbers of the presidential desk, his left hand still bearing the scars from the Taliban bullet, the tinnitus in his ears from the IED reminding him that he'd never truly be at peace. That was okay. Peace was not what he was after.

He'd already read two of the files, front to back. They were stacked to his left. Alec looked down at the two remaining folders. One was labeled Executive Order 12333. He flipped to part two, paragraph thirteen: Prohibition on Assassination. His eyes scanned the section of the order, a version of which had been signed or strengthened by every president since Gerald Ford.

No person employed by or acting on behalf of the United States Government shall engage in or conspire to engage in assassination.

The president then shifted his gaze to the last file. It had been delivered by the CIA that morning and passed to the national security advisor, who in turn had placed it on the president's desk. It was labeled

DIRECTOR OF NATIONAL INTELLIGENCE / TOP SECRET / SI-GAMMA / TK / HCS / RSV / KDK / NOFORN / HANDLE VIA EXECUTIVE CHANNELS ONLY.

Under those code words and control labels was a name: JAMES REECE.

The president flipped the page and began to read.

CHAPTER 5

John F. Kennedy International Airport
New York, New York

ALI REZA ANSARI MADE sure he wasn't the first to exit the Jetway. He didn't want to look overly eager to anyone monitoring the cameras or facial recognition programs constantly scanning every face deplaning in one of the busiest airports on earth. He'd specified with his travel department that he'd like a window seat near the rear of the business class cabin. That would be expected for someone in his position and would put him near the back of the first pack of deplaning passengers.

He'd been with BioDine Medical Systems for seventeen years. A global health-care company headquartered in Switzerland, it boasted research and manufacturing facilities in Germany, Switzerland, Ireland, Canada, and what they referred to as the Central Eastern European region. Ali had first interned with them as a graduate student pursuing dual-track business and pharmaceutical sciences degrees from Saarland University in Germany. BioDine was also one of the few bio-medical research companies with research and distribution networks in both the United States and Iran.

BioDine was a respected, progressive, and diverse company that traced its roots back to 1758, when it was founded as a trading business specializing in chemicals, dyes, and pharmaceuticals. It was called Andros & Sons then, and for their first hundred years they focused on producing alizarin blue and auramine dyes. It wasn't until the late 1800s that they developed a medical-grade pharmaceutical, an antiseptic for soothing arthritis. With that success, the company shifted to the research and development of medicines in their Basel, Switzerland, chemical plant. In 1971, they sold to Glencore Trading Company. That merger gave them international reach through research labs and manufacturing plants in Europe, North America, and the Middle East. In 1997 they merged again, this time with one of the largest health-care companies in the world, becoming BioDine, with biomedical research labs in Cambridge, Massachusetts, and Tehran, Iran, through a partnership with the Iranian Communicable Disease Research Center.

Ali got into the line for non-U.S. citizens and waited patiently for his turn with the Customs and Border Protection official, who opened his Swiss passport and compared the photo to the man on the other side of the glass. Ali offered a pleasant smile as the uniformed officer scanned the bar code and shifted his eyes to the computer. Why the United States did not screen passengers ahead of time like El Al, Ali would never understand. He'd also never fly El Al.

"What is the purpose of your visit?" the CBP officer asked.

"Business," Ali replied, with only the slightest hint of an accent, as he'd done at least a hundred times over the years.

"And what kind of business is that?"

"A medical device technology company," Ali replied, not offering any more than required. Pharmaceuticals had the tendency to be off-putting with so much bad press around the opioid epidemic in America. It seemed as if the venerable news program *60 Minutes* ran weekly segments on Big Pharma's shady lobbying and marketing practices, pointing out that opioids killed more Americans annually than were killed during the entire Vietnam War. What the West called *terrorism* had nothing on opioids. Even though BioDine did not manufacture the devastating drugs, Ali did not want to highlight the pharmaceutical side of the company to someone who might be related to one of the thousands affected by a highly addictive narcotic.

The official flipped pages in the passport, looking for stamps from Yemen, Afghanistan, or Pakistan, which would lead to additional questions and a possible secondary screening.

"How long will you be staying in the United States?"

"About a week," Ali lied.

The official found a blank page and stamped it with an entry date before returning Ali's passport under the Plexiglas partition.

"Enjoy your stay," he said, nodding to the next person in line.

Ali made his way casually into the international baggage claim, noting exits and careful to pay just the right amount of attention to the armed police patrolling the area. He was also sure to force a disarming smile when he passed by a police officer with one of the Americans' canines by his side. Americans loved their dogs. *Filthy animals.*

Senior lab manager with one of the world's leading medical technology companies was not the career field to which Ali aspired in his youth. He'd only wanted to kill Iraqis and Americans.

Ali couldn't even remember the last time he'd seen his father. He was still in the crawling stage when his dad was conscripted into military service. Two years later his oldest brother would leave for the front lines, followed five years later by his middle brother, who would fight in the final battles of the Holy Defense, a conflict the rest of the world insisted on calling the Iran-Iraq War.

His mother had not been notified by a knock on the door, as he'd seen in so many American movies. Rather, a list of the dead and missing was posted each week in the town square. The list was displayed a good distance from the Provincial Society office, the locally elected Islamic Council responsible for coordinating regional affairs with the Islamic

Consultative Assembly in Tehran; the politicians seemed more afraid of backlash from Iranian mothers and widows than they were of invading Iraqi forces.

Young Ali would accompany his mother to town each week in search of news. She would leave him in a chair by a butcher stand on the corner and push her way through the crowds to read the names, praying to Allah for the safe return of her loved ones. The stench of rotting meat behind the thin curtain would stay with Ali the remainder of his life. He could live with the smell. What haunted his dreams were the wailings of the women. Their screams as they read the names of husbands and sons they'd never see again would fuel his every decision. The list offered no cause of death. No locations. The bodies were buried on the battlefield out of necessity, often in mass graves. Rarely was it possible for the dead to receive a proper Islamic burial as mandated by sharia law. In wartime, one must make sacrifices.

They would mourn his older brother first, killed in the early days of the war in a human wave attack in the marshes of Basra in 1982. At fifteen years of age he'd received a week of training before being sent to the front lines. The cult of the martyr had become a powerful instrument of the state. Whether he was killed by artillery, rockets, tanks, or small arms fire, or hunted down by the devastatingly effective Mi-25 helicopters using the same "hunter-killer" tactics the Soviets had used against the mujahideen in Afghanistan, Ali would never know. His only connection to his older sibling would come years later in the Iranian Martyrs Museum in Tehran, where he'd found his brother's picture encased under a glass display.

Additional research would reveal that his father had been a victim of a sarin gas attack in the town of Halabja, Iraq, in March 1988. As a soldier and then university student, Ali would spend hours sifting through available photographs of the battle, trying to identify his father among the bloated bodies of the dead. Iraq's chemical weapon attacks would kill thousands of Iranians and expose even more to the deadly contaminants. Even thirty years following the UN-brokered end of hostilities, close to one hundred thousand Iranians were still receiving medical treatment for the lifelong effects of the toxins.

Open-source declassified CIA documents would confirm that by 1984 the American intelligence agency was aware of Iraq's use of chemical weapons in violation of international law. An ally of Iraq, the United States not only remained silent but ramped up their military and intelligence support of Saddam Hussein's troops, even using their clout with the United Nations Security Council to block condemnation of Iraq when UN investigators presented unrefuted proof of the use of banned weapons by the Iraqi regime. Free of condemnation, Iraq increased its use of weaponized neurotoxins through the end of the war in 1988.

Ugly things are done in times of war, Ali knew. Heads are turned. Reports are falsified. Evidence is buried. The United States should have done a better job at covering their tracks. It was U.S. satellite imagery provided to Iraq that allowed them to effectively target advancing Iranian troops that March day in 1988, the day Ali's father was killed. The Americans were responsible for the excruciating deaths that morning, bodies of women and children scattered among the soldiers, their faces contorted in agony. Gas was not a precision weapon system and did not discriminate between combatants and civilians.

In 1982, deciding that an Iranian victory was contrary to U.S. foreign policy objectives, President Reagan removed Iraq from the list of state sponsors of terrorism. The military-industrial complex about which Eisenhower had so solemnly warned was in full swing. War was big business. Reagan's actions opened the door to military equipment and munitions sales to include the dual-use technology that would allow Iraq to produce and weaponize the chemicals that would give them the upper hand against the Iranians, the same poisons that had altered the course of Ali's life.

In the popular press, Iran was portrayed as the instigator, which made it easier for the world to support the Baathists in Iraq. With a billion dollars a month flowing in from Saudi Arabia, Iraq was able to purchase weapons from the United States, the Soviet Union, and the countries of Western Europe. Howitzers, Exocet missiles, Gazelle helicopters, Mirage jets, Soviet tanks, Mi-24 attack gunships, mines, RPGs, and AKs flooded the country. MiG-25 Foxbats and Su-22 Fitters escorted Soviet-made Tu-22 Blinders and Tu-16 Badgers on bombing runs of Iranian cites in a strategy of total war. Saddam Hussein was the West's man in the Middle East. As American flags were burned in the streets of Tehran, American support flowed unfettered to their adversary. With the world aligned against them, Iran had stood strong; Allah was on their side.

In later training with his country's intelligence service, Ali would learn that even more unforgivably, the United States secretly supplied Iran with weapons in exchange for help securing the release of American hostages in Lebanon. The so-called land of liberty prolonged the conflict and profited by selling the instruments of death to both sides in a war of attrition. America was the world's most prolific arms dealer. They had abandoned their god and chosen to worship a false idol—the almighty dollar.

That the Great Satan and her European allies would switch course and betray Saddam just a few years later only confirmed their duplicity and hypocrisy, the height of which was using Iraq's WMD development program as a pretext for invading Iraq in 2003. When administrations change every four to eight years, the institutional memory is short. They had conveniently forgotten their country's complicity in the chemical atrocities wrought on civilian and military targets when it suited their objectives. Their constituents were easily distracted and had little interest in world affairs, particularly the plight of people beyond their borders. Ali would not forget.

The war between Iraq and Iran would end in a stalemate, with no change in territorial boundaries and no reparations. The only thing either country had to show for it was a million dead soldiers and civilians. Ali knew too well that the toll was much higher. The official numbers were an estimation and did not take into account the psychological impact of the war. That had been ingrained in Ali's mind when he found his middle brother swinging from a rope in their home by his neck. A veteran of the final summer of fighting at Tawakal ala Allah, one of the last battles of the war and a military disaster for the Iranians, he'd never mentioned it in the two years he'd been home. To his younger brother and widowed mother, he rarely said anything. Inside he'd been waging his own personal jihad, a struggle he couldn't win. He'd been dead for a few hours when Ali found him upon returning from school. Ali stared up at his naked brother, shit and piss already dried on his legs and on the floor under his suspended body. Ali was twelve. When his mother arrived an hour later the wailing began again. Suicide was prohibited in the Quran. Allah was the ultimate arbiter of life and death. It was not Allah who had called his brother to paradise. It was the Americans.

His father and brothers had died for nothing. They had perished in a war that would have been over years earlier had it not been for the U.S. support of Saddam. The infamous 1983 photograph of then special Middle East envoy Donald Rumsfeld shaking hands with Saddam Hussein was seared into Ali's mind. They would meet again in 1984 to cement the relationship and reassure the dictator that Iraq had complete U.S. support in the war against Iran, going so far as to restore full diplomatic relations. Ali would later read reports of a CIA front company in Chile delivering cluster bombs and chemical precursor agents to Baghdad.

When the United States invaded Iraq in 2003, Ali was a young soldier with the Islamic Revolutionary Guard Corps. He thought his time had finally come to kill Americans. The Ministry of Intelligence (MOI) had other ideas. The most powerful ministry in Iran, it falls under the direct control of the Supreme Leader and traces its history back to the eleventh century, when the Ismaili Shiite sect known as the Nizari used targeted killings as an instrument of power. They were called "Hashshasin" for the use of hashish in their training. To the Crusaders they were known as assassins. Within the MOI is a group known as Department 15. Their mission is to target and kill threats to the Iranian regime abroad. It was this group that recruited Ali Reza Ansari.

The Iranian intelligence service had studied the American response to 9/11. They read the 9/11 Commission report, and, along with the rest of the world, they watched the long lead-up to "shock and awe," where America's military prowess was confirmed with a quick conventional victory on Iran's doorstep. They then watched incredulously as the Americans snatched defeat from the jaws of victory, allowing themselves to be pulled into an insurgency of their own creation through an ineptitude born of arrogance. Iranian intelligence and political leaders observed in disbelief as the United States disbanded the Iraqi military and enacted a policy of de-Baathification put in place by that silly man at the Coalition Provisional Authority who wore combat boots with his suits. The United States had essentially handed Iraq to Iran. What the Iranians couldn't do in eight years of war, the Americans had managed to do in a period of months. Now they just needed American forces to leave them to it.

Almost immediately, the MOI began a covert program, arming and training militia movements in neighboring Iraq. From their safe haven across the border, Iran built and supported an insurgency. That was phase one. The second phase would include the introduction of the EFP, the devastatingly effective explosively formed penetrator. Developed in World War II, it had been refined by Hezbollah in Lebanon but took hold of the public consciousness only when used to target Americans. Introduced into Iraq in force in 2005, they would wear down public support for the war effort as more and more soldiers returned home in flag-draped coffins. America's sons and daughters once again paid the price as corporate shareholders benefited from increased revenue; armored vehicles didn't come cheap. Iranian intelligence built EFPs and smuggled them across centuries-old "rat lines" to Shiite militias and Badr Brigade splinter groups to defeat the Americans' technologically superior armor on the streets of Baghdad, Ramadi, and Mosul. Those attacks could weaken the giant, but eventually she would limp home to recover, adapt, and then continue a war against Iran that had begun with the fall of the Shah. To defeat her they would have to take other measures.

A small group of senior Intelligence Ministry officials met with the Supreme Leader in the summer of 2003. They presented a plan.

By the fall they were scouring the ranks for candidates with specific attributes for a special mission. They were looking for young soldiers who had scored high marks on academic exams, specifically in the sciences.

There was a long history of Iranian students traveling abroad to study. Abbas Mirza, the crown prince of Persia, first sent students to Europe in the early part of the nineteenth century. Iranian academic institutions retained close ties with European and American universities up through 1979. Those exchange programs, along with lavish donations, kept the lines of communication open until all Iranian universities were shut down from 1980 to 1983 as part of Iran's Cultural Revolution. When they reopened, instead of being modeled on the American universities they had emulated under the Shah, they now included a mandatory Islamic curriculum in a strict Islamic educational forum.

After the Iran-Iraq War, and with approval from the Islamic Council, relationships were reestablished with European and American institutions of higher learning under the guise of modernizing Iran. In reality, a long-term deep penetration program was being set up. Iranian students began to once again study abroad in programs financed through government scholarships, particularly in the areas of science and medicine.

At first, Ali had been furious that the government had pulled him from his unit. By that time, he was already a member of the IRGC, preparing to avenge his father by facilitating chaos in Iraq. He was training up to replace an insurgent leader who had been killed across the border by the Americans. He was finally going to get his chance. Instead, he'd been summoned to the capital for a meeting. A week later, still dreaming of infiltrating across the Iraqi border and leading Shiite militia against the invaders, he began his studies at the University of Medical Sciences in Tehran. He was twenty-three years old.

His military file disappeared and was replaced with an exemplary academic record. They promised him that if he excelled at the university and in his intelligence training, he'd get his chance to kill more Americans than he ever would smuggling IEDs across the border. It was going to take time. Their new student needed to learn patience.

During the day, he was on a premed track with a heavy emphasis on English and German. Following classes, he would practice surveillance detection techniques taught to him by his instructors in Department 15. At night and on his days off he learned to rent cars, check into hotels, and order dinner and drinks. And he learned to kill. He was taught dead drops, surveillance and countersurveillance techniques, covert communication, and improvised weapons and explosives. His interrogation training was conducted with political prisoners from Section 209 of the Evin House of Detention in Tehran. If the brutal interrogations went too far, no one would miss them; they had already disappeared. Most important, he was taught the dark art of assassination, studying the work of the *sicarios* in Mexico, the Italian mob, the Russian Bratva, and the Mossad.

After a three-year accelerated program in Tehran, he applied for and was accepted into the master's program at Saarland University. In his first year, he applied for an internship at BioDine. There was nothing out of the ordinary about an Iranian student studying in Europe and working for a European company. Thousands of Iranian students had done so since 1988. Settling into his new life, he continued to meet with his handler to develop his tradecraft on European soil. He was a precision instrument of the state, and like any tool he needed to be sharpened. Department 15 honed his edge through missions that eliminated threats to the regime. He had once killed an Iranian diplomat on his way to meet with a CIA case officer to hand over a thumb drive with documents proving Iran had systematically targeted U.S. soldiers in Iraq. The diplomat had been found floating in the Danube weeks later. No thumb drive was recovered from his body. Ali's handler was also in place to assess and ensure that he was not being corrupted by Western ways or courted by a foreign intelligence service. He traveled freely, improving his English and German and adding proficient French to his list of talents. He was a regular at football and rugby matches, always refining his counterintelligence skills. And he continued to study the United States, its successes and failures on the battlefield and in the diplomatic and political arenas.

Know thy enemy.

Through his internship at BioDine, he was accepted into the doctoral program in physical chemistry at the University of Lausanne, Switzerland. His classmates and employer knew he was from Iran, just as were thousands of other Europeans. When he accepted full-time employment at BioDine he applied for Swiss citizenship. His record showed no military history. He'd never been arrested. He was never photographed going into and out of mosques. He was clean.

The Hashshasin had successfully infiltrated the land of their enemy.

Ali retrieved his wheeled travel bag from the carousel and worked his way into the main terminal, stopping at a Hudson News kiosk to pick up a copy of the *Wall Street Journal*. As the deputy director for BioDine's Institute for Biomedical Research, he was responsible for programs run by almost six thousand scientists in seventeen facilities worldwide, including the Institute for Tropical Diseases, which focused on dengue, tuberculosis, and malaria. Eighty-six different pharmaceuticals developed through the BioDine Innovative Medicines Division were available in 186 countries, which made it one of the most profitable companies in existence. Even with that success, BioDine still received millions in research grants from the Bill and Melinda Gates Foundation. Eradicating infectious disease was a team effort.

Ali was not in the United States to treat infectious diseases, nor kill an errant traitor to the regime as he had done in Europe. He was in the United States to fulfill his destiny. Americans would die. Young American children would experience the pain he had felt. They would hear the wailing of their mothers. He was there to weaponize a virus.

Iran knew they could not defeat America in a conventional battle or through proxies using thirty-dollar IEDs and truck bombs. Removing the Great Satan from the world stage would require a long-term strategy. Much like the warriors hidden inside the Trojan horse, the attack would have to come from within. This required an indirect approach, one that could not be tied directly back to Iran. Proxies had proven extremely effective over the years, but the relatively small-scale impact of their attacks resulted in nothing more than a scratch to the United States. This attack would be different. It would be perpetrated by proxies who were citizens of the very country they sought to destroy.

COVID-19 had sped up the timeline. The religious counsel in Iran had seen the Great Satan falter. An invisible bug born out of a research lab in Wuhan, China, had devastated the world's most powerful economy. Unemployment was at an all-time high, race riots plagued the major cities, statues were being toppled; a once-strong nation was bowing to the mob. America was on the ropes.

Strike where and when your enemy is vulnerable.

Ali passed through the crowds that reminded him more of his home country than of the United States. Even the smells were reminiscent of his native Iran. America was becoming more like the Middle East every day. *Good.* That would only play into what was to follow.

He waited patiently in a taxi line with his suit coat over his arm, pulling his small roller bag behind him, briefcase in hand, taking note of any familiar faces from his stroll through the airport, just as his trainers in Iran had taught him. He glanced at people's shoes over the top of his Android device. It was easy for a tail to reverse a jacket or throw on a hat and sunglasses; changing shoes required more time.

He had a scheduled tour of the BioDine research facility in Cambridge at the end of the week. There he would sit down with the team to bring them up to speed on new company policies and initiatives in person. That night he planned to catch a soccer game; the New England Revolution was playing D.C. United. It would also serve as a venue to identify possible surveillance. It was hard for authorities to fake being fans of such an un-American sport.

The following day he would set in motion a chain of events that would bring America to her knees.

CHAPTER 6

Camp David
Catoctin Mountain Park, Maryland

IT WASN'T REECE'S FIRST time in a Super Huey. The CIA had used them in Iraq to ferry personnel to and from outstations to the Green Zone and to Baghdad International Airport. During the height of the war, flying over Route Irish was considerably safer than making the twenty-minute mad dash from the embassy on the banks of the Tigris to the freedom bird that would fly one home; even up-armored vehicles were not immune to the devastating power of the EFP.

The Agency maintained a fleet of innocuous planes and helicopters stateside, one of which was now carrying Reece to his destination. Painted to blend in with normal civilian air traffic, they were flown and maintained by front companies to provide some semblance of distance from America's premier spy organization. The rhythmic whir of the blades never failed to bring Reece back to his SEAL days in Iraq and Afghanistan. He always wondered how some operators could sleep while packed into a helo speeding toward target. As a combat leader, Reece took the time to focus, knowing that whatever plan they had submitted to higher command authority for approval was about to become the first casualty of a dynamic battle space. The enemy always got a vote. He was getting a similar feeling now.

As the Huey maneuvered its way north, Reece took a breath and admired the beauty of the Blue Ridge Mountains below. He was almost finished with his training at the Farm. Even though he had no intention of ever working as a case officer as his father had, these days the paramilitary officers of the Clandestine Service went through training at Camp Peary, Virginia, alongside the operations officers and collection management officers. This gave the Agency and the recruit more career options and fostered the relationships necessary to navigate the halls at Langley. His Clandestine Service Trainee class consisted mostly of graduate students proficient in a second or even multiple languages. There were also a select few his age, plucked from the military's most elite special operations units.

His class had commenced in D.C. practicing SDRs. These surveillance detection routes, both in vehicles and on foot, would be a part of every training scenario. Reece knew this was a skill he needed to refine. He was much more comfortable in paramilitary specific training—the shooting and driving portions that the students affectionately called "crash and bang." They went through two weeks of almost exactly the same static line jump training as the three weeks Reece had endured at Fort Benning, Georgia, as a newly minted frogman. Reece remembered his fellow jump students joking that the Army had managed to cram *two days* of training into *three weeks*; at least the CIA had successfully reduced it two weeks. They had a week of maritime training, unarmed combat, medical training, and a SERE/POW scenario that Reece hated even more than the first one he'd gone through at what was affectionately called "camp slappy" almost twenty-years earlier. And they were taught the basics of espionage: disguises, working in alias, dead drops, and how to assess and recruit based on vulnerabilities and motivations. They were being turned into spies.

The president of the United States has requested a meeting.

His supervisor had called Reece into his office and, without even offering him a seat, relayed the information as if it were a common occurrence.

Reece thought *requested* was a strange word to use. Then again, who turns down a *request* from the president?

Reece knew something of the new president's background but had not studied him in depth, having been preoccupied since his return from a personal mission in the wilds of Siberia. He had followed the politics of the recent election because it was difficult to avoid, especially when one's girlfriend was a prominent cable news contributor. After mourning the passing of so many friends and teammates, it disgusted him to watch politicians offer hollow promises to the masses in a bid to continue their hold on power, most forgetting they were employees of the people as soon as they reclaimed their thrones.

The helicopter banked to starboard as it made its approach, settling in through the trees and onto a helipad of bright green AstroTurf on the grounds of what was officially known as Naval Support Facility Thurmont. Situated just over sixty miles from D.C. and located near the border of Maryland and Pennsylvania in Catoctin Mountain Park, the two-hundred-acre retreat had been an escape for presidents and their families since World War II.

Reece heard the familiar sound of the engines going to idle. He unhooked his seat belt and removed his headset as someone he assumed to be a Secret Service agent ran toward the bird and slid open the door.

"Welcome to Camp David, Commander," the man shouted over the still turning rotors. "Follow me."

Reece grabbed his pack and hopped from the bird, instinctively ducking his head as he followed his greeter toward a waiting golf cart, where another Secret Service agent waited at the wheel. He heard the whine of the rotors behind him as the pilot increased their speed before pulling up on the collective and rising back into the clouds.

"Frank Sharp, Secret Service," the man in slacks and a light jacket said, extending his hand.

"James Reece."

"We know." Sharp smiled. "This is Agent Neely."

"Commander." Neely nodded.

Reece looked around, taking in the moss-green hangar nestled among the trees, his eyes coming to rest on a flagpole with the Stars and Stripes gently moving in the breeze.

"Is it what you expected?" Sharp asked.

"Guess I didn't really think much about it."

"It's got a nice campground-type feel, but as you can imagine, it's a tad more secure than the average campground."

"I bet."

"Sir, I have to ask, are you armed?"

"Pistol and blade."

"I'll have to ask you to transfer them to your bag and leave it with us. You'll be meeting with the president alone."

Normally being disarmed made Reece extremely nervous, but this was anything but a normal situation.

"Of course," Reece responded, removing his holster and weapon from the appendix carry position. He wanted to ask additional questions but held his tongue.

"Is that the XL?" Sharp asked, admiring Reece's weapon of choice.

"Yeah, I've been running it for a few months with the red dot and I have to say, I'm a fan."

"I've had my eye on one but 'the missus' thinks I have too many already. I've refrained from telling her she has a closet full of shoes that cost more and all look the same."

"Wise man," Reece acknowledged, as he unclipped the AMTAC Northman blade from his pocket.

"Mind if I wand you?" Sharp asked.

"Go right ahead," Reece said, raising his arms to allow the metal detector access. "I've been switching up between the XL and the 320 X-Compact. Both solid setups."

The wand gave a slight beep at his eyelets on his boots, at his belt, his watch, and his sunglasses.

"Thank you. Hop in. It's a quick ride."

"Where are we going?"

"Aspen."

"What's that?" Reece asked.

"The president's cabin."

CHAPTER 7

THE GOLF CART WOUND its way through the woods on gravel trails. It felt surreal to be on paths that held so much history. It wasn't that long ago that the establishment wanted Reece dead, sending special operators and contractors to kill him. Now he was about to have a one-on-one meeting with the man who currently led that establishment.

They came to a halt at a cabin with the same green exterior as the hangar, a sign designating it as "Aspen." A single golf cart was parked just steps away from the front door. Reece couldn't help but smile as he read a small plaque on its front: Golf Cart One.

Sharp noticed and said, "That always gets a few laughs. Forty-Three had it christened during his first term."

The Secret Service agent led Reece to the entrance and knocked three times. "Mr. President. Commander Reece is here." He turned to Reece. "President Christensen will be with you shortly. We'll be close."

"Thank you," Reece said as his escorts moved off down the path, leaving the former SEAL alone.

Reece heard the knob turn and a second later was face-to-face with the leader of the free world. He suppressed his military tendency to come to attention.

"Commander Reece, thank you for coming. I'm Alec Christensen."

"Pleasure, sir."

"Come in. I'm told the trees have eyes," he said, with a disarming smile.

Reece entered a room that reminded him more of his grandparents' house than a retreat befitting the commander in chief.

"I know, it's in dire need of an upgrade. Probably going to do it myself to save the taxpayers some money. Have you ever been to Camp David?"

"No, sir. But I think you knew that."

"I'd also be remiss if I did not thank you for your service to the nation. Had you not saved President Grimes in Odessa, I might not even be in this position."

"It was Senior Chief Freddy Strain, sir. He saved the president," Reece said, remembering his friend and teammate killed by a sniper on a rooftop half a world away, a sniper who was still out there.

"The country will never forget him, Commander."

"Thank you, sir."

"I want to show you something," he said, leading the way to the outside patio of the upper terrace, a location that offered sweeping views of the expansive property.

"Are you a student of history, Commander Reece?"

"I like to think so, Mr. President," Reece replied, looking down on the pool below.

"Beyond those trees," the president pointed, "is Holly Cabin. FDR and Churchill planned the D-Day invasion over cigars and highballs from that very porch. In fact, the only reason this place exists is because Roosevelt's staff was worried that his presidential yacht was going to be sunk by a German U-boat. He was on the USS *Sequoia* so often they called it 'the Floating White House.' Quite an appealing target for the Nazi war machine. In '42 the National Park Service was tasked with procuring him a more secluded location that was still close to D.C., so they found this old Works Progress Administration site from the thirties. FDR dubbed it 'Shangri-La' after the Tibetan paradise described in the James Hilton novel. Eisenhower thought that was a bit pretentious and renamed it in honor of his grandson, David. It's been Camp David ever since."

The president looked back to his guest.

"Forgive me, I get caught up in how many decisions impacting twentieth- and twenty-first-century history were made right here. The fates of nations have been decided on these very grounds."

Reece nodded politely, recognizing that the president was not yet finished.

"Eisenhower put in the golf course that doubles as the helo landing pad. It's really just a driving range with four tees. The Internet thinks it only has three. Shhh, don't tell anyone." He winked. "Khrushchev and Ike actually stayed in this cabin. They watched Westerns together, if you can believe that. JFK and Jackie liked to shoot clays right over there. Obama staged a picture there with a shotgun trying to appeal to gun-owning voters, but it didn't play well. Brezhnev almost crashed a Lincoln Continental while driving with Nixon around the perimeter one day in '73. Why Nixon let him drive is anyone's guess. Maybe his ego got the better of him after opening China in '72. Gorbachev threw his first horseshoe right here. Thatcher, Yeltsin, Blair, and even Putin have been guests. And now *you*."

"It's an honor, sir," Reece said, unsure of how to respond.

"The White House is for photo ops and press conferences. The *real* decisions are made out here. But you didn't come all this way for a history lesson on Camp David, did you, Commander?"

"I was told only that you requested a meeting, Mr. President."

The president tilted his head to the left, his eyes focused on Reece as they might read sentences in a book, comparing the man to the information from his files.

"I'd tell you to just call me Alec, but I can't get anyone to do it. That's one order they won't follow."

The president looked back out on the grounds of the presidential retreat and gestured to a fire pit a stone's throw away.

"In 1978, Anwar Sadat sat by that fire with Menachem Begin. Jimmy Carter played referee. Over two decades later, President Clinton would sit in those very same chairs with Ehud Barak and Yasser Arafat. *Twenty years* went by like that." The president snapped his fingers. "And what did they have to show for it?"

Not waiting for an answer, he continued in a tone that shifted slightly to one tinged with respect.

"This land holds secrets, Commander." His eyes scanned the tree line. "This cabin is one of the few places where my conversations are not recorded for posterity. Come inside. Can I offer you a drink? Whiskey?"

"No, thank you. I'm fine," Reece said.

"Hard to find a picture of JFK around here without a drink in hand. Times have changed. Let me fix you some coffee. Honey and cream, right?"

"That's right, Mr. President."

"The Secret Service has quite the file on you. As does the Navy, the NSA, the FBI . . . and the CIA."

Reece's eyes narrowed.

"Fascinating reading."

The president moved to the kitchen and dumped the morning's coffee.

"Are you surprised the president of the United States can make his own coffee?"

"Ah, well, not that you *can*, but that you *do*."

"Even more surprised it's in this old Mr. Coffee?" The president chuckled. "I like to do a few things for myself. They won't let me at the

White House, but out here I can get away with it. Reminds me of a morning in September . . ." The president's voice trailed off.

"Sir?"

"I made her coffee that morning, you know."

"Who, sir?"

"My fiancée. Jennifer. Looking back, there were so many mistakes."

The coffeemaker began to purr.

"I was working in California, and she had a job in New York. I was so invested in my company. I thought we had our entire lives ahead of us."

He poured Reece a cup and stirred in cream and honey.

"Thank you, sir."

"Do you believe in the Deep State, Mr. Reece?" the president asked as he made himself a cup, gesturing to a sitting area just off the kitchen.

"Sir?"

"Sit, please. The Deep State, or what people call the Deep State, anyway. Do you believe in it?"

Now it was Reece's turn to study the man before him. He was shorter than Reece expected. His hair was cut conservatively and was graying beyond the temples. A dark blue polo with the presidential seal was tucked into khaki pants, revealing the physique of a man who still kept in shape, his eyes blue and alert.

"I believe we've found common ground, Mr. President."

"I thought we would, Commander. The Deep State is real, though it's not what's portrayed in the movies. The deep state is *bureaucracy.* Power held by the few. The elite. The *intelligentsia.* It's our cultural institutions: academia, big tech, Wall Street, Hollywood, even professional sports. I scare them." He paused. "I wouldn't be surprised if I don't make it through my term. Does that surprise you?"

"Not much surprises me, sir."

"The Deep State is not a group of men in a bunker issuing orders. It's a remark, an offhand comment, plausibly deniable suggestions. It's donors. It's established media, right, left, and center. It's regulations and broad, sweeping laws. It's the power of the IRS, NSA, EPA, FBI, and your very own CIA. That's the Deep State, Reece."

"I don't understand, sir. What are you saying?"

"Are you familiar with William Ramsey's work on spiritualism?"

"I can't say that I am."

"In 1856, he wrote: *One of the most striking proofs of the personal existence of Satan is found in the fact, that he has so influenced the minds of multitudes in reference to his existence and doings, as to make them believe that he does not exist.* I found his work while studying the conceptual existence of evil after my fiancée was murdered. I was trying to understand and make sense of it all. Those words stuck with me."

The president put down his coffee and moved to the window, his back to his visitor.

"Can you keep a secret, Commander?"

"I wouldn't be here if you thought otherwise."

"True. You know, Ben Franklin had a saying, *Three may keep a secret, if two of them are dead.*"

"I'm familiar with it. The Agency has an unofficial motto from the Bible, 'And ye shall know the truth and the truth shall make you free.'"

President Alec Christensen made his choice.

"Nine-eleven was not just the work of nineteen hijackers and a man hiding in a cave in Afghanistan. Nor was it any of the wild conspiracy theories you may have heard. *Nineteen hijackers.* I never believed it." The president turned. "There were more: facilitators, enablers, financiers right here in the United States. The Deep State, they knew we needed a nice, tidy list to appease the American public. The nineteen hijackers were already dead. The public still needed a face. Someone to blame. Someone far away. Someone who could be eliminated to make them feel safe again. To restore their *illusion* of safety. Get them back in the malls. There was a hand at play, Mr. Reece, though it's not who you think."

The president reached down and picked up a frame that had been leaning against the wall under the window.

"Do you know what this is?" the president asked, throwing it to his visitor.

Reece caught it. He looked at the commander in chief and then down at the document encased in glass.

"Don't worry, it's a copy. I had it framed when I ran for my House seat. Read it aloud, would you?"

Reece looked back to the document in his hands.

"Public Law 107–40 107th Congress, Joint Resolution, to authorize the use of United States Armed Forces against those responsible for the recent attacks launched against the United States."

Reece's eyes moved back to the president.

"Skip to section one," he said.

"Section one. This joint resolution may be cited as the 'Authorization for Use of Military Force.' Section two. Authorization for use of United States Armed Forces. The President is authorized to use all necessary and appropriate force against those nations, organizations, or persons he determines planned, authorized, committed, or aided the terrorist attacks that occurred on September 11, 2001, or harbored such organizations or persons, in order to prevent any future acts of international terrorism against the United States by such nations, organizations or persons. Consistent with section 8(a)(1) of the War Powers Resolution, the Congress declares that this section is intended to constitute specific statutory authorization within the meaning of section 5(b) of the War Powers Resolution."

Reece looked up. "That's it?"

"That's it. Four days after the attack, President Bush met here at Camp David with a group that would set U.S. foreign policy for the next twenty years. Cheney was already here; this was his much-talked-about 'secure location.' Powell, Rumsfeld, Wolfowitz, Rice, Armitage, O'Neill,

Ashcroft, and Mueller, along with Tenet and Cofer Black from the CIA; all of them were here. None of the conversations were recorded. National Security Presidential Directive Nine came out of those meetings. It's now called 'Defeating the Terrorist Threat to the United States.' The notification on bin Laden also came out of meetings with Tenet and Black."

"Notification, sir?"

"The legal authority for our intelligence services to target and kill Osama bin Laden."

"I always thought the mission was a 'capture/kill,'" Reece said.

"A convenient semi-truth."

It was all starting to sink in.

"The resolution you just read was passed by Congress the following week, just seven days after 9/11. Two hundred and seventy-five words. It authorized President Bush to take us into Afghanistan and then into Iraq. Those words remain the sole legal justification to commit military forces to the Global War on Terror. It's been *twenty* years, Commander. Look at their intent. ISIS didn't even exist in September 2001. Yet the language in this document justifies U.S. presidents to order invasions of sovereign countries in their pursuit."

"Mr. President," Reece said slowly, "what do you want from me?"

Answering a question with a question, the president asked, "What do you think our adversaries have been doing while we've been fighting the War on Terror?"

Reece paused; he was in a job interview.

"They've been learning, sir. They've been adapting. China, Russia, Iran, and North Korea. They watched us destroy Saddam's military in 1993 when they went head-to-head with us in a conventional conflict. We did it again in 2003. Then they watched those same technological advances rendered ineffective by various factions and splinter groups wielding AKs, RPGs, and IEDs by insurgents whose goal was to run out the clock."

"That's right. We need to regroup, Reece. Our main state adversaries know how to fight us and win. We've shown them how over the past two decades."

"Sir, with all due respect. You can have these conversations with any number of policy wonks in the swamp. What am I doing here?"

"True, though only a select few really understand the nature of the conflict in which we are engaged and, more importantly, understand what you just so clearly articulated." The president stopped and lowered his voice. "The resolution was never fully utilized in accordance with the intent of Congress and the American people."

"Sir?"

"Read section one again."

Reece tilted the frame and read: "This joint resolution may be cited as the 'Authorization for Use of Military Force.' Section two. Authorization for use of United States Armed Forces. The President is authorized to use all necessary and appropriate force against those nations, organizations, or persons he determines planned, authorized, committed, or aided the terrorist attacks that occurred on September 11, 2001, or harbored such organizations or persons, in order to prevent any future acts of international terrorism against the United States by such nations, organizations or persons."

"Read that last part again, Commander."

"Organizations or persons he determines planned, authorized, committed or aided the terrorist attacks of September 11, 2001."

"We've gotten so far away from that original intent. Someone's face had to be plastered on TV and on those targets at gun stores across the nation. The American public needed to give evil a name, so we handed them nineteen dead hijackers and Osama bin Laden. Sure, there was a supporting cast of characters, but they were all overseas living in caves to be rooted out and destroyed by our new heroes in special operations. No one wanted to know the truth."

"What truth, Mr. President?"

"The truth is that the support network from 9/11 still exists."

The president reached across the small coffee table that separated them and set down three files.

"Have you heard of File Seventeen, Mr. Reece?"

"Isn't that the file President Obama declassified a few years ago that pointed to a Saudi connection to 9/11?"

"Yes, though it was more to placate some of the families of victims. It was all circumstantial and relatively benign. Barely registered in the public consciousness."

"What's this one?" Reece asked, picking up the next file.

"That's the twenty-eight redacted pages from the 9/11 Commission report. Also, mostly circumstantial and likely would only have hurt relations with the Saudis in the wake of 9/11, an ally we needed in the region."

"And this?" Reece asked, holding up the third file.

"That, Commander, is a target package. Open it."

Reece flipped the page and began to read.

"Take your time."

When Reece picked his head up, the most powerful man on earth was staring at him with an intensity born in battle.

"The terrorists in that package are still out there. They still live among us. They didn't fly the planes or slash throats of pilots and flight attendants, but without them, 9/11 would not have happened. Jen would still be alive, as would almost three thousand others, not to mention those killed on both sides in Iraq and Afghanistan. Reece, there was a concerted effort to convince the American people that there were only nineteen hijackers plus Zacarias Moussaoui, the twentieth hijacker. There were more; a network of facilitators. I always knew it. I want you to finish what we started in 2001. The country has lost its appetite. If we bring them to trial now, it's years of pain and political infighting. That joint resolution you just read gives the president of the United States the ability to bring all those who enabled the 9/11 attacks to justice."

"I think I'll take that drink now, Mr. President."

The president stood and returned with two tumblers.

"On the rocks, no water."

"Was that in my file, too?"

"No, just a guess."

"It was a good one."

"What do you know about Operation Wrath of God, Commander?"

"It was the Israeli response to the Munich Massacre. Eleven Israeli athletes were killed by Black September at the 1972 Olympics. Wrath of God was authorized by Prime Minister Golda Meir. Mossad hit teams deployed worldwide to kill those responsible and to send a message."

"That's right. What are your thoughts on targeted assassinations?"

Reece took a sip and looked around the room.

"Don't worry. Like I said, this is the one place I trust not to be recording my every word. It's one of the reasons we are meeting here and not in the White House. Plus, visitor logs are almost impossible to doctor these days."

"Isn't there an executive order that prohibits assassination?"

"There is, but legally that definition of assassination refers to a head of state. Individuals can be targeted with what's referred to as a 'notification,' just like with bin Laden. Reagan issued a directive in '83 for the mastermind of the Beirut embassy and Marine barracks bombings. There are new notifications in the back of the file, signed by me."

Reece set down his drink.

"Sir, are you asking me or ordering me to kill everyone on this list?"

"Think of this as an exploratory conversation. The seven people on that list were under surveillance for ten years as 'persons of interest.' We never put them on the no-fly list. We wanted to watch and observe to find out who else they were in contact with, to continue to gather intelligence to use them to disrupt any possible sleeper cells preparing for another wave of attacks. They never led us anywhere. Surveillance was called off in 2011 after the bin Laden raid."

"Maybe we were watching the wrong people," Reece countered.

"Spend some time with that file; we have the right people."

Reece took a long sip of his drink.

"Reece, do you know that the president of the United States does not even undergo a background investigation?"

Reece shook his head.

"Do you know why that is?"

"My guess is that none of you would pass it."

"An excellent deduction. And true. A president does not even have a security clearance yet has unfettered access to our nation's most closely guarded secrets. A president can read anything. He can classify or declassify anything. That's the power of this seat, Mr. Reece. That's why I'm here. To find out who made 9/11 possible and bring them to justice."

"Why me?"

"I think you know the answer."

Reece swirled the dark, smooth liquid in his glass.

"Because I've done it before. If things go south, you can point to me as a renegade CIA asset who went off the reservation. I have a history. This meeting is off the books. It becomes just another crazy conspiracy theory, like the Kennedy assassination. Anything tying me to you is lost in classified files just like Dallas. Those 'notifications' in the file disappear. If I'm successful and take them out quietly, it still gets classified in the mountains of files that only a president can access. Maybe I have an 'accident' to further muddy the waters in case anyone came looking."

Reece's head was spinning. Not long ago, when he thought he was dying, he'd killed on home soil. Some saw his actions as murder, others as justice. Believing he was already dead gave him a freedom to seal the fate of all those who had taken everything from him. That freedom to become an insurgent on home soil allowed him an effectiveness and efficiency through the acceptance of a fast-approaching death. He'd bottled that part of his life up and packed it away in the deepest recesses of his mind; his wife, daughter, and unborn son slaughtered in their home, his troop ambushed in the mountains of the Hindu Kush. It had been orchestrated by a cabal of senior military officers, political leaders, and private sector financiers, all of whom Reece put in the ground.

"Sir, I'll need to think about it."

"I understand." The president stood and started toward the door. Reece took the hint and followed suit. "We've prepared a cabin for you. Think it through. Get a workout in. The gym isn't bad. Shoot some clays. In the morning we can have breakfast. A helo will be here at ten to take you back to the Farm. If you decide against it, it will be like you were never here and I expect you to never breathe a word of our conversation to anyone."

They stopped at the entrance and the president opened the door for his guest. "And remember, don't trust anyone."

"Even you, Mr. President?"

"Trust no one, Reece."

Reece nodded.

"Oh, Commander, before you go, there is one other thing."

CHAPTER 8

THE GYM WAS EMPTY. Reece pushed himself hard in round after round of kettlebell swings, Turkish get-ups, and sprints. He lost track of the rounds and continued to push, spurred on by visions of the living and the dead, Katie, Lauren, Lucy, Freddy, faces of those he'd tortured and killed in a quest for vengeance. His mind came to focus on one person in particular, a sniper whose face he'd only seen in a surveillance photograph, a man whose finger had pressed a trigger and killed Freddy Strain, leaving his wife without a husband and his children without a father. A man Reece was going to kill.

Jogging back to his cabin he'd thought of Freddy's special needs child, Sam, now dependent on just one parent for his very survival. Freddy was dead because of Reece. The money Reece had used to fund Samuel Strain's special needs trust would ensure the child had a lifetime of medical care, but what he really needed was a father. What Joanie Strain needed was her husband. Reece had promised her that he would kill everyone responsible. To do that he needed the resources of the CIA.

As Reece lay on his bunk, watching the fan slowly turning in the shadows of the early evening light, he thought about what the president had asked of him as he left Aspen cabin.

Oh, Commander, before you go, there is one other thing.

On September tenth, Mohamed Atta and Abdulaziz al-Omri traveled from Boston to South Portland, Maine. It's been speculated that they did so because of a more lax security posture at Portland International Jetport, but that doesn't make sense. They still had to pass through security at Logan in Boston. Atta was even selected for additional screening. They made it through security just fifteen minutes before takeoff. Atta nearly missed the appointment for his own death. I want to know who they met in Maine, Mr. Reece. The FBI, CIA, no one has been able to figure it out. Find out. Find out and let me know.

With each turn of the fan, Reece saw pictures of the 9/11 hijackers imprinted in his brain, finally settling on the passport photo of Mohamed Atta. It had been broadcast across the world in the months after the attack: dark collared button-up over a white T-shirt, lips pressed together, the dead dark eyes. Forever frozen in time, at thirty-three years old he had been an instrument that helped change the course of history.

Who did you meet in Maine? Reece thought.

Whoever it was, Reece knew they'd be added to the president's list. If it was an agent of a foreign intelligence service, Reece could only imagine what the leader of the free world would do. A man in that seat wielded a power greater than anyone in recorded history. With ever-changing launch codes and the turn of a key, he could remove entire regions of the globe from existence. The Authorization for Use of Military Force and Presidential Directive Nine gave him that authority.

The president had entrusted Reece with a secret. The popular president was not in office as a servant to his nation. He had fought overseas and returned home to amass a fortune and run for the highest office in the land not out of duty, but out of a need for vengeance; to avenge one particular victim of 9/11.

Reece understood revenge, which is precisely why the president had chosen him for this mission.

As Reece closed his eyes and fought off the nightmares, he remembered the pastor at Freddy's funeral echoing the words from Isaiah 6:8 that he'd heard recited over the graves of so many of his SEAL brothers: *"Then I heard the voice of the Lord saying, 'Whom shall I send? And who will go for us?' And I said, 'Here am I. Send me!'"*

Reece was going back to war.

CHAPTER 9

Washington, D.C.

AS IRAN'S CHIEF INTELLIGENCE operative in the United States, Hafez Qassem had been conducting what amounted to a yearlong surveillance detection route. He'd been followed by agents from what he correctly assumed to be the Foreign Counterintelligence Squad of the FBI's Washington Field Office for the better part of a year when he first took the post, though he pretended not to notice. He did not meet with sources, nor did he do anything the least bit suspicious. He went to dinners, as would be expected of a diplomat of his station, attended soccer games, drank in moderation, and every now and again would stuff dollar bills into G-strings at Good Guys Gentleman's Club, on Wisconsin Avenue in the shadow of the United States Naval Observatory. He was setting the conditions.

The Iranian embassy in the United States had been boarded up since 1979 following the Iranian Revolution, the rise of Ayatollah Khomeini, and the ensuing hostage crisis that would usher in the Reagan era. Diplomatic matters were handled through the "Interests Section of the Islamic Republic of Iran in the United States," which was conveniently housed in the embassy of Pakistan on 1250 23rd Street NW in Washington, D.C. As part of a small Iranian contingency, Qassem enjoyed diplomatic immunity and could travel freely to and from Iran on one of the planes designated for the Iranian ambassador to the United Nations in New York.

As Iran's top spy in the United States, his job was *not* to spot, develop, and recruit spies; he had a network at the tactical level responsible for identifying potential assets. His job was to oversee that intelligence, to analyze it for exploitation, identify patterns, and detect possible double agents. It was well known that the NSA collected and read all electronic communications in and out of Iran, so Qassem's reports were sent directly to the Supreme Council of National Security via diplomatic pouch. Because he was not actively involved in recruitment, there was little the United States could do about him. As with every other embassy, to include those of staunch U.S. allies, it was expected for there to be an intelligence section to the diplomatic mission, just as the United States operated out of all of their embassies and consulates abroad. To the Americans, he was a boring bureaucrat, enjoying a drink or two beyond the watchful eye of the regime. Americans could understand that. It was the ones who never drank, prayed five times a day, and avoided scantily clad women who made them nervous.

After the first six months, his around-the-clock initial surveillance was reduced to what amounted to a "checkup," to ensure nothing had changed and that Qassem was still passing his time with nice dinners and soccer games. When the FBI did monitor his activities, they were easy to spot. Qassem had been a player in the game long enough to know when something was out of place. He hadn't met physically with an asset on American soil in almost twenty years, back when a meeting in a pizza restaurant in Maine had made his career and altered the destiny of a nation.

Following the U.S. withdrawal from Iraq, the up-and-coming spymaster had successfully turned it into a client state of Iran. CIA sources, as part of their deep penetration programs, eagerly switched sides after the American abandonment, believing their past CIA associations would come to light. They were looking for a new guardian. The intelligence windfall on CIA tactics, techniques, and procedures was a treasure trove for the regime. Qassem was rewarded with a promotion.

More recently, he had overseen the recruitment of U.S. Air Force Sergeant Monica Elfriede Witt. She defected to Iran in 2013, and still lived there today. Qassem had met with her numerous times over the years and spent untold hours reading her debriefings. The Americans had not realized what was happening until she was safely on Iranian soil. They should have killed her at the first hint of betrayal, before she was beyond their grasp. That's what Qassem would have done: raped, tortured, and killed her as a warning to others. If the MOI ever suspected changing loyalties, they would not hesitate to put a bullet in her head before she could cross the border, a condition of internment of which she was well aware. She would stay put. Not only had she provided the names of U.S. intelligence sources in Iran, but she also helped reveal a covert communication network code named COVCOM, used by the CIA to securely communicate with agents in Iran, China, Russia, and North Korea. It was the biggest intelligence coup since the end of the Cold War, and it was Qassem who had been its mastermind. Intelligence gleaned from COVCOM served another purpose—it confirmed that the United States did not know who Qassem was or the role he had played in 9/11.

Unlike some of his counterparts, he kept a low profile. Revolutionary Guard Quds Force Commander General Qasem Soleimani, Hezbollah chief of staff Imad Mughniyeh, Islamic Jihad leader Fathi al-Shkaki, and PLO Chairman Yasser Arafat had been relentlessly hunted for years. Only one of them had died of natural causes. It was important for the West to have their devils. Qassem planned to remain a ghost. He was more effective that way. While his contemporaries had become martyrs,

Qassem would rather live for the cause than die for it. He'd stay off the radar to increase his chances of remaining aboveground.

Not even he had known what was coming. In 2001 he was simply a messenger, tasked to pass along a word. He'd taken that word from Iran, to Turkey, to Germany, to the United Kingdom, to Canada, and finally into the United States, where he'd whispered it to the man with the dead eyes. Qassem had suspected a truck bomb near the White House in the months ahead, not a multipronged attack using commercial airliners as instruments of terror the following morning.

The Sunni-Shia rift was commonly pointed to by academics as the reason Iran could never have played a role in the attack on America. Qassem had listened to the experts on CNN, Fox, and the BBC for years. The accepted histories of the lead-up to that September morning focused on the Soviet-Afghan War, disenfranchised mujahideen, U.S. troops on the sacred lands of Mecca and Medina, the banishment of a Saudi son, and a Sunni group called al-Qaeda; a convenient history for those accessing the past from an ivory tower. Those academics failed to understand the bonds forged between al-Qaeda and Iran in Sudan after the son of the Saudi construction magnate was expelled from the Kingdom. Al-Qaeda and Iranian leadership were not concerned with a seventh-century dispute of succession; they had a common enemy in the twenty-first century.

Al-Qaeda operatives were sent from Sudan to train in Iran and with Hezbollah in Lebanon, adding tactics of terror to their battlefield experience from the land of the Pashtuns. The godfather of modern terrorism, Imad Mughniyeh, met with Osama bin Laden and Ayman al-Zawahiri in Khartoum, passing on the lessons of 1980s Beirut and the success of martyrdom operations against Western targets. Al-Qaeda was listening and learning. As Qassem worked his way up the ranks of Iranian intelligence, he would discover the lengths to which his country had gone in assisting al-Qaeda in the assassination of Ahmad Shah Masoud, commander of the

Northern Alliance in Afghanistan, just two days prior to 9/11. The Sunni-Shia divide was a convenient talking point for the so-called terrorism experts on CNN. The view from the foxhole told a different story.

Qassem had proven himself adept at orchestrating the proxy war against the Americans in Iraq while simultaneously infiltrating every ministry of the Iraqi government to include the office of the prime minister. Iran now dominated terrain from the Persian Gulf to the Mediterranean Sea and had done so right under the nose of the American soldiers and diplomats trying so hard to bring George W. Bush's vision of Jeffersonian democracy to the Middle East. Dick Cheney, Colin Powell, Donald Rumsfeld—their arrogance had cost their country dearly and allowed the regime to outwit the enemies of Islam in the new Great Game.

After his success pushing the Americans from Iraq, Qassem was transferred from the senior office of Iran's Ministry of Intelligence and Security to the Intelligence Organization of the Islamic Revolutionary Guard Corps, a more flexible entity established at the behest of the Supreme Leader in 2009. It gave Qassem the freedom to think and to plan. His mentors had taught him well. They had been the architects of a proxy war against the Americans for almost forty years, ushering in a wave of suicide bombings targeting the U.S. embassy and Marine barracks in Beirut. Their greatest achievement was contesting the religious ban on suicide bombings. Sunni organizations had eventually followed suit. They made martyrdom operations acceptable within Islam and successfully exported the tactic from the Middle East to the rest of the world. Qassem had studied their operations and identified the gaps in their ideology of terror. Truck bombs and airliners would not destroy a nation as prosperous and resilient as the United States. It would take something more. Fomenting chaos through proxies was what Iran did best. They were about to bring that expertise to the land of the free.

The contents of a diplomatic pouch are protected under Article 27.3 of the Vienna Convention on Diplomatic Relations, shielding them from any searches by a host nation government. Searching a properly marked diplomatic pouch including via x-ray was a violation of international law. And so it was that a pouch arrived in the mail section of the Pakistani embassy in Washington, D.C., properly marked as official correspondence with DIPLOMATIC POUCH clearly identifying it as protected material between Islamabad and its mission in the United States. Inside was another box labeled as property of the government of Iran and addressed to a member of their diplomatic staff.

Even though the contents of the diplomatic pouch were protected by the Vienna Convention, Qassem took his time opening the box; the small vial within contained the death of a nation. In many ways this was the most sensitive part of the operation. Once he passed the contents of the package to the asset, there was no turning back. There was no recalling it. There was no abort code. The poison would be released into America's bloodstream and just like a cancer-ridden patient, America would turn against itself, compounding the problems of racial discord, Marxist communist protests, a domestic insurgency, and the economic hit of COVID-19. This was the time to strike, before they could regain their footing or rally around a foreign threat. There couldn't be a country or organization to blame, bomb, or destroy. It had to look like a naturally occurring event, and *if* the plot were uncovered, the menace had to have come from within. Nothing could tie it back to Iran; on this, the Ayatollah had been clear.

Qassem had learned something else from the traitorous Air Force sergeant, a detail she didn't even know was important. It was why he continued his conversations with her. Initially he'd been interested in the U.S. cyber-warfare capability and what Iranian actions would trigger a U.S. nuclear response. Almost as an aside she'd mentioned another protocol, a nonnuclear OPLAN more secure than anything she knew about her country's designs on Iran. She'd learned about it during a briefing in Hurlburt, Florida.

Why, Qassem wondered, did the United States have multiple MC-130s from the U.S. Air Force Special Operations Command on standby in Florida armed with GBU-43/B bombs, and why was their mission a more closely guarded secret than the nuclear OPLAN for Iran?

MC-130s were not a traditional long-range strategic bombing platform like the venerable B-52, B-1, or B-2 stealth bomber. MC-130s needed to be forward deployed to a combat theater of operations to be effective. Why the secrecy surrounding this squadron in Florida always on standby? How far could they fly from their base in the panhandle? A Caribbean or Central or South America contingency? Maybe, but there had to be another reason to have those platforms on constant alert.

Qassem was missing something.

He made a trip to an apartment in the Tajrish neighborhood of Tehran. Located near good shopping and restaurants but still far enough from the chaos of city center, the third-floor apartment was the last stop for a man who had once been a senior biologist at the Institute of Medical Biotechnology in Moscow. Following the collapse of the Soviet Union, he had been one of those recruited by Iran to help modernize its biological weapons program.

The old scientist was frail and not completely lucid as he struggled to make tea for his guest. He'd given up trying to return to the Ukraine of his birth. He'd sold his soul to his masters in Tehran. This is where he would die.

Valeri Bakayev was not a young man when Gorbachev instituted his policies of glasnost and perestroika. With a wife who had left him for a more attentive suitor, Bakayev was alone in the world when the paychecks stopped arriving and the Soviet Union dissolved before his eyes. The Iranians had recognized their opportunity and pounced. When presented with the prospect of dying alone of starvation in a cold Moscow apartment or continuing his work in Iran for more money than he ever thought possible, Bakayev left Mother Russia with the clothes on his back and a lifetime of biological warfare knowledge in his head.

Contingency.

What do you mean, Doctor? Qassem had asked.

On this particular point the old scientist's memory had been clear. Using the Socratic method so popular with those in the legal and medical professions, he'd led Qassem to the answer.

What would you do if a deadly pathogen you'd developed in violation of international treaty escaped your lab and threatened to infect a town, a city, a nation, the world?

We'd contain it, Qassem answered.

What else? What if it escaped the containment zone?

We'd have to kill it.

Precisely. And how would you do that? How do you destroy what can't be seen?

It must be eradicated.

In Russia we had a protocol called yasnyy veter, *"cleansing wind," the old scientist said. All cities near our facilities studying the deadliest pathogens were on a target list. Biological weapon production facilities, bio-weapon research labs, storage facilities, testing grounds: Zagorsk, Pokrov, Kirov, Omutninsk, Vozrozhdeniya, Aralsk, Nukus, Vladivostok. In the eventuality that a pathogen escaped, the area would need to be obliterated before the contagion destroyed the entire country.*

The Soviet Union targeted its own cities for destruction?

It was the most efficient way to contain an outbreak that could have destroyed the country.

Are you sure?

My son, I developed the contingency.

Before he left the old man's apartment, a plan had started to form in the intelligence officer's head. He now knew what would lead a country to destroy its own cities. And he knew why those MC-130s were staged at the ready in Florida. Qassem would turn the might of the American military against itself.

Qassem remembered the long-term penetration program he had helped design years earlier, sending young students abroad to study medicine to help modernize the Iranian health system; he remembered one student in particular. He would be perfect.

First, he'd need to sell it through his superiors to the Ayatollah.

There was nothing electronic to tie Iran to the plan; no emails, no text messages, no cloud-based spy communications network like the CIA's foolish COVAIR system. This would be done the old way. The way of the Hashshasin. The way things were handled when the Persian Empire was at the height of its power. This attack would restore Iran to its rightful place in the world order, reducing what the Americans liked to call a "beacon of hope" to a legacy of ashes.

CHAPTER 10

Gillette Stadium
Foxborough, Massachusetts

THEY HAD MET ONCE before, at a football match in Germany. It had been a number of years, but Qassem and Ali had been trained by one of the most ruthless intelligence organizations in existence. They had not forgotten each other or the procedures for exchanging bona fides.

Security was tight with the Boston Marathon bombing still relatively fresh in the minds of those who attended sporting events in the Cradle of Liberty, but the plainclothes and uniformed officers were looking for something else, unaware that an attack was being set in motion in the very birthplace of the American Revolution.

The spymaster and the assassin did not do a brush pass or a dead drop. They made no attempt to avoid the multitude of cameras covering the event.

Leaving the bathroom, Qassem stopped next to a concession stand selling hats and jerseys to rub on hand sanitizer and adjust his mask. It was a blessing from Allah that the masks they were forced to wear at sporting events were now the accepted norm. Facial recognition software could take parts of the ears and eyes and put together partial matches, but it was not the tool of the state it had been just a year earlier. The Americans had tried to enforce six-foot distancing during the COVID-19 pandemic, obviously so they could build their databases, matching "partials" to build their sample volume and increase occlusion detection accuracy. Coverings were nothing new. Masks were just added to a list of facial obstructions including sunglasses, scarves, and hats so algorithms could make matches via an ear, an uncovered nose, or just one eye.

The Americans are such sheep.

If the intelligence services went back weeks from now and pieced together the meeting with partial matches from their facial recognition databases, it would already be too late.

"Excuse me."

Qassem turned and looked into the eyes he remembered from their meeting in Germany.

"Yes?" Qassem responded.

"Could you spare a few drops of that sanitizer? I seem to have forgotten mine in the car."

"Of course," Qassem said, holding out the small bottle.

"Thank you. Great game."

"Ha! Not quite like those in Europe but it will have to do."

"Agreed."

"Here, take this extra bottle, I have plenty," Qassem said, pulling another unopened bottle from his pocket.

"I couldn't."

"Please, I insist."

"Thank you."

"*Ma'al-salfāṃah,*" Qassem said through his mask. *With peace.*

"*Ff ' amfān Allfāh,*" Ali responded. *In God's protection.*

Ali touched his right hand to his heart and walked back to his seat to finish the game. For American *soccer,* it wasn't half bad.

One of the deadliest toxins ever developed had just been placed in the hands of an assassin.

CHAPTER 11

Club Aegis
Washington, D.C.

SENATOR EDWARD THWAITE'S BLACK Suburban stopped in the alley on the 700 block of 15th Street, not far from the Treasury Building and within easy walking distance of the White House. He dropped his phone and tablet into a leather pouch that he handed to his aide for safekeeping. Electronic devices were not allowed where he was going. His aide took them without a word, knowing not to speak unless spoken to. He'd never been invited inside. He knew his place: out here in the vehicle.

The driver stayed behind the wheel while the detail lead exited the passenger side and opened the door for the senator, escorting him to what looked to be the back exit to any number of businesses whose fronts faced Lafayette Square. The senator nodded to another man who waited by the door.

"He's upstairs, sir," the advance man stated.

"Thank you," the senator replied, taking a key card from his pocket and sliding it into the card reader affixed to the door.

He punched in a code that was also his membership number and stepped inside with his bodyguard, leaving the advance man in the street. The senator much preferred arriving through the main entrance and taking the private elevator up to the second floor. This back entrance was installed during Prohibition, when the same people who outlawed alcohol needed a speakeasy nearby to enjoy a drink; regardless of who controlled the House and Senate, hypocrisy was a constant. Today, the alley entrance allowed for additional anonymity but did require him to make the trek to the second level on foot, a journey that left him slightly winded.

It was almost a straight shot down Pennsylvania Avenue from Capitol Hill and offered a beautiful walk, though the senator had never exercised that option. Nestled in among the monuments, federal agencies, and museums for which Washington was famous, Club Aegis, or AG for those in the know, was the last true bipartisan private club in D.C. Membership was not based on political leanings. Republicans and Democrats were welcomed with open arms, if they could pay, if they had power, and if they could wait. The five-person membership committee was made up of three generations of the Marchetti family. Rumors abounded that there was a connection to what insiders called "the outfit." The rest of the world called it the mafia.

Power was the currency traded upon in the high-backed leather chairs of Club Aegis. If Los Angeles was about sex and New York was about money, D.C. was all about supremacy. *Aegis*, in Greek mythology, conjured up images of a protective shield from the *Iliad*, an image reinforced by statues of Zeus and Athena that framed the bar. Members thought of themselves as protectors of the republic, though the goal of most was to protect and grow their bank accounts.

Senator Thwaite was a second-generation Aegis member, his father having served in the Senate for thirty years before Edward took over the seat. In his father's day, one would look around and see Kissinger, Abrams, McNamara, William Weed Kaufmann, Harold Brown, John Rubel, Alain C. Enthoven, Maxwell Taylor, William Westmoreland, Olaf Helmer, Herman Kahn, and even a Kennedy or two until that idiot Bobby started going after the mob, the very people who had delivered the Italian vote for his brother. That sort of idealism and treachery saw them both to early graves. *The death of Camelot.* True power still came from the barrel of a gun. Mao had been onto something.

Today, men with the same pedigrees sat in the same seats. There were no fedoras in the coat room, but the windows were still covered with the same bloodred drapes to conceal the business within. The president could fool around in the White House all he wanted; it was here that deals were struck and budgets were allocated. Those who controlled the purse strings had the de facto power. What happened in the halls of Congress was theater, distraction for a gullible public who still believed in a government of the people, by the people, and for the people. No one would ever imagine that the world's most powerful nation was run from a sixty-year-old cigar club on 15th Street.

They entered through a dark corridor around the corner from the second-level bar. Thwaite handed his coat to the striking yet conservatively dressed hostess. His bodyguard took a seat at the far end of the best-stocked bar in the city and ordered an ice water from the tuxedo-clad bartender, keeping an eye on his principal in the reflection behind a sea of spirits.

Thwaite opened the glass door to the walk-in humidor and approached his personal humidity-controlled "locker." He produced a key and extracted a Fuente Opus X, holding it under his nose and savoring the aroma. To Thwaite it wasn't just a cigar, it represented his ability to impact the world. At sixty-four he still believed he had a chance at the coveted top job. It had been within his grasp until that brash young California Democrat started making moves. The new president was going to find out that it could get very lonely at the top.

Senator Thwaite closed the door behind him, intentionally avoiding the corner table where he knew his appointment waited. He needed to send a message as to who was the alpha male, though he doubted the man would care. It infuriated the senator that nothing seemed to faze the former military officer.

Doing his best to hide his annoyance, he made his way back out onto the floor, passing a waitress in a skimpy black dress. The all-male membership raised no objections to the staff's required attire, harking back to the building's original days as a whorehouse at the turn of the century. It had fallen into disrepair after Prohibition. There had been attempts at a few different restaurants, all unsuccessful, before an Italian family had purchased it in the late 1950s with outside investors from New York and Chicago. The downstairs home-style Italian food supported a profitable business, and the full menu was available to the private club on floors two and three. The club refused to adopt bylaws, which allowed them to reject membership applications on a whim without fear of a recriminatory lawsuit. It boasted a ten-year waiting list for those willing to pay an undisclosed fee that would horrify most.

Thwaite walked up to the third-level mezzanine, passing between a lion and a crocodile standing guard at the base of the staircase. Both floors boasted an assortment of African wildlife taxidermy and safari art donated by an early member, which gave the establishment the aura of a man cave on steroids. That same member had been hastily expelled and his membership revoked for getting drunk and grabby with a hostess. The arrangements made between the hostesses and club members behind closed doors were one thing, but making a spectacle in the club was grounds for immediate expulsion. They had kept his taxidermy as a final *fuck you* and a reminder to other members of the proper rules of etiquette.

Thwaite stopped by a table overlooking the bar to say hello to Pietro and Franco Beretta, who were enjoying a meal with two members of the Senate Armed Services Committee, one of whom was a senator from Tennessee, where Beretta had recently moved its U.S. manufacturing facility. Thwaite shook hands with them all. He thanked Franco for the kind gift of matched 20-gauges he'd presented to Thwaite's wife on a driven pheasant hunt outside Gubbio, when they'd been guests of the Beretta family the previous fall. Loosely adhering to the U.S. Senate gift rules, the shotguns were given to his wife as a "thank you" for a speech she had given to Beretta's employees in conjunction with her corporate consulting business.

In Club Aegis it would have been considered rude not to offer a quick hello. One acknowledged the other patrons one knew and then moved on to the business of the day.

He floated among the tables shaking hands and making his presence known, hoping his sojourn was causing the man in the corner to sweat. He made sure to acknowledge the Assistant Secretary of Defense for Special Operations/Low-Intensity Conflict, who sat drinking wine from the most exhaustive list in the swamp with an executive from Raytheon, an untouched bowl of calamari between them.

He only nodded to two tables of competing pharmaceutical companies, as even Thwaite found their ilk distasteful. He recognized a lobbyist for Purdue Pharma sitting with the chairman of the Senate Appropriations Committee, and though the second-generation congressman couldn't make out what he was saying, the unmistakable southern drawl of the chairman permeated the air. The Sackler family minions had been hard at work to minimize the financial impact of the two thousand state and local lawsuits filed to recover the losses associated with fighting the opioid epidemic. They had hired an army that included twenty-two separate lobbying firms to ensure they could continue peddling drugs to the most vulnerable segments of society, all the while reaping the financial benefits. To assuage some of that guilt, the Sacklers had plastered their family name over everything from university chairs to the wings of world-renowned museums. Thwaite wondered if that helped. The nail in their coffin was the recent publication of a book by Gerald Posner titled *Pharma: Greed, Lies, and the Poisoning of*

America. It was being hailed as the twenty-first-century equivalent of Upton Sinclair's *The Jungle*. Thwaite would be sure to reference it when the CEO of Purdue answered questions in Senate hearings later that month. Thwaite looked forward to watching him squirm.

Though it might seem like a very public place to discuss such sensitive and controversial topics, that was the magic of Club Aegis. Business was conducted in plain sight, conversations disappearing along with the tobacco smoke into the state-of-the-art ventilation system. When the participants parted ways, like an unfamiliar perfume lingering in the wake of a forbidden affair, the only evidence that remained from meetings in AG was a hint of smoke on the conspirators' clothing.

Bidding a good day to an executive vice president of Royal Dutch Shell, Thwaite descended the stairs. Returning to the second level, he took another three steps down off the raised bar area, leaving the original wood floor and striding onto a black carpet inlayed with gold tobacco leaves. He slid into a leather chair the color of the finest Connecticut shade tobacco leaf before finally making eye contact with his appointment. The man across from him removed a thick Cohiba Behike from between his teeth and slowly exhaled, the gray smoke finding its way into the vents above. Even though he had no love for the Cuban government, the man had no qualms about procuring his beloved Cohibas whenever he was beyond the borders of the United States. While D.C. had banned cigar clubs and indoor smoking a decade ago, Aegis was grandfathered in, due in no small part to the powerful political connections of its membership.

"And how is the most underappreciated champion of the people doing today?" the man asked.

Even though Thwaite had kept him waiting for more than forty-five minutes, Erik Sawyer did not look the least bit disturbed. He didn't steal a knowing glance at the large Hublot watch on his wrist or inquire as to why the senator was late. He acted as if Thwaite was right on time.

He was dressed comfortably in slacks and a sport jacket. As usual, he was not wearing a tie, something about it serving no useful purpose in a fight.

In his mid-fifties, he was a decade the senator's junior. His confidence bordered on arrogance, a trait unsettling to politicians accustomed to holding all the cards. His short-cropped salt-and-pepper hair betrayed a military background exacerbated by a physique more befitting a man who was decades younger. Erik Sawyer was a born businessman trapped in the body of a soldier, and though he might be getting up there in years, his eyes and mind were as sharp as ever.

He had read the tea leaves prior to the attacks of 9/11, merging the entrepreneurial spirit infused into him by a father who had left his children an inheritance they would not be able to spend in a lifetime with his experience on the ground as an Army Ranger in Mogadishu, Somalia, in 1993. He returned home with a vision: to create a privatized intelligence and security apparatus leaner and more agile than the CIA and the U.S. military, services for which he'd charge a pretty penny. His timing could not have been better.

Senator Thwaite's wealth came from owed favors; he was beholden not just to his constituents but to donors, to lobbyists, to other politicians, family members, and reporters. Sawyer, in contrast, did not owe anyone favors. He had the financial freedom to sit on a beach drinking fruity cocktails in the sun at the home he kept on the island of Mustique in the West Indies if he so desired, but that was not Sawyer's way. He could not stop building an empire that had grown to include government contracts worth billions over the past twenty years. He was both a patriot and a die-hard capitalist. He provided something of value. It was rumored that the intelligence wing of his operation had collected information on more than a few of Thwaite's competitors. The senator had attempted to buy the information from Sawyer in years past, but the former Ranger had only laughed. That information, if it existed, was not for sale. He called it his "get out of jail free card." He'd almost had to use it when a convoy of his contractors had hit an IED outside Gardez in 2005. Instead of retreating, they laid waste to a nearby village as a warning to not target their convoys. Unfortunately for them, a *New York Times* reporter had gotten wind of the atrocity and plastered photos of the dead, unarmed villagers across the front page. Sawyer had weathered the storm and even paid the legal expenses for the contractors involved. They'd still gone to prison, but the company had survived. As part of a public relations rebranding effort, Sawyer changed the business name to Masada. The following year, State Department contracts almost doubled and classified contracts with the CIA increased tenfold. Thwaite could only venture a guess at the value of the information in the files Sawyer had gathered over the years. He wondered what information the corporate warrior had collected on *him*.

"Just another day on the Hill, Erik. Thank you for waiting. I was held up by urgent business in committee."

He hadn't been, of course, but Sawyer nodded politely in that infuriating way that conveyed he believed not a word yet was not bothered in the least.

A waitress appeared to take a drink order.

"What is he having?" the senator asked, pointing to his companion, who casually took a sip from a crystal glass.

"Pappy 23, sir," the waitress replied.

Sawyer swirled the deep amber liquid around the one large ice cube he'd requested to release the flavor.

"I put it on your tab, Eddie," Sawyer said.

Attempting to not show his annoyance at being called Eddie, Thwaite stifled a grunt wondering how many glasses of the $2,300-a-bottle Pappy Van Winkle Family Reserve the old soldier had put away while he'd waited. They were both members of the club, and Sawyer certainly had no need to charge it to the senator's personal account. He did it to toy with the senior man. Everything was a chess move with Sawyer.

Thwaite pretended to take it in stride. He ordered a Bombay Sapphire martini with three olives.

"Will you be dining with us tonight?" the waiter inquired.

"Just drinks," the senator responded a little too quickly.

Sawyer smiled, knowing he'd gotten to the aging politician.

Mission accomplished.

The martini was delivered swiftly, and Thwaite took too big a sip.

Why does Sawyer make me so nervous?

Regaining his composure, Thwaite pointed to the flat screen set to a cable news channel with the sound off and positioned in a way that only their section of the club could see it. A fellow senator was being publicly crucified. Allegations of sexual misconduct with female staffers and interns had surfaced along with sexually explicit text messages. The Senate majority and minority leaders had referred the allegations to the Ethics Committee. The news commentator cited anonymous sources stating that he would resign rather than face the further public embarrassment of being censured and stripped of committee assignments; due process in progressive America. *Mob rule. Cancel culture.* Thwaite almost felt bad for him, but the accused was a Democrat and the senator would take his wins where and when he could.

Thwaite then raised his martini to the screen. "And once again, pussy remains undefeated."

Sawyer chuckled and took another pull from his Cuban cigar.

"How is the detail working out?" Sawyer inquired.

The team protecting Senator Thwaite was a Masada contract. In the violence that had ensued the following year, many politicians had added additional security to their routines, Thwaite among them. Sawyer didn't discriminate in taking contracts and even found satisfaction watching a politician call for additional gun control at rallies while armed Masada contractors stood just feet away protecting that same politician with the very gun they wanted to ban. They were all such hacks. Sawyer would gladly take money from both sides.

"My driver has a lead foot. This isn't Baghdad," the senator said, feeling like he had to say something disparaging.

"I'll be sure to let him know," Sawyer said, having no intention of doing so. "Not even sure why you need the detail with that six-shooter on your left ankle."

Erik was one of the few people who knew about the senator's pistol, and now Thwaite regretted ever telling the former Army officer, as he never let an opportunity pass to disparage the heirloom.

"You know that was a gift from my father. He carried it all his years in the Senate and I continue the tradition."

"When was the last time you shot it?"

Thwaite fumed, struggling to maintain his composure.

"Why don't you come down to the Masada training facility and let me get one of our armorers to work up a Glock for you: trigger job, full wrap stipple, barrel, slide cuts, RMR, the works. We will get you all set up with a *real* pistol. We'll even put you through some training, on us."

"I appreciate the offer," the senator replied, knowing the only reason Sawyer wanted him on the range was to humiliate him. "I think I will stick with my paid security and continue my business of running the country, thank you."

"As you wish, Senator. Now, I'd love to drink bourbon on your tab all evening, but I do have other business to attend to. What can I do for you?"

"Don't *fuck* with me, Erik, I'm not in the mood."

He finished the martini and signaled the waitress for another.

"What if you could fight a war without firing a bullet? Is it still a war?" the senator asked.

Sawyer studied the elder statesman sitting across from him, raised an eyebrow, and took another sip of bourbon.

"That, Senator, is the highest level of warfare."

"This country *is* at war."

"Yes, I'm aware."

"Not overseas, Erik. Here at home."

Sawyer knew when to let others talk. Interrogators often found that by being silent they allowed their subject to fill the void with information they would never have extracted via more ruthless methods.

"We are in the middle of a war for our very existence, a war of subversion. Bullets are not flying between north and south, east and west, red and blue, but we are already in the midst of a civil war, make no mistake."

Sawyer watched the senator clip the end off his cigar and strike a wooden match from a matchbox on the end table.

"This war does not require bullets or assassinations in the traditional sense. It doesn't need a Che Guevara to raise a guerrilla army. The leaders have already been elected to state, local, and federal governments. Sympathizers have been infiltrated into our media establishment, entertainment industry, big tech, academia, even professional sports. Breitbart was right, 'politics is downstream from culture.'

"You don't need to take up arms in this war. Their weapons are hurled from social media platforms from which there is no defense and the assassinations are character assassinations. Public executions come not from a slice of the guillotine but by tweet, gleefully cheered on by the mob. You can fight it from your mom's basement as you eat Cheetos and collect an unemployment check from the very government you seek to destroy. It doesn't take courage, moral or physical, nor does it take resiliency. In fact, it takes the opposite of those once-lauded traits. It takes apathy. You don't have to be creative, well-read, in shape, resourceful, or strong. The weaker your mind and body the better. You can be taken advantage of. You are ripe for recruitment. Racism is the witchcraft of the twenty-first century, and cancel culture is the stake at which you are burned."

Thwaite caught his breath as his next martini arrived.

"It's a cancer. It's infected its host. It was a slow-growing lesion and could have been removed decades ago, but was allowed to fester under the guise of the very principles it seeks to destroy. Now it is going to kill the carrier and there is nowhere for the remaining healthy cells to go. The U.S. was the last bastion of freedom. It was an experiment. That experiment has failed. The very ideals it sought to uphold are the ones that are allowing our ultimate demise. This is our last stand."

"Nice speech, Eddie. You should think about becoming a politician."

The senator waved a hand of dismissal and rolled his cigar between his nicotine-stained fingers to ensure an even burn.

"This president must not win a second term, or the country is finished," Thwaite stated.

"You can vote him out in three years," Sawyer said.

"Don't give me that *bullshit*, Erik. The Russian election interference is no joke and they've only refined their techniques since the last election. This kid in the White House is only there because his friends in Silicon Valley manipulated their social advertising algorithms and swayed the election."

"Really? Are you sure it wasn't creative marketing and a war hero's resume that crushed *you* at the ballot box? Or perhaps his opponent just wasn't likable."

Thwaite's face flushed red but he pressed on, pointing back to the cable news program.

"Those pundits keep warning of a coming civil war. It helps ratings but it's disingenuous. That civil war is here. They just don't recognize it for what it is."

"Let's say you and Yuri Bezmenov are right, Senator," Sawyer said, referencing the KGB defector who had warned the United States of a long-term Soviet subversion program to undermine free democratic societies of the West. "What do you intend to do as the *savior* of the nation? You had me tear apart Christensen's past in the lead-up to election. All it did was cost you much-needed funds that could have been used to bolster your campaign."

"Drastic measures are necessary, but we need to take the White House to implement them. The president met with someone yesterday at Camp David. I want to know what they talked about."

"Let me look into it. Who did he meet with?"

"James Reece."

Erik Sawyer leaned forward and set his drink down on the table between them.

"James Reece? *The* James Reece who dismantled the Capstone Program a few years ago? *The* James Reece who saved the former president in Odessa? *The* James Reece who allegedly hunted down that CIA spy in Siberia last year?"

"I see you are familiar with his work."

"He actually made Masada millions when he took out those Capstone contractors on Fishers Island. All their contracts fell through when the company went down the tubes. We picked them up. I should be paying him a retainer."

"Find out what the president talked with him about at Camp David. Something doesn't smell right about it. He's an assassin and he met privately with the president. All we need is the hint of a scandal and we can turn the tables. This cancel culture so popular on the left might finally work in our favor. Find me something I can use to bring down a president."

CHAPTER 12

University of Colorado School of Medicine
Denver, Colorado

SEBASTIAN PHILLIPS KNOCKED ON the door of his department chair of the Department of Immunology and Microbiology at the University of Colorado School of Medicine to say good-bye.

Behind a desk strewn high with books and papers, a small-framed Jewish woman sat across from a second-year female student from India. He recognized her from a thesis laboratory he'd supervised earlier in the year.

"Have a wonderful weekend, Seb. Any big plans?"

The Indian student turned in her chair and smiled.

"Might get some mountain biking in before the snow hits. Other than that, I'll probably just be working on my dissertation," Sebastian said, tucking an unruly strand of his long, curly black hair behind his ear.

"I'm looking forward to reading the finished product. Take care."

Sebastian waved and nodded to his fellow student before making his way into the shadows of a late fall afternoon. He found himself wondering if either of them would survive what was to come.

He made his way through campus, messenger bag over his shoulder and hands stuffed into the pockets of his bright blue puffy jacket. He still had a lot of research to do on his dissertation and was falling behind. He'd been distracted by another project lately.

He tossed the bag into the passenger seat of his used forest-green Subaru, his mountain bike still affixed to the roof rack, and slid behind the wheel to start the engine. He lived walking distance from campus, but as a fifth-year immunology student he'd finally gotten a parking place because of the teaching duties associated with his degree requirements. He'd been driving a lot more recently. If anyone asked, he'd be able to point to his bike and use it as an excuse, saying he was going for a ride in the Rockies, which were still a bit of a trek from the Aurora, Colorado, Anschutz Medical Campus in a suburb of eastern Denver.

Pulling onto I-225, he drove north before hitting I-70 West, passing the Bass Pro Shops and Safeway Distribution Center, the Nestlé Purina plant, and the Coliseum. He then merged onto I-25 South and drove by Coors Field, REI, the Aquarium, and the Children's Museum, finally exiting the freeway and working his way to a house he'd purchased in Central West Denver near Paco Sanchez Park, in a neighborhood time had forgotten.

Just over a year ago he wouldn't have been able to safely make the drive as Denver, and even the streets of Aurora, had erupted in riots. He briefly wondered if what he was about to do was even necessary. America seemed content to destroy itself without any provocation from a warrior of Allah.

Sebastian looked forward to using his given name someday, but he knew the reason his parents had changed it before enrolling him in public school in Phoenix. It had been explained to him by the imam. Shahram Pahlavi was a name that made the infidels nervous. After he finished his studies, he'd revert to his given name and make the pilgrimage to Mecca during the twelfth month of the lunar calendar, as all Muslims must do at least once in their lifetime in adherence with the fifth pillar of Islam.

His program in the Department of Microbiology in the School of

Medicine had recently merged with the Integrated Department of Immunology. It was now a joint venture between the School of Medicine and National Jewish Health in what was obviously another move by the Jews to increase their power over the U.S. health-care system. They already controlled the governments of most Western nations and had a monopoly in the international banking community. Shahram Pahlavi would be remembered for striking down the Zionist occupation government. That the very movement he sought to destroy was giving him the skills to strike a blow for all Muslims around the globe was an added bonus. He was almost ready.

Parking in the driveway of the run-down single-story home, he locked his car and looked up and down the street as he fumbled through the keys until he found the right one. Weeds infested what had once been a lawn. The decades-old lime-green paint was peeling away from the siding as if trying to escape a community that wouldn't quite let it go. The bars on the windows matched the other homes in the neighborhood and added a layer of security Sebastian found comforting.

The young PhD student locked the front door behind him and walked through the house as he'd been instructed, looking at his telltales to ensure nothing had been tampered with. Satisfied that everything was as it should be, he opened the door to the basement and descended the stairs.

The basement had not been converted to a game room, home theater, bar, or man cave. Instead, Sebastian had used his knowledge of immunology and microbiology to build a high-tech virology lab. Clear poly sheeting lined the floor, ceiling, and walls. High-flow hoods with heat ventilation chambers wound via ducts to high-intensity UV exhaust ports that off-gassed like any home heating and cooling system; he did not want to accidentally obliterate the neighborhood. He intended on causing more damage than a single explosion could possibly produce. Anything he couldn't buy at Home Depot had been sent to his off-site mailbox at a UPS Store in Denver and arrived from a variety of different life sciences and laboratory equipment companies so as not to trigger the suspicions of the FBI.

Sebastian was pleased with his work. An expensive ultracentrifuge culture cabinet cell separation hood, a device that resembled an uber-sturdy photographer's light box with flexible thick, clear plastic partitions, was on a metal table against the wall next to a Nano-Images Model 4500 scanning electron microscope. The microscope was a far cry from what he'd used in his high school biology class in Arizona. It could easily be confused with an industrial-strength espresso machine and was linked to a high-resolution computer monitor.

He had followed his instructions to the letter. Whoever was directing the operation clearly knew what they were doing. Sebastian had not been told why he was building the clandestine laboratory, only that he must stay on schedule. The young doctoral student had spent months speculating about what he was preparing in the name of Allah.

Patience.

Lā 'llāha 'lllā Allah, Muḥammadun Rasūl Allah
There is no god but God. Muhammad is the messenger of God.

The lab was fully functional when the African monkey kidney cells had arrived. He'd ordered them through the university lab as part of the research necessary for his dissertation. There was nothing out of the ordinary about ordering cells to one of the premier medical research universities in the country. A biosafety level one product, they had arrived frozen in liquid nitrogen and had taken almost a month to prepare. He had separated them into fifteen independent cell lines and had confirmed they contained no contaminants and exhibited stable growth factors.

Sebastian knew he was close. All that was missing now was a sample.

A sample of what?

Seb looked at the two DuPont Level A hazmat suits and respirators hanging on the wheeled pipe clothing rack at the base of the stairs. It was amazing what one could order from Amazon. Whatever it was, its handling called for fully contained biohazard suits, the same suits used in bio-containment level four facilities. That there were two indicated that Sebastian would not be conducting the next phase of the operation alone.

Sebastian knew that he was waiting on someone who would bring a sample that almost certainly contained a deadly pathogen. In this makeshift lab, he and his unknown benefactor would transfer small amounts of what was undoubtedly an infectious disease in sample blood plasma to the cell culture plates of the monkey kidney cells.

From there, the cells would replicate until they were ready for weaponization.

After that, Sebastian could only guess.

CHAPTER 13

Landini Brothers Restaurant
Old Town, Alexandria, Virginia

"SO, WHAT ARE YOU having?" Reece asked.

Katie peered at him over the top of the menu and raised an eyebrow. "Hmm . . ."

"Your usual?"

They were on the first floor, seated just past the bar at a corner table in their favorite restaurant, a Tuscan landmark in the heart of Old Town. It made Reece uncomfortable that there was no back exit. If something happened, at least he wouldn't waste time deciding where to go; they would fight their way to the front door. Reece's back was to the wall, and even though he knew the layout by heart, he'd still made his security assessment as he walked in. He couldn't help himself. It was ingrained. He told himself it wasn't paranoia; it was situational awareness. He'd lost his family because he had not been there. He wasn't going to let that happen to Katie.

"Cheers," Reece said, raising his glass.

It irritated Katie that Landini Brothers didn't allow corkage, relegating patrons to their expensive wine list, which for some unknown reason didn't list the vintage. She tolerated it because the food was delicious, the charming old-world atmosphere appealed to her, and unfortunately there were few great restaurant options in Old Town. Additionally, it happened to be walking distance from her condo. Looking at the wine list, Katie noticed two great "Super Tuscan" choices that happened to be among her favorites—Tenuta dell'Ornellaia Masseto, which was egregiously overpriced even though it was a tremendous wine, and Tenuta San Guido, Sassicaia, which was similarly an excellent bottle. With a smirk at the sommelier, who clearly had no idea what he was doing, Katie ordered the Sassicaia, which was mistakenly priced at half of what they should have charged.

So much for no corkage policy.

"To what are we drinking on this fine evening?" she asked.

"Uh, a weekend back from the Farm?"

"Can't you think of anything more romantic than that?"

She liked to make him sweat. She'd seen him under pressure before, and it never failed to amuse her that someone who could be so calm, cool, and collected when the bullets were flying struggled to find words when it came to matters of the heart.

"Um, to uh . . ."

"Let me help you." Katie smiled. "To us."

"To us," Reece said, relieved.

"See, that wasn't so bad. I thought they were supposed to be turning you into a *suave* secret agent down there. I was expecting you to come back all 'shaken, not stirred.'"

"They're working on it," Reece said with a smile. "I'm proving to be a tough case."

It had been almost a year since Reece had returned from Siberia. Katie was less than pleased when Reece had gone off the grid, hunting the man who had killed his father and orchestrated the Russian hit team that had targeted and almost killed them both in the mountains of Montana. Reece was a man with grit. It was a trait she respected. It also terrified her.

"Before I forget, Caroline Hastings emailed me. She wants us to come back to the ranch as soon as we can. Her exact words were 'Your cabin awaits.' She says Raife is getting antsy and wants to take you on a hunt. He still has a bit of a limp that she says he is very good at hiding from everyone. She also said the house is as good as new; all the bullet holes have been patched and the glass replaced. She made a point of telling me they've also emplaced additional security; I think she wanted me to feel safe."

"Let's do it. I love Montana in the winter. Most people head south, which means there is just more of it for us to enjoy."

"Wine by the fire beyond the grasp of *these* does sound nice," she said, holding up her phone and making a point of dropping it in her purse so Reece knew he had her full attention.

As she was hanging her bag on the back of her chair, a guy at the bar chatting up a young woman spilling out of a dress a couple of sizes too small caught her eye and gave a little wave. Katie nodded back politely and turned back to Reece, rolling her eyes.

"Ugh, that guy is the *worst*."

Reece shifted his eyes from Katie to the Romeo at the bar, recognizing him as a cable news personality, light on substance and heavy on hair products.

"Not to be gossipy," she said conspiratorially, "but he is such a creep."

Reece raised an eyebrow.

"That girl is a new producer, about a year out of college. Guess how he met his third and current wife, who is at home with the kids?"

"Producer?" Reece ventured.

"Exactly."

"Doesn't he have a book out?"

"Oh yes, a *New York Times* bestseller. Guess how that happened?"

"No idea."

"You need to suffer through an evening of cable news. That should be all you need to figure it out. I wouldn't mind as much if he wasn't so slimy. I refuse to even do his show. It's guys like him that make me seriously consider getting out of the news business."

"Sounds like a real treat."

"On to more pleasant topics. How was your week?" Katie asked, knowing Reece would have to be guarded about his final weeks at Camp Peary. "Are all those grad school coeds behaving themselves?"

The CIA's Camp Peary was commonly known as the world's most exclusive dating service. Recruits were typically in their mid- to late twenties, with graduate degrees from the nation's most elite bastions of academia. That they were under intense pressure for the better part of a year and were restricted from talking about their training with anyone outside the circle made for some intense relationships. The Farm was responsible for more than a few marriages, as well as a slew of divorces.

Katie was familiar with government agencies. As one of the most recognizable journalists in the Beltway due to her book about the embassy annex attack in Benghazi, aptly titled *The Benghazi Betrayal*, Katie had interviewed a host of current and former CIA staff officers and contractors. Her exposé on the conspiracy to kill Reece's team in the mountains of Afghanistan by a cabal of government-connected financiers only raised her profile as one of the country's most respected investigative journalists.

"Well, it was, uh, interesting."

"Oh, do tell," Katie teased.

"I met with the president on Tuesday. So, have you decided? Want an appetizer?"

Katie dropped her menu on her plate.

"*You what?* You mean he came down from D.C. to address your class?"

"No, I mean he sent a helicopter and flew me up to Camp David. What do you think? Calamari or caprese?"

"Are you serious? What did he want?"

"That's classified. I think I'll start with the carpaccio. Salads look good, too. I love this place."

"James, how long were you there?"

"About twenty-four hours. Did you know that Brezhnev almost crashed a Lincoln with Nixon in the passenger seat joyriding around the perimeter?"

"I was not aware," Katie said, suddenly serious.

"What are you thinking for your main? Fillets here are fantastic."

"James Reece, the president of the United States does not just summon a CIA recruit to Camp David to give him what I'm sure is a fascinating history."

Reece put down his menu and looked into the deep blue eyes of the woman with whom he'd fallen in love.

"True. He wanted to discuss the events in Odessa. He said he might not even be in the seat if it hadn't been for Freddy saving President Grimes."

Reece felt more than a tinge of guilt for not telling Katie the whole truth, but what was he supposed to say? *The president of the United States got himself elected to the highest office in the land to wage a personal war of retribution against those he believed helped facilitate the attacks of 9/11 that killed his fiancée?*

"Did he ask you about Russia?"

"Interestingly enough, that didn't come up. Did you know that FDR and Churchill planned D-Day there?"

"I *did* know that," Katie acknowledged, still skeptical.

Their waiter interrupted just in time.

"Have you decided?" he asked.

"What are the specials tonight?" Reece asked, trying to draw out the disruption. He smiled at Katie, who shook her head, knowing exactly what he was doing.

Men could be so transparent.

They ordered appetizers and main courses, handing their menus back to the waiter before leaning back toward one another to continue their conversation.

"Change of topic," Reece declared. "What have *you* been up to this week?"

"Well, I most certainly did *not* meet privately with the president. But I am in the middle of a fascinating investigation that my friend Haley Garrett is helping me with."

"Isn't she the one that works at the CDC?" Reece asked, using the acronym for the Centers for Disease Control and Prevention.

"That's her. We were roommates at Davis before I changed my major and transferred to Berkeley. She was on the premed track, always talking about wanting to work with Doctors Without Borders, which she eventually did. She volunteered with them in the Democratic Republic of the Congo. It changed her."

"How so?" Reece asked, taking a sip of his wine, remembering how Africa gets in your blood.

"She was always a free spirit but seeing so many people, particularly children, die of malaria, Ebola, Zika, cholera, yellow fever, even bubonic plague, took her down a different path. She came back and got a master's in public health and did a residency in internal medicine. She's now at the CDC specializing in infectious diseases."

"I'm glad somebody does it," Reece said.

"As you may or may not have noticed, I have been devoting columns to Russian government–mafia collusion."

"I hadn't noticed," Reece responded, with a hint of sarcasm. They'd had more than a few conversations on the subject, Reece advising her against poking the bear and Katie standing strong for the principles of her profession. It was her way of fighting back. When the Bratva tried to kill them both in Montana, Reece went to guns. Katie's weapons were her words and her platform.

"Haley and I were talking about that very same thing."

"What did she say?"

"She sounded an awful lot like you, Mr. Reece," Katie said, swirling her wine in her glass and holding it up to the candlelight.

Before changing majors, Katie had been in the viticulture and enology program at UC Davis. She knew her wines.

"I like her already."

Their appetizers arrived and Reece dug into the carpaccio while Katie picked at the caprese, choosing her next words carefully.

"She also said something that got me thinking."

"And what was that?"

"When she was in the Congo, they heard about a village a couple hundred miles northeast where there had been an outbreak of hemorrhagic fever."

"Like Ebola?"

"Yes, what do you know about it?"

"We did some training in bio and chemical weapons in the Teams in case we were ever tasked with hitting a WMD facility. Did some full mission profile exercises out on a base in Utah that's set up for that type of scenario. *Not* a mission any of us were dying to do. Other than that, just what I read in *The Hot Zone*. True story if I remember correctly."

"That's right. It was about a scare they had just down the street in Reston, Virginia, back in 1989. They contained it. It didn't get out of control. Anyway, she told me that they had heard rumors of Russian military advisors working in the area. When I heard that, I put my reporter hat on."

"And?"

"Russian arms dealers and advisors have been going in and out of

Africa for a generation. It is one of the least-talked-about battlegrounds of the Cold War, so that wasn't surprising. What was surprising were the other rumors."

"Other rumors?"

"That the Russians had been using villages as test subjects for their bioweapons programs since the early sixties."

"Test subjects?"

"I hadn't really thought about it before, so I did my research. Between 1976 and 2020 there were twenty-eight documented hemorrhagic fever outbreaks in Africa. All were assumed to be natural occurrences. Typically, the World Health Organization and various NGOs go in to treat infected people, take samples, and conduct research. There are firsthand reports of Congolese soldiers massacring entire villages and burning them to the ground to control the spread."

"I hate to say this, but that's not shocking. Human life tends to have a different value in certain parts of the world."

"And sometimes in our very own part of it," Katie concluded.

Though it had not been her intent, Reece's memories flashed back to the smiling faces of his young daughter and beautiful wife.

"Very true," Reece said, looking into the cherry-red wine in his glass.

"When Haley and her team arrived at the village the following day, do you know what they found?"

"I hate to even speculate."

"Nothing."

"Nothing?"

"The village had been incinerated, not just burned to the ground, but wiped off the map."

"You said that was common practice."

"Yes, but Haley said this was different. There was a huge crater where the village should have been, and the jungle was a charred ruin for what seemed like miles in every direction."

"A crater? From a bomb?"

"That's what she said."

"Did she get any pictures?"

"They did, but it was back before everything was cloud based. On their way back to Kinshasa they were stopped at a roadblock. They were accused of being spies. She swears there were Russian mercenaries assisting the indigenous military personnel manning the checkpoint. All their phones, cameras, and computers were confiscated. They were ordered out of the country the following day."

"They're lucky they weren't killed. African dictators don't mess around over there," Reece said, remembering his own experience with Raife working on a hunting concession back in their college days.

"I did a little more digging. What she's describing could have been the result of an FAE."

"A fuel air explosive?"

"That's right. Do you know how they work?"

"I don't have much experience with them, but I've seen video of some tests the Air Force did at China Lake; huge canister dropped by a parachute. If memory serves, an initial charge disperses the fuel over the target and then multiple secondary charges ignite it. Looks like a nuclear explosion."

"That's the general idea," Katie confirmed. "We used them in Vietnam. The Soviets used them in a border dispute with China in 1969 and in Afghanistan in the eighties. In fact, it is the largest nonnuclear device in our arsenal and in the arsenal of Russia. The Russians call them vacuum bombs."

They both took a moment to collect their thoughts as the waiter placed their main courses on the table.

"Can I get you anything else?" he asked.

Reece eyed the bottle of wine. "I think we are good for now. Katie?"

"This looks delicious. Thank you."

Their server nodded.

"You think the Russians used an FAE to control an outbreak?" Reece asked when their waiter was a safe distance away.

"Yes, but I believe there is more to it."

"Such as?"

"It's possible these outbreaks are not naturally occurring."

Reece slowed his chewing and chased the tender meat down with a large sip of wine.

"You think the Russians were testing a bioweapon on villagers in Africa and when they got what they wanted they cleaned it all up with an FAE?"

"We know that back in the Soviet days, the Russian military began collecting various strains of hemorrhagic viruses in Africa. They were and still are embedded in a host of African nations. I think they took samples back to the Soviet Union and weaponized them. More information on the Soviet bioweapons program has come to light in recent years. It even had a name: *biopreparat*. We are now finding out that there were hemorrhagic virus outbreaks in the Soviet Union in the seventies and eighties that were covered up. These are tropical diseases, Reece, not something you find outside Africa. The Russians were weaponizing some of the deadliest pathogens known to man. They also needed to test them. What better place to test a bioweapon than in a place where its effects would look like a naturally occurring event to the rest of the world? They refined their weapons in human test subjects, and if it looked like it was going to spread, they wiped the test village off the face of the earth."

Reece took it all in.

"And you want to expose it?"

"I do, but I need proof. I need to talk with a doctor involved in the program or a pilot who dropped a bomb."

"And what brought all that up to begin with?" Reece asked.

"There was another outbreak."

"In Africa?"

"Yes. In Angola. Every time hemorrhagic fever breaks out, the World Health Organization is alerted. The CDC monitors the outbreak. They do what they can working with NGOs to treat infected people and contain the spread. Depending on the severity, Haley will take a team in to assist and bring back samples to study and compare to previous outbreaks, looking for mutations. Viruses adapt just like the enemy, Reece," she said, framing it in terms he would understand.

"Do I remember that her husband worked at Fort Detrick? A scientist or doctor as well, right?"

"Ah, you do pay attention when I talk about my friends."

"Steel trap," Reece said, tapping his temple with his finger and giving her a wink. "What are your next steps?"

"I need to track down some Russian defectors."

"There's nothing I can do to discourage you from doing this, is there?"

"Nope."

"I didn't think so."

"Well, be careful. While you are working to prove that a major world power violated an international bioweapons treaty, I have another week of training. My class is going to Harvey Point in North Carolina. That might be classified, but if you want any specifics you can just google it. All the information is out there in cyberspace. I know a lot of the instructors. It's the improvised weapons course. James Bond and MacGyver stuff. The grad students love it."

"Well, don't you go getting all smitten with any of those young female spies," Katie said, pointing her fork at the former SEAL.

"Speaking of smitten," Reece said, pulling a box from his pocket.

"It's not a ring, so don't get nervous," he said, smiling. "Just a little something . . ."

Katie put her hand to her heart.

"James, you did not have to do that."

She opened the box and looked down at a gleaming diamond pendant in a platinum setting with chain.

"But I'm glad you did. It's beautiful, James. I love it!"

"I know I missed your birthday while I was away. And I wanted to say I'm sorry."

"You're sorry? For what?"

"For leaving the way I did. I was so focused on the mission, I didn't stop to think about anything else. I had the opportunity to go after Grey and finish it. I couldn't have him coming after you again."

Katie saw the candlelight reflected in the dark green eyes of the man who had killed for her. She swallowed knowing that he was capable of intense violence and intense passion; she had firsthand experience with both.

"I had one of Raife's outfitters bring it down from the Northwest Territories. I had no idea Canada was such a big player in the diamond industry. Jonathan Hastings knows Martin Katz, so he set the stone for you."

"So fancy," she said. "I had no idea you had such refined taste."

Katie pulled the stone from the box and brushed her blond hair aside as she tilted her head to clasp the catch behind her neck.

"Well, what do you think?" she asked.

"It's striking. But not nearly as stunning as who's wearing it. You look beautiful."

"Oh, stop it, Mr. Reece. You are going to make me blush."

"What do you say we settle up and get out of here?" Reece asked.

"You think this diamond means you're getting lucky tonight?"

"One can hope."

"I thought you told me that hope is not a course of action."

"I did, hence the diamond," the former frogman said, pointing to the rare gem around the reporter's neck.

"Your place or mine?" Katie asked, with a gleam in her eye.

Reece signaled the waiter for the check.

"Yours is closer," he said.

"We can have dessert at my condo."

"I'm in. What are you serving?"

"You're looking at it."

CHAPTER 14

THEY HIT THE STREET arm in arm, bundled up against the evening chill. Katie noted Reece's eyes scanning up and down the street, moving their way back over the windows and rooftops. Old habits die hard. He had been a little more on edge lately, perhaps due to the CIA training. Katie knew it involved a lot of basic spy tradecraft, surveillance detection, driving, and asset assessment and recruitment.

Katie had been unsuccessful in getting him to open up about his trek across Siberia. She knew he was alone for six months and had somehow made it from Medny Island, off the Kamchatka Peninsula, more than a thousand miles into the interior in search of his prey. She could only imagine the demons he'd wrestled alone, cold, tired, and hungry. How he had ventured from the Russian interior to the Central African Republic remained a mystery. She knew that from the American embassy in Bangui, the CIA had stepped in and brought him home.

Since his return he'd made a point of taking her to the range and running drills with her Glock 19 and Bravo Company AR topped with an Aimpoint Micro red-dot optic. She was pleasantly surprised that tonight's gift was jewelry and not a blade, gun, or weapon of some sort.

Both her firearms were legal in Virginia, but if she forgot and drove over the invisible boundary into the District of Columbia, she risked imprisonment. *Beware of the government that fears your guns.* In less than the distance of a foot, she'd go from law-abiding citizen to felon. Citizens could be trusted in Virginia but not in D.C., though even that could change. Virginia had been trending away from the state motto so boldly emblazoned on their official state seal and flag: *Sic semper tyrannis—Thus always to tyrants.*

She'd written a few articles for *Town Hall* and *National Review* on the irony of politicians calling to defund the police, while surrounding themselves and their families with armed security paid for by the taxpayers. More often than not, these were the same politicians taking active measures to ensure private citizens could not own firearms. The irony seemed to be lost on the mob, but not on Katie. She proposed that any politician who supported legislation to defund law enforcement should also be responsible for funding their own security. How they could live with themselves in a constant state of hypocrisy, Katie would never comprehend. As long as she had a platform, she was going to hold them accountable. That was the responsibility of a free press, or what was left of it.

Knowing that husbands or boyfriends were inevitably the worst teachers due to relationship dynamics, Reece had his buddy, Ox, come up to run them through drills in individual and team tactics, working barricades, training in vehicle dynamics, room clearing, malfunctions, tactical communication, and combat medicine.

Rick "Ox" Andrews had been around the block a time or two. Closing in on sixty years old, he'd earned his nickname as a young Ranger weighted down with a mortar tube across his shoulders and belts of linked M60 ammo crisscrossing his chest, sprinting across the Port Salines Airport runway in Grenada. He'd eventually serve as a sergeant major in Delta Force before he retired into the waiting arms of Ground

Branch, continuing to put rounds into terrorists and insurgents the world over. When not deployed with the CIA, he trained up new recruits stateside at the Farm and conducted more specialized training at a black site in Florida. As luck would have it, he was running the basic rifle and pistol courses for Reece's clandestine services class and was available to help teach Katie the way of the gun.

Katie was a quick study and was feeling more and more comfortable with her pistol and rifle. She learned to win the fight before rendering aid to her partner, regardless of how horrific the wound. She now had RATS tourniquets in her purse, car, and condo. At home, they trained to both barricade in place and clear the two-floor structure. Reece had even made them test out their pistol and rifle-mounted lights, shining them against the off-white walls to ensure the bright beams wouldn't reflect and blind them in a stressful situation. Ox also ran them through scenarios in personal protective detail tactics and vehicle dynamics with Katie as the principal moving to cover in the event of an attack.

Katie thought a lot of it was overkill. Then she remembered being bound and gagged on the floor of Secretary of Defense Hartley's Fishers Island mansion, being thrown to the ground on the streets of Chinatown in LA with an assassin moving in for the kill, and taking aim at a Russian mafia hit man with a rifle through a sliding glass door of the Hastingses' Montana home. It did not escape her that the common denominator in all of that violence was Reece. The devastating loss of his family was directly related to the weapons and tactical training he was so intent on putting her through.

She had come to terms with the idea that being with Reece was inherently dangerous. Could she live a life of constant vigilance? The closer they became, the more she found herself asking that question. She also knew he longed for the wilds of Montana and Alaska. With a country that seemed more divided with each passing day, she was more amenable to leaving her life as a journalist behind and moving with Reece to the mountains. That meant abandoning the possibility of hosting a prime-time cable news show, but it would allow her time to focus on research and writing. Maybe it was time? Would Reece begin a new life with her? Would he start a new family? Those were questions she had yet to explore. She knew he wasn't ready. There was something he still needed to do; she could sense it. She had respected his privacy and not pushed; there was still a demon in Reece's crosshairs.

Katie moved to Reece's left side, his support arm pulling her close, leaving his right hand free to go to the gun, his mind subconsciously noting cover, concealment, and avenues of egress, storing the information away in the event he needed it. To Reece, it was as natural as breathing.

• • •

Even with his preliminary and secondary scan of the area, Reece didn't notice the nondescript dark blue minivan with Maryland plates half a block down. Nothing made it seem like anything other than a run-of-the-mill grocery getter for a local soccer mom. It certainly did not stand out as a specially designed rolling surveillance vehicle, with miniature cameras installed and concealed to record in 360-degree high definition.

"Target's moving," a man dressed in the dark casual clothes of the season said into a mic attached to an encrypted radio.

"Copy. I have visual," a voice responded.

The operative in the back of the minivan didn't ask why his team had been tasked with surveillance of a killer who was once the most wanted domestic terrorist in the country. Charlie Crimmins had been out of the military for only a couple of years. The drug charges didn't stick, but they ruined his Marine Corps career. The former sergeant found refuge in private contracting, and right now that paid the bills and let him strap on an M4 in the same places where he'd once deployed as a leatherneck.

He'd heard rumors that their target had terminated an entire protective detail on an island off upstate New York before killing the secretary of defense a few years back. The former SEAL didn't look so tough now as he walked with his lady friend through the early winter snow. Crimmins felt himself begin to perspire, thinking that one day he might get a chance to take out a frogman.

The founder and CEO of Masada wanted him surveilling James Reece. He hoped the company would order him to take things to the next level and install listening devices in the hot reporter's apartment, better yet, audio *and* video. He'd like to see what she looked like out of those tight clothes they made the female reporters wear on cable news. He'd make sure he suggested that to his boss. For now, he'd have to be content just to imagine.

They'd been told to avoid detection at all costs, to get photographs of anyone he met, and to track his every movement. The surveillance team had been reminded that James Reece had a close relationship with violence. And to increase their chances of being witness to the next sunrise, they'd be wise to keep it professional and do their jobs from a distance.

If the news reports from three years ago were any indication, James Reece was not a man you wanted to cross.

CHAPTER 15

White House Situation Room
Washington, D.C.

SECRET SERVICE AGENT FRANK Sharp held the door open and the president of the United States entered the Situation Room.

"Keep your seats," the president said, as he made his way to the head of the table.

Officially called the John F. Kennedy Conference Room, the secure area in what amounted to the basement of the West Wing of the White House had been in operation since 1961. It was installed following the Bay of Pigs fiasco, to ensure the executive branch would have a secure facility to monitor sensitive world events and military operations in real time. Finally updated in 2007, the fax machines and computers that were state-of-the-art during Reagan's second term were replaced with encrypted communications equipment and flat screens. The room was layered in sensors to detect illicit monitoring. Lead-lined cabinets for smartphones and tablets were built in by the entrance as a reminder to leave unsecure devices on the outside.

Six black leather swivel chairs were arranged on each side of the rectangular mahogany table and additional chairs lined the walls. There was one seat at the head. The presidential seal affixed to the wall behind it made clear who controlled the room. This was no Knights of the Round Table. Responsibility and accountability fell on the shoulders of only one man, the commander in chief of the United States armed forces.

The president had entered precisely at 6:00 a.m., balancing a cup of coffee he'd been handed on his way into the secure conference room. Veterans of previous administrations sometimes still called it the "Sit Room," a term this new generation only knew from books, movies, or fireside chats with their grandparents. It was now called "WHIZZER," for "White House Situation Room."

The young president glanced at his watch, still set five minutes ahead, and smiled at the memory of his father. The room itself was really a collection of rooms manned by a rotating team 24/7, 365 days a year. The staff was assigned for two-year cycles and occupied a Watch Floor just off the main conference area, where they constantly monitored world events for the National Security Council. There were additional offices and breakout rooms for private calls and conversations, one of which had been immortalized in the photo of President Obama's national security team the night U.S. special operations forces killed Osama bin Laden. Though the area occupied more than five thousand square feet, it still felt surprisingly cramped to those who met there to discuss the government's most sensitive secrets.

President Alec Christensen ran his hand down his bright blue tie out of habit and leaned forward in his chair.

"Thank you all for coming. I know this is not our usual morning crew, but the vice president is attending a funeral in Japan and I wanted to have a more limited discussion today."

The president still found it odd not to shake hands with everyone, but the previous year's coronavirus pandemic had shifted some of the country's cultural norms. The nation had still not recovered from the devastating impact of an almost complete economic shutdown. It was Alec Christensen's job to lead the way back to financial prosperity and create the conditions for small businesses to revive. The country had seen technology giants flourish, increasing the distrust between rich and poor, a divide exploited by both parties for political gain. As a Democrat who came from the one percent, the president was acutely aware that any move he made would always be scrutinized through the lens of his past life, privilege offset by service in Afghanistan.

During the economic shutdown, the power of big business and the technology sector was highlighted on a daily basis. Blue-collar workers read headlines to learn a tech mogul dropped $165 million on a Beverly Hills mansion for his new wife, while regular people wondered how they were going to pay the rent and feed their families. Disdain for the ultrarich grew, their wealth increasing as unemployment soared. The middle class had been decimated, and there were those who blamed a progressive ideology that advanced its base only if Americans became increasingly dependent on government. Christensen understood the theory. Before his foray into politics, he would have categorized it as a fringe conspiracy, but after fifteen years in the swamp he now understood the draw of absolute power for power's sake. This game was all about control.

It was the president's job to bring the Democratic Party back to the ideals that embraced the values of working-class American voters, the people his party claimed to represent, but who in reality had been left behind for Wall Street, Hollywood, tech titans, and media elites long ago. If he succeeded, there was still hope for the country. A predecessor of his had run on a campaign of hope and change only to further commit the United States in the Middle East and escalate a drone war that fed the enemy's recruiting efforts. If Afghanistan had taught the new president anything, it was that the country needed more than hope. It needed a leader.

The president went around the table greeting the participants by name. His national security advisor sat to his right, across from the director of national intelligence. His White House counsel shuffled papers opposite Janice Motley, the director of the Central Intelligence Agency. The president's eyes settled on a man to her left and one of the only people not usually present for the president's morning briefing.

"Mr. Rodriguez, thank you for taking the time out of your morning to be here. I know you have a full plate running the Special Activities Center."

"Of course, Mr. President. It's an honor."

"Greg?" the president said, acknowledging his national security advisor.

Greg Farber's dark blue suit and red tie were offset by prematurely white hair that lent him an air of distinction usually befitting a much older statesman. He'd been a major in the Army's Reserve JAG Corps, which let him practice law in the private sector between government appointments in both Democratic and Republican administrations, to include chairing a commission on justice reform in Afghanistan and a successful term as the Special Presidential Envoy for Hostage Affairs.

"Before we delve into the PDB," Farber said, referencing the highly classified President's Daily Brief, "we wanted to convene this working group. The administration is conducting a review of the past extreme rendition programs run by the CIA and targeted drone strikes by both the CIA and armed forces."

Motley's face betrayed nothing, but Terrance Lowe, the director of national intelligence, to whom she reported, turned to her and interjected, "It is time to take a look at these programs to determine what lessons we can learn from the past as we forge ahead."

Motley nodded. Director of National Intelligence was a position created out of the 2004 Intelligence Reform and Terrorism Prevention Act. Prior to 2004, the director of the CIA had overseen the U.S. intelligence apparatus. Now the CIA director was solely focused on her agency, while the DNI was responsible for seventeen different intelligence agencies to include the CIA. The DNI also produced the PDB, the most exclusive and restricted document in the world.

Terrance Lowe was new to the job. He'd been a SEAL admiral and the commanding officer of the Joint Special Operations Command the night his forces had crossed into Pakistan targeting the world's most wanted terrorist. After his tenure at JSOC came to a close, he had accepted an offer from his alma mater, Texas A&M University, to serve as president. There he quickly built up his Democratic bona fides, publishing a popular SEAL leadership book and becoming a roundtable regular on the more progressive Sunday morning political talk shows. Some suggested he was building a resume in the hopes of becoming a vice presidential pick to help turn Texas blue. Instead, the president had decided on a female running mate from Florida to bring that swing state into play. He still wanted to reward the former flag officer for his support, which is why he now sat at the commander in chief's left side. Some editorials were already suggesting the retired admiral planned to challenge the new president in the next election cycle.

Lowe had given Motley a heads-up prior to the meeting, so she was prepared to field any questions that came her way. She and Vic were the only two holdovers from the previous administration in the room, and both agreed with the need to continually assess the effectiveness of their programs.

"Just to be clear," the president said, "I want to ensure we are conducting ourselves in a manner befitting the ideals we want to exemplify to the rest of the world. We now have twenty years of data to examine; it is imperative we weigh the results against the unintended consequences. Just because we've always done it one way doesn't mean we will continue to do it that way. This briefing serves as much as an education for me as it does for all of us to study a decades-old program spanning what is now four administrations."

"Thank you, Mr. President," Farber continued. "I think all of you know Mitch Cohen, White House counsel."

Mitch pushed his wire-rimmed glasses up onto the bridge of his nose and cleared his throat. His wrinkled suit looked like he'd slept in it, which he probably had. A thin man with unkempt hair, his appearance had caused more than a few to underestimate what was a superb legal mind. During his time at Harvard Law School he clerked for a justice of the Supreme Court of Israel when they heard a challenge to what their press called *Chissulim*, eliminations. Though his success in private practice focused on commercial litigation, intellectual property, defamation, and antitrust trade regulation, he'd never forgotten the lessons he'd learned in the land of his parents' birth, a country his grandparents had helped carve out of the desert when the tattoos on their forearms were just beginning to fade.

"As you are all aware, the legal basis for both our extreme rendition program and our targeted strike program comes from the AUMF, the Authorization for the Use of Military Force, passed into law on September 18th, 2001. The oft-cited prohibition on assassinations from Executive Order 12333, United States Intelligence Activities, does not legally apply to legitimate military targets. It applies to heads of state. The targets are selected by our seventeen intelligence agencies led by the DNI, along with intelligence from the DoD, CIA, NSA, NRO, and NGA. Our criteria was based on the Israeli program, but unlike the United States, the Israeli intelligence services and military branches were given direction by their supreme court. All eliminations require adherence to four criteria: one, the target must be designated a combatant and more importantly the targeting agency must have evidence that the target is a combatant; two, the targeting agency must present reasons why arrest is not a feasible course of action; three, the targeting agency must consider collateral damage; and four, there must be an investigation after the fact."

"Excuse me, Mitch," the president interrupted to address the group. "I want to run a cost-benefit analysis on these strikes and renditions. Are they worth the return on investment, not of the missile that kills them but of the political and moral capital of the United States? Are we creating more terrorists for our next generation to fight both at home and abroad?"

The president's wording struck Vic as peculiar. *At home? Targeting on U.S. soil?* If anyone else noticed, they did not bring it into the discussion.

"Go ahead, Mitch."

"In the United States we have operated by three principles since the attacks of September 11th, 2001. In accordance with the AUMF, a targeted individual must pose an imminent threat to the nation; their capture must not be feasible; and the operation would be conducted in accordance with the principles set forth in the laws of armed conflict."

"But no requirement to investigate after the fact." It was a statement, not a question.

"No, Mr. President."

Christensen looked to the DNI.

"Admiral, in your experience at JSOC and since coming on board as DNI, have we followed those three requirements?"

"Yes, Mr. President. The collateral damage assessments are crucial to a green light. Our policy is not to authorize a strike if there is the possibility of *any* noncombatant casualties. The enemy knows this and have incorporated that information into their order of battle. They keep women and children close. I'm not saying we haven't made mistakes, but collateral damage is always at the forefront of the decision-making process."

"Thank you, Admiral. Mitch, please continue."

"Yes, sir. The president has the authority to authorize targeted elimination operations and indeed has the responsibility to do so, which is derived from his constitutional authority to protect the American people. Targeting a U.S. citizen is lawful if that citizen has joined al-Qaeda or an associated terrorist organization or is providing support for imminent terrorist operations. The Supreme Court has found that the use of force is justified against U.S. citizens who have taken up arms against their country or pledged allegiance to a terrorist organization; it is consistent with the Fourth and Fifth Amendments. Targeting a citizen posing a clear and present danger would not violate criminal provisions, nor would it constitute a war crime. Congress has authorized the president to use all 'necessary and appropriate' force against al-Qaeda and its associated terrorist organizations through the AUMF. Also supporting this opinion is the national right to self-defense via international law, specifically UN Charter, article fifty-one."

"Are there any territorial parameters?" the president asked.

"Sir, the AUMF does not specify geographic limitations. It's termed a 'non-international armed conflict.'"

"What constitutes an imminent threat?"

"If there is a gray area here, that's it, sir. As we all know, war with proxies, nonstate actors, and super-empowered individuals like bin Laden is not a conventional war between nation-states with clearly defined areas of operation. Terrorist organizations are continually planning. If they conducted an operation in the past there is a high probability that they are still in the network and planning future attacks; therefore a targeted elimination would not be an act of revenge, but an act of self-defense to protect the American people from violence."

"If I may, sir," Farber interjected, "the concept of imminence is subject to interpretation, meaning it must be formulated and argued. Does imminent constitute a day, a week, or a month? And there is no guarantee that a window to strike based on actionable intelligence, which might also be the *only* window, will align perfectly with a predetermined criterion of imminence."

"Thank you, Greg," the president responded, turning back to the

White House counsel. "If it has been determined that members of a terrorist organization have planned attacks in the past, then legally, whether a day has passed or twenty years, they remain viable targets. Is that correct?"

"Legally, yes," Cohen answered.

"And rendition operations fall into that legal framework?"

"Yes, sir, providing adherence to the law-of-war principles: necessity, distinction, proportionality, and humanity, i.e., collateral damage."

"Have they forfeited their rights as U.S. citizens?" Admiral Lowe asked.

"Yes, actions hostile toward the United States constitute a forfeiture of citizenship. Legally, they would still be targetable with lethal force due to imminent threat, but to answer your question directly, a U.S. citizen gives up his or her citizenship, what the law calls a 'loss of nationality,' when he or she engages in hostilities against the United States. U.S. citizenship does not guarantee immunity in armed conflict. The Supreme Court has held that the president may authorize lethal force against a U.S. citizen who is an enemy combatant. It is considered an act of treason; a capital crime. A lawfully targeted elimination is consistent with the principles of national self-defense. The important takeaway, Mr. President, is that lethal force cannot be used as a punishment for past acts, only to prevent future acts, as with Admiral Yamamoto in World War Two."

"I'm clear on the legality. Ms. Motley," the president said, addressing his CIA director. "What is the position of the CIA?"

"Mr. President," Motley said, "my organization operates in accordance with strict criteria: the target is confirmed as present and there are no noncombatants within the blast radius, capture is not feasible, the foreign government is not capable of addressing the threat to the United States, and no other reasonable alternatives exist."

"And in terms of effectiveness? Are we just creating more terrorists in a game of whack-a-mole?"

Janice Motley had risen through the ranks on the Hill, first as a legislative assistant before becoming the lead staff attorney for the Senate Select Committee on Intelligence. It was in that position where she had caught the eye of the then CIA director, who began grooming her for an executive position in America's premier intelligence organization. She would eventually become the staff director of the SSCI, before accepting a position on President Obama's national security transition team, which would lead her to acting director of the National Clandestine Service and then into the role of America's top spy. She was the second female director in CIA history and the first African American woman to hold the position. Those who briefed her would walk in familiar with her background and reputation as one of the smartest people in the Beltway. They would walk out with a newfound respect; in addition to being a brilliant strategist, she was tough as nails.

"That is certainly a probability, Mr. President."

"Then why do we continue to execute a policy with long-term results inconsistent with the investment?"

Without missing a beat, the director of the CIA answered the query: "Previous administrations have continued the program and even escalated it to keep the enemy off balance, Mr. President. Our signals intelligence supports the contention that while it does assist in enemy recruitment efforts, it also continues to disrupt the planning process. I'll have my office send over a classified white paper detailing the threats to the homeland prevented by the strike program."

"It's insurgent math, Mr. President," Admiral Lowe offered.

"Insurgent math?"

"For every terrorist killed, we create ten more. Stan McChrystal arithmetic, Mr. President."

"I see."

"Administrations of *both* parties have operated under the president's constitutional authority to protect the nation," Cohen added. "These actions are supported by *Al-Aulaqi v. Obama* and *Hamdi v. Rumsfeld*, the inherent right of the United States to protect itself under international law, and the congressional authorization for the use of military force against AQ and associated groups."

"I'd like to hear Mr. Rodriquez's thoughts," the president said.

In his early fifties, Vic was the most junior member of the group. He remembered asking new members of his Special Forces ODA for their opinion during debriefs when he was a young SF captain with 7th Special Forces Group. The president was a veteran and was doing the same thing.

"Sir, my team has studied this at length in accordance with the office of the general counsel at CIA. As you are aware, my department offers another option if the conversation in question is specific to the effectiveness of using unmanned aerial vehicles to deliver a lethal payload. The enemy can use Google just like the rest of us. They have studied our tactics and know exactly what we just discussed in this secure conference room. They know our aversion to collateral damage, which is why you rarely find senior al-Qaeda or ISIS leadership alone. They surround themselves with noncombatants, specifically women and children. My office offers a different option, one that is much more personal and also more dangerous from a commitment of forces standpoint. A single operative or a small team from my side of the house can, at times, be a viable alternative."

The president looked at his national security advisor and then back at the leader of the CIA's paramilitary division.

"Assassins?"

"No, Mr. President. Hunter-killers. Ground Branch operatives who understand the nature of the conflict necessitates them getting close to eliminate the threat, limiting collateral damage that can't be positively identified from a Reaper firing a Hellfire at fifty thousand feet. A covert action statute authorized under title fifty of the U.S. code is an option we've exercised in the past."

"Director Motley."

"Mr. President, this agency is not in the business of creating more terrorists. The targeted killing program under President Obama rose to levels inconsistent with desired end results. Human intelligence networks with proxy forces targeting the enemy run by Ground Branch operators are high risk, but they lower the potential of creating more terrorists vis-à-vis the insurgent math Admiral Lowe referenced. When a Hellfire hits a moving vehicle from out of the blue, there is only one country to blame: the United States. An IED or well-placed bullet, on the other hand, well, responsibility for that type of operation offers plausible deniability."

Alec Christensen leaned back in his chair and touched both forefingers to his lips.

"My duty as president of the United States is to protect the American people. Having fought in Afghanistan I am distinctly aware that we now have soldiers patrolling those same mountains who were not even born on September 11th, 2001. They are fighting the sons of men we targeted in the opening years of the war. It is my job to see that the grandchildren of those I fought don't put Americans in the sights of their AKs. Find me solutions. I want a briefing on the Disposition Matrix, the kill list for lack of a better term, with best- and worst-case scenarios attached to each target. And I want options other than UAVs," he said, looking directly at Vic. "Greg will coordinate a follow-up meeting. Now, let's go through today's PDB."

For the remainder of the briefing, questions were directed to Motley and Lowe by the president and his national security advisor. Vic's mind focused on the fact that his office might be getting a lot busier in the weeks and months ahead. It scarcely registered that the President's Daily Brief contained information on a hemorrhagic virus outbreak in Angola and that 457 people had perished before it had been contained by the World Health Organization.

• • •

Director Motley and Vic Rodriguez exited the Situation Room and took the stairs up to West Executive Avenue, where the director's motorcade was waiting to take them back to Langley. They did not speak until the heavy door to the up-armored black Suburban closed behind them.

"That was interesting," Vic said.

Motley nodded, still deep in thought.

"I know you have teams downrange working through host nation forces, but from the tone of the briefing we might be taking a more unilateral approach."

"It certainly sounded like the president does not favor relying on UAVs as the preferred method of engagement," Vic agreed.

"I'll have counsel compile a history of the legal justifications for each targeted elimination and rendition since the AUMF. We certainly don't want any of our people in the hot seat at the change of administrations like we had with enhanced interrogations."

That she immediately thought of protecting those on the ground doing the nation's work was why she had the respect of the case officers, paramilitary officers, and contractors she led. It was a rare quality in Washington.

"I agree. I get the feeling the president is after more than just finishing what was started under the Bush administration," Vic noted.

"I had that feeling as well."

"Did you catch the U.S. soil comment?" the former Special Forces officer asked his boss.

"I did."

"There's something else at play," he said.

"What do you make of it?"

"I think it has something to do with James Reece."

CHAPTER 16

Denver, Colorado

DR. ALI REZA ANSARI pulled his rental car close to the curb in front of the aging home. A green Subaru, extremely popular in these parts, was parked in the driveway. Ali noted that it had not been backed in. The bike was on the roof rack, signaling that it was safe to approach. Still, Ali was cautious. If the FBI were onto them, this would be the time they would make their arrests, before the deadly virus could be replicated.

Ali had supervised the construction from afar. The *hawala* network transferred more than funds; it passed information. The network of couriers had no idea what they were passing, or why. The messages had been hand carried from Switzerland into the United States. Ali suspected he would have to make a few adjustments, but as long as all the materials were there, and the monkey kidney cells had been prepared as he had instructed, he would be able to complete the next phase of the operation. His priority was to use the scanning electron microscope to ensure the cells contained no contaminants and exhibited the stable growth factors necessary to cultivate the virus.

He had informed BioDine that he'd decided to take two weeks and tour the United States before returning to Europe. He would be reachable for Zoom conference calls and would be answering his emails.

The drive from the East Coast had taken four days. He could have done it in two, but he'd explored along the way, not because he was interested in the sights and history between the Atlantic seaboard and the Continental Divide, but because he was looking for surveillance. He was certain that the Americans were not conducting physical surveillance, but these days, with drones and the interconnected web of the surveillance state, it was nearly impossible to tell if they were tracking you electronically. Ali had always been careful. All his military, intelligence, medical, and business training had culminated in what he was about to do. This was his moment of truth.

Ali approached the front door and knocked three times. The door opened immediately. The young student had been eagerly waiting.

"*As-Salaam-Alaikum*," Sebastian said.

"Never use Arabic or Farsi with me," Ali said, pushing past the young medical student and making his way inside.

Worn hardwood flooring in dire need of attention led to a small living area, where a couch too small for the space faced an old brick fireplace that at one point had been painted white in a failed attempt at modernization.

"Do you have a cell phone?" Ali asked.

"Yes, but it's in my apartment. I've never taken it here."

"Good," Ali said, still weary, as he entered the small kitchen.

An avocado-green refrigerator hummed away next to a four-burner electric stove, and a microwave sat at an angle on the rust-colored countertop.

Ali parted the thin drapes above the sink and looked into the street beyond the yard. Nothing seemed out of the ordinary. No vans with tinted windows, no unmarked Crown Victorias desperately trying to fit in.

"Show me," Ali said.

Sebastian led the way to a door off the hallway and unlocked the dead bolt. His hands trembled for just a moment in anticipation.

Ali knew all about Shahram Pahlavi. The regime had groomed him since birth, through his parents, who were long-term penetration agents. The Americans were so stupid. Why they kept allowing the sons and daughters of those who wanted to destroy them inside their country baffled him. You did not see Americans flocking to Iran, Russia, China, or North Korea to conduct subversion operations and change the fabric of those societies. That is why those countries would endure and why America was doomed to fail.

Shahram seemed eager to please. By design, he knew next to nothing about the BioDine executive who now followed him into the makeshift lab. No name, no background. Ali already had a plan to kill him, after his usefulness expired.

Ali surveyed the virology lab: clear plastic sheets, the ventilation system duct-taped to the outside vents. The state-of-the-art lab equipment he had ordered through intermediaries was all set up and running.

"I need to check the cells," he said.

Sebastian tapped the space key and brought the computer monitor to life. The high-resolution black-and-white image came into focus, displaying what looked like a worm with one end curled into a ball.

"Just as I was instructed. They've been growing for twenty-eight days. Fifteen separate cell lines. No contaminants."

Ali moved in front of the keyboard and zoomed in on the cells, confirming what the younger man had told him.

Nodding, Ali asked, "What do you know about Marburg Variant U?"

Sebastian swallowed. He knew the story. It was a case study in improper safety protocols when handling level-four pathogens.

Marburg Variant U? His visitor couldn't have a sample of that. Could he?

"Marburg. A virus first discovered in a lab in Marburg, Germany, in green monkeys from central Africa. They were working with kidney cells just like these," Sebastian said, nodding at the cultures just beyond the clear plastic slats.

"That's right. That was 1967. Monkey handlers in Marburg, Frankfurt, and Belgrade were all infected. They died in ways the researchers had not seen in their previous experiments. The virus liquefied organs and brain cells. Almost ten years later 430 people died in Zaire and Sudan with similar symptoms to what had been observed in Marburg, but this was another filovirus."

"Ebola."

"Ebola Zaire and Ebola Sudan," Ali corrected.

"I've studied Ebola," Sebastian said. "Under a microscope like this one, filovirus strains look almost the same."

"Ebola's mortality rate is between seventy and ninety percent. For our purposes, we needed something even more toxic."

"Marburg?"

"Not just any strain of Marburg. Variant U."

"That is one of the most closely guarded pathogens on the planet. Only the Russians have a strain, if memory serves."

"Not just the Russians, Sebastian. With the fall of the Soviet Union, their scientists were more than willing to sell it. China has it. North Korea has it. Iran has it. And, most importantly, the Americans have it."

"Where did we get this strain?" Sebastian asked.

Ali paused.

"Where do you think?"

"Iran?"

Instead of confirming, Ali continued, "What do you know about bioweapons?"

"My studies have all been on virology and immunology, not weaponizing viruses."

"I will guide you through this. Before we begin, it is important for you to understand just how careful we need to be. You've done a more than adequate job setting up the lab in accordance with my instructions. What we don't have is a decontamination station. I didn't have you build one because it wouldn't matter. If you prick yourself while handling Variant U, you have less than two weeks to live."

Ali had to hit the right psychological tone to ensure Sebastian believed he was a part of the team and would survive the mission.

"At its height, the Soviet State Center for Virology and Biotechnology, also called VECTOR, was one of the most advanced bioweapons labs in the world. In 1977 Dr. Nikolai Ustinov was injecting Marburg virus into a guinea pig when he accidently injected the virus into his thumb. The animal was not strapped to a board and Dr. Ustinov was not wearing the proper biohazard suit or gloves required for the experiment."

Sebastian whispered a prayer to Allah.

"As you know, all viruses have unique characteristics. That is what allows us to differentiate them from one another and develop vaccines specific to the particular disease. The more deadly they are, the harder they are to spread, killing their host before they can move on to another body with healthy tissues to destroy. High contagion rates such as H1N1, flu, and COVID-19 have kill rates between 0.01 percent and perhaps as high as 0.2 or 0.3 percent. By contrast, the 1918 Spanish flu and the swine flu in 2009 caused worldwide panics because of the respiratory nature of the spread. Hemorrhagic viruses, like Marburg, only spread through direct blood-to-blood contact or secretions with broken mucous membranes, making them difficult to transmit. Once contracted, however, Marburg is a true killer, with an infection fatality rate of 85 to 90 percent and death in thirteen days."

"Forgive me, if it only spreads through blood-to-blood contact, what is all this for?" Sebastian asked, pointing to the equipment he'd so painstakingly prepared over the preceding months.

"Because the variant extracted from Dr. Ustinov can be aerosolized."

"*al-Ḥamdu lillāh,*" Sebastian whispered.

"Dr. Ustinov was immediately quarantined in the facility behind pressure-locked doors. As his body and brain liquefied over the next two weeks he kept a diary, documenting the progression of his deterioration. It started with a headache, fever, and nausea, followed by toxic shock as his eyes filled with blood and the capillaries throughout his body began to hemorrhage. Near the end he was literally bleeding through the pores of his skin, to say nothing of the blood and liquefied organs oozing from his nose, mouth, penis, and anus. The blood- and mucus-stained pages were collected and transcribed before being incinerated. When Ustinov's body had nothing more to give the invading filoviruses, when his cells had all burst, he finally succumbed. His body was doused with a chloramine disinfectant and welded into a metal box to seal the deadly African pathogen inside."

"But not before the Russians took samples from his organs," Sebastian deduced.

"That is correct. Additional testing showed something interesting. Do you know what it was?"

Sebastian took a moment before responding.

"The virus had adapted. Lab-grown viruses are often more potent than those found in nature."

"Not only was it more deadly, it was also more stable. They named it Variant U after its creator. Do you know what they did next?"

Sebastian didn't hesitate this time: "They weaponized it."

"Yes, they weaponized it for an aerosolized delivery via vapor. They tested it on monkeys in a facility in Kazakhstan and on human test subjects in Africa. It became the most potent bioweapon in the Soviet arsenal."

"And you have it with you?"

"I do. It's time to make a weapon."

• • •

Dressed in full Level A hazmat suits with respirators, Ali and Sebastian went to work. Ali's hands moved deliberately in the encased glove box as he carefully cut open the bottle of hand sanitizer that he'd received from Hafez Qassem. He slowly extracted a small test tube of plasma under the vented hood, plasma originating in Dr. Ustinov's dead body in 1977. The most deadly pathogen in human history was now in the basement of a run-down house in Denver, Colorado.

Over the next three days, Ali and Sebastian transferred Variant U blood plasma to the cell culture plates in a process called transfection. A virus that had been sitting dormant for decades had been given a host. It had been lurking in the shadows, waiting for its opportunity to multiply. When Ali injected it into the cell culture, the virus was resurrected. The doctor would have liked a real-time x-ray fluoroscopy to confirm the procedure was working, but the samples they observed under the electron microscope indicated it was growing.

Within a week, each of the culture disks contained millions of copies of the disease.

Variant U had come back to life.

CHAPTER 17

Interstate 90

REECE HAD NEVER DRIVEN from Virginia to Illinois. When he was stationed on the East Coast, he and Lauren had big plans to explore Maine, the Shenandoahs, New River Gorge, the Okefenokee Swamp, and the Florida Keys. Instead, the newlyweds never left Virginia Beach, a series of back-to-back workups and deployments taking precedence. He smiled at the memory of buying their first home together on the water in the SEAL-dominated Chick's Beach area and of the night Lauren had shared the news that they were expecting their first child. He thought they would all have plenty of time to travel together. He had been wrong. Lauren and Lucy were dead, murdered because of a government-private sector conspiracy that Reece had dismantled piece by piece. His wife and daughter had been murdered by the same government Reece now served.

Not forever. I'm going to do this job, get the intelligence from the Agency I need to find Nizar Kattan, and put him down. Then I'm out.

The former SEAL had never been the biggest fan of flying. Even in SEAL training it had always been a relief when the red light switched to green and the jumpmaster pointed at the exit ramp or door. He'd had to touch down on more than a few airfields that required excessively aggressive landings where there was nothing for Reece to do but brace for impact. That, and pray. Reece would much rather be in control of his own vehicle, on the open road with access to his weapons. On this particular drive, he needed to think.

As the miles clicked by on the odometer of his old 1988 Land Cruiser, Reece attempted to shake the memories of the dead. Lauren had always rolled her eyes at the classic off-road vehicle. She knew that Reece loved the car for some reason and that it was just part of the package. His old FJ62 had recently been upgraded with a Corvette LS3 engine, giving it more power than most modern trucks and SUVs. From the outside it looked like a standard 1980s four-by-four. That vintage exterior cloaked what was on the inside an entirely new machine. Restored by the experts at ICON in California, the old truck was a sleeper.

Grey Man Tactical rigid MOLLE panels were attached to both seatbacks and held a fire extinguisher, medical kit, tourniquet, knife, and Winkler tomahawk. The firearms conveniently secured to the black plastic panels had been transferred to Goose Gear overland storage drawers. Reece had installed them in the back of the vehicle, in preparation for his drive to Virginia from Montana before his Clandestine Services Class had kicked off. It was better to keep the AR, shotgun, and scoped long gun out of sight, even if he did have U.S. Marshals Service credentials in case he was stopped. That was one of his asks of the president. He had once been issued a Marshal's badge as part of an operation on U.S. soil when he was in the SEAL Teams. It opened doors and kept the operators out of trouble with local law enforcement in case they were rolled up. U.S. Marshal creds were also federal, meaning he would not have the issues that Texas Rangers Frank Hamer and Maney Gault had when they left the Lone Star State hunting down Bonnie and Clyde. The arsenal that Hammer carried around in the backseat of his 1934 Ford Model 40B in pursuit of the infamous killers actually dwarfed what Reece had hidden in the back of his Land Cruiser. The former SEAL needed to be a bit more subtle.

Get in the game, Reece.

He'd been taught the basics of surveillance and surveillance detection routes in the SEAL Teams as part of his training in PSD, or personal security detail, operations. His team had been the first tasked with protecting the interim Iraqi government officials after the invasion, a mission most of them thought would be suicide. He had also done some work with the FBI's Hostage Rescue Team on close target reconnaissance, which included driving into enemy territory to gather intelligence prior to a hit. Reece's troop had two HRT members and two field agents assigned to them in Iraq, investigating connections to planned terrorist operations in the continental United States. Of all the missions Reece had conducted over the years, the ones that gleaned intelligence on threats to the homeland were the ones of which he was the most proud. More than a few acts of terror had been thwarted on foreign soil before they had a chance to take flight.

He was never a fan of the PSD mission. Reece preferred to be on offense, taking the fight to the enemy rather than standing next to a politician with what was essentially a target painted on their back. The year of training he had recently completed at the Farm built on the lessons he had learned in the SEAL Teams. The CIA was all about their SDRs. Using the SDR techniques had become second nature. They augmented his proficiency acquired through operations in Iraq, Afghanistan, Mozambique, Albania, Ukraine, and Russia. That real-world experience was enhanced with the scenarios they'd put him through at Camp Peary. He knew that to execute his current mission successfully, he'd need an entire team conducting both physical and technical surveillance to build a pattern of life and confirm they were targeting the correct individual. With that information, they could then decide upon the time and place of the elimination. Then why was Reece driving to Chicago alone?

He needed time to think.

The president of the United States has asked you to complete a mission.

You could say no.

Or was saying no not an option?

Reece had raised his right hand to protect and defend the Constitution of the United States against all enemies, foreign and domestic.

Protect and defend the Constitution . . .

Protect and defend . . .

What are you doing, Reece?

You are protecting the country you swore to defend.

Are you?

Or, are you an instrument of vengeance, the personal assassin for the most powerful man in the world?

Are you working for the very government that had a part in killing Lauren and Lucy?

Are you doing this to avenge the attacks of 9/11? Attacks that would pull the country into a twenty-year war and see your friends and teammates die in battle?

Are you doing this to prevent a future attack?

Or, are you doing this so that the president of the United States will owe you a favor? Is this about getting the support you need to kill Nizar Kattan, the sniper who put a bullet through Freddy Strain?

Are you doing this so you can use the power of the executive branch to decipher the letter your father left you? The letter you found the night you called Vic Rodriguez and agreed to join the ranks of the CIA's paramilitary branch?

Or, are you doing this because all you know is the kill?

Later. Focus on this mission.

These terrorists helped plan 9/11, Reece.

They could be planning future attacks.

Twenty years later.

What are you, Reece?

A soldier, an intelligence operative, a hunter of men? An assassin?

You told the president you would do it.

For God and country.

God and country.

As the truck pushed westward, Reece convinced himself that what he was about to do would bring justice to those who had perpetrated the most devastating attack on the United States in modern times. The Japanese had attacked Pearl Harbor before Hawaii was even a state. They had bombed military targets. The Twin Towers were not a legitimate military target. Deliberately targeting civilians was the very definition of terrorism.

Reece thought of all those who had jumped to their deaths rather than face the prospect of being burned alive; fathers and mothers, sons and daughters, brothers and sisters. All they had done was go to work one sunny Tuesday in September.

He thought of the president's fiancée. Had she jumped? Had she perished of smoke inhalation? Had she been burned alive? Had she been trampled to death in a stairwell? Or had she died in darkness, hunkered in the corner of an office as the North Tower imploded around her? The president would never know. No one would ever know. But there was something he could do about it now.

The animals who attacked the nation deserved what was coming, regardless if one day had passed since that fateful morning or twenty years. The president thought so, too. There was a reason he'd issued a presidential directive, notifications based on the Authorization for the Use of Military Force. These were legitimate military targets. Though it was not clear that they posed an imminent threat, it was not clear that they did not, either. They needed to be removed from the battlefield so that they could not be used to enable further attacks. The president was sending a message, one that would not be broadcast on cable news channels, but one that would be received by the terrorist network loud and clear.

CHAPTER 18

Chicago, Illinois

ALI WOULD HAVE PREFERRED to spend a few more days in the area, but time did not allow for that luxury.

Out of necessity, he had taken a circuitous route to Chicago. Borrowing Sebastian's Subaru, he first drove to Richardson, Texas, just outside Dallas, where he met with a man named Mahan Faramand, a sleeper agent of the regime. Ali had passed him the delivery mechanism and specified his objectives: first multiple restaurants and grocery stores, then two days later, a hospital in Richardson. It was imperative they target hospitals. Timing the releases was critical.

The green Subaru would undoubtedly be caught on video at some point in the journey. Avoiding every camera in the western United States was an impossibility, so Ali was going to use the power of the surveillance state to his advantage. If an enterprising investigator or intelligence officer began to put the pieces together, it would lead back to a radicalized virology student in Denver.

He had then driven back to Colorado, returned the Subaru, and passed a second device to an asset in Denver. The operation was in motion and nothing could stop it.

He'd studied the Colorado asset for two days to confirm that the intelligence he'd been sent by Hafez Qassem through a local mosque was indeed true; he was a true believer. They'd met in Cheesman Park, across from the Denver Botanic Gardens, where Ali had explained the simple instructions to a man who had two weeks left to live. Again, public locations followed by hospitals were the key.

Though they didn't know it, as soon as they depressed the plungers on the CO_2 cartridges, releasing Marburg Variant U into the atmosphere, they were as good as dead. No loose ends.

Ali had given them two special inoculation pills and told them to wear N95 masks as an added precaution. In actuality, the pills were two tablets of vitamin D from Walgreens and the masks would do nothing to stop the aerosolized five- to twenty-micron droplets, each one containing one hundred viral strands of the deadly pathogen.

They would strike a blow for Allah and would die martyrs.

The delivery mechanism had been designed by the Iranian and Russian scientists at Damghan, a bioweapons research facility about 185 miles east of Tehran. Disguised as a bottle, it looked like a piece of trash. All the asset needed to do was press down on a handle that resembled a Corovin, a wine bottle sampling and preservation device that used a needle and Argon gas cartridge to tap wines without removing the cork. A needle powered by a cartridge containing the gas would puncture a rubber seal on a small glass vial inside the bottle, aerosolizing the virus and forcing the liquid to rapidly deploy through a nanofiber mesh filter to produce a vaporized cloud of droplets. The resulting whitish-yellow puff contained billions of viral particles. Released through a ventilation system, it could infect entire shopping malls, office buildings, or in this case, hospitals, in minutes.

With most contagious viruses like COVID-19 or H1N1, thousands of viral particles need to be inhaled or touched and transferred to the nose or mouth to initiate the infection. Marburg was in a league of its own.

As little as one or two viral particles were enough to contaminate a host. A single droplet from an aerosolized spray would generate a fatal illness with an incubation period of less than forty-eight hours. Death would follow within days.

It was vital that the attack not look like an attack at all. Though Marburg was not "airborne," as the American press liked to call viruses that could be spread with a cough, it was imperative that they believe it was. It needed to look like it had originated in Angola, the result of a naturally occurring hemorrhagic virus the Americans were always making movies and writing books about. The infidels never did anything other than confirm it was contained on a continent they largely ignored. All they really cared about was that African diseases stayed in Africa. What made this outbreak different was that it had made it to the homeland and had gone airborne, or so they would believe. They would connect the dots from Cabinda in northern Angola, to the Quatro de Fevereiro International Airport in the capital, to a flight landing in the United States. Ali needed at least two of the four target cities to be hit with the same infection. The virus would be traced to Angola, a country with a history of infectious tropical diseases. The most sophisticated intelligence agencies in the world would never trace it back to Iran. Of course, "never" was a word that made Ali cringe. Every plan needed a contingency. If the U.S. intelligence community did discern that the virus was not a naturally occurring disease, it would be traced back to homegrown terrorists inspired by what the talking heads liked to call an "ideology of hate."

That Sebastian Phillips had grown up in the United States and worked in a university bio lab would only fuel the conspiracies. With COVID-19 having dominated the news cycle for so long, most of the country had at least heard the very real possibility that the coronavirus had first originated in a Chinese bio-containment facility in Wuhan. Either way, regardless of whether the United States traced the virus to Angola, or if they discovered it was released into the environment by a terrorist organization made up of U.S. citizens, the result of an airborne pathogen with the infection and death rates of Marburg was the same. The only choice was for the United States government to release the antibodies that would destroy it. In this case, those "antibodies" were on standby in Hurlburt Field, Florida: MC-130s armed with the largest nonnuclear payloads ever developed. To save the country from an invisible virus, the United States would have no choice but to attack itself and incinerate the disease threatening to destroy the entire nation. As with a host whose immune system attacks an invading cancer, oftentimes that host did not survive. The United States was already on edge from COVID-19 and had almost destroyed their economy for a virus that was actually doing them a favor: killing off the weak.

Pulling to the curb three blocks from his meeting location, Ali put the car in park and looked at two small children playing in the front yard of a house across the street. The home was neglected and the yard full of weeds, but the smiles on the children's faces were no different than the smiles of children the world over. An older boy looked on, possibly their brother tasked with keeping an eye on them in this neighborhood just outside Chicago. He was about the same age Ali had been when he'd found his brother swinging from the noose, eyes bulging, tongue protruding from the left side of his mouth, a casualty of war.

The wailing of his mother.

Ali had been told that the asset in Chicago had been unreliable in his communications. The imam had expressed concerns. There were indications that the asset had been corrupted by Western *values.* There were no signs that he had been contacted by American law enforcement or intelligence officers, but one could never be too certain. Ali would be the arbiter of his fate.

CHAPTER 19

THE DOOR OPENED AND Kareem Talib looked suspiciously though the crack, a thin chain linking the door to the frame.

"*Salām,*" Ali said, with a disarming smile.

"Salām, chetori?" the smaller man replied.

"I am well, Kareem. May I come in," Ali said, switching from Farsi to English.

"Of course," Kareem responded, bowing his head and pushing the door closed to disengage the chain barrier before holding it open for his guest. He had been expecting the visitor.

"*Moteshaker hastam.* Are your wife or children home?" Ali asked.

"No, they are at the park. I don't expect them for another hour."

"Good. Let us talk, Kareem. May I have some tea?"

"*Man rā bebakhsh,* yes," Kareem said, nervously putting his hand to his heart. "Please, follow me."

Ali trailed behind the shorter man down a hallway and into a small kitchen with aging linoleum floors.

As Kareem filled a pot with water and set it on the electric coil stove, Ali pulled a photo from a magnet on the refrigerator.

"Is this your family, Kareem?"

"Yes, my wife and two sons."

"They are handsome boys," Ali noted. "How old are they?"

"Four and six."

"You seem too old to have such young children."

"My first wife died in childbirth. Our daughter did not survive. I did not remarry for many years."

"I am sorry, Kareem. Even the prophet Muhammad, peace be upon him, lost six of his seven children."

"They await, and I will see them again on the Day of Recompense," Kareem whispered, placing a mesh strainer into a small ceramic blue teapot.

"Ah, that you will, Kareem. Allah will ensure you will once again be at peace."

Kareem nervously watched as his guest examined the photos and drawings on the refrigerator and inspected the small living area just off the kitchen.

"How do you like your tea?"

"Strong, Kareem. Do you know why I am here?"

Kareem's hand quivered, some of the boiling water spilling down the side of the teapot as he poured the hot liquid over dried leaves and rose petals.

"I was told only to expect you. That you would have a job for me."

"Not just any job, Kareem. A mission from Allah."

Ali watched his subject cover the teapot.

"We will let it steep for about five minutes."

"I understand you have not been to your mosque in quite some time, Kareem."

"It is best not to be noticed coming and going from mosques in Chicago. The American agents are everywhere."

Ali folded his arms. Chicago had one of the fastest-growing Muslim populations in the country. Close to half a million children of Allah called the Windy City home, and fifteen new mosques had been built in the past decade. Chicago was not a city where a Muslim would have a hard time blending in.

"Have the American authorities ever tried to contact you?"

"No. As far as I can tell, I am still clean."

"Ah, I see. And where do you and your family practice *salat*?" Ali asked, referring to the five daily prayers that were the second pillar of Islam. He intentionally looked down the hall and into the living room.

Kareem slowly removed two clear glass teacups from the cupboard and set them on the counter, gathering his thoughts.

"Has faith left your heart, Kareem?"

Kareem drew in a deep breath and whispered "no" with as much emotion as he could muster.

"Have you not come to terms with what you did for Allah?"

Kareem pushed his hands together in an attempt to steady them.

"Here, let me help," Ali offered, gesturing to the small kitchen table, where his host reluctantly took a seat.

The assassin took charge and poured a splash of tea into both cups to warm them and check the brew for consistency. Judging the tea was strong enough for his liking, he then poured them back into the pot before filling both cups to the halfway point, adding a dash of hot water to each.

Kareem did not notice the small wax-infused wafer that his visitor slid into his cup. It dissolved immediately and Ali placed the steaming hot liquid in front of his asset.

"*Mersi*," Kareem said, thanking his unwelcome caller, thinking back to the day his adopted country was attacked: an attack he had helped facilitate. An attack that occurred on the day his wife died in childbirth: September 11, 2001.

"*Khāhesh mikonam*," Ali responded. "Why are you nervous, Kareem? Allah has chosen you to finish what you started twenty years ago."

Kareem took a sip of the dark tea to steady his nerves.

"Please . . ." His voice trailed off.

"If you are no longer devoted to the cause, I can understand that, Kareem. You have a nice life here in Chicago. Do you want me to leave?"

"I am not the person that I was. Allah now has a different calling for me: to raise my two sons. I am sorry."

"I am sorry, too, Kareem."

Kareem felt his pulse begin to race. He looked into the eyes of the man who he now knew had decided to kill him. He gazed back into his tea, struggling to focus, feeling an unnatural sweat beginning to permeate his glands.

"How do you feel, Kareem? You do not look well."

Ali had used the technique before. In Europe he had concentrated natural-occurring regulatory neuropeptides that control stress, emotions, and arousal into high doses—doses large enough to cause heart attacks, seizures, and strokes. He had looped the DNA sequences into a simple bacterial culture for delivery via spray or wafer. It was completely undetectable in an autopsy, as peptides are so efficiently metabolized by the body that they are gone seconds after absorption. The concoction had sent more than a few enemies of Iran to paradise.

Kareem looked at Ali in horror as his body began to react to the overdose of neuropeptides. As he struggled to breathe, the cold sweat was replaced by a bout of nausea; his chest felt like it was being crushed by an invisible block of iron. His vision blurred and he made a feeble lunge for the kitchen counter, knocking over his tea before collapsing to the floor.

Ali took a sip of the dark liquid. He would have preferred it stronger. He crossed his legs and watched as Kareem struggled to breathe on the dirty linoleum tile. He waited another five minutes after Kareem had stopped breathing and finished his tea. He then washed out his cup in the sink using a paper towel to turn on and off the water and also to dry out his cup before replacing it in the cupboard. He then exited the home and walked the three blocks back to his car. Chicago would be spared. No matter. This contingency had been built into the plan. Ali had another city to visit.

He made his way out of Chicago and merged onto I-65. Setting his cruise control to the speed limit, he drove south toward Atlanta.

CHAPTER 20

Chicago, Illinois

REECE HAD DONE ONE drive-by of the target house and then circled back onto West Devon Avenue, passing a Dunkin' Donuts, a Domino's Pizza, a tobacco shop, a Honda dealership, a hookah lounge, and ironically the Iraqi Mutual Aid Society, located within a stone's throw of the Tel-Aviv Kosher Bakery. This one street on the outskirts of Chicago was a multicultural microcosm of American society where Italian, Mexican, and Chinese restaurants shared the street with Lahore Food and Grill and the Salvation Army. He passed a synagogue, a mosque, and a church within blocks of one another. Driving by a business awning signage that read BAGHDAD HAIR SALON, he did a double take and almost missed his turn, flashing back to a mission on the streets of Iraq's capital city in a thin-skinned HMMWV.

The West Ridge neighborhood of Chicago was far enough outside "the Loop" that it had been spared the rioting and looting of the previous summer. Reece couldn't help but think how much better the country might be without politicians stoking the coals of division. They excelled at stirring up hate and discontent to advance partisan political agendas in an attempt to persuade their voting blocs that they were the answer to the very problems they were creating.

Those who sell the panic, sell the pill.

Those politicians might be responsible for more deaths than your target, Reece.

The former frogman was acutely aware that his Land Cruiser stood out. He could have gotten away with it in a few California seaside surf communities or the back roads of the Pacific Northwest or a ski town in the Wasatch or Rockies, but in suburban Chicago, vintage off-road vehicles were not the order of the day. If he was going to go through with this mission, he would need to do it right. That meant a team. It meant "indigenous" vehicles. It meant technical and physical surveillance. It meant building a pattern of life and getting creative with the method of termination.

Then what the hell are you doing here?

Reece's attention was drawn to a woman descending the steps of the small single-story home with two young children in tow. He watched them disappear down the street and found himself thinking of Lauren and Lucy walking to the park in Coronado together; beauty, innocence, and hope shattered at the business end of an AK. Shifting his focus back to the house, Reece wondered if his target was inside.

Am I about to do to this family what was done to mine? At the behest of the same government?

According to the file, this man facilitated 9/11, Reece. He deserves what's coming. Justice. Justice? Or, retribution?

Just over twenty years ago, Kareem Talib had lived in Florida. He'd taken flying lessons at Huffman Aviation in 1999 but dropped out well before he'd completed the thirty-five hours required for a private pilot's license certification. He was not a U.S. citizen at that point and had moved to Chicago shortly thereafter. A year later, Mohamed Atta, Ziad Jarrah, and Marwan al-Shehhi applied for training. Talib had conducted what was known in special operations circles as an advance force operation. He had confirmed that a dark-skinned Muslim on a student visa could apply for flight training in the United States without getting a visit from the FBI.

By all indications, Talib had been living his life as a U.S. citizen for almost two decades without any negative interaction with law enforcement or U.S. intelligence agencies. Had he reformed, or was he just biding his time, waiting for his next assignment? That was not Reece's department. This man was a foreign agent, responsible for the deaths of almost three thousand Americans, citizens with families and dreams just like Lauren and Lucy. His actions had forfeited his right to citizenship. It was time for him to die.

The man who knocked on the door to the home wearing what most people still called a "COVID mask" could have been anyone: a friend, relative, neighbor, or business associate. He spoke briefly to the man who opened the door and then disappeared inside.

Shit! I should have had my phone ready, or even better, had a high-resolution camera with a zoom lens. Rookie.

Twenty minutes later the man reemerged alone and casually made his way down the street away from Reece's position. The camera on Reece's iPhone wasn't bad, but it was not made for taking surveillance photos through windshields at over a hundred yards. Something about the way the man moved put Reece on edge. He'd seen it in the instructors at the Farm, men and women who had been trained to blend in while still remaining situationally aware in nonpermissive environments. He took a burst of photos and resisted the urge to follow the visitor.

Stay on target.

Reece forced down a sip of coffee from the 24 oz. Yeti Rambler in the seat next to him. The mini-mart where he'd filled up hadn't had any honey so he'd been forced to substitute with artificial sweeteners and

French vanilla creamer. Reece made a mental note to dig out his Black Rifle Coffee travel kit and keep it in his vehicle.

The woman and children returned around noon.

Less than ten minutes later the first police car arrived.

Reece continued to snap pictures with his phone as a fire truck roared down the street and came to a stop in front of the target house, an ambulance and another police cruiser close behind. The paramedics entered the home with two large medical packs as two EMTs pulled a wheeled stretcher from the back of the ambulance and maneuvered it inside.

What the fuck is going on? Reece wondered.

In less than five minutes the medical team reemerged with a body strapped to the gurney. They loaded the patient into the back and sped off with sirens blaring. Moments later the woman and children rushed down the steps and into an aging Civic, taking off after the ambulance.

Reece exited his vehicle and approached a police officer who was talking to a firefighter.

"Hey, guys," Reece said, holding up his Marshal badge. "I was just driving by. What happened?"

"Heart attack," the officer responded.

"That's too bad," Reece said. "Will he make it?"

The officer looked to the firefighter, who shook his head.

"He's gone. We still rush them to the hospital as a matter of protocol. He'd only been out for thirty minutes or so. Probably could have saved him if he'd been able to call 9-1-1."

"Did the wife find him?" Reece asked.

"Kids found him first. Always tough."

Reece contemplated telling the cop that he'd seen a man leave the house just minutes before the family had returned, but that would have led to additional questions. Reece had already pushed it enough.

"So rough," Reece agreed. "You guys stay safe. Thanks for holding the line."

"You, too, Deputy."

Reece crossed the street and walked back toward his Cruiser.

There is no such thing as a coincidence was a popular saying in spy novels and movies. In real life, Reece knew that coincidence *was* a real thing; that is why it was a defined term.

Then what is this?

Who is the man who arrived just prior to Talib's family returning?

Had he killed the first target on Reece's list?

Though he knew it was a fruitless effort, Reece took his time getting out of town, slowly weaving his way through the surrounding streets on the off chance he might see the man in the mask.

Still perplexed by the mysterious visitor, Reece turned south onto the interstate toward the next name on his list.

CHAPTER 21

CHARLIE CRIMMINS HADN'T EXPECTED Reece to bolt out of town. They certainly had not expected him to drive from Virginia to Illinois, but the tracking device they'd attached to his Land Cruiser allowed them to stay far enough back so as not to be noticed. Reece's sudden road trip could be the incentive Masada leadership needed to approve installing audio and visual recording devices in that reporter's bedroom where Reece and Katie spent a lot of their time. Crimmins was looking forward to that assignment.

He switched driving duties with his partner, a former police officer from Ohio who had been removed from the force after a suspect died in his custody. He had already been on thin ice after one too many excessive force complaints. No charges were filed because the one and only witness was dead. After a stint as a bouncer at a local strip club, he'd been hired on with Masada and completed a three-month contract in Afghanistan and another in Colombia. The cocaine habit he'd picked up on guard duty in South America only fueled the delusions he had of himself as a special operations warrior, now having spent time in the *'Stan*, as he liked to call it. That his experience there consisted of manually opening and closing a compound gate was not something anyone needed to know.

"Woody," Crimmins said to the former police officer in the back of the minivan. "He still parked?"

"Huh?"

Crimmins turned around and looked into the heavily modified passenger section of the dark minivan.

"Put that bullshit gun porn down and pay attention," Crimmins snapped.

Woody threw his *Recoil Magazine* to the side and refreshed the screen on the monitor.

"Still there, boss," Woody said. "What the fuck is this guy doing here? Think he's got some *strange* on the side?"

"Quit thinking about pussy. He's got that smoker of a reporter in D.C. He's out here for something else."

"Is Sawyer going to have us whack him or what?"

"We are going to do as we are told."

"Fuck, man, I hope we get to ice him. It's been too long. I got my blaster right here," Woody said, tapping the appendix holster. "Taran Tactical Glock. John Wick version."

Crimmins could only listen to so much from the wannabe super soldier.

"I'm hungry," Crimmins said. "I'll take over for you. Why don't you run back to that kebab place we passed a couple blocks back and pick me up a tandoori chicken?"

"Fuck that *haj* shit! I had enough of that in the sandbox."

"First of all, you didn't do shit in the *sandbox*. Secondly, it's Indian food, and thirdly, you can go wherever you like but you'll grab me a tandoori chicken."

"*Fuck!* You want a drink?" Woody asked, moving his steroid-assisted bulk into the front passenger seat.

"Dr Pepper, and have them throw in some—"

His order was interrupted by a siren. Crimmins watched in the side-view mirror as a police cruiser sped past and turned onto the street where their tracking device pinpointed James Reece.

"Where's he going?" Crimmins wondered aloud.

"Oh man, I miss that rush," Woody said. "Probably going to smash some skulls."

A fire truck, ambulance, and another police car passed in close succession.

"What else you want with that *haj* food?"

"Forget it. Get in the back. Hit the recorders."

Woody maneuvered into the commander's swivel chair in the back, which allowed him access to the technical surveillance equipment that lined one side of the van.

"We're good," he confirmed.

Glad that the equipment was almost idiot-proof, Crimmins started the engine and slowly merged onto the street. Doing a drive-by with the Maryland plates was a risk. Thankfully, he'd already requested another Masada team to assist with surveillance. A second vehicle in the rotation would help keep them from getting burned.

"Target vehicle still hasn't moved," Woody said.

"Roger."

Crimmins turned onto the street and immediately identified the emergency response vehicles in front of a home just down the road from their target vehicle. He recognized Reece talking to a police officer and firefighter in front of the house and continued to drive past, collecting 360-degree video. He drove four more blocks before pulling over.

"What the fuck was that about, boss?"

"Not sure. Keep an eye on that monitor. Let me know if he moves."

Crimmins pulled a phone from his pocket, selected a name, and brought it to his ear.

• • •

Erik Sawyer listened to the report.

"Send me the address and stay on him," he ordered, before ending the call.

The address appeared in his messages a moment later. Sawyer forwarded it to an assistant and within minutes had a name and criminal history from a publicly available background check.

Sawyer picked up his encrypted KryptAll secure mobile phone, which was used to communicate only with people who owned the same devices, and placed a call.

Senator Thwaite answered immediately.

"What do you have for me?" he asked.

"James Reece drove to Chicago. He parked outside a house owned by a man named Kareem Talib, a naturalized U.S. citizen with no criminal record."

"And?"

"And, Kareem Talib died of a heart attack while Reece was parked outside."

"That gives me next to nothing."

"If I were you, Senator, I'd use your contacts at whatever government agency owes you a favor and find out all you can about Kareem Talib."

The senator terminated the call and did just as he was told.

CHAPTER 22

Atlanta, Georgia

SOHRAB BEHZAD WAS STILL security conscious, not just because of what he *had* done but because of what he *continued* to do.

Emigrating from Morocco in the early nineties, drawn to Nevada by the low cost of living and growing Muslim population, Sohrab's father had started his American dream as a cabdriver. He soon had to quit because of the distasteful practice the company had of "long hauling" tourists to cheat them for a higher fare. That, and dropping drunks at strip clubs, ran counter to his beliefs. A failed rental property business followed, and for a short time he drove a trailer advertising scantily clad "escorts" up and down Las Vegas Boulevard until he could no longer stomach it.

Speaking fluent French, English, and Arabic, his wife found a good-paying job at one of the upscale hotels and acted as an interpreter when the various "princes" from the Kingdom and other parts of the Middle East rented out the penthouse suites for a week of sin. Her work paid for close to two years of schooling at a local community college for her husband, who learned the art and science of stenography. When he graduated, he could transcribe more than two hundred words per minute and was hired on at the Las Vegas Municipal Court, Criminal Division. The elder Behzad was proud of the life he carved out for his family in the land of opportunity. For the teenage Behzads, the mecca of sin provided other temptations.

Sohrab had been young in the spring and summer of 2001 and had already spent time in the Clark County Juvenile Detention Center for possession with intent to sell. His older sister had been disowned by their parents, the lure of the Vegas Strip proving stronger than the teachings of Allah. It was her pimp who had introduced Sohrab to the drugs; the money and women that came with them were hard to resist. It wasn't easy being a Muslim so near to the gambling, fornication, and gluttony of Sin City.

The Behzads lived fifteen minutes from downtown, a distance that proved not far enough. There was only a single mosque when his parents had arrived from Morocco, and they raised their children to be stringent adherents of the faith. When Sohrab's sister had been brought before the judge as part of a prostitution sting operation, their father dutifully took notes as a court reporter. When he returned home that evening, they had boxed up all her belongings and removed them from the house, stacking them by the garage. She had picked them up a week later with a strange man who loaded them into a lowered van. Her mother watched from the window, but her father refused to even look at her. All her photographs were discarded and she was never spoken of again.

Sohrab continued to sell drugs at his high school. He was paid in sexual favors by the pimp's prostitutes and given money that, to a seventeen-year-old kid, seemed like a fortune. All the while he continued to go to the mosque and pray with the men. He wasn't yet ready to be kicked from the nest.

His parents did not disown him as they had his sister when he returned from the juvenile detention facility. He had found a deeper connection to Allah while incarcerated, which they saw as a blessing. His time in the state-run facility had two unintended results: he had learned to fight with improvised weapons, and he had been recruited.

It was rumored that the imam from their mosque in the Vegas suburbs had fought the Soviets in Afghanistan, but he didn't look like a battle-hardened warrior to Sohrab. When the imam called upon him one evening after prayers, he had expected a lecture on the dishonor his criminal activity had brought to his family. Instead they discussed worldwide Muslim persecution. The same country that had locked him up for a minor drug offense was actively murdering Muslims across the globe at the behest of the Jews.

The respected imam had given him a mission. Four men would be coming to Las Vegas and Sohrab would be their guide. It was important that they not attract attention. He was to provide them with a list of hotels and Internet cafes with no security cameras and he was to help them get around while they were in town. If Sohrab was successful, the imam would have further assignments, assignments that paid. In exchange, Sohrab would have to swear to Allah that he would stop selling drugs.

The four men visited Las Vegas six times over the next few months. Each time Sohrab did his duty. They were not interested in strippers, gambling, or cocaine. Instead they stayed to themselves, meeting in the dirty rooms of shitty motels in the seedier sections of the city just off the Strip. They also spent long hours in the Cyber Zone Café.

It was Sohrab's responsibility to make sure they could get to and from their destinations in a way that wouldn't attract attention. That, and teach them how to fight. They wanted to learn the skills Sohrab had acquired in jail. They were particularly interested in training with box cutters. Sohrab adapted what he'd learned as a ward of the state. He taught them how to use the short-bladed cardboard-cutting tools as instruments of death. He didn't think it unusual when he saw Mohamed print off flight schedules in the cyber cafe. Nor did he think much of it when he drove them to the Hoover Dam. He did find it strange when the one called Marwan wanted to move to the St. Louis Manor. Only after the attack did Sohrab realize that the new hotel put him a block from the Stratosphere, the tallest building in Vegas.

In the days following September 11, he saw their pictures on the news: Mohamed Atta, Hani Hanjour, Marwan al-Shehhi, and Ziad Samir Jarrah. Rather than disgust or guilt, he felt a power; he was a warrior of Allah. He walked with a newfound swagger. He trained harder in the ring and in the weight room, feeling a great sense of pride when the hookers commented on his physique.

Sohrab stuck to his schedule after the attacks, continuing to work out at the boxing gym, pray at the mosque, and smoke weed with prostitutes. He kept his word and never sold drugs again. Using them was another story. When the imam called him to his office, he did not mention the men who were now known the world over as the 9/11 hijackers. Instead, he offered Sohrab another job.

The mosque would recommend him for employment with the Islamic Relief Society of America. One of their objectives was to provide security to mosques in the United States and Canada. They would train him as a safety and security operations officer, even bringing in the Arab American Police Association to conduct a seminar titled "Protecting Our Places of Worship." Violent anti-Islamic backlash was expected as part of the fallout from the attacks, and mosques needed to be prepared. Sohrab accepted. Without leaving his adopted country, he could be a warrior for the faith.

Almost two decades later, Sohrab was one of the leading experts on mosque security in the United States. His skills had improved over the years, as he added Brazilian jiujitsu and firearms training to his regimen of boxing and weight lifting. The Islamic Relief Society sent him around the country conducting mosque vulnerability and risk assessments, writing armed-carry authorization policies, providing emergency medical training, developing active threat engagement strategies, instructing de-escalation courses, and teaching incident response and crisis management. His favorite days were those training staff and volunteers for what were now called active shooter scenarios. After a day of force-on-force UTM paint cartridge training, he was ready for a night of ganja and female companionship.

The "dating" apps on his phone made it so much easier to connect to call girls in the cities he visited across the country. He liked to end his seminars with sex he paid for. He favored the transactional nature of the relationship. He could fuck them and kick them out, just like his parents had abandoned his sister.

All these years after the planes had hit, Sohrab felt the same power he had when he'd first seen the four martyrs on TV. He imagined them using the box cutters to slice the throats of the pilots, some of whom had military experience and had probably bombed innocent Muslims in the Middle East. He pictured the sharp razors at the throats of the whore flight attendants. He was proud of the skills he'd taught the martyrs.

Sohrab was more energized now than he had been in years; the imam at the Atlanta mosque had passed him a message. He was to have a meeting. He was to receive a mission. That excited him. He might spend a little extra on a hooker tonight, maybe keep her for a few extra rounds before getting rid of her. The warrior in him preferred to wake up alone.

CHAPTER 23

REECE HAD TAKEN HIS time with this one. The file detailed the target's background in security. *Never underestimate your opponent.* Sohrab Behzad took different routes from the extended-stay hotel to the mosque in East Atlanta. That indicated he was taking precautions. He spent each day in the mosque with a lunch break between his morning and afternoon training sessions.

Reece was staying in the same hotel, which allowed him to access camera locations, entry and exit points, and study the doors and locks. Making entry to rooms with electronic door locks was much easier than hotel chains wanted guests to realize. At the Farm, Reece had been taught how to surreptitiously enter and exit hotel rooms bypassing the electronically coded RFID key cards. That would have been the way he made entry but for the camera at the end of the hallway. Instead, the sliding glass door that opened onto an absurdly small balcony would be his way in. Reece had practiced breaking into his own room from the balcony, a fairly simple procedure that called for lifting the door from its track with his Dynamis Combat Flathead while pulling the door open with his free hand. It was possible that his target had put an obstruction in the base of the slider, and if so, Reece would regroup and continue surveillance. He wouldn't know until he tried.

Reece had built a pattern of life on his targeted individual over the past few days. Sohrab had been getting back to his room late each night between midnight and 1:00 a.m. Tonight Reece would be waiting.

The third-story room was obscured from view of the highway by large trees that also helped dampen the noise of freeway traffic. There were no cameras observing that particular side of the four-story structure, and the curtains were pulled in the two rooms he would have to bypass on his way to the third floor.

Having checked out of his room the day before, Reece pulled his Land Cruiser onto a side street away from the outdoor hotel parking lot in a position to observe the area. There were no lights illuminating the two rooms he would climb past on his way to the third-level terrace. He could see the approach to the hotel and noted that his target had not returned earlier than expected. At 11:00 p.m. Reece moved from his vehicle, down the street and across a grass- and tree-studded park to the edge of the hotel. After pausing to ensure a late-night walker had not compromised his approach, he climbed to the edge of the first-floor railing and jumped, pulling himself up onto the second-floor veranda. Once again, he stopped to look and listen. Confident he had not been discovered, he heaved himself up and onto the balcony of his target. He knelt down out of sight and listened, closing his eyes to further enhance his sense of hearing.

Nothing.

He gave it a full two minutes before moving to the sliding glass door, being sure to stay low and out of sight. He jammed the sturdy flathead into the lower portion of the tack, pushing down on the tool to leverage the door out of its track while yanking it open with his left hand. It pulled free of its safety catch and Reece entered the room.

• • •

What the hell is he doing in Atlanta? Crimmins wondered.

They had been on Reece for almost a week and Crimmins didn't know how much longer he could put up with his partner, whom he'd nicknamed "Worthless Woody." Reece had checked into the extended-stay hotel, far enough outside the trendy Buckhead area to keep the price down. It was an inexpensive option for those unwilling to pay the five-hundred-dollar-a-night prices of the hotels near the bars, restaurants, and nightlife of the uptown commercial district. It catered to road crew construction teams, families on cross-country road trips, and cheating spouses looking for a discreet midday rendezvous, an illicit fling during an extra-long lunch break.

The two Masada teams were staying at the Westin and kept tabs on their prey electronically. The crews rotated every eight hours, with the on-duty team setting up across Peachtree Road in a mall parking lot where they could change positions periodically without attracting too much attention. Though they didn't have "eyes-on," they were in a position to follow their target when he left the hotel, which he did each morning, taking one of three different routes to East Atlanta. Their surveillance notes indicated he spent much of his time in his vehicle around the Atlanta Masjid of Al-Islam Mosque.

What are you up to, you son of a bitch?

Their target's movements coincided with another guest at the hotel, a man driving a midsize rental car who appeared to be working at the mosque. Crimmins had "Worthless" capture high-resolution stills and video of the new person of interest and forwarded those to Masada higher headquarters.

Hours later the Masada surveillance detail received a report and were told to continue shadowing their primary target.

Tonight, Reece's Land Cruiser was not in the hotel parking lot. It was parked just down the street. That put Crimmins on edge.

In Iraq, Crimmins had noticed similarities between how their ground intelligence teams had developed target packages and how his uncle had taught him to hunt whitetails in the Tennessee of his youth. Humans and animals were creatures of habit. It was all about identifying patterns. He'd been involved in enough surveillance details at home and abroad to know what Reece was doing.

He was hunting.

CHAPTER 24

REECE WAITED IN DARKNESS.

He'd wetted down the Dead Air Odessa-9 suppressor with water from the bathroom sink to further dampen the sound. The suppressor was threaded onto the True Precision barrel of his SIG P365. Contrary to what Hollywood had programmed moviegoers to think, silencers didn't actually "silence" a gunshot. Rather, they suppressed the noise to more palatable levels, which is why the military community called them suppressors, in contrast to Hiram Maxim's original patent language, which called them silencers. Reece planned to take one well-aimed head shot as his target entered the room.

No plan survives first contact with the enemy, Reece.

That's why you have more than one round. Be prepared.

Reece glanced at the vintage Rolex Submariner on his wrist.

Anytime now.

At the sound of a woman's voice Reece jerked his head from his watch.

What the fuck? I know I'm in the right room.

Bolting from the chair in the corner, Reece bounded past the bed and peered through the peephole before quickly retracting and throwing his back against the wall in the dead space behind the door.

Shit!

Sohrab Behzad had a woman with him.

Reece's mind raced.

Take a breath and make a call, Reece.

The former frogman pulled his pistol down against his abdomen into the *Sul* position to get as flat as possible. *Sul* was Portuguese for "south" and had been developed in Brazil as a way to move more safely through crowds with a handgun without drawing the type of attention one would otherwise generate at the low ready or high port. Right now, Reece used it in an attempt to melt into the wall as the door swung open on its automatic commercial closer.

Shit!

Before the door had even shut to give Reece the time he needed to bring the pistol up for a shot, Sohrab had grabbed the woman and pulled her through the small entry toward the bedroom. He tore off her leather jacket as he spun her around and drove her toward the bed. Had he not been distracted by her artificially enhanced breasts, he might have taken the time to professionally assess the room. Sohrab was thinking with his dick.

Slow is smooth, smooth is fast.

Emerging from his position against the wall, Reece moved into the bedroom, slowly working to get an angle that wouldn't endanger the woman. Her jacket was on the floor and her tight top was pushed up, revealing a lacey bra that struggled to contain her tits. She had Sohrab's full attention. His left hand held her head to his, his face buried in the side of her neck, his other hand forcing its way down the front of her tight skirt between her legs.

That attention shifted in an instant when the woman opened her eyes and screamed. A creature had materialized from the entryway, a creature holding a gun. Sohrab spun, instinctually throwing the girl at the threat.

No shot.

Reece retracted his pistol to a position of retention and deflected her momentum with his forearm, sending her crashing into the closet.

Win the fight.

Reece charged forward, driving his opponent facedown onto the bed, still attempting a single shot to minimize the risk of discovery. Holding him down with his support hand, Reece struggled to index his muzzle on the back of his adversary's head, which would have worked on an untrained opponent. It didn't work on Sohrab.

With a violent twist, Sohrab threw Reece off balance, elbowing him in the side of the head and pushing him back off the bed just as Reece's trigger finger sent a shot into the mattress. The mosque security man was now in his element, using a leg sweep to take Reece to the ground between the wall and the bed. Falling to the floor with his attacker, Sohrab pinned Reece's pistol to the wall by the suppressor while raining down a succession of hard blows with his free hand.

Covering his head with his left hand in an attempt to counter the hits, Reece drew his left knee up and to the inside, creating space as Sohrab went for the mount. That was the opportunity Reece needed to draw his blade from appendix carry with his left hand in a reverse grip and stab it directly into Sohrab's groin. He retracted it quickly and thrust it into his target's diaphragm.

Feeling the sharp intrusion, Sohrab's body reacted. His hand loosened on the pistol he still had pinned to the wall, allowing Reece to rip it back and fire two rapid shots. The first went into Sohrab's leg just above the kneecap. The second went into his upper thigh, tearing through muscle, sinew, and bone, with the largest bullet fragments finding their way into his hip. Desperately wanting to get out from underneath the surprisingly heavy man, Reece thrust his pelvis up and to the side, sending his target forward and smashing his head into the bedside table. Aggressively turning to get to his feet, Reece moved to cover by the closet, pushing the still-screaming woman back toward the entryway and sending two more shots at the man who now had a pistol in his hand.

Where the hell did that come from?

Sohrab took one of Reece's bullets to the groin and another to his lower abdomen while shooting three rounds into the wall as Reece disappeared into the entryway. The sound of the unsuppressed pistol was deafening in the small space.

Shit, I hope that didn't kill anyone sleeping next door, Reece thought. *End this.*

Preparing to get the angle and put Sohrab down, Reece felt the flurry of blows from behind. He spun, obstructing the girl's punches, first knocking her to the closet and then kicking her into the bedroom. The force of the kick sent her flying past Sohrab, who fired two shots at the movement, both of which missed and again impacted the wall.

Taking advantage of the misdirection, Reece went to a knee to change levels. Emerging from cover, he put two well-placed shots into Sohrab's upper thorax. Pouncing from the kneeling position, Reece closed on the man who had helped facilitate 9/11. With the blade still in his support hand he stabbed Sohrab in the hip, exploding upward and opening the left side of Sohrab's body from his pelvis to his chest. With his knife embedded in his enemy's deltoid, he used his elbow to check Sohrab's gun off line, trapping him at the door of the bathroom across from the bed. Moving the suppressor of his pistol under the wounded man's chin, Reece looked him in the eye and pulled the trigger.

CHAPTER 25

ALI ANSARI WAS FULFILLING his due diligence. Of all the assets in place across the United States, he had the most specific information on Sohrab Behzad. The man worked for the Islamic Relief Society of America and had been in and out of mosques developing security plans for almost twenty years. According to the file, Sohrab came from a devout Islamic home. The family had disowned his sister years ago. *Lucky for her she didn't live in Afghanistan.* Ali knew that when she left the world of the living, she would spend eternity in the fires of *al-Nar.* In fact, *Jahannam* might be the next place the siblings were reunited.

Ali pulled his car to a stop across the street from the extended-stay hotel. He'd tailed Sohrab from the hotel to the mosque to dinner at the home of the imam and then into an area of the city one wouldn't want to spend much time in unless it was absolutely necessary. Ali wondered why Sohrab didn't pick one of the more upscale gentlemen's clubs in Atlanta.

Two hours later, Sohrab exited and picked up a woman by the back entrance. It was not difficult to discern that she was a whore just like his sister. No matter. Sohrab would soon be dead. They had an appointment in Briarwood Park the following day. There Ali would pass on the Marburg dispersal device along with the vitamin D tablet "antidote." Atlanta would suffer the same fate as Denver.

Ali was about to start up his car and return to his hotel, his curiosity satisfied, when he heard the gunshots. Instantly alerted, he focused his attention back on the four-story establishment. His breathing intensified as he wondered what was happening and if he should get out of the area before the police arrived. Catching movement in his peripheral vision, he watched as a side door swung open and a man and woman swiftly moved into the dark wooded area just south of the hotel. The woman was the same one who had entered with Sohrab, but the man was someone new.

What is this?

The man kept his head down but was obviously alert, his arm around the women who stumbled along next to him.

Ali took pictures with his cell phone before they vanished into the darkness.

For a moment, Ali didn't know whether to follow the man and the whore, stay observing the hotel to find out what happened to Sohrab, or turn tail and put as much distance between him and the gunshots as possible.

Trusting his instincts, he hit the start button and eased into the night. As his headlights illuminated his marks, Ali was careful not to change speed. He passed them getting into a Land Cruiser. Had it been a different car, Ali might not have noticed, but it was a vehicle prevalent in the land of his upbringing and not so prevalent in the United States. He had also seen it before, outside the house of Kareem Talib in Chicago.

Ali's heart raced faster than his mind. A nervous sweat caused him to take a tighter grip on the wheel, his eyes darting to the rearview mirror and out the side windows looking for any sign of the American FBI.

If law enforcement were onto him, they would not have allowed him to pass the device to the assets in Texas and Colorado. Were they following him? Was he leading them to the entire cell? Had all his hard work been for nothing? No, the Americans would have stopped him. This was something different.

Ali drove exactly the posted speed limit, watching the cars around him. He pulled into a gas station on the outskirts of the city. He still had a mission. He carefully screwed a time-release mechanism onto the virus dispersal device and left it in an overflowing trash can. It would not be as effective as what Ali had originally planned for a local hospital, but in this business one had to adapt.

The cold perspiration continued to intensify until he pulled into a motel just over the Alabama border. Acting as naturally as possible, he checked in and went to his room. He requested one with a view of the parking lot and immediately parted the drapes at the window, half-expecting to see a fleet of American police cars descend upon him. He opened his BioDine work computer and selected a VPN. He then entered a username and password for a photo-sharing account, activating a protocol to be used only in the case of extreme emergency.

Via Bluetooth, he shared the photos he'd taken of the man and the hooker as they exited the hotel, along with the video he'd taken as he passed them in the street. He uploaded both to the photo-sharing service and into an album of innocuous photographs of national parks, flowers, mountains, and monuments, photos that looked like any other photo-sharing account storing vacation memories.

Why had the Land Cruiser been at the location of two of Ali's assets? Surely the Americans would have used a more innocuous vehicle for a professional surveillance detail. The fact that Ali had not been arrested suggested that something else was at play.

As per their prearranged procedures, Ali's uploaded photo and video to their shared database meant there was a problem. If Ali uploaded a photo, the receiver knew it was a picture of someone who threatened the mission, someone who had to be eliminated.

• • •

Hafez Qassem received the alert that new photos had been uploaded to the shared account the following morning. An hour later he had confirmation that the man in the photo was a former commando with an interesting history. Qassem had a face, a name, and a vehicle. If Ali had risked sending the photo, he needed the man dead. Qassem hit a button on his desk phone, summoning an assistant who appeared a moment later.

The Iranian intelligence chief was about to activate a sleeper cell on American soil. By the end of the day a team of assassins would have orders to kill James Reece.

PART 2

INFECTION

"Marg bar āmrikā"

"Death to America"

—ALI KHAMENEI, IRAN'S SUPREME LEADER

CHAPTER 26

Camden, North Carolina

ERIK SAWYER FINISHED READING the report for the fourth time and tossed it onto his desk, leaning back in his Wegner swivel chair and interlacing his fingers behind his head.

Lieutenant Commander James Reece, what are you up to?

Save for the lavish chair, his office as founder and CEO of Masada Security Solutions was no different than the nine other offices that dotted the administration building of the largest paramilitary training facility in the United States.

Just across the Virginia border in North Carolina, Masada's eight-thousand-acre flagship compound boasted indoor and outdoor shooting ranges, a driving track, a lake for waterborne insertion operations, two sniper ranges, an airfield, "kill houses," a maritime interdiction trainer, and a multipurpose K9 complex. They had also constructed what they called the "Tactical Training Laboratory," a huge state-of-the-art indoor facility housing multiple buses and airplane fuselages. Lighting, audio, fog, and temperature could be configured from a control room that filmed the practice runs for later debriefings and assessments. They even had a 150-foot ship available to rent for Visit, Board, Search, and Seizure "underway" training docked in Norfolk. Located within driving distance for special operations units based in Fort Bragg and Virginia Beach and the FBI's Hostage Rescue Team in Quantico, Virginia, Masada was a playground for the best operators in the world. It was also the headquarters of Sawyer's private army.

Sawyer preferred his office to look just like those of "the boys," the retired operators and spooks who ran the day-to-day operations of what had popularly become known as a PMC, or private military company. His employees were called contractors in Western parlance. The rest of the world called them mercenaries. Behind his back, he was disparagingly called the "Whore of War" by those critical of outsourcing America's wars to for-profit companies. Sawyer wore the moniker as a badge of honor.

He had purchased the property with a sliver of his inheritance after his return from Mogadishu. It had come a long way. The years following 9/11 saw an explosion of growth in the security sector, and Sawyer was positioned to pounce. He used the new influx of capital from overseas contracts to expand the North Carolina complex, also adding off-site facilities in California, Illinois, and Florida. Maritime, air, and intelligence divisions were run from offices in McLean, Virginia, near his most profitable clients, the U.S. Department of State and the Central Intelligence Agency. The privatization and outsourcing spurred on by the Global War on Terror had been good to Sawyer. The spartan offices on the edge of the Great Dismal Swamp stood in stark contrast to the building in McLean where politicians could stop by for bourbon, and military and intelligence officials could marvel at the impeccably decorated conference rooms and offices. Maybe there was an office waiting for them in retirement if they approved a multimillion-dollar security contract?

When Sawyer was in North Carolina he wanted to train. He'd hit the obstacle course with a group from Quantico early that morning, impressing even the most fit agents in the group. When HRT moved on to the Tactical Training Laboratory to practice bus takedowns, Erik had challenged his COO of the training division to a shoot-off. The COO was a crusty master chief who kept the range schedule packed with well-paying clientele. He also happened to be on the streets of Mogadishu on October 3 and 4 of 1993. They ran a stress course competition in full kit. Erik won the speed game but lost by ten points when they scored their targets.

"Fast is fine," the master chief chided his boss, "but accuracy is everything."

"Wyatt Earp, I believe," Erik said, citing the attributed source of the quote.

Though he didn't mention it to the old SEAL sniper, Erik knew his first shots were on target well before those of the aging master chief. He counted it as a win.

Originally incorporated as Talos, named for the bronze god who guarded the island of Crete, the company name had subsequently been changed to Masada following the unfortunate 2005 Gardez incident. In Greek mythology, Talos had a weakness: an unprotected vein in his ankle held his ichor, the lifeblood of the gods. It was a reminder to Sawyer that even the most powerful and well trained among them had flaws. The country had weaknesses, as did his company and each individual operator who now worked for him. The key was acknowledging those weaknesses and then taking steps to turn them into strengths.

Rebranding his company after an incident on par with the My Lai Massacre in Vietnam, he had chosen the name Masada for the great fortress in southern Israel overlooking the Dead Sea, a fortress occupied by warriors who defied the Romans. It was occupied in A.D. 66 by a Jewish sect known as the Sicarii, for the small *sicae* daggers they carried concealed in their clothing. At the end of the First Jewish-Roman War, as the Romans prepared to overrun the citadel, the Sicarii set Masada ablaze and committed mass suicide rather than become slaves of the Roman Empire. Sawyer's twenty-first-century Masada in North Carolina was his personal fortress and his operators were his Sicarii.

Sawyer registered Masada offshore in Barbados as a tax-exempt corporate entity. With daily flights to Bridgetown from Miami, Charlotte, Dallas, Philadelphia, New York, and Atlanta, it was easy to host meetings away from the prying eyes of investigative journalists employed by the *New York Times* and *Washington Post*. Though Sawyer wouldn't be caught dead on a commercial carrier, his clients could fly into Grantley Adams International Airport and then transfer to a Twin Otter for the short flight to the island of Mustique, a Caribbean hideaway for those willing and able to pay for its veil of privacy. Sawyer's father had purchased property there in the late sixties, property that was now endowed by a trust attached to an innocuous LLC.

Sawyer had printed out the report from the surveillance team assigned to James Reece the night before, mulling it over in preparation for his upcoming call to Senator Thwaite. Rather than reading important documents on his monitor, he preferred to print them off. He needed the visceral experience of reading from physical paper in his hands. It helped him process and think. He circled sections and made notations with his S. T. Dupont fountain pen, handcrafted to honor the warriors of feudal Japan. It had been a gift from a Japanese businessman after Sawyer had provided him with revealing photographs of the CEO of a rival company. The pen always reminded the founder of Masada that the Sicarii predated the assassins of ancient Japan by centuries.

Sawyer had gone straight to the gym from the range, his ten-point loss to the master chief driving him to a new personal record on the classic 21-15-9 thruster and pull-up Fran CrossFit WOD. He showered and dressed in jeans with a black polo embroidered with the Masada company logo: crossed curved *sicae* daggers. His custom Zev Technologies Glock 19 and two extra magazines were at the ready on a thick nylon belt.

Sawyer picked up the phone and dialed the senator's office number, patiently waiting for fifteen minutes on hold for Thwaite to finish a "meeting" that Sawyer knew didn't exist. It was the senator's way of trying to exert his power over the former Army Ranger. Sawyer was determined not to mention the delay as he knew no reaction irritated the senator to no end.

"Erik, sorry to keep you waiting. I was in with members of the Intelligence Committee."

"Call me back in five," was Sawyer's response before hanging up.

Sawyer's KryptAll buzzed three minutes later.

"Okay, we are secure," Thwaite said. "What do you have for me?"

"Have you read the report?"

"Yes, it is interesting in all but the recommendations. Those were perceptibly missing."

"I am more than happy to charge you for recommendations. The contract was just surveillance, not analysis and recommended COAs."

"COAs?"

"Courses of action, Senator."

"You've given me next to nothing, Erik. I need text messages, pictures, something to build a story to leak to the media."

"What we have, Senator, is James Reece meeting privately with the president of the United States. That intel is from your source, so our report is basing its findings on that assumption."

"He did. I have it on good authority."

"Of course you do, Senator. Soon thereafter Reece drives to Chicago, where he stakes out a house belonging to a Kareem Talib, who then dies of a heart attack. Reece then drives to Atlanta and stays at the extended-stay hotel in Buckhead for six days, driving to and from the Masjid of Al-Islam Mosque in East Atlanta every morning. He checks out, but our tracking device puts his vehicle a block from the hotel when Sohrab Behzad, a mosque security consultant with the Islamic Relief Society of America, is killed. Cause of death: stab wounds and seven bullets from a firearm chambered in 9mm Parabellum. The surveillance team trails Reece out of Atlanta and observes him dropping off a woman at a gas station outside Braselton. The follow-on surveillance team confirmed she was a stripper and prostitute. Masada has Reece's phone and text records. There were no communications with any numbers other than investigative journalist Katie Buranek and a number in Montana belonging to a hunting operation; nothing to indicate what he was doing in Chicago or Atlanta. He is now back in the D.C.-Virginia-Maryland area."

"Like I said, Erik, this just makes me wonder what I'm paying you for."

"Time and place connect him to the deaths of Talib and Behzad, both Muslim males."

"Circumstantial evidence doesn't cut it, Sawyer. I need something I can use."

"What did you find out about Talib and Behzad? I would think the chairman of the Intelligence Committee would have the power to look into their backgrounds."

Thwaite ignored the comment.

"Talib was under surveillance for years after 9/11."

Sawyer leaned forward in his chair.

"Really?"

"Yes, really," Thwaite said, finally enjoying a small victory.

"Why?"

"Something about taking, or I should say, attempting to take flying lessons at the same school as the hijackers."

"At the same time?" Sawyer asked.

"No, about a year before."

"Why was surveillance dropped?"

"Clean record. No contact with anyone on a terrorist watch list or no-fly list in person or electronically. No extremist website activity."

"When was it dropped?"

"After the bin Laden raid."

"And Behzad?" Sawyer asked.

"Juvenile record for drugs in Vegas. Looks like he committed to Islam in prison and has been clean ever since. He was one of the country's foremost authorities on mosque security."

"Country of origin?"

"Parents are from Morocco. Immigrated to the United States in 1992 and settled in Las Vegas. Father is a court recorder and the mother is employed by one of the casinos."

"Any government surveillance similar to Talib?"

"If there was, it's not in any government records."

"I see."

"I'm going to need more, Sawyer."

"Recommend we stay on Commander Reece. It appears he was surveilling both at the time of their deaths. There is a connection. We will find it."

Sawyer could buy one coincidence. Two, on the other hand?

Fool me once, he thought.

"Find the connection. Build the story. Get me what I need to destroy this president."

"Senator, these secure phones we use . . ."

"What about them?"

"Talos."

"What?"

"There is always a weakness," Sawyer said.

"What are you talking about?"

"I'll be in touch. Clear your calendar in the evenings all next week. I'm coming back to D.C."

CHAPTER 27

Richardson, Texas

DR. JAY DROPPED HIS day pack onto the cracked leather passenger seat of his slate-gray 1970 Porsche 911S and turned the key to crank the engine. It sounded more like a lawn mower than a high-performance sports car, but it was now more than fifty years old and built in a time when it was still possible to turn wrenches on motors instead of plugging them into computers for expensive diagnostic checks at the dealership. Today, its specs were dwarfed by even the most average of economy cars, but back in 1970 it was the pinnacle of performance.

Gripping the wheel always brought him right back to the dinner table of his family's small Centralia, Pennsylvania, home, where he would spend hours talking with his father about race cars. The family had neither a vehicle nor a television, but that did not stop them from dreaming. One of Dr. Jay's most pleasant memories was of taking the bus into Pottsville to watch *Le Mans*. For the first three minutes and forty seconds of the film as Steve McQueen throttles his Porsche through France, the legendary actor is uncharacteristically upstaged by the 200-horsepower machine.

Dr. Jay had no idea how many previous owners his 911S had known before ending up on a used car lot outside Fort Sam Houston in Texas, where he had seen it rotting away, dented and unloved. The financing interest rates had been atrocious, as they are at all car dealerships in military towns where slick salesmen in cheap suits love to take advantage of young E-3s who have steady paychecks for the first time in their lives. Dr. Jay was already a major when he pulled a U-turn and drove onto the used car lot. He knew better, but purchased the German classic automobile anyway and kept a promise he'd made in that movie theater with his father when his age was not yet in double digits.

His given name was Julius Mieczkowski, but because his last name was difficult to pronounce and because there was already another recruit of Polish descent assigned to the same barracks who had been given the name "Ski," he became "J" for Julius, a nickname that stuck. Upon graduation from Air Force boot camp at Lackland Air Force Base, "J" had become Airman First Class "Jay" and then Senior Airman "Jay" before receiving his commission to the United States Air Force Academy in Colorado Springs.

The path into service had started in what was now a forgotten relic of an America that no longer existed. The Mieczkowskis had held on in the dying Pennsylvania mining community for three generations until 1984, when Congress offered buyout options to relocate the desperate residents of what was becoming a ghost town. A mysterious fire had been burning underground for decades, slowly killing an area and economy rooted in coal. His parents accepted a modest payment from the federal government, purchased a used station wagon, and headed to Texas for opportunities in the oil business. They arrived just as oil fell below twenty dollars a barrel, sending thousands of previously thriving companies out of business.

Julius's mother found work as a checkout clerk with a local grocery store and his father took odd jobs as a handyman. All five kids were working by middle school in a time and place where labor laws were not strictly enforced.

Julius still remembered the taste of the fried Spam he was eating when he heard that devastating cough. He would never forget the look on his mother's face when she heard her husband try to mask it by pretending to clear his throat. Mining families could immediately differentiate the cough of a common cold from the one that meant death. Pneumoconiosis plagued the mining community. More commonly referred to as "black lung," once you had it there was no known medical treatment. His father died on Christmas Day, when Julius was in his first year of high school.

It was that cough that spurred Julius to take his MCATs and pursue a career in medicine, first becoming Major Jay and then Dr. Jay. Trained in internal medicine and general surgery, he transferred into the Air Force Reserves in the late nineties. He wanted to provide a solid financial foundation for his wife and children, a foundation young Julius had never known.

As a lieutenant colonel Air Force Reserve doctor, he was mobilized after September 11, 2001, and soon found himself in Afghanistan running a field hospital. An assignment establishing the hospital in the Green Zone in Baghdad would follow. When he had his three years under his belt as a colonel, he retired and accepted a position at the Richardson Methodist Medical Center just northeast of Dallas. He didn't want his kids to grow up without a father.

His experience in Afghanistan and Iraq lent itself to emergency medicine, and working in the small regional emergency room with a level-one response team provided all the stimulation he needed. At this stage in his career he worked 9:00 a.m. to 9:00 p.m. shifts for four days straight but was then able to enjoy ten days off with his family. The boys were getting older and would soon be in college, pursuing dreams of their own. He and his wife had a few more years with their youngest daughter and he intended to make the most of them.

He was conservative in his investments and the family lived well below their means. The Porsche was the one indulgence he allowed himself, a promise to a seven-year-old boy in a Pottsville, Pennsylvania, movie theater eating popcorn with his father. Now in his mid-fifties with two sons in high school and a daughter in eighth grade, a reserve military retirement check that would kick in a few years down the line, and a secure job at the hospital, he finally felt like he'd built the life he wanted.

No matter how much he loved the familiar sound of the German engine and the slight aroma of gasoline in the cabin, he couldn't keep his mind off work. It was a bit unusual for an early flu spike, yet the hospital had seen more than the usual number this year. The entire country remained on edge from the COVID-19 pandemic still so fresh in the collective consciousness, and with flu symptoms so closely mimicking the fever, chills, headaches, and body aches of the coronavirus, Richardson Methodist Medical Center had invested in an Abbott ID NOW point-of-care testing system. The procedure and testing provided coronavirus results in less than fifteen minutes. So far, all patients exhibiting flu-like symptoms had tested negative for COVID. This had to be just an early flu season.

It was 9:35 p.m. when he pulled the Porsche that his kids affectionately called the "time machine" into the garage. He kicked off his shoes and took the four steps up into the main house. He called out a quick hello to his wife and whichever kids happened to be home before taking the stairs two at a time to the second-level master bedroom to jump in the shower.

His family was accustomed to this routine. "Too many bugs in the emergency room," he always told his teenage girl.

By the time he was out of the shower, his wife was just saying good night to their youngest. He stuck his head into her room and whispered, "I love you, honey. Sweet dreams." He then said hello to the boys, who had been back from Friday night's football game for a couple of hours and were having a second dinner as teenage football players were apt to do.

"How did you play?" he asked his oldest.

"Caught a touchdown pass, but we still got creamed."

"Well, that happens in life, son. How about you?" he asked his middle child.

"I'm off the bench. Finally starting. Just JV," he said.

"Fantastic! I'll be there next Friday. Good night, boys. Don't stay up too late."

"We won't. Good night, Dad."

He entered the living room and gave his wife a kiss before sitting down to join her for a glass of wine.

"What happened to keeping the dog off the couch?" he asked, reaching over to pet the old golden retriever behind the ears.

"The same thing that happened to the 'not feeding her from the table rule,'" she replied. "You all clean? There are leftovers in the fridge if you're hungry."

"All clean," he confirmed, looking back into the kitchen. "And as far as leftovers, I think the monsters have devoured them."

"They tend to do that, don't they?" she said. "I can make you something."

They had been married for twenty-five years, surviving multiple wars and a residency she categorized as tougher than the deployments.

"I'll see what I can scavenge after the boys vacate the premises. How was the day?"

As they caught up, he grabbed his laptop. The doctor in him couldn't help but scour a few medical sites to check for reports of flu spikes. He noted a few cases around the country but nothing too out of the ordinary.

Before going to bed, he ensured the house windows and doors were locked and that the alarm was set.

Just after 1:00 a.m. his phone vibrated to life on the nightstand. He grabbed it and slid his finger across the screen to answer. He listened in silence.

"Dr. Jay, something is going on," his head ER nurse said, with an unusual edge to her voice. "We are being flooded. Everyone is so sick."

Julius swung his feet from the bed and worked his way to the bathroom in darkness, carefully closing the door so as not to disturb his wife.

"Sorry, Nancy, just waking up. What's going on?"

"I don't know. I've never seen anything like it. It's like the flu but much worse, and everyone has it at once."

"What do you mean, *everyone*?"

"They look so sick."

He could tell she was looking at patients as she spoke.

"Nancy, what do you mean, *everyone*?" he repeated.

"I mean we are running out of places to put people. The waiting room is completely packed, and they just keep arriving."

"Take a breath. I'll be there in thirty minutes."

"I apologize, Doctor. I know you are off today, but we are going to need you. This is *different*."

There was something about the way she said *different*.

He ended the call and looked at himself in the mirror, noting the dark bags under his eyes, the result of working too many vampire-hour shifts over the years. Running his hand over the gray stubble on his chin, he decided to forgo the shave. He moved as quietly as he could from the bathroom to the walk-in closet and dressed before reentering the bedroom.

"Is everything okay?" his wife asked, pushing herself up on her pillow.

"Oh yes, don't worry," he whispered. "The ER is just a bit overworked tonight. Typical Friday in Texas. I'm going to go help out for a few hours. Go back to sleep. I'll see you in the morning, and then we have ten days off."

He leaned over and gave her a kiss.

It didn't enter his mind that he would never see his family again.

When he arrived at Richardson Methodist Medical Center, his parking place was blocked by a truck with the engine still running. Vehicles occupied every space in the lot. Most were double-parked. Two ambulances were unloading patients in the arrival area, the lights swiveling with reds, yellows, and blues. A third pulled in as Dr. Jay passed.

This couldn't be from the flu, could it?

Not wanting to add to what was a palpable and growing panic, he stifled his desire to run. Instead he walked swiftly past the growing line and into the ER, his brain flashing back to the field hospitals of Iraq and Afghanistan as he processed the scene. Nurses and doctors moved from patient to patient, stepping over piles of vomit that orderlies hurried to clean up, maneuvering mop buckets from one mess to the next. Nancy was right, this was different. People were everywhere: in the hallways, waiting rooms, and examination rooms, some supported by worried family members with terror in their eyes. Children, babies, the middle-aged, and elderly of all races endured their wait together. Whatever was happening certainly did not discriminate.

The unmistakable stench of bile overwhelmed his senses. He found himself wishing he was home, showering away the smells and memories of trauma wards and war zones.

Dr. Jay remembered an attending physician early in his residency telling his interns, *The pungent smell of stale blood gets on you and sticks with you, and you cannot wash it off no matter how many showers you take.*

That physician had been right.

Blood in the vomit? The olfactory system in his "old brain" was warning Julius to get out and get away from the smell, away from the danger.

Not today.

Dr. Jay clicked into military mode and began barking orders.

"Nancy, set up an area in the cafeteria to isolate," he said, pointing down the hall.

"We're on it," she said, delegating the task to two junior nurses so she could take on the role of Dr. Jay's executive officer.

"We need to get this cleaned up," he said, pointing to the vomit, remembering the blood on the floor of the field hospitals overseas. "Make it a priority."

The staff had seen Dr. Jay like this before in the trauma room during emergencies.

"Nancy, get me the BioFire results from last shift of the flu patients. The labs from last two days. Get them, *now*!"

The BioFire Assay was a blood test that checked for twenty-six known virus strains. The hospital had been testing patients with flu-like symptoms in the wake of COVID. BioFire was one of the biotech companies that had made it big during the pandemic and had developed the standard test to check for COVID, H1N1, rhinoviruses, and agents known to cause viral illnesses.

"Here they are, Doctor," Nancy said.

Julius pulled down his "readers" and stared at the results. All the patients were negative.

"What the *fuck* is going on," he whispered, leaning against his office door, looking from the data to the chaos of the hallway. This wasn't a plane crash, vehicle accident, or shooting, but it was without a doubt a mass casualty event.

"Get me the CDC hotline, and numbers for the sheriff's department and mayor's office," he said.

"Julius, are we going to be okay?"

"We will be fine."

Dr. Jay was not a good liar.

A nurse passed by in the hall, assisting a patient to an exam room. He looked up while attempting to cover a cough. Julius saw red hemorrhage in the conjunctiva of his eyes.

"And get every staff member in full PPE: gown, gloves, goggles, and

N95 masks. Do it now, and don't touch anything or anyone until every member of the staff is protected."

"You've got it, Doctor," she said before moving off down the hall to carry out her orders.

Julius watched her go and then rushed to the lavatory, thoroughly washing his shaking hands before donning his PPE gear.

A hemorrhagic fever outbreak in Texas?

Before emerging into what was now ground zero, Dr. Julius Mieczkowski dropped to his knees and began to pray.

CHAPTER 28

The White House
Washington, D.C.

SECRET SERVICE AGENT FRANK Sharp did not have to work the night shift. He was senior enough to avoid that duty. He was known as an agent who did not mind getting his hands dirty and liked the example it set, especially if he took the duty on a weekend, which he did at least once a month. He'd be relieved in a couple of hours and have the rest of Saturday and Sunday off. He was honored to hold the line, a sentinel in an agency whose motto, "Worthy of Trust and Confidence," still filled him with pride.

Authorized by President Lincoln in 1865, the Secret Service was established under the U.S. Department of the Treasury and tasked with suppressing counterfeit currency. After the assassination of President McKinley in 1901, that mission was expanded; the Secret Service has been standing guard ever since, though now it was part of the Department of Homeland Security. The threats had changed, the enemy had adapted, and yet one element remained the same: a Secret Service agent with a gun standing next to the president of the United States.

Sharp looked at his watch. It was just before 6:00 a.m. He knew the president was up; a light was visible under the door. Two more hours and

Sharp would be on his way home. He'd already been divorced twice and knew that if he didn't want to make it a hat trick he should be spending the night at home rather than electing to stand guard outside the president's door. He was debating how to make it up to wife number three, when his earpiece cracked to life with a code word that would significantly alter his plans. It was a code word that had never before been used.

He immediately turned and gave two sharp knocks on the door to the president's bedroom.

"Yes," Sharp heard the president say from the bedroom.

Sharp opened the door and scanned the room. The president approached from the bathroom, attaching a second cuff link to his dress shirt, socks and shoes off, preparing for the day.

"Sorry, Mr. President. We have to go to the Basement."

"What's going on?"

"Unknown, sir."

"Not the bunker?" the president asked, referring to what was officially designated the Presidential Emergency Operations Center, or PEOC. Located under the East Wing of the White House, it was originally constructed during World War II for FDR, to protect the president and his staff from possible German rocket bombardment. Eisenhower upgraded it in the 1950s and it remained relatively unchanged until September 11. Those attacks confirmed that it was time for another upgrade.

In 2010, fences with attached privacy screens went up around the North Lawn of the White House. All construction workers underwent extensive background checks and signed nondisclosure agreements. The administration announced that it was a long-overdue infrastructure upgrade. In reality it was to build the most secure facility ever constructed. It was protected by concrete thick enough to withstand the radiation of a nuclear bomb and had its own air supply to combat a biological or chemical weapon attack. Stocked with food and water to last over a year and utilizing the most advanced communications suite available, the Basement was designed as a final fallback position to be used only in case of war. Each president since its completion was given a tour upon taking office. None of them had ever been evacuated to it during a real-world crisis.

Had different code words been used, a scrum of agents would have materialized around the president and escorted him to the PEOC or the White House Situation Room. Though rumors abounded, the Basement was officially known to only a select number of individuals in government. Agent Sharp was one of them.

Agent Neely joined his partner and fell in behind the president as they made their way to a hidden elevator with its own power supply to begin their journey underground.

"What did they tell you?" President Christensen asked.

"Nothing, sir. Just *Sentinel* and *Ender*."

Since the days of Camelot, the first family had been assigned call signs. The White House Communications Agency provides a list to candidates. Before he could choose his own, Christensen had been assigned *Spirit* as a nod to the *New York Times* article and photo that had shot him to prominence. He thought that was on the pompous side, so his national security advisor had suggested another name from the list: *Sentinel*.

Ender was a code word everyone briefed on its significance prayed they would never hear.

Agent Sharp put his finger to his ear. His normal radio was about to go dark as they descended toward the EMP level-four protected facility. Once they entered the Basement their only connection to the outside world would be through a hardened stand-alone communications system.

"The national security advisor, DNI, and CIA director will be here in twenty minutes," the Secret Service agent said.

The president nodded. He would not know more until they arrived. The vice president was still on a tour of Asia. Depending on what he learned in the briefing he was about to receive, she might be ordered back to the United States to lock down at NORAD in Colorado. An *Ender* meant they would not be colocated until the crisis, whatever it was, subsided.

The elevator doors opened, and Agent Sharp led the way through a cold concrete tunnel. Agent Neely took rear security. Pipes and emergency lighting guided them to a steel blast-resistant door that resembled a bank vault. It was open as per protocol to facilitate a faster evacuation of the president. Neely closed it behind them as Sharp walked through an anteroom to another set of doors. Sharp entered a code, pressed his thumb to a biometric reader, and looked into a screen that scanned his iris. The president did the same. The locking mechanism disengaged, and the door swung open on its massive hinges. Neely maintained his position in the anteroom to meet the incoming members of the executive national security team as the door closed, locking the president and Agent Sharp five stories beneath the White House.

CHAPTER 29

Fairfax, Virginia

HALEY GARRETT'S PHONE WENT off with an unknown government number coded 00011 just before 7:00 a.m. She looked over at her husband, but he had already snuck off for his morning run. She answered on the third buzz.

"Yes?"

"Is this Dr. Haley Garrett?"

"Yes, who is this, please?" she asked, already irritated at the tone of the caller's voice.

"Doctor, this is Deputy Director of CISA Isaac Glover."

CISA?

Haley searched her memory filled with government acronyms as she shook the cobwebs from her head.

The Cybersecurity and Infrastructure Security Agency?

"What can I do for you at"—Haley turned her phone in her hand to look at the clock—"six forty-seven on a Saturday morning?"

"We understand that you are the lead on a hemorrhagic virus outbreak in Angola."

"That's right. I *was* point on that outbreak. It burnt itself out. My office would be happy to forward you the report."

"I've read the report, Doctor. There has been another outbreak."

"Damn it. Same area?" Haley asked, rubbing sleep from her eyes and still wondering why the deputy director of CISA was calling her so early on a weekend.

"No." Glover cleared his throat. "We are going to need you at CDC now. You will be briefed when you arrive. CISA will be handling all responses from here. You are not to discuss this with anyone."

"Discuss what? You haven't told me anything," Haley said, raising her voice.

"This has been designated a national security critical infrastructure threat. Any violation of these orders is an act of treason."

Is the deputy director of CISA reading from a prepared document?

"What are you talking about?"

"A CISA representative will be at your office shortly to coordinate. Thank you for your cooperation."

"Hey . . ." Before she should get another word out, the line went dead.

CISA?

She knew that CISA had been created in 2018 and that it was a stand-alone agency reporting to the Department of Homeland Security. She had taken part in an exercise a year ago in which CISA co-opted control of the CDC in a simulated bioterrorism attack against the United States. Her part in that exercise had consisted of sending a couple of emails. She had not thought much about it at the time.

Nothing in Deputy Director Glover's voice indicated this was another exercise, but she wouldn't know for certain until she got to work.

She slipped out of bed, splashed cold water on her face, dressed, and texted her husband a message saying she'd been called into work. He'd see it when he returned from his morning run promptly at 7:30 a.m.

As she waited for the coffee machine to do its magic, she began connecting the dots. If CISA was confirming that she was the lead on the Angola outbreak and was calling her in on a Saturday morning, there really was only one reason; the outbreak didn't die out on the Dark Continent. It was alive and it was now on U.S. soil.

Without waiting for the coffee to finish, she grabbed her purse and headed for her car.

CHAPTER 30

The White House
Washington, D.C.

DIRECTOR MOTLEY WAS THE first to arrive. She had been given a familiarization tour of the Basement, as had all members of the National Security Council, but just like the president, this was her first time entering the secure facility in a time of crisis. National Security Advisor Greg Farber and Allen Cruse, director of the Cybersecurity and Infrastructure Security Agency, emerged from the tunnel talking in hushed voices, followed by the secretary of state, the secretary of the Treasury, the secretary of defense, the director of national intelligence, and the chairman of the Joint Chiefs of Staff. They were all flanked by Secret Service agents.

Each of them typed in a code, pressed their fingers to the biometric scanner, and stared into the screen that read their irises to confirm identities and access.

Cruse looked more like a construction foreman than he did a government bureaucrat. His height and girth suggested a past-his-prime linebacker when in fact Motley knew he was one of the smartest people in Washington. With a background in secure data storage, he was instrumental in advocating and building the "cloud" a decade before most had ever heard of it. Oracle often took a backseat to Microsoft and Apple in name recognition, but that didn't bother the founder, executives, or shareholders. Few realized that a sliver of every electronic interaction around the globe touched an Oracle platform, including those of Microsoft and Google. It was imperative that those transactions be secure.

For the data that powered the nation's military and intelligence apparatus, security was even more paramount. Oracle had cornered the market for secure government data storage long ago. Cruse had been in on the ground floor, learning from Oracle's founder and helping him turn his vision into a reality. As the landscape in Palo Alto began to change, Cruse didn't jump ship for Google, Facebook, Uber, or Airbnb. He continued to adapt and build the Oracle "cloud" into the most secure data storage platform available. He had been rewarded with multigenerational wealth. He could have been enjoying a life of leisure but had decided to serve, first as the senior advisor to the assistant secretary of homeland security for infrastructure protection and later as senior advisor to the secretary of homeland security. In that role he had applied his intellect to the study of emerging threats to the United States, threats that included nuclear, chemical, and biological weapons.

The previous administration had identified a vulnerability and the president had recognized Cruse as a talent. Truth be told, Motley had identified the vulnerability and recommended the creation of the Cybersecurity and Infrastructure Security Agency with the sole task of protecting government infrastructure. Cruse was the first person nominated to lead the new agency and still the only person to hold the post. Motley now wondered if she had created a monster.

"Take your seats, please," the president said. He stood at the end of a large conference table. "Greg, bring us up to speed."

"Mr. President, apologies for not being able to brief you ahead of the meeting, but the situation dictated swift protective action due to the nature of the threat. Let me assure everyone that in all likelihood we will not remain underground all year, or even all week. There are not incoming missiles from Russia or North Korea, nor is Iran detonating a dirty bomb in the capital. Before I go on, I'll give you the bottom line up front: there has been what we suspect to be a naturally occurring outbreak of hemorrhagic fever in the United States."

"We've seen this before," Terrance Lowe, director of national intelligence, broke in, clearly annoyed he'd been pulled back to the city on a weekend.

"Not like this, Admiral," Farber responded. "This one is airborne."

"Please continue, Greg," the president said, looking at Lowe and regaining control of the meeting.

"Mr. President, four hours ago the CDC emergency hotline received a call from a hospital in Richardson, Texas, just outside of Dallas. Late last night that hospital started admitting patients exhibiting signs of severe flu. They were overrun in a matter of hours."

"What made them think it's not just the flu?" the president asked.

"The hospital invested in an on-site array for symptomatic infectious disease testing during the COVID-19 pandemic."

"What does that mean?" Lowe broke in.

"It means that they can rule out twenty-six viruses, including the flu and COVID. It's a presumptive diagnosis with all twenty-six tests being negative."

"So, it could be anything," Lowe said.

"*Not* the twenty-six negatives," Farber continued, beginning to get irritated with the retired admiral. "The on-site physician is a former Air Force doctor. He observed hemorrhaging in multiple patients' eyes along with blood in vomit, all symptoms consistent with a hemorrhagic fever diagnosis."

"Wait, when you say hemorrhagic fever, you mean Ebola?" Lowe asked.

"Blood samples were sent to the CDC in Atlanta and here in Washington. Possible hemorrhagic strains include Ebola, Marburg, Lassa, and Crimean-Congo."

"Aren't these strains usually limited and spread via bodily fluid transmission?" Lowe asked.

"True," Farber conceded, "*but*, we've never seen an airborne variant."

"How do we know it's airborne?" Lowe asked.

"On the way into this meeting the director of the CDC called confirming this appears to be a new strain of Ebola. His senior infectious disease specialist compared it to various strains of hemorrhagic fever in the level-four host site lab in Atlanta. It doesn't match any known samples, which indicates it is a strain that has evolved. The number of patients exhibiting symptoms in Richardson suggests it is airborne."

"*Jesus* . . ." Lowe whispered.

"Also, just before I called this meeting, we received a call from a hospital in Denver. Same symptoms. Director Motley?"

"Mr. President, I received a call from Mr. Farber this morning on the developing situation. As you recall, thirteen days ago you were briefed on a hemorrhagic fever outbreak in Angola."

"I remember. It burnt out as I recall."

"That is correct, sir. My analysts linked the Angola outbreak with flights from Quatro de Fevereiro International Airport to the United States. Depending on a variety of factors, if we assume that the hemorrhagic fever from Angola is the same contagion now in the United States, it would mean that an infected passenger boarded a flight in Luanda sometime between ten to fourteen days ago. There has been one flight a day since the outbreak from Angola to Johannesburg. From Johannesburg, there have been two flights a day to JFK and Atlanta, with connecting flights to the rest of the country, not to mention the flights out of Johannesburg to the rest of the world. My agency is working with the FBI to track the passengers and flights from Angola to South Africa to the United States. We are reaching out to our counterparts worldwide to find out if there are any other outbreaks. Preliminary analysis suggests that connecting passengers during the time frame in question did take connecting flights to Dallas and Denver."

The gravity of the threat momentarily turned a meeting of the National Security Council into a prayer service as silence gripped a group not accustomed to silent reflection.

"Director Lowe," the president said, addressing the DNI. "Give me some options."

"Sir, certain protocols automatically engage in the event of a threat to critical infrastructure from nuclear, biological, or chemical attack. This naturally occurring event falls under the parameters of that executive order. I'll turn it over to Director Cruse, who is versed in the details."

Cruse stood and addressed the room.

"Mr. President, as you are well aware, CISA's mission was envisioned during the Obama administration out of concern for attacks on critical infrastructure. The previous administration officially formed CISA as a component of the Department of Homeland Security, but in times of crisis as an independent agency with direct report to the executive branch for action. The world has never dealt with a respiratory-spread hemorrhagic fever. If the CDC confirms that Ebola is in fact airborne, it has the potential to spread at a rate unparalleled in the history of infectious disease."

"What kind of mortality rates are we talking about?" the president asked.

"Without containment measures it has the potential to kill ninety percent of the country, over two hundred and ninety million people."

For the first time in as long as he could remember, the president was at a loss.

"Greg, do we have contingency plans for an outbreak of that magnitude?"

"Sir." Farber hesitated. "The sensitivity of those plans requires a smaller audience."

"Smaller than this?"

"Sir, we are in uncharted territory," Farber said.

"This is the National Security Council," the president said, reasserting his authority. "We will *all* be briefed on the contingencies."

"Yes, sir," Farber said. "General?"

General Nathan Seifert stood to address the room. Even though this was an emergency meeting on a Saturday morning, he was clean-shaven, and his uniform was immaculate. Though it was obvious he could no longer pass the Army PT test, he was stern and direct. By his way of thinking, at this stage of his career, the American people were not paying him to pass a two-mile timed run. They were paying him to advise the president of the United States and the members of the National Security Council as the highest-ranking military officer in the country. Though he hid his contempt, he maintained no regard for those senior-level officers who hid their intellectual ineptitude behind their annual PT scores.

"Mr. President, by way of background, in the years following World War Two it was revealed that the Nazi and Imperial war machines had experimented with bioweapons as a way to destroy the enemy without firing a shot. President Eisenhower tasked the United States military to develop protocols in the event a biological weapon were released in the continental United States. Those containment and eradication plans have been updated on a periodic basis since inception in 1954."

"Containment *and* eradication?" the president inquired.

"Yes, Mr. President. To stop the spread of either a bioweapon or a naturally occurring highly contagious virus that threatened to destroy the county, a fail-safe last-resort plan was developed in the 1950s. Only a select number of people have ever been briefed on the contingency."

General Seifert looked at the secretary of defense, who nodded.

"Mr. President, there are protocols in place to isolate areas, to include cities, in the case of a contagion event. Troops are staging as we speak in advance of a containment order."

"And eradication?" the president asked.

"If the pathogen escapes the perimeter and threatens to infect and destroy the nation, we can rapidly expand the containment zone. There are MC-130 aircraft on standby in Hurlburt Field, Florida. Those planes are equipped with GBU-43/B Massive Ordnance Air Blast Fuel Air Explosive munitions, the most devastating nonnuclear bombs in our inventory."

The president leaned forward and cleared his throat. "General, are you telling me we have had plans in place to destroy our own cities since the early days of the Cold War?"

"That is correct, sir. Even the pilots and crews don't know their mission. The squadron believes they are on standby for a Cuban contingency, more specifically a Chinese buildup in Cuba. Their CAE flight simulators are only programmed for OCONUS contingencies."

"And why am I just finding out about this now?"

"Sir," the national security advisor offered, "there are several military contingency plans in place, their existence only revealed through a triggering event."

Christensen's head was spinning.

Dear Lord, give me strength.

"If I may, sir," Cruse interjected.

The president nodded.

"Mr. President, you may remember Operation Jade Helm in 2015. It was a continental U.S.-based exercise. Twelve hundred troops mobilized across twenty Texas cities. Under the guise of a military exercise surrounding a potential asteroid strike, FEMA tested citizen response to martial law. In 2017, a similar exercise called Operation Gothic Shield moved military forces into and around New York City. This time the cover was an exercise to combat a potential nuclear threat to Manhattan. Martial law was again tested on the citizenry. Based on the findings of Jade Helm and Gothic Shield, CISA was created in 2018 to coordinate a whole-of-government response to a cyber-warfare attack, but its charter more broadly applies to all acts of terrorism against U.S. critical infrastructure. During the COVID-19 crisis CISA conducted trial runs in Portland and Chicago."

"What were the findings?" he asked.

"That small pockets of resistance emerged, organized primarily through social media. Algorithms are now refined and in place through our partners in the technology sector to reduce the spread of information intended to incite violence."

The president leaned back in his chair.

Jesus.

"Continue," the president said, weighing the implications.

"The Bioterrorism Act of 2002 first delegated authorities to HSS. Ill-equipped to handle a crisis of this magnitude, the Department of Homeland Security was tasked with building response mechanisms to a bioterrorism attack. Those same protocols apply to a naturally occurring event like a respiratory-spread hemorrhagic fever in the continental United States."

"And what was designated as critical infrastructure?" the president asked.

"That was and is a 'living document,' Mr. President," Director Cruse said. "There are multiple lists at various government agencies that all vary, not so much as to the definition, but to the entities actually listed."

"Explain," the president said.

"Under Presidential Directive Seven, there are sixteen infrastructure sectors critical to the defense of the United States, our economic security, and our public health and safety."

"What are they?" the president asked.

"Nuclear, chemical, agriculture, health care, water, energy, critical manufacturing, communications, dams, commercial facilities, emergency services, financial services, government facilities, transportation systems, information technology, and the defense industrial base."

"That doesn't really narrow it down. What's not on that list?"

"Initially, critical infrastructure was designated by a working group from Homeland Security. When COVID-19 shut down the country, those on the critical infrastructure list continued to operate. That put 'critical infrastructure' on the radar for most Americans, some of whom owned companies and were politically connected."

The president knew exactly where this was headed.

"Political donations began pouring in, followed by requests for certain businesses to be added to the critical infrastructure list through special interest groups and lobbying firms. Today the list includes shopping malls, gaming operations, and stadiums in addition to the list created by Homeland Security working group."

The president shook his head and leaned back in his chair.

"Typical Washington."

He looked around the room, his eyes coming to rest on his national security advisor.

"Greg, approve containment for Richardson and Denver. If it's respiratory, everyone on those planes could be infected. God knows where they are now."

"Yes, sir."

"Recommendations," the president said to the table, his eyes coming to rest on the director of the CIA.

"Mr. President," Motley said, "my agency is working with the FBI to confirm we have the manifests from all flights to the United States from Angola. We are coordinating with Homeland Security to quarantine and test those individuals, and with your authorization will institute executive contact-tracing protocols with the technology sector so we can determine how far the virus has spread."

"Is that legal?" Christensen asked his national security advisor, noting for the first time that the White House counsel was conspicuously absent.

"We have memorandums of understanding in place to acquire that information; however, it will take an executive order to mandate isolation for confirmed contact traces. The previous administration prepared one for COVID-19. We can use it as a model and cite it for precedent."

"When will we know if it has spread outside of Denver and Richardson?"

Farber nodded to Motley.

"We will know in the next twenty-four to forty-eight hours."

The president looked to his secretary of defense, William Dagher, a quiet and thoughtful former Marine flag officer often uncomfortable in a city where most speak before even bothering to study their history or form a coherent opinion. Born in Oregon of Lebanese descent, he had been one of the few general officers who spoke Arabic when the United States committed large-scale forces to the Middle East and Central Asia. A graduate of the United States Naval Academy, during his time in uniform he earned a master's in Middle Eastern studies at Harvard before being selected as an Olmsted Scholar studying at the University of Jordan in Amman. Upon retirement he accepted a position at the Hoover Institution at Stanford and a board position at the president's former start-up, now one of the most powerful and profitable companies in history. Christensen tapped him for SecDef early in the transition process and his confirmation hearings were the most civil in recent memory.

"Bill, what does it take to launch the MC-130s? If it comes to that, will those crews drop on an American city?"

"Mr. President, I have instructed the Fifteenth Special Operations Squadron at Hurlburt to forward me SF-86 security paperwork for each crew to determine if they have family in the affected areas. Your executive order will also allow us to access their social media accounts. Those with family and friends in the target cities will be pulled from the rotation and replaced."

Turning back to his national security advisor, the president asked, "And, to confirm, so far there are no cases outside of Richardson and Denver?"

"Correct, Mr. President."

"Greg, I am going to address the nation."

"Yes, Mr. President, the Basement is designed with that provision."

"Not from the Basement. From the Oval Office."

"Sir, I strongly recommend remaining on lockdown until we have a clearer picture of how fast this is spreading."

"Greg, the American people need to know we are not in a panic. Staying in an actual basement did not play well for leaders during COVID-19. I need to inform the American people that military forces will be containing areas in Texas and Colorado *before* they see it on the news or walk outside and see HMMWVs and Bradley Fighting Vehicles staging in their local Walmart parking lots. General Seifert, what is the status of troops in Texas and Colorado?"

"They are moving to bases in closer proximity to the affected areas to await your containment order."

"Then we don't have much time. I want to head this off. I don't see a viable alternative to containment, but by God we need to move heaven and earth to avoid eradication. Let me be clear, there is *nothing* we will not do to ensure we never have to face the possibility of eradication. We are all going upstairs. I am going to address the nation from the Oval Office at 9:00 a.m. Eastern. Make it happen."

CHAPTER 31

Richardson, Texas

THE RESPONSE CAME UNUSUALLY fast for a town typically mired in the sludge of the literal and figurative swamp. The president's address from the Oval Office was broadcast live at 9:00 a.m. Eastern. By the time those on the West Coast were pouring their first cups of coffee, it was the talk of cable news. With no shortage of "experts" to choose from after the experience of COVID-19, every channel had panels of talking heads expounding on pandemics, epidemics, hemorrhagic fever, vaccines, masks, shutdowns, and the legality of contact tracing. The hashtag "outbreak" began trending on social media and the 1995 Dustin Hoffman movie of the same name experienced a resurgence on Hulu.

The events of September 11, 2001, had not only put the country on war footing, they had set in motion a flood of convoluted congressional directives and acts resulting in a series of new authority chains, departments, and agencies that effectively handed additional power to the executive branch. The president now had more control and discretion on applying military force than at any time in the nation's history. In order to streamline and expedite certain decisions, CISA had automated initial steps in the decision-making process to protect critical infrastructure.

In the case of a naturally occurring virus, forces identified as essential to containment measures were put on standby before the president had reached the secure space under the North Lawn.

As part of their classified mission set, the Air Force Global Strike Command at Barksdale Air Force Base in Shreveport, Louisiana, was put on alert. Tasked with continental United States unconventional responses, they notified component commands and began to consolidate forces at predetermined staging locations across the country. The United States Northern Command at Peterson Air Force Base in Colorado Springs activated the unified-action layered defense strategy OPLAN federalizing the troops of Special Operations Command–North. This brought special operations personnel, trained to fight an enemy overseas, under the control of a command focused on maintaining peace and security within the borders of the continental United States.

While the commander in chief was addressing the nation from the Oval Office, the First Special Forces Command, established in 2014 at Fort Bragg, was activating the recall of intelligence, psychological operations, civil affairs, and sustainment assets for follow-on movement to Dyess Air Force Base in Abilene, Texas. Black Hawks and Little Birds from the Special Operations Aviation Regiment in Fort Campbell, Kentucky, were loaded into C-130s and lifted off to stage within striking distance of the affected areas. They had been flying in major U.S. cities and population centers for years as part of exercises termed "Realistic Urban Training" with Special Mission Units out of Virginia Beach and Fort Bragg. In Florida, C-130J transports were wheels-up from Eglin Air Force Base en route for Dyess and Buckley Air Force Base in Aurora, Colorado. As the president closed out his address, local news outlets were already broadcasting videos of tanks, Bradleys, helicopters, and troop transports staging for what looked like an invasion, giving rise to a number of conspiracy theories across the new media. A crisis was always good for news outlets and their advertisers.

Dyess and Buckley Air Force Bases were converted to military command centers. By the time the president approved the order to contain the outbreak, forces were already in place to respond. All flights in and out of Dallas, Denver, and surrounding areas, to include private aviation, were grounded while restricted airspace designations were immediately put in place via NOTAMs, notices to airmen.

Though the president never mentioned martial law in his address, it became the topic of the day. Never mentioned in the Constitution, not clearly defined by an act of Congress or by Supreme Court ruling, martial law has been enacted more than sixty times since 1776, perhaps most infamously by General Andrew Jackson in New Orleans during and after the War of 1812. Lawyers, pundits, and military analysts debated the merits of the Insurrection Act, posse comitatus, along with Title 10, Title 32, and Title 50 of the U.S. Code. As they talked, argued, and cycled through commercial breaks, the United States military took up positions outside Richardson and Aurora.

CHAPTER 32

RICHARDSON, TEXAS, WAS A small, affluent suburb east of Dallas with a population of 121,323. Home to the University of Texas at Dallas, the idyllic suburban community also hosts a high concentration of telecommunication industries. AT&T, Cisco, Samsung, and Texas Instruments headquartered there due to the quality of life and the ability to recruit a highly educated and motivated workforce. It was the regional hub of Blue Cross Blue Shield and UnitedHealthcare, boasted an outstanding public education system, and was a short distance from Dallas via DART, the Dallas Rapid Transit System. It was consistently ranked by *Forbes* as one of the top suburban areas to live in the United States. It was about to be isolated from the rest of the world.

The drive from Dyess air base to Richardson was just over three hours. The military's experience on the ground in Iraq and Afghanistan suggested that three hours could be an eternity. Dallas Love Field airport was less than twenty minutes away.

The call came in just after 8:00 a.m. Central time. Having already suspended all air traffic an hour earlier, the director of operations at Love Field listened in disbelief as he was ordered to sequester all nonessential personnel and all civilians waiting on what were now canceled flights.

Troops in full combat gear were posted at every entrance and exit. Checkpoints were set up on roads leading to and from the airport. Psyops vehicles announced the immediate evacuation via loudspeakers as soldiers cleared and locked down terminals. Essential air traffic controllers were co-opted by the Department of Homeland Security as HMMWV gun trucks secured the runways. Fifteen minutes after ground forces had commandeered the airport, C-130s and C-17s began landing and unloading Abrams tanks, Bradley Fighting Vehicles, Stryker Infantry Carry Vehicles, helicopters, and additional troops.

The now-federalized troops began separating the travelers into groups based on cell phone locational data. The group who had been in Richardson were separated from those who had not. They were loaded onto buses for transport to isolation facilities for treatment.

The airport director stood in the tower overlooking the terminals, apron, taxiway, and runways in a state of shock. He had just relinquished control to a man in a camouflage uniform with a silver eagle rank insignia on his chest. Love Field was now the forward operating base for a complete martial takeover of Richardson.

• • •

Dr. Jay closed his office door and took a seat at his desk. Cases continued to mount in the emergency center and ICU at Richardson Methodist Medical Center. He picked up the phone and hit the direct connect to the nurse's station.

"Nancy, please get me the latest numbers and results from BioFire."

He then dialed his wife's cell from his office phone, only to hear a busy signal. He tried his eldest son with the same result. Fishing his cell phone from his backpack, he noted it was connected to the hospital Wi-Fi and tried his family again: no luck. He attempted to connect to a news website with no success, even with a full-strength Internet connection.

Having had significant exposure to medical contingency operations in the military, Dr. Jay knew what was happening. The hospital was being isolated.

He got up and maneuvered through the throng of sick patients crowding the hallways, the smell of blood and vomit even heavier in the air than when he'd arrived. He passed through the waiting room and noticed that the televisions mounted strategically in the corners were dark. He exited the hospital, pulling his mask to the side to inhale air not tainted with the infection inside. The dying leaned on the side of the building, against cars, and sat at the base of the few trees that grew outside. He turned off Wi-Fi and looked at the cell service bars. Nothing. He usually had full bars at the front of the hospital.

Hearing the familiar sound of rotors, he held his hand up to block the sun, still low in the sky.

Black Hawks.

Containment.

Even though he knew it was useless, he tried to call his wife again, his heart in his throat.

Take the kids and get the hell out!

His phone would not connect.

All cell, Internet, landlines, TV, and radio were down. No text messages or ways to connect on Facebook, Twitter, or Instagram. It was a complete blackout. Full electronic isolation had already been initiated.

God help us all.

CHAPTER 33

BY 8:30 A.M., RICHARDSON, Texas, had become a prison. Military and law enforcement personnel had sealed the city from 635 to the south, 380 to north, Route 75 Addison to the west, and Route 78 to the east, creating a noose with a three-mile radius. A soft boundary was set at the two-mile mark with no entry or exit permitted. No one, for any purpose, could exit the one-mile containment zone. Wire mesh barricades and twelve-foot walls had been assembled and installed around the hard one-mile perimeter. Only authorized personnel with full credentials and hazmat gear were allowed between the one- and two-mile rings. Armed Little Birds from TF-160 patrolled the perimeter of the lockdown area. Communications were now via secure channels only. More than eighty thousand people were restricted to the central core of the city.

An evacuation area was set up to the south on the University Park Field, manned by personnel in full hazmat gear. A fifty-thousand-square-foot tent was erected with massive air filtration systems sealing it off from the outside world, the internal section bathed in UV light for sterilization. Patients were transported into the facility and escorted to a predesignated cot. Each man, woman, and child was heavily sedated with morphine and then restrained to their beds. Fingerprints, pictures, and DNA swabs were taken. Wallets, phones, and personal effects were confiscated, sealed in clear storage bags, and labeled. In an ominous prelude to the expected body count, refrigerated trucks and trailers were positioned on the streets behind the field.

By the end of the day, 457 people had been transported to the holding facility; 108 of those were now in body bags and stored in refrigerated trucks.

Outside the three-mile perimeter, news trucks, media, and family members with loved ones trapped inside the containment zone were met with harsh orders to return home and await further notifications.

The president's address was thus far the only official statement given to the nation. A second address was planned for 9:00 p.m. Eastern time. In the meantime, the White House press secretary did the best she could to field questions from a hostile press, each reporter looking to get their thirty-second sound bite in the hopes it would go viral and increase their personal follower profile. Representatives of both parties called press conferences looking for much the same results as the reporters at 1600 Pennsylvania Avenue. Sensational video and photographs coming in from the outskirts of Richardson and Aurora were played on cable channels as commentators bloviated to fill the news cycle. The rumor mill was in full swing as shock jocks, trolls, and far-right and far-left conspiracy theorists spread conjecture as fact, adding to the hysteria.

When a Channel 4 Fox News Skycopter from Dallas attempted to penetrate restricted airspace for exclusive video, the pilot was intercepted by two black A/MH-6M Little Birds. The mounted machine guns and snipers on platforms on either side of the fuselage were enough to turn him around.

Other rotary-wing aircraft with high-power loudspeakers instructed residents to stay in their homes. If anyone in the house experienced flu-like symptoms, they were to wave a white shirt from a window, roof, or front yard. An ambulance would be dispatched to transport the infected individual to the field hospital.

Those who took to their cars or trucks in an attempt to escape the containment barrier were met with a show of force and in some cases warning shots from .50-caliber machine guns.

The first complete containment of a U.S. city in the twenty-first century had been accomplished.

CHAPTER 34

U.S. 50 West
Maryland

THE LAND CRUISER'S OLD yellow plastic headlight coverings had been replaced with clear lenses and modern LED bulbs that cast a bright whitish-blue light across the dark road ahead. The truck barreled down U.S. 50 West toward the CIA safe house in Maryland that Reece currently called home. With the country on the verge of another lockdown due to the emerging threat of a new pandemic, coupled with the peculiar death of the first target on the kill list, Reece's mission was on hold. The president wanted him to stand down while they got a handle on the situation.

"This is just too eerie," Katie said from the passenger seat. "There are hardly any other cars on the road. It's a Friday night. We are not even in a mandatory lockdown here. There have been no cases in D.C., Virginia, or Maryland."

"COVID made us all gun-shy and ultrasensitive to any sort of virus," Reece said. "Even though the outbreak seems to be isolated in Denver and Richardson, locking down en masse has become the norm. What does your friend Haley at the CDC have to say?"

"You can ask her yourself. She's going to stop by for a drink tonight.

She wants to talk with me about a story. She's at the forefront of this and hasn't slept since the first cases appeared. Just like the president said, it appears that it's a new strain of Ebola originating in Angola. They are still looking for the index case, but it looks like one of the people who died in the Angola outbreak a few weeks ago infected a traveler who then boarded a plane to the U.S. We've never had a strain of hemorrhagic fever go airborne, so this is something new."

Depending on traffic, the drive from D.C. to the house on the Severn River was between twenty minutes and an hour. Reece had picked Katie up at the Washington bureau, where she was part of a panel on the constitutionality of government-mandated lockdowns and using active-duty troops to quarantine cities without congressional approval in violation of the Posse Comitatus Act. The president's actions in Richardson and Denver had brought up serious legal issues about the power of the federal government in dealing with pandemics. It was her last live show of the workweek, and Katie was not scheduled to appear again until Sunday morning. They planned to pick up a pizza from Neo's before it closed and enjoy a lazy Saturday morning together in a house in one of the nicest neighborhoods in the country. Maybe they would even get out on the Chesapeake in the Agency sailboat docked across the lawn.

• • •

"What the fuck was that?" Woody asked as their minivan swerved slightly to the right.

"*Asshole*," Crimmins said.

"What?"

"Not you, *asshole*. These other *assholes*," Crimmins said, nodding ahead toward the two vehicles that had just sped past them.

"Oh," Woody said from his captain's chair in the backseat, where he continued to monitor the Land Cruiser. "When the *fuck* are we going to do something other than monitor this guy? This shit is *boring.* I signed up for the action. So far all we've done is follow him around the country and sit outside while he bangs his chick."

"Our mission is to surveil him, record his movements, take notes, and send reports to higher. That's it. If you want something more, I can tell Sawyer you are unhappy with the assignment. I am sure he will have absolutely *no* trouble replacing you."

"*Fuck* you, Crimmins. I'm good. Just miss the 'Stan."

Crimmins shook his head as he watched the van and the mid-nineties Chrysler speed out of sight.

• • •

"What do you want on your pizza?" Katie asked, pulling her phone from her purse.

"What do you think? Neo's, right? How about a Great White or Florentine?"

"Florentine it is. How are we on wine?"

"Luckily we already worked our way through the CIA's stash."

"A truly horrid experience," Katie confirmed.

"Ha! That it was. Vic told me the last person they had sequestered in there was a Venezuelan intelligence officer who had an affinity for Two Buck Chuck. I had Raife raid Jonathan's wine cellar for us. It only took two reminders that I saved his life in Russia. He shipped out a box of assorted selections, which should get us through the night. He included a few from Beckstoffer."

"Don't tease me, Reece," she said, giving him a mischievous look.

As she hit the number for Neo's on her phone, Reece looked at her and smiled. The diamond he'd given her at Landini Brothers still graced her neck. She hadn't taken it off.

As soon as it's done, Katie. As soon as I finish what I started, then it will be time for us.

Reece's eyes caught a reflection in the rearview mirror and he intuitively inched farther to the edge of the right-hand lane.

Probably nothing. Relax, Reece. Only someone rushing to get home from D.C., just like you.

As Katie placed their pizza order, Reece switched his attention from the rearview to the side-view mirror.

It was tough to tell in the dark, but the approaching vehicle looked like a sedan, the dim yellow lights giving it away as an older model.

Reece glanced in the rearview mirror again, noting a larger vehicle following it a few car lengths behind.

The violent impact to the left rear section of the Land Cruiser sent the off-road vehicle into an immediate spin.

Katie dropped her phone, desperately grasping the dashboard and reaching for the handle on her door.

Reece attempted to counter-steer out of the spin when the sedan accelerated and hit them between the driver's and rear driver's-side doors. The large all-terrain tires caught the pavement and sent the Toyota into a sideways roll. Reece's head smashed into the side window as it disintegrated in an explosion of glass fragments, Katie's screams mixing with the violent impacts of steel and glass meeting road.

The car rolled again, cartwheeled to the right, and plunged down the embankment.

CHAPTER 35

"*WHOA!*" WOODY YELLED FROM the back where he monitored the tracking device.

"What?"

"The *fucking* thing just went off the road!"

"Speak English. What's happening?"

"I don't know. He was driving along, and the tracker just flew off the road."

"Could he have found it earlier and thrown it out the window now?" Crimmins asked.

"Maybe. Let's find out. You want the rifle?"

"Just stay cool."

Crimmins and Woody had been monitoring from a few miles back so as not to spook their prey. They hadn't thought about what to do if their target had an accident.

"As hard as it is, try not to do anything stupid," Crimmins told his partner. "We are going to roll up, assess the situation, and make a report. Is it still pinging in the same location?"

"Yeah. It hasn't moved. From the satellite map I think it's down in a ravine or something. Two miles ahead."

As much as he wanted to find out what was happening, Crimmins maintained the speed limit as he approached.

"Pass me the NODs," he said to Woody, who passed up a bump helmet with PVS-31s attached.

Woody watched the night-vision-capable monitors as Crimmins switched off the headlights and activated the IR beams, which allowed him to see clearly through the white phosphor image-intensifying tubes of the NODs.

"Wish I had those in the badlands," Woody said. "Just think of all the *muj* I could have slain."

"Shut up and tell me what you see."

Woody turned back to the monitors and zoomed in on the area ahead as Crimmins pulled to the side of the road.

"Two vehicles on the shoulder. One van and one sedan. Lights on. I count four, no, make that five MAMs," Crimmins said, using the military term for Military Aged Male. "They're looking down what appears to be a ravine or gully of some sort. Think he went off the road?"

"*Shit.* I don't know. Maybe he crashed."

"*Wait!*" Crimmins said. "Guns."

Crimmins adjusted his NODs to more clearly focus on the people standing outside their vehicles.

"What's your count?" Crimmins asked.

"I see two handguns and three long guns—correction, six MAMs, two handguns, and four long guns. What the *fuck* is going on?"

"Keep watching," Crimmins ordered. "I'm calling it in."

This was not a contingency they had planned for. Crimmins had one AR in the back, and he and Woody each had pistols.

What the hell?

"This goddamn van is like a clown car. They just keep piling out. I now count eleven. *Shit!* Most of them have long guns. Hard to get an accurate count. They are all looking off the right-hand side of the road."

Eleven armed men in Maryland? Following James Reece? What the fuck is happening?

"These dudes are going to poach our kill. What do you want me to do?"

"I want you to *shut up* and let me think."

"Charlie, two of them, the two with pistols, are moving down the embankment. Whoever they are, they are going to *fucking* kill him."

CHAPTER 36

"JAMES! JAMES!"

It wasn't Katie's screams that roused him from unconsciousness, it was the gunshot.

Upside down, suspended by his seat belt, Reece reentered the world of the living. In predeployment workups, SEAL platoons were put through helo-dunker training at Miramar in which a simulated helicopter fuselage hanging from a specially designed crane over a deep pool was dropped into the water and spun upside down. They were taught to unhook their restraints, find a reference point, and then pull themselves to safety. That was all well and good until they were then given blacked-out goggles to simulate a nighttime crash. Reece's takeaway had been that if they survived and were not knocked unconscious in a helo crash in the middle of the ocean at night, with mere seconds to unhook and find a window in which to escape, most of them were not going to make it.

With his left eye swollen shut and caked with blood, his right eye focused on a gun. Katie was screaming and thrashing in her seat, pinning the weapon to the dash with both hands. Even in the ambient light he could tell it was a Glock 17. A second shot tore through the steering column.

Katie!

There was no time to process what just happened. They were upside down in the dark, still restrained in their seats, trapped in the wreck, with at least one person trying to execute them.

Reece lunged forward to grab the pistol Katie so desperately grappled with in the passenger seat, but his seat belt prevented him from reaching it.

Just a few inches shy.

The gun fired again, sending a round in front of Reece's face.

Just one more second, Katie.

Reece reached behind the passenger seat, felt for the corner of the Grey Man Tactical rigid MOLLE panel.

Reference point.

He stretched farther and unhooked the bungee holding his Winkler-Sayoc tomahawk securely in place. His hands choked up around the familiar wood just under the axe head and ripped it from his sheath.

Time to kill.

Reece punched the spike on the axe head into the inside wrist of the man holding the gun, aggressively corkscrewing through the tendons. Screaming in both agony and surprise, the hit man dropped the pistol, which fell through the broken windshield and slipped out of reach.

Don't let him go, Reece.

Reece lunged across the center console and trapped the would-be assassin's hand to the dash. He then pushed the hawk into his leg, forcing his hand to the base of the shaft, and then used it to extend his reach. Thrusting it past Katie and hooking the curved butt of the axe head around the neck of their assailant, he pulled him into the vehicle through the broken window. Changing tactics, the hit man crawled over Katie, whose fists pounded on the aggressor as she continued to curse and scream. Reece choked up on the axe head, grabbing a handful of the man's hair and pushing his head against the dashboard, firing short, powerful punches with the front point into his attacker's face. Each blow crushed more of his temporal bone, penetrating deeper through the skull and into brain matter. The man rolled past the dash and onto the vehicle's headliner.

"JAMES! JAMES!"

Katie's screams pulled him from his rage-induced psychosis.

Ears ringing from the gunshots in the confined space of the vehicle, Reece turned his attention to the new threat. He heard shouting in Farsi, feet sliding down the rock- and dirt-strewn embankment above, and the unmistakable sound of incoming gunfire.

Get off the X!

Still upside down and restrained in his seat, Reece switched the axe to his left hand and arched his back, drawing his SIG X-Compact from appendix carry. His good eye found the red dot and he destroyed the target in his optic, which in this case were the knees and lower thighs of a fast-approaching threat. The man fell face-first screaming into the dirt. As he attempted to push himself up, Reece took a second to get steady and put a 9mm round into his face.

Reorienting himself, Reece reached down and sliced through the seat belt where it attached to the frame. He then quickly cut through his lap belt, freeing himself from the safety harness and unceremoniously falling on top of the man he'd just killed. Hearing more shouting in Farsi over the distinct sound of incoming gunfire, Reece adjusted to the circumstances. On his side in an awkward half-crimp position atop the dead man's body, Reece identified the muzzle flash of a rifle behind a tree halfway up the slope and sent five rounds in response.

"Katie! Are you okay?"

"What?"

Reece spun around, his face inches from Katie's.

"Let's go," he said, slicing through her seat belt and attempting to soften her fall.

More rounds cracked above them.

"Get ready," Reece said, twisting around on his back, lying as flat as possible to give him the angle he needed to shoot uphill from the upside-down cab of the Land Cruiser. His working eye focused on the optic and he pressed the trigger, sending three bullets into the chest of a man running down the slope with a rifle toward the overturned Land Cruiser.

"Get out on your side!" he yelled to Katie. "Get out *now*!"

Experience had taught him that vehicles had a tendency to turn into bullet sponges in gunfights. Reece had no idea about the numbers and skill level of the opposition. The fact that they had rifles but had instead led with men using pistols to make sure their marks were dead gave Reece a data point. Had Katie not grabbed the gun when he stuck it inside to finish them off, they would both be dead. A professional would have used the distance and executed them without sticking the muzzle into the vehicle. Pros would have led with the rifles. That information told Reece he was probably not dealing with a professional hit team.

Crawling over her dead attacker, Katie felt a shard of glass slice into her upper leg as she dug her fingers into the damp ground and pulled herself through the broken passenger-side window.

Reece pivoted on the dead body and crawled after her, emerging into the night. He quickly put himself between Katie and the wheel well and engine block, taking stock of their injuries and the situation.

"Are you hurt?" Reece asked, quickly giving Katie a once-over before sliding the axe into the back of his belt. He performed a tactical reload, ensuring the pistol was at full capacity and stowing his partially used magazine for future use.

Even in the darkness he could tell Katie was shaken. Blood matted her hair to the side of her face and was already starting to clot around her nose. He felt safe in concluding that the hit team did not have night vision. If they did, he and Katie would be full of holes and the assaulters would be pouring effective fire into the overturned vehicle.

"James, your face," Katie said.

"It's okay. Do you have your Glock?"

"No, I was in D.C."

Shit.

Reece knelt back down and leaned into the vehicle. He rolled the body to the side and stood back up, holding the dead man's pistol. He released the magazine and pressed down on the top round to ensure that the gunman hadn't expended his last couple of rounds in the struggle. He reinserted the magazine and performed a one-handed press check, feeling for the chambered round in the darkness.

"This 17 works just like your 19," Reece said, handing Katie the pistol. "Now, just like we practiced with Ox. We are going to move across the open space behind us and hardpoint in that building."

Katie turned her head and saw a brick building up a low hill behind them.

Gunshots and yelling in Farsi brought their attention back to their attackers.

"Cover and move," Reece said, repeating what Ox had taught them when training in team tactics.

"Cover and move," Katie affirmed, nodding. Her frantic screams while trapped and struggling for her life in the overturned Cruiser had been replaced with an air of resolve.

"When I start firing, sprint to that set of trees at the base of the hill."

They both knew that a moving target was a lot harder to hit than a stationary one.

"Go!" Reece barked.

Leaning out from behind the vehicle in a low kneel, Reece started sending rounds at the muzzle flashes of the enemy shooters.

As soon as he heard Katie's Glock go to work, he spun and took off at a sprint across the open grass, throwing himself behind a tree next to Katie.

"Follow me," Reece said in a hushed voice.

They had broken contact. It was time to go black and not give their attackers anything to shoot at.

Moving from cover to cover, tree to tree, Reece and Katie maneuvered into the unknown.

CHAPTER 37

"WHAT'D HE SAY?" WOODY asked.

"He said to continue monitoring and ensure we are getting video," Crimmins responded.

"Are we just supposed to let these guys kill him?"

"We are *supposed* to follow orders. If you'd done that, you'd still be a cop."

"Fuck off."

"Are we recording?"

Woody turned his attention back to the main terminal in front of him.

"Yeah, boss. It's recording in both FLIR and IR. We'll have some good footage, at least of the two guys still standing around the vehicles."

"Good. Don't *fuck* this up. If you can keep your mouth shut and do your job, I'll put in a good word for you with Sawyer. He might even move you back to an overseas detail where you can get your kill on."

"*Fuck yeah!* We'll have good video. Don't you worry. Be a shame if they whack that blondie. Sucks we never got to install that video camera in her condo."

"Stay focused," Crimmins ordered.

"Think they'll see us?" Woody asked.

"Don't think so. We are far enough back even though these optics make it seem like we are right there. If they start coming this way, we'll get out of here."

Crimmins turned his attention back down the road toward the two vehicles, his IR headlights illuminating them in the night.

Who the fuck are these guys?

• • •

"Moving!" Reece hissed, grabbing Katie's hand and placing it on the back of his belt.

She latched on, remembering the training they had done together with Ox to prepare for a scenario in which they had to defend themselves from multiple armed attackers. Her job was to watch the six o'clock position as Reece concentrated on the terrain ahead.

They moved together across the dimly lit parking lot of a two-story brick warehouse.

Always improve your fighting position.

Reece didn't know how many assailants they faced. He had put down three and needed to hardpoint in an advantageous position. His iPhone had been in the cupholder and Katie had dropped hers on initial impact. His encrypted KryptAll was in his backpack in the backseat. All were somewhere in the wreck, on the street, or the embankment.

No comms.

Reece trained his pistol ahead, keeping it just below his line of sight. Where his one good eye went, the pistol went.

Reaching the side of the warehouse, Reece noticed an exterior stairwell. He paused at the base of the stairs to take stock of their situation. His left eye was completely swollen shut and he felt the pressure building on that side of his head. Katie was limping and the right side of her face was caked in blood. They both needed medical attention, but they were breathing, ambulatory, and determined.

Win the fight.

"We're going up," Reece said. "We've got to find a phone and hard-point until the cavalry arrives. I'll cover. See if that door is open."

Katie's eyes reflected the light from a lamppost that cast a dim glow over the parking area. The horror she'd experienced in the over-turned vehicle and the mission of moving through the darkness were beginning to give way to shock. Reece had to get her upstairs and take a look at her leg.

"We're going to be okay, Katie. Check that door," he said, turning back to the tree line.

He could hear her moving up the stairs behind him.

You can't lose her. Not now, Reece. Focus.

"It's locked," Katie whispered downward as loudly as she dared.

Shit.

"Coming up," Reece responded. "Hold on the tree line."

Katie forced herself to kneel, pointing the Glock in the direction of the last known threat as Reece raced up the stairs. She moved her left hand to the top of her pant leg and turned her palm to see it wet with blood.

Reece examined the door and lock, holstered his SIG with practiced precision, and reached to the back of his belt for the axe.

Inward-opening door. Master lock.

The base of this particular tomahawk was not designed for breaching, so Reece jammed the back spike on the head of the axe into the latch of the padlock, prying it violently to the side and popping the lock free.

Five rounds from Katie's pistol caused him to spin back around in time to see a man with an AR-type rifle scamper back into the tree line.

Fuck!

Reece steadied himself on the landing railing and drove a mule kick into the exterior door. It flew open, exposing a small office with an interior open door in the back-right corner. He redrew his pistol and cleared the room as best he could without a light, not wanting to hit a light switch that would backlight them.

Clear.

"Katie, move," Reece said, training his weapon on the open interior door and expecting her to move past him.

"Katie!"

He looked back and saw her struggling to her feet.

Shit!

Reece turned and helped her up. Not knowing the extent of her injuries, he reached down and picked her up in a fireman's carry over his shoulder, left arm around the back of her legs, SIG in his right hand, up and at the ready. He kicked the door closed behind them and moved into the room.

You have got to win the fight, Reece. Yeah, but if she dies, it doesn't matter.

Reece pushed one room deeper, clearing it from left to right. This room was bigger, with a number of cubicles set up in its center. A couch was against the wall to his left by a water cooler and countertop with a sink and microwave. It looked like a poor substitute for a break room.

Reece dropped Katie onto the couch.

"Where are you hurt?"

"I think just my leg. James, don't worry about me. Find a phone."

Reece ripped the Rapid Medical Tourniquet from under his belt.

During the medical portion of their training at the Farm, his class had been taught to carry low-visibility tourniquets in certain situations. Hidden by the outer belt, the thin elastic band attached on itself with a locking mechanism in the front. Reece assessed the wound as best he could in the hazy light creeping through the dirty windows. If it was a femoral bleed, Katie would already be dead. The wound probably didn't require a tourniquet, but efficiency was of the essence. He would normally have packed the wound with gauze before throwing on the tourniquet, but the aid bag was in his truck, so he ripped off his plaid button-up and quickly cut a strip of fabric to stuff into the cut. For now, his makeshift bandage and the tourniquet would have to do.

"You'll be fine, Katie. It's not bad," he said as he locked the tourniquet in place on her upper leg.

"What's going on, James?" Katie asked, unable to control her reporter's instinct to ask questions. "Who are they?"

"I heard Farsi. We'll figure it out. Right now, I need you to hold on the door. Anyone comes through, start shooting. I'm going to find a phone and call 9-1-1."

As Reece turned to find a phone, a shadow fell across the open door from their initial entry room. Reece put his finger to his lips and stepped back to the side of the door.

The man led with the muzzle of his AR.

Mistake.

Reece grabbed the barrel, trapping it to the man's body. While pulling his SIG back into the position of retention angled just above his right hip, he fired three rapid rounds into the attacker's midsection. Reece moved his pistol up for a head shot but it snagged on his opponent's shirt, his momentum continuing to carry him forward. Reece pressed the trigger again, sending a 147-grain Speer Gold Dot hollow point into the man's heart.

Reece didn't need to reengage with another shot to know that firing into clothing at contact distance had caused a malfunction; he felt it. At such a close range, clothing, bone, and skin could work their way into the mechanism, preventing the weapon from going back into battery with the following round. He also knew there was another attacker right on his heels.

Throwing the lead assaulter into the doorframe, Reece checked the next intruder's gun to the side, smashing his now-inert pistol into the face of a man who did not expect to be in a hand-to-hand fighting situation when he had a rifle. As the assailant put his hands up to instinctually block his face from the onslaught, he also turned his back.

Reece snaked his left arm around his opponent's neck, putting in the initial move of a rear naked choke. Instead of sliding his left hand into the crook of his right inside elbow to sink in the submission, Reece tapped the base of his magazine on his right leg. He then angled it so the rear sight would catch on his belt, racking it downward in a violent motion to clear the stoppage. He could tell by feel that it hadn't helped.

Work the problem.

Instead of losing time clearing a type two malfunction, Reece went for his secondary weapon, which in this case was his Winkler tomahawk at the back of his belt.

Katie's Glock exploded behind him, firing eight times in quick succession.

What the fuck?

Katie!

Reece's hand found his hawk, freeing it from his belt line. He spun it so the sharp front spike was facing him, then sliced it across the abdomen of the man he was locked with in a primal dance of death. He sliced back and forth three times, feeling the sharp implement working its way deeper and deeper into the bowels. Releasing his choke hold, Reece sank the man to his knees, spun the hawk, and implanted the axe blade through the top of his attacker's head.

He turned to Katie, who still had her Glock trained on the doorway, then to a third man lying on the floor. Reece knelt next to his pistol. He laid the hawk on the floor, ejected the magazine from the SIG, and racked the slide three times, clearing whatever clothing or body parts had fouled it. He reinserted the magazine, racked the slide again to chamber a round, and then performed a press check before picking up the tomahawk.

How many assassins did they send?

Not professionals but professional enough.

Reece moved to the closest body and bent to pick up the AR. His attempt at a battlefield pickup was interrupted by the sound of footsteps running up the outside metal staircase. Reece reacted.

How many?

Doesn't matter.

They tried to kill Katie.

I am going to kill them all.

Rushing back toward the staircase, Reece met the first aggressor with a shot that caught him just below the nose and sent him crumbling to the deck.

Reece was overcommitting to the problem, but he was on autopilot set to rage. Visions of his dead wife and daughter forever imprinted on his soul drove him forward. His tomahawk caught the rifle of the number two man and checked it toward the ground. The violent impact of bodies and weapons clashing together in battle caused the intruder to shoot several rounds into the ground. With the AR trapped, Reece fired three rounds into the man's stomach. He then changed angles and sent three more into his upper chest. Bringing the pistol up in an unconventional position, he fired one last round into his face.

Slide lock.

Shit.

Another threat entering the room.

Reece dropped his pistol and charged at the third person in the element, impaling his hawk into the upper arm of the new threat and forcing him back onto the second deck landing.

Control the gun, Reece.

The assailant's finger contracted around the trigger and sent a fully automatic burst into the building—into Katie's room.

Reece sliced down the man's arm with the ancient weapon until it met the metal of the AR. With the axe pressing on the rifle, Reece pulled the man toward him and then slammed him into the outside wall, using the blade of the axe to scrape down through the hand controlling the trigger.

In a primal panic, the assailant pushed off the wall and sent them both careening into the outside railing. Running the blade of the axe back up the man's arm, Reece pushed it behind his neck, grabbing either side of the axe and putting his head in a clinch. Reece fired several knees into his opponent's groin and midsection, dropping him to the grated landing. Releasing his grip with his left hand and freeing the axe from behind the man's neck, Reece raised it above his head and delivered a massive blow to the side of his face. His assailant's head fell forward and Reece ripped the blade free, slamming it into the back of his neck, severing the spinal cord and sending the lifeless body onto the grate.

Knowing that too many warriors throughout history had been killed by people they thought were dead, one final blow ensured the man would never move again.

Reece's eyes went to the stairs, the parking lot, and then to the tree line.

If there were more in this element they would be shooting.

Or they are calling in reinforcements.

That's exactly what you should be doing.

Katie . . .

Reece charged back into the building.

"Katie! Katie!"

She sat on the couch, Glock still trained on the man she had killed. The cocktail of epinephrine and cortisol coursing through her body from the fight was starting to subside.

"It's okay, Katie," Reece said, kneeling in front of her. "Are you hit?"

Katie blinked her eyes as they came to focus on the man before her.

"I'm going to find a phone. You are doing great. Keep holding on the door, but use this," he said, reaching down and retrieving an AR. He released the magazine, checked it for rounds, reinserted it, gave it a quick tug, and then press-checked the chamber, feeling for the round before letting go of the charging handle and hitting the forward assist. He handed it to Katie.

Reece holstered his pistol and slid his axe into the back of his belt. He then unslung another AR from a dead assailant and ensured it was loaded with a round in the chamber before moving to a desk and picking up a phone. No dial tone. He checked a second and then a third. Nothing.

"Well, looks like whatever this business was, it is shut down. The phones aren't working."

Reece checked the three dead bodies for phones and wallets. Clean. He then moved into the front room and checked the others before returning to Katie.

"No cell phones. No identifying information."

Katie had regained her composure and Reece helped her to her feet.

"How does it feel? Can you walk on it?" he asked.

"Yes. It's not bad. I can do it. Think those gunshots will bring police?"

"Probably, but they could also bring reinforcements for the bad guys," Reece said, gesturing to the bodies. "I don't know what this is all about, but now is the time to get someplace safe. Let's get back to the road."

"Your car is totaled."

"True, but I've heard Toyota made more than one," he said with a smile, knowing the power of humor on the battlefield. "These fuckers had at least one vehicle, and judging by the numbers here I think they had a follow car with hitters. I didn't find car keys, so I'd bet they left at least one person back at the road."

Katie nodded.

"How do you do it, James?"

"What's that?"

"This," Katie said, looking over the trail of bodies that littered the two rooms of the second-floor office.

Reece paused.

"It's time to go, Katie. Just like we practiced. Are you ready?"

Katie knew this was not the time to attempt to analyze the psyche of the man she loved. Could she live with someone so attuned with death? That was a question for another day. Right now, they needed to survive this one.

"On me, Katie."

Reece made his way across the office to the opposite side exit door. *Outward opening.* Kicking it open, he pied the door, using angles to clear as much of the outside space as possible.

Internally, Reece shook off Katie's question. This wasn't the time.

He knew the answer. He'd always known.

They maneuvered swiftly down the stairs, rifles up searching for threats, then moved across the parking lot and into the darkness.

CHAPTER 38

"DUDE! THAT'S GUNFIRE, BRAH!" Woody said from his captain's chair in the back of the minivan.

"I know what it is, Worthless."

"Well, let me go mix it up out there. I *need* to get after it."

"Keep it in your pants. I'm texting Sawyer."

"*Fuuuuck!* I'll prep the bang stick just in case."

"You do that," Crimmins said, tilting up his NODs and starting to text.

"Who do you think they are?" Woody asked, as he opened the pelican case and extracted a Daniel Defense M4.

"No idea," Crimmins responded, concentrating on his text.

"Can't tell for sure on the FLIR but they look like *haj* to me."

"Is that so?"

"Yeah, I used to watch them in Afghanistan. These goat fuckers are holding their guns just like the host-nation-force dudes we trained up."

"You mean the ones you watched on guard duty?"

"*Fuck off*, Crimmins. All I'm saying is that they move the same."

"Ever heard the adage that 'everyone looks guilty under NODs'?"

"What's that mean?"

"Never mind," Crimmins said, finishing his text.

"What'd he say?"

"I just sent it. Cool your jets."

Crimmins moved his NODs back into place. As dumb as Woody was, he might have a point. They actually did move like the host nation forces Crimmins had worked with in the Marines, though he wasn't about to concede the point to his partner.

Crimmins heard the bolt go forward on the rifle behind him as his phone buzzed.

"Sawyer says to just keep recording."

"Fuck!"

"It could be anyone out there, Woody. Those could be cops, Agency, who the hell knows."

"They're *haj*, bro. You know it."

Maybe, Crimmins thought.

"Just do your job and ensure we are recording. In the meantime, hand me that rifle."

CHAPTER 39

REECE AND KATIE MADE their way deliberately down the wooded slope, with just a sliver of a moon to guide them. Reece angled west.

He who flanks first, wins.

He paused at the base of the embankment. His Land Cruiser was visible about seventy-five yards to the east.

Sorry, old girl, Reece thought.

Turning his attention from the wreck, he looked up toward the road. In the darkness it was hard to tell if anyone was in an overwatch position.

"Katie, stay on rear security. I'm going to go up and get us some transportation. If something happens or you see anyone but me come back over the rise, make your way back to the west. Use the road as a guide. Keep moving. That will keep you warm. Keep going until you find a house. Then call 9-1-1 and tell them everything."

Reece looked into her eyes and then down at the diamond that still hung from her neck.

When she spoke there was no panic, no fright, no uncertainty in her voice.

"Come back to me, James."

Reece nodded and moved up the rise.

• • •

"Charlie, we have something here," Woody said, staring at the monitors.

"What is it?" Crimmins asked, adjusting the focus on his NODs.

"I think it's *him*."

"Who's *him*? Be more specific," Crimmins ordered, focusing in on movement closer to the minivan than he expected.

"It's *fucking* Reece."

Crimmins brought his NODs back into focus on a figure moving over the low guardrail between his position and the two vehicles he had been watching.

Shit. Though he couldn't be sure, the figure in his NODs seemed to pause and look directly at him.

He can't see you, Charlie. He's just checking his flank. Isn't he?

"Fuck, Charlie. That's James Reece. Clear as day. What happened to the nine tangos who went after him? Think he killed them all? *Damn*, that's one bad *motherfucker*."

"Don't *fucking* move, Woody."

"He can't see us in here. This thing is all blacked out and high-speed. If he sees anything it's the outline of an abandoned minivan."

Charlie swallowed. He knew Woody was right, but something about the way the figure turned and looked right through him made him uneasy.

"Just keep recording, Woody."

"I'm on it. He's moving to the vehicles. He has what appears to be an AR."

"My NODs are a little hazy at distance; what do you have on FLIR?"

Forward-looking infrared had come a long way in the past twenty years. The optics available even on the civilian sector market put the heat-sensing technology from the first half of the war to shame.

"I have one tango standing by the lead vehicle smoking a cigarette. The other guy is in the driver's seat of the van. Appears to have the heat on."

The crack of a rifle shot broke the night air.

"Oh shit!" Woody exclaimed. "He just straight up murdered that dude with the cig. *Fuck!* One shot! He's not even wearing a shirt. What a beast! That was *fucking* awesome!"

"Just tell me you recorded it."

"Oh, I got it all right. This is *fucking* sweet. I'm going to rub one out to this shit later. Wish I was out there stacking bodies with this dude."

"Keep recording."

"*Oh damn*," Woody said, playing announcer at a UFC fight. "He just shot the driver in the van through the passenger window. *Fuck*, now he's leaning in . . . oh, bro, he shot him again!"

"I can see that."

"What's he doing now?" Woody wondered out loud. "He's clearing the van . . . now the sedan. He's walking to the first guy. *Oh shit!* He just shot him in the head again. This dude is a *fucking* savage! He's leaning down. Going through his pockets. He just picked him up. Fuck, that's some cold shit."

They watched as Reece carried the dead man to the back of the van. He opened the rear door and tossed him inside. He then moved to the front driver's-side door and pushed the man he'd just killed between the seats. He then got behind the wheel and reversed toward the minivan.

"*Oh, fuck*," Woody said. "Let's get ready to get out of here or shoot or something."

Crimmins was already on it. The vehicle was outfitted to drive with no illumination when in IR mode. No brake lights or reverse lights would give them away.

The van came to a stop where Reece had climbed over the guardrail. They watched as he exited the vehicle and appeared to call down the slope. Moments later Katie Buranek emerged. Reece helped her over the rail and put his arm around her. She walked with an obvious limp. Reece assisted her into the passenger seat and then walked back to the driver's side. He stopped again, only momentarily, to look back down the road to the west.

Crimmins tensed in his seat, preparing to step on the gas to reverse out.

Be cool. He can't see you. Just be cool.

"He's looking right at us," Woody whispered. "Probably just checking the road behind him. We are ghosts, brah."

"Shut up and don't say another *fucking* word."

Reece got back in the van and a second later it sped off down U.S. 50 toward Annapolis.

CHAPTER 40

City Tavern Club
Georgetown, Washington, D.C.

"YOU COULD HAVE AT least worn a tie," Thwaite said as he joined his companion in the private third-floor room of the City Tavern Club, a private club located north of the "Grand Old Ditch," otherwise known as the C&O Canal near M Street and Wisconsin Avenue in Georgetown.

"Not tactically sound. Serves no purpose."

Sawyer was dressed in his normal D.C. attire of slacks, button-down shirt, and navy blazer. He stayed seated and didn't offer a hand when Thwaite entered the room. He nursed what Thwaite could only assume was an expensive glass of bourbon.

"Pappy 23? On my bill I assume."

"No. Cognac tonight. Louis Treize. And yes, of course it's on your bill. I'm not a member. I doubt the former CIA officers who restored this place would be happy I'm even having a drink here."

"Probably not."

A waiter approached and set a Bombay Sapphire martini on the table in front of the senator before leaving the two men alone in a private room usually reserved for functions with a minimum of fourteen people.

"Your usual?"

"*Fuck you*, Erik. I ordered on the way up."

The building was one of the last remaining examples of American Federal–style architecture in D.C. With a history dating back to 1796, its early patrons included George Washington, Thomas Jefferson, and John Adams. When a group of CIA Clandestine Service officers stumbled across it in the late 1950s it was scheduled to be demolished and turned into a parking lot. The enterprising officers on the verge of retirement formed an association to save the historic building. In 1962 they reopened the restaurant as a private social club, continuing its legacy of exclusivity, catering to Washington's political and social elite, its red brick housing furniture and relics from the country's earliest days.

"I wonder if Jefferson discussed the Barbary Wars in this room?" Sawyer said, admiring the fixtures and flooring that dated back to the eighteenth century.

"America's first war on terror," Thwaite said, draining half his martini in the first sip.

"There you go again, Eddie. Remember, I've heard your speech before."

"You could have at least waited for me in the Receiving Room or Jefferson Library."

"One never knows how long your *vital* work for the people will take, Senator. Besides, we are in the private room for a reason."

"Erik, the president is destroying this country. Our economy is in shambles. People across the nation are sheltering in place to avoid a virus that so far has only affected Texas and Colorado."

"Are you not worried it might spread?" Sawyer asked.

Thwaite finished his martini and looked for the waiter.

"Yeah, I'm worried it's going to spread. The president has evoked executive powers put in place after September 11th and strengthened by each administration since, Republican and Democrat. His administration is keeping Congress and the American people in the dark. Who knows what this thing really is, though we might find out tomorrow. The president is going to address Congress in a closed-door session. It's about time. The country is tearing itself apart and all he's done is address the nation from the Oval Office, reassuring us that 'the government' is doing everything in its power to safeguard the American people. Meanwhile he's got tanks and armored personnel carriers holding two entire cities hostage."

"I'm not a constituent, Eddie, and didn't you vote for the Patriot Act?"

"*Fuck you*, Sawyer. Those laws are in place to *protect* the American people."

Sawyer signaled their waiter through the glass door that two more drinks were necessary.

"I also believe you reauthorized it twice."

"*Goddamnit*, Erik. We are not here to talk about my voting record. I need to know what you have on James Reece and the president."

The waiter entered with two additional drinks. Sawyer's phone buzzed as his third glass of Louis XIII was placed before him.

"Would you like to know the specials?" the waiter asked.

Thwaite waved him off with a dismissive hand and he backed out of the room.

"Something more important to deal with?" Thwaite asked.

"Maybe," Sawyer said, returning the text and placing the phone on the table next to him.

"That is the perfect segue. It's time for you to pull your weight, Senator."

"Excuse me?"

"You've been in Washington a long time. You are a swamp creature. You head the Senate Select Committee on Intelligence. Your party controls the Senate."

"What do you want, Sawyer?"

"We need a FISA warrant on James Reece's secure phone."

"Oh, for Christ's sake. How do you know he even has one?"

"He's not communicating with anyone at the CIA or in the executive branch with his iPhone. We know that. He's got to be communicating somehow. He knows what we know about secure comms. The president uses a KryptAll. I'd be willing to bet my next government contract that Reece does, too."

Thwaite took a slower sip of his martini.

"And, how do you suggest we justify it?"

"Bring in one of your stooges. I can find someone, believe me. I have plenty to work with as leverage. We gin up a suspected Russian intelligence threat. Reece did spend six months in Siberia after all, and somehow got back to the United States. Someone with ties to Russia in close contact with the president and CIA? Call it a counterintelligence operation or a national security investigation. You know all the correct buzzwords. Get me the contract to run it as an 'independent' investigation. You want the president and James Reece? This is how we do it."

Sawyer's phone buzzed again.

"Do you mind turning that thing off? I know it's secure, but it still makes me nervous."

Sawyer diverted his attention to the phone.

"Sawyer."

"You are going to want to see this," Sawyer said, pushing his phone across to the senator.

Thwaite removed his glasses from the inside pocket of his jacket and perched them on the end of his nose, blinking as he adjusted the angle of the screen to get a better view.

"What am I looking at?"

"Unless my operatives are mistaken, you are looking at James Reece committing murder."

CHAPTER 41

Annapolis, Maryland

WITHIN AN HOUR OF their pulling into the CIA safe house on the banks of the Severn River in Annapolis, additional vehicles began to arrive. To the casual observer passing by, it would look like just a normal Friday night get-together. Had they looked closer, they would have noticed that all of the guests were male and that not one them seemed out of shape. As they parked and approached the entrance, a more studious observer would take note that none carried bottles of wine or plates of appetizers. They were not focused on the front door, nor did they joke or even talk as they approached the house. None of them looked directly at the home; instead their heads were on swivels. Closer inspection would indicate that the one on the right looked to the right, ahead, and behind while the one on the left looked to the left, ahead, and behind. They were dressed in earth-tone clothing and each carried a backpack. These were anything but ordinary men.

"Jesus, Reece. Where did you get your medical training?" Logan asked to lighten the mood.

Katie sat on the couch in the main room. A large kitchen was to their left and huge windows opened onto a deck that overlooked an immense grass lawn. Lit up by lights to discouraged intruders, the yard sloped gently down toward a dock with a sailboat secured next to a Boston Whaler.

As soon as they arrived an hour earlier, Reece had cleared the house and ensured all the doors and windows were locked and that there were no signs of forced or illicit entry before tending to Katie's wounds and throwing on a T-shirt.

"He makes up for his lack of medical expertise with his bedside manner," Katie joked.

Both men laughed, knowing that a sense of humor is a good sign when confronting the physical and emotional trauma of battle.

"Big hole, big patch. Small hole, small patch," Reece teased back. "What else do you need to know?"

Logan rolled his eyes and smiled at Katie.

"Not sure how you put up with this guy," Logan continued, as he inspected Katie's head and leg. "You are going to need some stiches."

Logan pointed a penlight into each of Katie's eyes.

"I don't think you have a concussion, which is a small miracle, but I'd still like you to refrain from having anything with caffeine and to stay away from alcohol until we are sure," he said, looking at the glass of wine next to the journalist.

Katie frowned.

"And you, Reece, sit down and let me take a look."

"I'm fine."

"You are not fine until I say you are fine. Now sit down and let me do my job."

Reece reluctantly sat and let the former Air Force PJ give him the once-over.

After clearing the house, Reece had used the landline to contact Vic at the CIA. Within twenty minutes the first car had arrived, a retired Ground Branch contractor living in Forest Meadows. Four more vehicles had pulled up over the next hour. Reece knew most of them, all former operators now working for the paramilitary side of U.S. intelligence. They now stood guard around the house, sentinels of the republic, allowing Logan to tend to Reece and Katie's wounds.

While Logan examined the gash on Reece's head, a GB contractor opened the door for Vic Rodriquez. Vic crossed through the foyer and extended his hand to Katie, the spymaster outwardly suppressing the shock of seeing Katie and Reece covered in dirt, sweat, and blood.

"Ms. Buranek, so good to see you again. I wish it were under better circumstances. How do you feel?"

Vic was addressing Katie but looked to Logan, who nodded reassuringly.

"I think I need more wine," Katie replied.

Vic chuckled.

"How is he?" Vic asked Logan, knowing he would never get the truth out of the frogman.

"He's going to need some stitches in his head, and he's certainly got a concussion. Other than that, he just needs a shower, and possibly a shave and a haircut," the Air Force medic jested.

"I'm fine, Vic." Reece winced as Logan parted his hair, inspecting the cut matted with dried blood.

"You look great," Vic deadpanned. "Let's talk. Katie, will you excuse us?"

"Of course, I'm going to get cleaned up," she said.

Ever the gentleman, Vic offered his hand and assisted the journalist to her feet.

Vic nodded to Logan and motioned for Reece to follow him to the kitchen.

"What the *fuck* is going on, Reece?"

Reece moved around the counter while Vic took a seat on a bar stool. He opened a drawer and removed a clean dish towel, which he ran under warm water before applying it to his face to remove some of the blood.

"Is this room wired?" Reece asked.

"It is, but it's not recording."

"You sure?"

"I'm sure."

Reece ran the now-bloody towel under the water again, watching the rose-colored water disappear down the drain.

"You want a drink? After I read you in on this, you are going to need it."

CHAPTER 42

WHEN REECE FINISHED, VIC closed his eyes and rubbed the bridge of his nose.

The president of the United States ordered assassinations on U.S. soil. Jesus Christ.

"And the two dead guys are still in the van?" Vic asked.

"They are. I went through their pockets. No wallets or cell phones, but it was just a cursory search on the side of the road. You might have better luck with a forensic team."

"I'll coordinate it."

"And, if you don't mind, I have an AR in a storage drawer in the back of my truck, and my secure phone is in my pack, which was in the backseat. There are a few other things in there I probably shouldn't have had in D.C."

Vic nodded. "I'll take care of it."

Reece paused.

"You're wondering why I didn't try to take one of those last two on the road alive, aren't you?"

Vic studied his newest recruit.

"It sounds like you are wondering that yourself, Reece."

Reece dropped the bloody towel in the sink.

"I saw the killers who took Lauren and Lucy from me in each of the men who came after us tonight. I couldn't let that happen again, Vic. I've put Katie in danger too many times. She almost died out there. She killed a man. She's acting tough, but as you know, the post-traumatic stress from events like tonight can manifest years afterward."

Vic nodded knowingly.

"I *should* have taken one. I *could* have."

"You don't know that, Reece. You made a tactical battlefield decision to eliminate the threat. Simple as that."

Both men knew it was not as simple as that.

"Regardless, it's done," Reece said. "No bringing them back. The question remains, who were they, who sent them, and why? I was worried about a faction of the Bratva tracking me down, maybe even Russian SVR. This crew was clearly speaking Farsi."

"Could it have something to do with anything you did in the Teams?" Vic asked.

"I guess it's possible, but you know how that works; you are banging targets every night, grabbing people and bringing them back to the FOB for interrogation. A lot of guys did that."

"Not a lot of guys then got caught up in the Capstone experiment and were labeled a domestic terrorist by the U.S. government, only to have their picture splashed across cable news and social media outlets for months."

"There is that," Reece agreed.

"If they knew about this safe house, they would have hit you here. They could have come in by water or the road or both. Too many variables to do a VI en route from D.C. to Annapolis," Vic said, using the abbreviation for "vehicle interdiction."

Reece looked at the stairs that Katie had just walked up, and then back to Vic.

As if reading his mind, Vic said, "Unless they were after Katie."

"It's feasible. I don't know. Things are not adding up. I go after a network that helped facilitate 9/11, one of the targets in Chicago has a heart attack as I'm surveilling, I take one out in Atlanta and then get told to stand down by the president as this airborne hemorrhagic virus paralyzes the country. I come back to Northern Virginia to recalibrate and suddenly get targeted by nine guys speaking Farsi? If what I was doing was Agency sanctioned, I'd say we have a mole in our midst, but this was *not* Agency sanctioned. This was me and the president."

"For the moment, I'm going to set aside the debate over legalities and chain of command and usurpation of authorities and the myriad laws you broke. Don't worry, we will revisit those later. Right now, I'm more concerned about foreign hit teams on U.S. soil targeting you and possibly others from Ground Branch. I have a cleanup crew coordinating with local law enforcement on scene. If any of these hitters are in the systems of any Western intelligence service, we will know in a few hours."

"Am I interrupting anything, gentlemen?" Katie asked hitting the base of the staircase and walking toward the kitchen.

She had cleaned up as best as she could. The blood that had dried on the right side of her face was gone and she was in fresh clothes.

"Not at all, Ms. Buranek, please join us," Vic said, standing and pulling out the counter chair.

"Please call me Katie, Mr. Rodriguez."

"Vic, please."

"Vic," Katie said. "Since we are forbidden from drinking the nectar of the gods for another night, can I get anyone some decaffeinated tea?"

"Let me," Reece said.

"You will probably ruin it with cream and honey," Katie said with a smile. "I've got it. Vic?"

"No, thank you. I need to coordinate with the cleanup crew and see if we can get some answers on who these guys were."

"You might want to wait. I called my friend Haley Garrett at the CDC to let her know I was alive. She was planning to stop by tonight to help me with a story. She's on her way over now. I tried to discourage her, but she does not dissuade easily. She also has some information she wasn't comfortable sharing on the phone."

"What do you mean?" Vic asked.

"I don't have specifics, but she doesn't think this virus originated in Angola. She thinks it's a bioweapon."

CHAPTER 43

HALEY GARRETT ARRIVED THIRTY minutes later. Even though Katie had warned her about the additional security, she looked a little perturbed by the armed men in the driveway. The two old friends shared a warm hug.

"Katie, oh my God, are you okay?" Haley asked, shooting daggers at Reece.

"Yes, I'm fine, just some scratches. Haley, you remember James. And this is Victor Rodriguez."

The two men shook hands with Haley, who studied them both the way a witness would analyze perps in a lineup from behind a two-way mirror.

"It's okay, Haley. Like I explained on the phone, these are two of the good guys."

Haley continued to take stock of the CIA operatives. She was dressed in running shoes, jeans, and a UC Davis sweatshirt. Her black hair was tied back and retro-vintage Ray-Ban prescription eyeglasses were perched precariously atop her head. She had the stern look of someone who could win any argument simply by wearing down and outlasting her opposition.

"I think we should sit down for this," she said, making her decision.

They moved to the spacious dining room and sat around the far end of a long rectangular table.

Reece looked up and noted that the ceiling was adorned with hand-painted roses.

Sub rosa.

Appropriate, Reece thought.

"Mr. Rodriguez, what exactly do you do for the government?" Haley asked.

"I work for the State Department."

"Ah, of course," she said. Everyone in Washington knew that State Department was a euphemism for the Central Intelligence Agency. "Well, in that case you just might be the perfect person."

"Perfect person for what?" Vic asked.

Haley looked at Katie, Reece, and then back to Vic.

"This virus is *not* 'airborne' in the way we've become conditioned to understand the term, and I doubt it originated in Angola. I also suspect it is connected to the attack on Katie and James tonight."

"I'm sorry, Ms. Garrett, I'm not following."

"Neither are my bosses at the CDC. Hysteria has gripped not just the populace but also the scientific community. My job is to follow clues, much like a detective. So, we have a suspected index case in Angola; almost five hundred people die, but the virus burns itself out like we've seen in the past. So far, nothing unusual. Only this time, a carrier boards a plane at Quatro de Fevereiro International Airport and brings the virus to the United States. It's happened before with the virus burning out on U.S. soil, but something is different about this. The virus has mutated. It has evolved. It's a new strain. How do we know? Because as of tonight close to three thousand people have died in Colorado and Texas, people who in no way could have had blood-to-blood contact. We know the Angola flight landed in Johannesburg and then from there flights departed to JFK and Atlanta, with follow-on flights around the nation to include airports in Dallas and Denver. Therefore, it's airborne. Our worst nightmare, right?"

"That is my understanding," Vic said.

"Then why do we not have cases in Johannesburg? Why no cases in Europe or the Middle East? In South Africa, passengers from Angola transferred to flights going to Dubai, UAE, Frankfurt, London, and Barcelona, but we only have cases in Dallas and Denver?"

"Maybe the carrier was not yet contagious until they got to Dallas or Denver?" Reece offered.

"I admit that is a possibility, but I submit that it is much more likely to be in either one specific location or to have spread to multiple areas around the world. Isolated to two cities is peculiar."

"We see that in Africa, don't we?" Vic asked. "Isolated to a single village."

"Yes, but typically villagers aren't traveling, which helps contain the spread," the doctor countered.

"I read that the CDC officially identified it as a new strain of Ebola," Reece said.

"That's true," Haley said. "It looks like a new mutation of Ebola under a microscope."

"A new strain that's airborne," Vic said, confirming the official account.

"Yes, but airborne does not mean that it's being spread via respiratory means," she said.

Vic leaned back in his chair and crossed his arms.

"Please elaborate," Vic said.

"Okay, let me break it down for those of you with Y chromosomes. It's possible for something to be 'airborne' but not necessarily spread via respiratory pathways. Think of it in terms of getting sprayed with perfume by one of those annoying salespeople at a mall. We are all old enough to remember malls, right? Well, you smelled the perfume, sometimes even tasted it, but you didn't cough the perfume onto someone else an hour or even days later."

"Are you saying someone wants us to think this virus is spread naturally from human to human, but it was really intentionally released to infect people?" Katie asked.

"A bioweapon," Reece stated.

Haley looked at Reece.

"That is my theory. It's only 'airborne' in that it is spread by contact with direct aerosol droplets released by a controlled pressure device, through a mist or a cloud of droplets. After that, it can only be spread as any standard hemorrhagic virus, with direct blood-to-mucus-membrane contact. It's actually difficult to spread with limited precautions."

"That's what makes it an effective bioweapon," Reece offered. "If you release a virus with that kind of death rate it does you no good if it then spreads back and infects the country that released it."

"That's right. Most importantly, it is incapable of human aerosolization like COVID-19. It's the perfect bioweapon. It strikes with incredible efficiency but its genius is that it doesn't continue to spread past those initially infected."

"That would defeat its purpose," Reece said, thinking aloud. "So, how do we kill it?"

"You don't kill it. It has infected everyone it's going to infect."

"Unless someone is still out there releasing it manually."

"Correct."

"So, to stop it, we find whoever is releasing it and we stop them," Reece stated. It wasn't a question.

"Yes," Haley said slowly. She had never heard the word *stop* used in a way that so naturally implied "kill."

"Can you prove it?" Vic asked.

"No. It's just a theory. To prove it we would need to first know what type of virus we are dealing with, and by that I mean what *specific* virus we are looking at. Right now, we are working off data that suggests it is a new strain of Ebola because that is what it most closely resembles under electron magnification and because it matches a sample from a recent outbreak in Angola. If it is in fact an engineered bioweapon that is not in our system, we would have nothing with which to compare it. Some of these viruses were weaponized going back to World War Two. Bioweapon research from Germany and Japan was absorbed by the Soviet Union and the United States, who then built on that research to develop their own programs; all highly classified. After we knew the type of virus, we'd then need a sample of the original bioweapon to compare to a sample from Colorado or Texas."

"And what does the CDC think of this hypothesis?" Vic asked.

"So far it has fallen on deaf ears. We started with the premise that this outbreak originated in Angola because the mutated strain from samples in Richardson and Aurora match the sample taken from Angola to a T. After it was identified, we, the scientific community as a whole, set out to develop an inoculation the way we did with COVID-19."

"You mean making a vaccine from one of the infected patients?" Reece asked.

"That is by and large a Hollywood myth. You just can't pull antibodies off the shelf and inoculate three hundred million people. It doesn't work that way. The point is, all our efforts went into developing a vaccine. No one stopped to ask why the spread rate is deviating from every other contagious disease ever documented."

Sensing that those around the table were not grasping the concept, she continued, "Usually the spread rate is inverse to the mortality rate."

"That does not sound good. What exactly does it mean?" Reece asked.

"The faster pathogens spread, the slower they kill. That preserves the host and gives the virus a chance to spread, to survive. By contrast, this virus *may* have adapted to spread via respiratory droplets. Someone can pass it through a cough, rather than direct blood-to-blood contact as with your garden-variety hemorrhagic virus. It's hard to infect another human when a disease is transmitted through blood. But, if this virus maintains its mortality rate of 85 percent to 90 percent in its current mutation, then it is no longer a flu or H1N1 outbreak with a 0.01 percent mortality rate or even COVID with a 0.1 percent or 0.2 percent mortality rate. If this outbreak continues on its current path and escapes the isolation measures in Richardson and Aurora, we are talking 280 million people dead, and that does not take into account international ramifications."

"The sixth wave," Katie whispered.

"The sixth wave?" Reece asked.

"Holocene extinction," Haley explained. "Planetary extinction of the human race. Earth has witnessed five previous mass extinctions. The last one was approximately sixty-six million years ago. Many scientists believe we are due for another."

"Dr. Garrett, you do not seem as distressed about this possibility as one would expect," Vic noted.

"That's because this is *not* that event, but we are being manipulated to believe it is for a reason that I don't yet understand."

"Explain," Vic pressed.

"Are any of you familiar with mathematically modeling R0?"

"The what?" Reece asked.

"R0, reproduction number, you may have heard it called 'r-naught.' It's a mathematical term used to describe the intensity of an infectious disease and therefore indicate its rate of transmission. Think of it as a spread rate. One-to-one transmission is a one. If it rises higher than one-to-one, the result is what we call logarithmic growth at uncontrolled speed. Below one-to-one, it burns itself out."

To the blank stares of her audience, Haley continued: "A situation where, on average, each infected person spread the illness to one other single person would establish an R0 of one."

"You lost me," Reece admitted.

"Simply put," Haley said. "If the R0 is over one, it's on a logarithmic escalation. That number does not change by the day; rather it takes weeks for curves to be established."

"You are saying that Texas and Colorado deviate from the established model," Reece said, processing the data and wrapping his head around the implications.

"That's right. The rate of spread in Richardson, thousands of patients all at once, would put the rate off the map. The r-naught would be twenty, thirty, or possibly higher, but then it jumped to another location with a smaller subset. That is too high a variance within the virus. They do not mutate or adapt that quickly."

"Meaning?" Reece asked.

"Meaning that the logarithmic growth rate would indicate the entire country should be infected by now, but we are not. Somebody, possibly a group of people, is releasing it in aerosolized doses trying to mimic a respiratory-spread contagion."

The repercussions of Haley's theory settled over the table.

Vic broke the silence first. "To be clear, you are saying this could be a coordinated release, mirroring a respiratory-spreading virus with a ninety percent mortality rate. A bio-terrorism attack."

"Yes, but it's not really all that well done, to be honest."

"How so?" Vic asked, leaning forward.

"As I said, think of me as an infectious disease forensic investigator. I tried to find the index case in Angola. That's harder than one would think. All the bodies were incinerated to prevent the spread of the virus. However, in this country we keep detailed medical records and in the case of a new strain of airborne Ebola, some of the HIPAA restrictions are lifted by executive order. The CDC tracked down flight manifests from Angola and cross-referenced those with patients here in the United States. Up until this point we've only looked at this through the public health lens because of the CDC's initial reporting from Angola. As far as

I know, the CIA and the FBI have not convened a task force because as of yet no one has explored it from a national security angle. And, based on what we have seen thus far, it seems cut-and-dried at face value; the virus index case is one of 457 people incinerated in Angola but at least one carrier boards a plane and from Africa travels to the United States."

"What we've been concerned with up to now is tracking down and testing passengers for the disease to contain the spread, not scrutinizing their backgrounds," Katie said, thinking aloud.

"That's right," Haley confirmed.

"I'll get detailed backgrounds on the passengers," Vic said.

"From your connections at the *State Department*?" Haley asked.

"Yes," Vic confirmed.

"Whoever did this made a mistake. I should have found a name on the manifests that matched a name in hospital records."

"Unless the U.S. carrier is dead in their house and has not yet been identified," Reece observed.

"True, but if you are a terrorist, you'd want us to tie a name on a flight to a name in a hospital and wrap it all up nicely to hand to the American public."

"Why wouldn't they do that?" Katie asked.

"OPSEC," Reece said.

"Excuse me?"

"OPSEC. Operational security. If we found them before they died, there is the possibility we could turn them and trace the attack back to its origin."

"There is no getting around the fact that a carrier might be deceased in his or her bed and as of yet undiscovered. But it's also possible that person doesn't exist, that it was not brought in from Angola," Haley said.

"There are still a lot of missing pieces here," Vic said.

"Also true, but I found something else of interest, and it only came to me after Katie told me about what happened tonight and that her attackers were speaking Farsi."

"Which is?" Katie asked.

"The first person admitted to Richardson Methodist Medical Center was Mahan Faramand. I did some digging. He's a second-generation Iranian American."

"Interesting," Katie conceded. "Is he still alive?"

"No, unfortunately he was one of the first to succumb to the virus. Do you know what's even more interesting? The first group of patients in Aurora had two names that stood out, Izad Turan and Sebastian Phillips. Turan has been in the country for twenty-five years. Guess where he's from?"

"Iran," Vic stated.

"What about Sebastian Phillips?" Katie asked. "He doesn't sound Iranian."

"His given name is Shahram Pahlavi. Where do you think his parents are from?"

"Iran," Katie said, remembering the gunshots and the screaming in Farsi reverberating through the dark warehouse, now echoing through her mind.

"Do we know if Izad Turan and Sebastian Phillips are still alive?" Reece asked.

"They are," Haley confirmed. "At least as of two hours ago."

"Did you check all the names from Richardson?"

"I did, of all patients thus far, anyway."

"And?"

"And there were three patients with Iranian surnames: Mahan Faramand, Reza Abed, and Hashem Shirazi."

Reece swallowed as the blood drained from his face.

"Reece," Vic said, "are you okay?"

Reece stood and walked to the windows overlooking the Severn River. He felt the pull of the ocean.

Take Katie and get out! Get on that boat and sail away!

To where? Anywhere but here . . .

Vic stood and moved next to Reece at the window.

"Reece?"

"Vic," Reece said, the tone of his voice matching the darkness beyond the shutters. "The names."

"What names?"

"Faramand, Turan, and Pahlavi."

"What about them?"

"Those are all last names on the 9/11 target list the president gave me."

"Dear God."

"Vic, get me a list of names from Angola. Highlight anyone with Iranian ties. Tell the president what's going on."

"I'm going to wake up the director. We will brief the president at the PDB. I'll get a team of Agency doctors on this immediately."

"Vic, if Dr. Garrett is right and there is an Iranian connection to the hit tonight that is also linked to this outbreak or bio-attack, they are not going to stop. Can you get Katie somewhere safe?"

"Of course. What are you going to do?"

"I'm going to do what I do best. First, I need someone with an infectious disease background."

Reece turned back from the window.

"Haley, are you up for a trip into the hot zone?"

"James," Katie said, a tinge of nervousness in her voice. "Where are you going?"

"I want to talk to Izad Turan and Sebastian Phillips. And, Vic?"

"Yes?"

"I'll need to borrow an Agency jet."

CHAPTER 44

Denver, Colorado

THE AGENCY GULFSTREAM 550 landed at Denver International Airport and taxied to a private terminal set up by the Department of Justice after 9/11 to receive government aircraft and officials needing to avoid public air travel. The fleet of taxpayer-funded private aircraft had received scrutiny in recent years after the high-visibility firing of FBI Director James Comey, who was photographed boarding an FBI G550 in Los Angeles for a flight to D.C. As with most outrages, it was short-lived as another hot topic distracted the media the following day.

Reece and Haley were met by a young CIA analyst, who was the Agency liaison to the FBI Denver Field Office.

"Mr. Ree . . . I mean, Mr. Donovan, Dr. Garrett, I'm Ken Daniel. I have your credentials and hazmat suits in the Suburban. The subjects have been moved from the hospital to two separate Chem-Bio Protective Shelters outside the main field hospital. As requested, they are under guard, though I have been told that was an unnecessary precaution."

"Why is that?" Reece asked.

"They were some of the first patients, sir. They don't have much time left. They'd already been triaged to the expectant area."

Reece nodded.

"Expectant" meant there was no hope. Usually annotated with a black badge, those in the expectant category of military triage were given pain medications and left to die while resources were allocated to those patients who had a chance.

"Thanks, Ken. The guards are there to keep anyone from killing them before we can question them," Reece said.

"Oh, I see."

Ken wiped sweat from a brow that carried a look of perpetual nervousness. He was young, thin, with a mop of blond hair that Reece suspected drove the FBI agents in the field office nuts.

"What do you do for the Agency, Ken?" Reece asked as they made their way to the black Suburban parked on the edge of the tarmac.

"Analyst, sir. Collections."

"Do you have time overseas?"

"Not yet, sir. I've been in Denver for the past year, mostly answering emails and trail running."

"How far is the hospital?"

"About ten minutes. Everything south of the 70 is shut down from the Denver Zoo to Buckley Air Force Base. I'm sure you've seen the rioting. It's getting bad. I'm worried the military is going to kill more people just keeping containment than this virus would."

Reece and Haley shared a look.

"That's why we're here, Ken," Haley said.

"Do the two people under guard have something to do with this?"

"We are going to find out."

Reece's phone buzzed.

"Excuse me," he said, hitting "accept." He put the phone to his ear and stepped away from his colleagues.

"What do you have for me, Vic?"

"Confirmation that Sebastian Phillips is Shahram Pahlavi. His parents emigrated from Europe in the mid-nineties. Both doctors. Settled in California and then Arizona, where Shahram was born. Prior to medical school at University of Leuven, Belgium, they were citizens of Iran. I just put them under surveillance in Phoenix."

"The father was on my list. Shahram would have been just a kid on 9/11. Anything else?"

"Shahram rents an apartment near the university, but he owns a home in Denver. Tax records do not indicate any rental income from either property. I'll text you the addresses. I'm working to get local LE and FBI on those locations, but they are overtaxed right now with containment, protests, and rioting."

"Understood. How about Izad Turan?"

"NSA went through his email and browsing history. It's clean. They went deep and found an old Hotmail account set up in 1999. It never sent an email. Its draft folder was accessed but the contents deleted, and it hasn't been touched since 2001. It was so long ago that the NSA has not been able to recover or restore the deleted files."

"Back when using the draft folder with two or more people having the log-in information was the preferred method of communication for terrorists. What about cell phone tracking data?"

"Turan does not appear to own a cell phone. Not that we could find anyway. Shahram's locational data was turned off for the most part, but as you know we can still track. That data indicates a pattern of life that centers around his apartment and campus, with occasional trips to the Rocky Mountains."

"What does that tell us?"

"The report indicates that on multiple occasions he left his phone at the apartment when we have him active on university computers."

"So, he's leaving his cell phone in his apartment?"

"Yes, it's possible he's just forgetful," Vic conceded.

"It's also possible he doesn't want his phone carrier capturing locational data on the days he leaves it at home," Reece said, remembering the phone he left on his dresser in Coronado, California, as he started crossing names off his terminal list.

"It's feasible."

"Those are the days he's going to the house in Denver," Reece said.

"I concur. That is a valid assumption."

"What else do you have for us?"

"Reece, the hitters in Maryland, they all had Iranian ties."

Reece took a breath, calculating.

"That fits. Is Katie locked down?"

"She's not happy about it. Ox and the boys are standing watch."

"Good. How'd it go with the president?" Reece asked, changing topics.

"I can't say much on this line other than there is staunch opposition to Haley's theory. People are scared, Reece. There are drastic measures on the table."

"More drastic than isolating American cities and letting everyone inside die?"

"Reece, these phones are secure, but like every electronic device, only to a point. I am going to violate procedure and tell you something that could end my career, but you need to know."

"I'm listening."

"There is an option to eradicate a virus that threatens to destroy the country. It's been used before by the Soviets and then the Russians in Africa."

Reece remembered his dinner conversation with Katie in what seemed like another life.

"FAEs?"

"That's right, Reece."

"On U.S. cities? *Jesus.*"

"Not to put any additional pressure on you, but the very real fate of the nation rests on what you find out from Shahram and Turan."

Reece looked back to Haley.

"Reece? Are you still there?"

"I'm here. Headed to the field hospital now."

"Call me as soon as you have anything."

"Roger."

Reece terminated the call and walked back toward Haley and Ken, who stood waiting next to the Suburban.

"What did he say?" Haley asked.

"He said this is all up to us."

CHAPTER 45

ON THE DRIVE TO Buckley Air Force Base, Ken briefed Reece and Haley on the procedures for entering and exiting what was now referred to as a hot zone. Like Richardson, Aurora had become a prison, and it was increasingly evident to the residents that all those trapped within its borders would eventually die. Ken explained that the containment plan had called for a complete encirclement of a geographical area, with those on its borders moved four miles inward to create a no-man's-land buffer zone, a DMZ. Those without family and friends were put up in hotels in Denver and in tents on Buckley Air Force Base.

The plan had not taken into account the power of American resolve and natural disdain for authority. The weapons that had at first been pointed in to keep those in the containment area from escaping were now augmented with additional forces holding back waves of protesters and family members from outside the isolation zones who wanted to know if their relatives were alive. Skirmishes had erupted between the military and citizens trying to break out of the hot zone and some trying to break *into* it. Americans had been shot and killed, and even the military had not emerged unscathed. Americans were dying on both sides of what some were starting to refer to as a civil war. Reece could only imagine the confusion of a young eighteen-year-old kid, embalmed in a claustrophobic hazmat suit with a fogged-up gas mask, holding an iron-sighted M16 or behind a 240 Golf on the back of a HMMWV as his fellow citizens approached with guns, knives, baseball bats, skateboards, bricks, and Molotov cocktails.

Ken explained that criminals had taken advantage of the chaos and were again rioting and looting shopping districts in Denver under the pretense of protesting government incursion a few miles east. Those with the means to do so had fled the state. A panic had gripped the nation. Cities across the country were descending into chaos, with rioters and looters protesting the actions in Richardson and Aurora. The virus, government response, and subsequent rioting had sent the economy into a tailspin. An enemy had breached the gates.

Second- and third-order effects, Reece thought. As with Iraq and Afghanistan, plans that looked good on paper rarely, if ever, survived first contact with the enemy. The men and women in hazmat suits tasked with protecting the country by containing entire cities were feeling the results of those unintended consequences. They had turned their weapons on the very people whose taxes paid their salaries and provided the rifles and ammunition now being used against them.

Imagine what happens if they find out this is not a naturally occurring virus, Reece thought. *They are going to demand someone pay: a population, a country, someone . . .*

The Suburban pulled through three separate checkpoints as it made its way onto the Air Force base, finally passing through the Sixth Avenue gate. Ken parked the SUV in the large parking lot just inside the perimeter where temporary tents had been set up. It reminded Reece of the early forward operating bases from the War on Terror.

A four-vehicle convoy consisting of two HMMWVs and two Strykers awaited them. Reece couldn't help but notice the 30mm cannons atop the Strykers and the .50s in the HMMWV turrets. They were lined up, engines on, ready to roll. All personnel were suited up in tan CBRN military hazmat suits with full-face gas masks.

Reece turned to Haley.

"Are you sure you want to do this?"

"I'm a doctor, Reece. I study infectious diseases. This is my theory. I'm going with you."

Reece nodded.

"Okay, but if anything happens, just stay behind me. Listen to what I say and do it."

"Deal. Now let me show you how to put on your suit."

CHAPTER 46

LEAVING BUCKLEY AND ENTERING the hot zone was akin to departing Baghdad's Green Zone after the al-Askari mosque bombing in 2006. It was game on. The convoy sped through the streets, abruptly switching lanes under overpasses in case they were targeted by Molotov cocktails or bricks from above. The drivers had clearly been downrange. A car defying the isolation orders was forced to the side by warning shots from the lead HMMWV.

Reece wondered how long those rounds would remain warnings before lighting up any person or vehicle outside their homes.

The military has occupied the United States of America.

They sped down State Highway 30 and turned into the Aurora Hills Golf Course, which had been commandeered by the military and transformed for hospital overflow. Passing through another three heavily armed checkpoints, they entered the grounds of what two weeks earlier had been a place to relax, tee off, and enjoy a day with friends. It was now a morgue. Two huge tents with accompanying diesel generators and air filtration systems dominated the course. Refrigerated semi-tractor trailers packed the parking area.

For the bodies.

The vehicles came to a stop and were met by three soldiers in the same tan CBRN military hazmat suits worn by those in the convoy.

"You ready?" Reece asked across the rear passenger seat of the HMMWV.

Their gas masks had been fitted with new removable filters. Reece had instinctually screwed his into the left side of the mask, which would let him bring a rifle to his right shoulder if need be.

Old habits.

The integrated speech diaphragms allowed them to speak to one another without shouting, a vast improvement from just a few years before. CBRN stood for chemical, biological, radiological, nuclear. The suits and gas masks were designed to protect service members from toxic industrial chemicals and chemical warfare agents, to include radioactive dust, noxious gas, and vaporized pollutants. They were an unfortunate necessity of the modern battlefield. None of those wearing them today thought they would ever don them on U.S. soil combatting American citizens.

"Let's do it. If I believed this was a respiratory-spread virus, I wouldn't even let you come in with me without the required training. *But*, this was spread in an aerosolized form like my example of the mall perfume samples."

"How sure are you?"

"I'm willing to bet both our lives on it but nothing is a hundred percent, Reece."

"Terrific," Reece said, exiting the vehicle to meet their escorts.

"Mr. Donovan, Dr. Garrett, I'm Captain Grady," the soldier said through his gas mask.

"Captain," Reece acknowledged.

"This was sent for you," he said to Reece, handing over a file.

"Thank you," Reece acknowledged, taking a quick scan of its contents.

"Sir, ma'am, both patients were moved from Kindred Hospital to separate tents this morning. I do have some unfortunate news; Izad Turan is dead."

CHAPTER 47

REECE AND HALEY ENTERED a small tent connected to a larger Chemical, Biological Protective Shelter through a self-sealing door. Part of an Army procurement program based on the requirement to treat U.S. troops infected after a chemical or biological attack overseas, the Smiths Detection CBPS Model 8E1 was designated the M8A4. Adapting to emerging threats, the program was later effectively diverted to National Guard units for use in the event of a chem-bio weapon attack on the homeland. Attached to a tan six-wheeled behemoth with a red cross painted on the side to identify it as a medical vehicle entitled to protections under the Geneva Conventions; the mobile self-contained protection system was designed to provide a contamination-free working environment.

The black laminated sign on its side did not go unnoticed by either of them.

Inside the first tent was a large clear plastic and stainless-steel box with duel airtight locking doors.

"Let's hope this works," Haley said through her mask.

"What is it?" Reece asked.

"It's a mobile level-four bio-containment module."

"That sounds serious."

"These CBRN hazmat suits don't provide the requisite level of protection for what we will be dealing with in there."

"They're good enough for the military guys but not for us?" Reece asked. "Typical."

"If this was a respiratory-spread pathogen, which it's not, and as long as they are not directly interacting with infected patients, those MilSpec hazmat suits would work and do what they are designed for, namely protecting soldiers from anthrax, mustard gas, and sarin. They are not designed to provide protection from a level-four pathogen and there simply aren't enough self-contained level-four suits to outfit everyone in the military. That's why the military is on the *outside* and not interacting with anyone *inside* the containment area. You ready to get naked?"

"Naked?"

"Just follow my lead. This first module is positively pressurized. We'll change out of this CBRN equipment and into fully self-supportive bio-containment suits with their own oxygen supply before moving into the CBPS."

"The what?"

"The Chemical Biological Protective Shelter. It's negatively pressurized."

"Why is that?" Reece asked.

"In this case, it's to keep the virus inside. Just do what I do if you want to live."

When they emerged, Reece thought they resembled astronauts. Each of them wore a small canister of oxygen on their back to pressurize the suit and allow them to breathe. Large clear plastic face shields were incorporated into the PPE and they were fitted with microphones for external communication. They passed under UV lights and pushed aside the heavy plastic flaps and fitted door to enter the negatively pressurized CBPS. In contrast to the desert tan exterior, the inside was stark white. It was constructed to eliminate the need for protective clothing. In contrast to the original intent, it was now being used to contain the virus itself, so anyone entering the space was required to be in full level-four PPE. The four hundred square feet of usable treatment space held only one patient.

Cots lined the interior, cots that Reece knew would soon hold more expectant bodies after Shahram Pahlavi was zipped into a body bag and moved to a refrigerated semi-truck.

A guard in a level-four suit stood watch and exited when the pair entered, as he had been instructed.

"Stay behind me," Reece ordered more out of habit than out of any concern that their target would attempt to attack them or escape.

Pahlavi was on a wheeled gurney behind another plastic covering that reminded Reece of cheap shower curtains. Reece stood outside with Dr. Garrett and took stock of the patient. An intravenous morphine drip was connected to a vein on his hand and an electronic vital-sign monitor beeped away atop a portable stand. It was evident that Shahram Pahlavi was going to die. Blood had dripped from his nose and over his mouth, mixing with the yellow vomit that had accumulated on his chin and chest. His eyes were closed, but his body shook as it used what little reserves of energy it had left to fight the fever that ravaged his body and brain. He had been covered with a blanket; as Reece and Haley watched through the opaque plastic, it slipped to the floor, exposing arms and hands purple with internal hemorrhaging. He was sweating blood.

Reece was not a trained interrogator. In fact, on his list of skills, interrogation was ranked at the bottom. He'd attended an interrogation school in the SEAL Teams, and his takeaway had been that he should leave tactical questioning to the professionals. It wasn't until his assignment to a CIA covert action program that he had been introduced to the darker arts of what they called "enhanced interrogation," lessons he'd applied after his family had been violently taken from him. Reece shook off the memory. Those lessons in interrogation and torture were not going to work on a man about to touch the face of God.

Even with Dr. Garrett's assurances, Reece was hesitant to engage.

What if she's wrong?

Too late. This guy is somehow connected to the virus and to the attack on Katie.

Do it.

Reece nodded at Haley and then entered the domain of the virus.

Reece kicked the gurney.

"Shahram!"

He kicked it again.

"Shahram!" he said louder, to overcome the slight muffle of the microphone built into his suit.

Shahram's eyes fluttered open and Reece fought back the urge to recoil.

The eyes had sunk into their sockets, the skin around them purple with broken capillaries, his entire body hemorrhaging from within as the virus liquefied organs in its quest to find a new host. The pathogen had its own mission: to live.

Shahram closed his eyes again, his breathing shallow.

"My name is Sebastian," he whispered.

"Your name is Shahram Pahlavi. Your parents are from Iran. You are a terrorist and you are about to die," Reece said without the slightest hint of sympathy.

"*Shahada*," the figure said, appearing more like a zombie than a man.

There is no God but Allah.

"I want you to listen to me closely, Shahram," Reece continued. "You do not have much time. That means you are going to have to think clearly."

Reece stepped toward the machine monitoring vitals and controlling the morphine and sedative on a timed release with intravenous fluids. He turned both machines off.

"Cremation is forbidden in Islam, Shahram. You know that. Those who are cremated go to Hell. That's what I am going to ensure happens not just to you, but to your mother and father after I kill them. Take solace in the fact that you will see them again soon, not in paradise but in the fires of *Jahannam*."

Reece could sense Haley staring at him through her gas mask. He took a knee, bringing his face closer to that of his subject.

"Your body will not be washed in accordance with your faith, nor will it go to a mosque for *Salat al-Janazah*. It's going to be packed in a refrigerated box truck along with hundreds of dead infidels, infidels that you helped kill. You will be stacked between other bodies for days, maybe months until you are incinerated."

With startling speed Shahram spit a bloody chunk of bile into his interrogator's face. The frothy red liquid hit Reece's face shield, slowly sliding down onto his suit.

Reece resisted the urge to pull back, aware he could not afford to give his target a psychological edge.

Trust the suit, Reece.

Reece slowly rose to his feet. He opened a manila folder and held up a photo. It was a beige home built against a red rock hill with a cactus dominating a small rock garden.

"Your parents' home in Scottsdale," Reece said, dropping it onto the dying man's chest.

He pulled out another photo of a woman pushing a shopping cart in a strip mall outside a Whole Foods.

"Your mother."

He dropped it onto Shahram's chest, where it stuck to the sticky vomit.

He extracted another of a man getting out of his car in the driveway of the house with the cactus.

"Your father," Reece continued. "Both will be dead in hours if you do not give me what I want. And, I'll make sure to stack their bodies with nonbelievers; better yet, I'll stack them with the Jewish bodies and then burn them together to ensure they spend eternity with you in Hell."

"Reece?" Haley said.

Even through the mask he could see the horror in her eyes.

"lā 'ilāha 'illā," Shahram recited.

There is no god but Allah.

"Enjoy your final prayers, asshole. Remember, it won't be me killing your parents. It's you."

Reece turned to leave, passing a stunned Dr. Garrett.

"Wait."

Reece turned.

"What was that?" he said.

"I don't know all of it. Just please, promise me you will bury me in accordance with sharia and not harm my mother and father."

"That is all up to you, Shahram. Your position in the afterlife and what happens to your parents all depends on what you tell me right now before you leave this world. You can't save yourself in this life, but you can save your mother and father."

"They wanted me to build a lab."

"A lab?" Reece asked.

Shahram closed his eyes.

"Who, Shahram? Your family is depending on you," Reece said, holding up the photo of his mother, now stained with blood and vomit.

"I don't know. I was just told to build a lab."

"A lab?" Haley asked, stepping forward. "What type of lab?"

"Virology. That's my specialty."

"What kind of equipment?" she asked, taking control of the interview.

"Electron microscope. Centrifuge culture cabinet. Heat vents. UV exhaust vents."

"What for?" Haley asked.

"For the kidney cells."

"Help us help you, Shahram," she said. "What kidney cells?"

"Green monkey. From Africa."

"Shahram, this is important: Did you separate them into independent cell lines? And did you introduce a sample?"

They had clearly surpassed Reece's infectious disease knowledge. He was now a spectator as Haley dove into the specifics.

Shahram coughed, more blood trickling from his mouth and nose. Reece noticed blood beginning to drip from his ears as Haley pressed on.

"Shahram, we need to know," she said, her voice calm and compassionate.

"Think of your parents, Shahram," Reece injected.

Haley turned and gave him a stare that told him to back off.

Shahram closed his eyes again.

"ašhadu 'an lā 'ilāha 'illa-llāhu, wa-'ašhadu 'anna muḥammadan rasūlu-llāhi."

I bear witness that there is no deity but God, and I bear witness that Muhammad is the messenger of God.

Reece was getting impatient. The constraints of the suit and the claustrophobia of the mask were pushing him closer to the edge. The man before him was responsible for a virus that threatened to ignite a new civil war and, more important to Reece, he was somehow connected to the assassins who had targeted him and Katie in Maryland.

Stuck upside down in the overturned Land Cruiser, drawing his pistol, eye picking up the red dot, knees exploding from the impact of the bullets, head shot.

"*Fucking talk, Shahram!* Fucking talk or I swear to God, I will fillet your mom in front of your father, before dismembering them both and burning their worthless bodies. Their souls will never find peace. They will haunt you in the afterlife."

"I . . ."

"Fucking talk!"

Haley stared at Reece in disgust, then turned back to the patient.

"Just take a breath, Shahram. Think and tell me the nature of the sample that was introduced."

Shahram's bloody eyes drifted from Haley to Reece. His vision blurred from fever and a virus that was liquefying his brain, but through the haze he studied Reece, seeing not a man but Azrael, the angel of death.

"Mar . . ." His voice trailed off, more blood dripping from his nose.

"What?" Haley asked, trying to encourage him.

"Marburg."

Haley felt the blood draining from her face.

"What type of Marburg?"

"Variant U."

Dear God in heaven.

"Where did you get it?"

Gasping for breath, his body shuddered and he retched a greenish yellow vomit mixed with tinges of dark blood onto his pillow and chest.

"Where did you get it?" Reece shouted, reinserting himself into the interrogation. "Was it this man?"

Reece shoved a blurry photo in front of Shahram, a photo he'd taken in Chicago of a figure leaving the house of his first target.

Before Shahram could avert his eyes, Reece saw the recognition.

"And the lab, Shahram. Is it in the house you bought in Denver?"

Shahram remained silent.

"Shahram," Haley said, needing more information. "How does it spread? Did you aerosolize it?"

He gave a slight nod.

"Can it be passed from human to human?"

He paused.

"Your parents, Shahram!" Reece barked.

"I don't know where it came from. How is it spread? Direct bodily fluid contact, contaminated blood. Is it a respiratory disease? I can't be certain. It was released in aerosolized form. I don't know why."

"To cause this?" Reece said, gesturing to the cots awaiting bodies against the green canvas walls of the tent.

"I don't know."

"Who knows? This man?" Reece asked, pointing to the surveillance photo he'd taken in the Windy City.

"I don't know, please." His voice was getting weaker.

"You are a *shitty* liar, Shahram. Tell me about him. Who is he?"

"Praise be to Allah, I do not know."

"He lied to you, Shahram. Did he tell you that you were part of the team? That you were a warrior of Allah? Is this how a warrior of Allah dies? He killed you, Shahram. He killed you to tie up loose ends. You were always a liability, an expendable asset. This is a man you want to protect?"

"*No,*" Shahram murmured without conviction.

"Where can I find him? How did you contact him?"

"I didn't. He came through the mosque. Please . . ."

"What mosque?"

"Please . . ."

"The FBI is raiding your house now. We are going to find everything, Shahram."

"This is all I know. *al-Ḥamdu lillāh.*"

Praise be to God.

His breath was coming in shorter gasps, eyes rolling back into their blood-filled sockets, red drops of what should have been tears trickling down his face.

"*'innā li-llāhi wa-'inna 'ilayhi,*" he whispered.

Verily we belong to Allah, and verily to Him do we return.

Reece bowed his head and whispered the *Istirja* before flipping the morphine and vital sign monitor back on and signaling to Haley that it was time to go.

They pushed their way through the clear plastic curtains and walked toward the exit, leaving Shahram Pahlavi to die a martyr, wondering if Azrael, the angel of death, would keep his promise.

CHAPTER 48

West Colfax, Denver, Colorado

THE KEY WAS TO make it look just enough like an accident to raise questions.

He'd used fire once before, on a houseboat in Amsterdam. That had been easier. He had started it in the engine compartment of a small boat moored alongside. This was different. If, *if,* authorities suspected that the virus was not naturally occurring with an index case in Angola, then a suspicious fire in a house on the outskirts of Aurora belonging to one of the first casualties might prompt some enterprising American detective or intelligence operative to start asking questions. That, or at least it would add fuel to online conspiracy theorists who would muddy the waters enough to cause even the staunchest government supporters to question the official narrative. It would be Angola or homegrown terrorism. Even though the perpetrator was of Middle Eastern descent, he was a U.S. citizen. No nukes would rocket toward Tehran, no U.S. boots would set foot on Persian soil. An America in ruins. A reshuffling of the world order.

Ali had already found antigovernment conspiracy websites theorizing that the virus was concocted in a U.S. lab, as many believed had been the case with COVID-19 in Wuhan, China. Twitter was ablaze with conjecture from shock jocks and conspiracy theorists speculating that the virus was intentionally released as justification for a federal power grab; gun confiscation was surely next, followed inevitably by reeducation facilities and, for the real troublemakers, concentration and death camps. The Bill of Rights was bound for the dustbin of history.

Ali loved the power of a free press. Its power was amplified when everyone had a voice. Theories without a foundation in facts or basis in reality could take flight and go viral. No barriers to entry. No editors. No fact checking, or if there was, it couldn't be trusted; "fact checkers" had biases and agendas, too, after all. The loudest voices dominated the chaos that was social media hysteria, and all of it contributed to the chaos. Suppression and censorship only fueled the flames.

If the Angola angle began to look dubious, Ali was setting the conditions for another, equally compelling narrative; a U.S. citizen had conducted the plan, using university assets to build a virology lab and unleash a devil upon the populace. Whichever way one leaned, the end result remained the same. The United States would continue to turn against itself, and by the time they found out the virus was not actually a respiratory-spread contagion, it would be too late. Two American cities would be destroyed, and the country would never recover. Pity that Chicago would be spared, but that could not be helped now. Even the Atlanta numbers didn't support the destruction of that city, but the few cases that had surfaced reinforced the perception that this new "Ebola strain" spread through the air. Iran would have her revenge, and no one would be the wiser. Ali would avenge the deaths of his father and two brothers, killed by an American war machine that profited from *Defā'e Moghaddas*, the *Holy Defense*, the Iran-Iraq War. Yes, Islam would be blamed if they connected Sebastian to the plot, but everyone who unleashed the virus would be gone. Investigators would hit a dead end. Two American cities would be smoldering embers without Iran ever firing a shot.

The very pinnacle of warfare.

He'd tasked Sebastian with destroying the lab. Better to keep his own involvement to a minimum. Ali had stayed behind to ensure it was done. He had not expected the virus to take hold of the young PhD student so quickly. No matter. Adapting to a changing environment was paramount. It was also why the warriors of Allah had an advantage over the entrenched bureaucracy of their enemy.

The house was so old, even the floorboards had rotted through in places. It was a prime candidate for an inferno. With so many assets allocated to investigating the fires and destruction connected to the riots and looting in downtown Denver, this incident could easily be explained away as having been started by someone building firebombs to target police. Molotov cocktails and fireworks had become popular with American insurgents in the summer of 2020. Ali even had an Antifa flag to leave behind for an arson investigator to discover in the rubble. The point was to muddy the waters with further conjecture and confusion.

He just needed to dismantle the computer in case Sebastian had been careless and left electronic evidence that could possibly implicate Ali or Iran. A fire would not destroy everything. That was part of the plan. There needed to be just enough evidence left behind to feed the conspiracies dominating social channels. He'd suit up, take what he needed from the basement, set the fire, and be out of the state before anyone connected the fire to the outbreak, if they ever did. The world gave the Americans too much credit. They had grown stupid and weak. A generation of fast food and instant gratification had left them soulless.

He thought of all he had accomplished. He remembered the wailing of the women, the rotting meat permeating his olfactory nerves, his brother hanging by his neck, legs stained with piss and shit. He briefly thought of traveling south to kill the former secretary of defense in New Mexico, the man who had prolonged and armed both sides in the *Holy Defense*, the Iran-Iraq War; the man responsible for the death of his father and two brothers. He pushed that notion aside. Rumsfeld would be dead soon. He was an old man now. Ali wanted him to see his country burning before he descended into the fires of Hell.

Ali stifled a cough. Was he coming down with something? There is no way he could have contracted the virus, was there? He'd taken precautions, unlike that idiot Ustinov. All he needed to do was dismantle the computer, start a fire, and drive east for his flight back to Europe to watch America destroy itself on Al Jazeera.

Ali grabbed a screwdriver from a drawer in the kitchen and was halfway down the stairs when he heard the knock on the door.

CHAPTER 49

Interstate 70
Denver, Colorado

"WHAT DID YOU FIND out, Reece?" Vic asked over the encrypted connection.

The Suburban sped down the deserted highway toward Denver. Ken was behind the wheel and Haley was in the backseat, quiet and still fuming at Reece's behavior with Shahram.

"This virus is not, I say again *not*, from Angola. Shahram built a virology lab in that house he bought in Denver. The man I photographed leaving my first target house in Chicago was his contact."

"Do you have a name?"

"No, but we are going to the Denver house now. Is SWAT or HRT on scene?"

"Reece, this is an unprecedented situation. SWAT and HRT have their hands full. The country is descending into chaos. Politicians are at each other's throats. Coordinating with local authorities and even federal offices is bottlenecked. Request for SWAT was approved but they are not yet on-site. There should be a black-and-white on scene now, but I have not received confirmation."

"*Shit!* Understood."

"Did he verify the type of virus. Is it airborne?"

"It's something called Marburg Variant U. Haley says it was originally from Africa and weaponized by the Soviet Union in the seventies. They were working on an aerosol delivery system."

The Suburban's brakes locked up and Reece was thrown forward in his restraint.

"What the *fuck*? What are you doing?" the commando shouted at their driver.

"Protesters, sir. They've shut down the highway."

"*Damn it!* Keep going. Just keep it slow and try not to kill anyone."

"I'm not trained for this, sir."

"Keep the doors locked, and slowly edge through them."

"What's going on, Reece?" Vic asked.

"Crowd of protesters blocking the highway."

"*Jesus Christ!*"

"Vic, you have got to tell the president this is not a naturally occurring virus. We are going to upend the Denver house and find a connection to the man in Chicago. He's the key."

The Suburban slowly approached the protesters. Their voices became louder, antigovernment signs, chants.

"Uh, Mr. Donovan," Ken said nervously from the driver's seat.

"Don't stop, just move slowly."

"Vic," Reece said back into the phone. "Tell the president not to order the strikes until we can confirm if this thing is airborne. If it's not, he's going to kill half a million people for nothing."

"The president is under serious pressure from both sides of the aisle to stop the spread, to do the unthinkable."

"What? I thought the final option was a closely guarded secret?"

"It was, but it leaked. It's not out in the public yet but enough people are talking about it in Congress that it won't be long."

"Uh, sir?" Ken said.

The Suburban was completely surrounded. Protesters pounded on the hood and windows as the large black vehicle crept forward.

"I don't like this, sir."

"Neither do I. Just keep going."

Antifa signs repurposed from the events of the past year were held aloft by men and women in black hoodies with masks. One man climbed up over the hood and onto the top of the slow-moving vehicle, slamming his fist onto the roof and screaming obscenities.

"Keep it slow," Reece said. "Just don't stop."

"Surprised you don't just plow through them," came Haley's voice from the passenger row.

"I don't want to hurt these people. I understand their position. That being said, I will not let them keep us from our mission."

Reece and Haley were still dressed in the CBRN suits they had changed back into as they reversed the sanitization and sterilization process on their way back through the mobile level-four biocontainment module. Their masks were off as soon as they were well out of the containment zone and DMZ.

"What's happening, Reece?" Vic asked, the strain in his voice obvious.

"Still working our way through these protesters."

"Get to that house. Find me something that confirms this is not airborne. Something concrete. If not, I fear the president will have no choice. If destroying these cities saves the country, possibly the world, he's got no choice."

"Just hold him off. Do not drop. Give me time."

Even at the slow pace, Reece jolted forward in his seat when Ken slammed on the brakes again.

Reece looked ahead and saw why they'd stopped.

The crowd had parted. Four armed men blocked the path, pointing shotguns and ARs directly at the front window of the Suburban.

CHAPTER 50

REECE DIDN'T HESITATE.

OODA—Observe, orient, decide, act.

Weapons. Enemy. Threat.

Reece picked up his left leg and pushed it over the center console, slamming it onto the gas pedal. At the same time as all 420 horses leapt to life, he grabbed the steering wheel.

Their vehicle had become a weapon.

Steel shot from the scattergun impacted the passenger side of the windshield, which spiderwebbed across the screen. Two of the ARs barked, one missing completely, the shots going wildly high over the vehicle and protesters. The man with the second AR found his target just before the large vehicle connected with him and sent him careening to the side. The driver's side of the windshield diverted the trajectory of the bullets but not enough.

Ken's body absorbed a round that drove down into his stomach. A second hit his headrest. A third entered his shoulder and fragmented into the top of his heart. A fourth passed through his throat, spraying blood across the steering wheel, dashboard, and the left side of Reece's face.

Haley screamed as the large vehicle thumped over the man with the shotgun, dragging him for a few yards down the road before the right rear tire caught his leg and spit him out.

"Get down!" Reece yelled at Haley.

He kept his foot on the gas, driving from the passenger seat, putting distance between them and the threat as bullets whizzed overhead and along the pavement beside them.

Ken's body slumped forward in his seat belt, body draining of blood, draining of life. Reece elbowed him back in his seat and kept him pinned in place as he put more distance between them and their attackers, the Suburban speeding up past 100 mph.

Reece moved his elbow from Ken's chest and attempted to apply pressure to the throat wound with his left palm, while keeping the car on the road, his hand slick with blood.

He took his eyes from the highway to assess Ken's wounds. Instead of a young, freshly shaven face with an unruly mop of blond hair, he saw a young bearded SEAL in body armor and helmet behind the wheel of a Hilux truck on a dusty road on the outskirts of a village in Afghanistan, Reece holding the wheel while attempting to stem the flow of blood spurting from his Teammate's neck, just before another AK round tore his head off.

"Reece! Reece!"

Haley's screams brought him back to reality and he swerved to keep the Suburban on the road.

"Stop the car, Reece. Stop the car!" she shouted.

Reece looked in the still-intact rearview mirror and confirmed they were off the X and about two miles down the road from the ambush. He pulled to the side of the empty freeway and turned his attention to Ken, holding pressure on his throat and sliding a finger through the blood to plug the hole.

"This thing should have a trauma kit!" Reece yelled to Haley. "In the back. Find it!"

Haley threw open her door and ran to the back of the Suburban.

"It's locked! Hit the unlock button!"

Shit!

Reece moved farther across his seat, pushing a finger from his left hand into the hole in Ken's neck, his right hand slippery with blood, searching desperately for the button on the driver's-side door to release the back lift gate.

"Got it!"

Reece heard a beep as the rear lift gate arched skyward, Haley reaching underneath to accelerate its power-assisted movement.

She appeared at the driver's side door and Reece grabbed the handle to open it.

"I've got him," Haley said, tracing Reece's fingers to the hole in Ken's neck and packing it with gauze from the kit.

As Reece felt Haley replace his fingers with gauze, he pushed himself back to the passenger seat and exited the vehicle, his eyes scanning in all directions for threats as he rushed to Haley's side and helped ease Ken to the ground.

Haley continued to stuff Ken's neck wound with gauze while Reece took a knee and ran his hands over Ken's body looking for additional injuries, finding the entry wound in his shoulder and immediately applying pressure.

"Another entry wound. Left shoulder!" he shouted.

"Reece," Haley said calmly.

"Do we have more gauze?"

"Reece," she said again.

This time Reece picked his head up.

"He's gone, Reece."

Reece looked back to the shoulder wound, then to the throat, and then into the eyes.

Ken's face was ashen. There was no rise or fall of the chest. No beating of the heart.

Reece looked at his hands, then to Haley. The left side of his face was covered with what was now drying blood. Ken's blood.

He saw a young SEAL lying in the red Afghan dirt. The left side of his head was missing.

"Reece, he's gone," Haley said again, the compassion in her voice directed at the former SEAL commander.

Reece shook the Afghan memory from his mind.

Without another word, he stood, hoisted the young CIA analyst to his shoulder, and laid him in the back of the Suburban.

"Load up. We have work to do."

CHAPTER 51

West Colfax, Denver, Colorado

REECE PULLED THE SUBURBAN to the curb a block from the target house.

The street was deserted, though this was not the type of neighborhood whose residents would have second homes in Aspen or Telluride. These families were sequestered to protect themselves and their loved ones from the unseen threat of a virus with an epicenter only miles away.

"Which one is it?" Haley asked.

"That one," Reece said, pointing. "See the beige Crown Vic?"

"Yeah."

"That's an unmarked police car."

"I don't see the cop," Haley observed.

"Neither do I. One car in the driveway," Reece continued, looking at the dark late-model Jeep Cherokee backed up to the garage. "Can you tell what state those license plates are from?"

"New York, I think," Haley said, squinting through her glasses.

"That's what it looks like to me, too. Maybe a rental?" Reece said aloud.

"Could be."

"Haley, I don't know what to say. We would not be here without you."

Reece paused.

"I need to tell you something that's highly classified. It's probably going to break into the news cycle soon anyway. I just need you to know why we're doing this."

"To find the source of this virus. I know why we're are doing it."

"That's part of it but I'm talking consequences. Haley, if the president and Congress think that a virus with an eighty-five to ninety percent mortality rate is airborne, highly contagious, and confined to two U.S. cities, they, or I should say, the commander in chief, has an option at his disposal to contain the spread."

"Not a vaccine. We talked about that. There isn't one yet and you don't miraculously create one by finding a monkey or index case like in the movies."

"No, not a vaccine. A more drastic solution."

"I don't understand. There is likely evidence in this house to prove that the virus is aerosolized, that someone has to physically come into contact with the aerosolized virus. Those infected can only spread it the same way Ebola is spread, through direct blood or bodily fluid contact, not via respiratory pathways. Once we have that evidence, I get it to the CDC, and we let the American people know it's not contagious in the way they've been led to believe. We continue to treat the infected but without the fear that a cough or sneeze will spread it. If we prove it's a bioweapon and that it was aerosolized in an attack on Aurora and Richardson, we can move forward rationally."

"We are on the clock, Haley, and so is the president. If we can't prove beyond a shadow of a doubt that this is not being spread from person to person, the president is going to incinerate the containment zones to prevent the spread."

"*What?* Just like I saw in Africa?"

"What choice does he have? It's either two cities or 280 million people in the U.S. alone."

"*We wouldn't destroy our own cities, would we?*" Haley said in utter disbelief. "How do you even do that? Nuke our own country? The radiation would be devastating far beyond the borders of the containment zones."

"Not a nuke. A fuel air explosive. The largest nonnuclear device in the arsenal."

"How long have you known this?"

"Just before we questioned Shahram."

Haley's eyes glistened over, her breathing pronounced, her mind weighing the options and possibilities.

"I need to make one more call, and I'm going to show you how to use this thing," Reece said, holding up the KryptAll mobile phone. "Then I'm going in that house. If anyone other than me comes out, tail them and call Vic. Help vector the cavalry in but stay back. You've gotten us to this point. No one knows more about what's going on and what's at stake than you do."

Haley watched in silence as Reece showed her how to use the encrypted phone to dial the CIA.

"Vic, run this plate: Echo, Bravo, Foxtrot—Eight, Four, Seven, Three."

"Stand by, Reece," Vic said. Reece could hear him passing the information to an analyst in the background.

"Vic, we lost Ken Daniel. Shot by the protesters. I'm so sorry."

Silence.

"Vic?"

"*Shit.* Reece, I . . ." Vic paused and took a breath. "SWAT is en route to your location. I'd ask you to stay outside and wait but I know you won't, so I'll refrain from wasting my breath."

"What's the status on the final option?"

"Just came from the director's office. She bought us until the end of this cycle of darkness. Then he's launching. Congress was informed via an emergency session. They are all in mandatory lockdown on Capitol Hill but the word will get out. They are all thinking about protecting their constituents and what happens if ninety percent of them die. This is going to leak, Reece. When it does there will be mass chaos and the president will have to speed up the timeline. If those trapped in Aurora and Richardson get wind of this, there will be a mass rush on the containment barriers and the virus will get out."

Reece closed his eyes and whispered a quick prayer.

"Reece, are you there?"

"I'm here."

Reece heard mumbling on the other end of the phone.

"Okay, that car is a rental. Enterprise. Rented by an Ali Ansari through a corporate account of a company called BioDine out of Switzerland. Doing a deep dive on Ansari now."

Reece's mind was spinning.

"Reece?"

"I'm here, Vic."

"I don't need to tell you what happens if Ali is the connection to this virus. If he has the answers that can save Aurora and Richardson."

"I know, Vic. We need him alive."

"Do what you can, Reece. I'll keep the director up to date so she can relay this to the White House."

"I'm giving Haley this phone so she can contact you if something happens to me. I'm going in."

"Godspeed, Reece."

He hung up and looked at Haley. Her revulsion at his actions with Shahram had been replaced with a newfound respect.

"Be careful, Reece. Remember, you are going into a bio lab, more accurately a virology lab, and if what Shahram told us is true, one of the deadliest pathogens in the history of the world was grown and converted into an aerosolized weapon in that house. Wear your gas mask. It might not be enough; we are dealing with too many variables and unknowns to be sure."

"If I don't come back . . ." Reece cleared his throat. "Um, Katie knows how I feel but, um, could you, uh . . ."

"I'll tell her, Reece."

Reece nodded, press-checked his SIG, and exited into the brisk afternoon air.

CHAPTER 52

REECE HELD HIS PISTOL by his right leg as he approached the target house.

To anyone watching from the windows of the surrounding homes, it must have been a peculiar sight, though perhaps less so after the events that had recently engulfed the nation. A man in a tan hazmat suit, with a gas mask in his left hand and pistol in his right, walking down the street in broad daylight.

Reece passed the Crown Vic and glanced inside. Empty.

He worked his way up the driveway, clearing the Cherokee as he passed.

He moved to the front door and attempted to turn the handle. Locked.

Fuck! This is the last time I go anywhere without my picks.

Reece was tempted to kick in the door, but if he had not yet given up the element of surprise, he wanted to maintain that tactical advantage as long as possible.

His mind briefly flashed back to a compound in the Hindu Kush, then a cartel drug house in Tijuana, tomahawk in hand . . .

Focus, Reece.

He backtracked down the front steps and to a side gate to a small backyard overgrown with weeds. He reached over the top and flipped up the latch on the other side.

An HVAC unit blew hot air out from a basement.

Reece moved to the corner of the house and took it wide, working the angles.

Tactical movement is a problem of angles.

The backyard was empty but for a rusty swing set and cracked concrete pad with an old Weber charcoal grill. A chain-link fence separated it from its neighbor. A sliding glass door allowed access to the home and Reece could see that it opened into a kitchen.

He crept to the side of the glass. As he'd been taught in sniper school all those years ago, his eyes scanned near to far through the glass. Lying on the floor between the kitchen and the hallway that led to the front door was a body.

Reece pushed on the sliding door. Locked.

The smell of smoke reached Reece's nostrils at the same time he saw movement through the glass. The sixth sense worked both ways. A man in a level-four bio-containment suit and mask stepped over the body and turned toward Reece.

Reece's brain registered the gun moving toward him. He ducked to the side of the sliding door as four rounds pierced the glass and impacted the stucco wall of the adjacent home.

Reece changed levels, taking a knee, and at an angle sent two 9mm projectiles toward the shadow that sprinted across the kitchen entrance. Standing, he made his decision.

The man inside was wearing a self-contained suit. *Shit!*

Reece donned his gas mask, grabbed the small Weber grill, and sent it careening through the sliding glass door, already damaged from six bullet holes. Reece entered right behind the grill, glass cascading to the floor. He held on to the open door that led to a small hallway. A quick glance told him the dead body was a police officer and that his gun was missing from his holster.

Reece looked to his right and noticed smoke coming from under a door.

Win the fight, Reece.

If this is Ali and you kill him, you have also killed half a million of your countrymen.

Fuck!

You have a terrorist in a barricaded position whom you have to capture alive.

You have no body armor, no helmet, no technical or tactical advantages.

You are fighting in a CBRN suit and mask with a pistol in a house on fire, possibly contaminated with a deadly pathogen, the fire destroying evidence you need to save the country.

Never pay attention to the odds.

Reece turned and worked his way back into the kitchen and to a closed door off the pantry.

Slow is smooth, smooth is fast.

The smoke is getting thicker, Reece. You can't stay in here forever.

You'll stay in here as long as it takes.

The door opened into a bedroom.

Clear.

Where are you, motherfucker?

Reece felt the heat building under the floor through his suit and shoes, the inside of his mask fogging up with condensation.

Think, Reece.

He moved back into a small hallway, weapon up, searching, scanning, attempting to override his instinct to shoot center mass, knowing he had to somehow take his prey alive.

Laundry room.

Another door.

Possibly to the garage?

Reece deliberately pushed the door open to find a garage stacked with boxes. He registered they were labeled with the names of companies in the scientific space.

Don't rush to your death.

Make your enemy rush to his.

Reece looked at the wall and saw the button for the garage door. He hit the button and heard the door lurch upward on its tracks. Seeing sunlight leak into the dark garage, Reece moved back into the house toward the flames.

CHAPTER 53

THE INFLUX OF AIR from the broken sliding glass door and the open garage door had its intended effect. The fire had heat. It had fuel. And now it had more oxygen.

The old rotting wooden floor beneath his feet began to seep gray smoke, flames visible through the floorboards.

Reece positioned himself down the hallway, where he had a semi-clear field of view. He would be able to see if Ali made a break for the garage, front door, or backyard. The backyard was a confined space. The front door would take a moment to open. The path to the garage was the most likely avenue of egress.

The question was, who could stand the heat the longest?

Sweat dripped down Reece's face. He could feel himself beginning to cook, feel the suit beginning to melt.

Come on, Ali. Come out.

Be still, Reece.

Patience.

You are a sniper.

Wait.

Movement.

There!

The man in a full level-four bio-containment suit rushed for the open garage door.

Resisting the urge to shoot, Reece sprinted down the hall.

Action is faster than reaction.

With the mask blocking much of his peripheral vision and in the heat and smoke of the fire, Reece hit his opponent from the side just as he was about to bolt through the laundry room door to freedom. Reece struck him just above the waist with his shoulder, taking him back into the smoldering hallway.

The impact snatched Ali's breath away, his hand instinctually moving the gun toward the man who had taken him to the ground.

Reece heard the bullet impact the ceiling and immediately pivoted to control the weapon hand.

A sharp pain in his shoulder told Reece that there was another weapon in play. Violently twisting the pistol from the terrorist's grip, Reece smashed it into Ali's mask, the self-contained unit absorbing much of the blow's impact. Instinctually Reece trapped Ali's other hand, which held a screwdriver.

Reece now had a gun in each hand that he couldn't use, weapons that were making it hard to control the screwdriver in Ali's left hand. Even when not trapped in a burning house with noxious gases filling the air, a screwdriver could be just as deadly as a blade. Still entangled on the ground, Reece shifted to control the left hand and felt Ali's right reach up to grab the air filter on his mask in an attempt to rip it from his head.

Gas. Fire. Virus. Panic.

Reece pulled back and jumped to his feet, pulling his mask from Ali's grasp. He threw Ali's gun down the hall behind him and brought his gun up.

"Stay down, motherfucker. Don't move!"

Ali looked up at the man pointing the pistol at him.

Shit, he knows I can't shoot him. He's the connection.

Ali got to his feet, screwdriver still in hand.

Flames leapt from the door at the far end of the hall.

Reece threw the SIG down the hallway behind them and charged forward to take the fight to his enemy. Two steps into his sprint, the rotting floor gave way beneath him and his left leg broke through the floor, pulling him toward the fire below.

CHAPTER 54

ARRESTED IN PLACE, REECE regained his balance in time to parry the attack by his adversary, blocking the screwdriver with his left arm and sending Ali into the hallway wall.

Attempting to yank his foot from the hole, seeing flames through the disintegrating floor beneath him, he saw Ali recognize that he was trapped. The terrorist lurched toward the pistols at the end of the hall.

No fucking way, Ali.

With his foot still trapped in the hole, Reece fell backward and grabbed Ali's foot with his left hand, tripping him to the ground. Reece wrapped the leg and pulled the lighter man back toward him.

Understanding the strength of his attacker, Ali redirected his movement, and instead of pulling away he turned back toward Reece with the screwdriver. The sudden change in direction freed Reece's foot, which he yanked back out of the hole, the leg of his suit melting into his flesh.

Both men scrambled to their feet, struggling to breathe in the heat of their suits, Reece positioned between the man and all exits from the burning building.

When backed into a corner, animals will either run or fight. Ali had nowhere to run. With astonishing speed, the screwdriver slashed for Reece's neck. Blocking it with both hands, Reece quickly reached over Ali's bicep, grabbing his forearm and putting him in a figure-four arm lock, controlling the weapon and torquing his shoulder to the outside of his body. Reece stepped into his attacker, throwing his right foot around the back of his opponent's leg, sweeping him to the ground. The small oxygen bottle strapped to Ali's back sent a debilitating nerve pain through his spine when he hit the floor. Reece followed him down, landing on top of him with a knee on his stomach. Still controlling the arm with the screwdriver, Reece switched knees, redirecting Ali's energy and stabbing the screwdriver into the terrorist's thigh. Even through the suit Reece could hear Ali scream in agony. Transitioning to his other knee, Reece improved his position and drove a palm strike into the back of the tool, imbedding it even deeper into the muscles of Ali's leg. Writhing in pain, Ali reached up and frantically grabbed at Reece's mask. Reece parried the first hand and landed a palm strike to the face, the pressurized suit once again absorbing much of the hit.

Thrashing in a primal fight for life, Ali grabbed Reece's mask with two hands.

Virus. Smoke. Death.

Panic.

Regain control, Reece.

Reece trapped Ali's hands to his own mask to prevent him from pulling it off. Vision obscured by his enemy's fingers and palms, Reece's free hand went back to the screwdriver still embedded in Ali's leg. Pulling the tool from Ali's thigh, Reece surgically indexed Ali's top hand with its side, slowly inserting the flathead between the metacarpal bones of Ali's hand, careful not to punch it through his own mask.

Feeling the side of the screwdriver pressing though his gloved hand, Ali let go of Reece's mask and snatched his hand back to cover his face. Too late. Reece pinned Ali's arm under his knee, indexed the back edge of the tool on Ali's forearm, and filleted his arm to his biceps, pressing it deep into his shoulder socket.

Jerking the tool up to Ali's elbow, he used his left hand to control the wrist, forcing the man to roll over onto his stomach. With his knee firmly planted on Ali's back, Reece retracted the screwdriver and dug it into the Ali's other elbow, using the leverage to pull the arm out and behind the back.

Fuck! I need some handcuffs.

Detecting a moment of hesitation, Ali exploded out of the submission with an animalistic scream, knocking Reece off balance and shooting in on him from the floor. Still on his knees, Reece sprawled, snaking his right arm across his opponent's throat, latching on to his left biceps in an anaconda choke. Reece flattened the man out and rolled toward his left side, using the hallway wall to walk his hips into the attacker, tightening the choke.

Seconds later, Reece felt Ali's last flutter of resistance as he went limp.

Starved for oxygen through a filter not designed for smoke inhalation, Reece peeled himself away from Ali's unconscious body. Feeling lightheaded from the smoke and heat, Reece looked back down the hall toward the body by the front door. Not trusting how long the blood-deprived brain of his opponent would stay shut off from the world, Reece grabbed Ali's right arm, feeling it pull from its socket, and dragged him down the smoke-filled hallway. Reece knelt by the downed police officer and checked for a pulse. Nothing. He then reached around to the back of his belt for his handcuffs.

It was only after he cuffed both of the terrorist's hands behind his back that he noticed the bright red arterial blood spraying from Ali's femoral artery.

CHAPTER 55

NOT KNOWING EXACTLY WHAT to do when she saw the house start to go up in flames, Haley had called 9-1-1 to report a fire.

She breathed an audible sigh when the door flew open and she saw Reece rush outside. He had a man in a bio-containment suit on his shoulders.

"Shit!" she said, hitting the start button and putting the large vehicle in drive.

Reece stopped at the base of the driveway, looked to Haley approaching in the black SUV, and continued across the street to get away from the heat of the growing inferno. He dropped the man unceremoniously to the ground as Haley screeched to a halt, blocking a neighbor's driveway with the Suburban.

"Oh my God! Reece, are you okay?" she asked, exiting the vehicle and taking in his injuries.

Reece ripped the mask from his face and sucked in the cool Colorado air. He put his hands on his knees to steady himself and then straightened back up, looking from Haley to the still-unconscious form at his feet.

"I'll live. I think," Reece said, rolling his shoulder from where the screwdriver had impacted and looking down at the burns on his left leg.

"Get me out of this thing," he demanded, pawing at the neck seal on his suit.

"Here, let me," Haley said, helping him remove what was left of his protective equipment.

With the suit off, Reece was able to access the Northman blade in his pocket. He knelt and cut the plastic attached hood and face shield off the terrorist's bio suit.

"Do you have that phone?" Reece asked, holding out his hand.

"Yes, right here," Haley said, handing it to him. "I also called 9-1-1 when the house started to go up."

Reece glanced up and down the street. He could hear sirens in the distance. He saw neighbors now looking out at the fire from their windows and at the strangers in the street, still afraid to come outside because of the confusion surrounding the virus.

"Good move," Reece said, a plan forming in his mind.

"He's got an arterial bleed on his right leg. Apply pressure."

Haley took Reece's hazmat suit and placed a portion of it over the terrorist's wound, pushing down with both hands in an attempt to stem the flow of blood.

"He's not going to make it long if we don't stop this," she observed.

"I know."

Reece took multiple photos of the man the Jeep in the driveway suggested was Ali Ansari and sent them to Vic via encrypted message along with the text: "Ali Ansari? Confirm."

"Where's your gun?" Haley asked.

"Melting inside."

The sirens were growing louder.

"Haley, we need to get out of here and back to the airport. Whatever is in that house is gone. Ali here is our only link to the virus and he's bleeding out."

Haley stared at the man before her: left pant leg shredded with what were obviously serious burns in need of attention, bloody shoulder, drenched in sweat. And possibly the only man who could prevent a disaster unprecedented in American history.

"I'm in, Reece. Let's stop this thing."

"Wait here."

Reece dashed back across the street to the Crown Victoria, holding up his arm in a vain attempt to block the heat of the burning home. He bent down, pulled a stone from the dirt- and weed-infested front lawn that bordered the driveway, and threw it through the driver's-side window. He reached in, unlocked the door, and opened it. Quickly searching for the trunk release, he pulled it and ran to the rear of the vehicle. Among a few bottles of water, jumper cables, trauma bag, police windbreaker, and a black plate carrier with body armor was what Reece was looking for: a 12-gauge Remington 870. He pulled out the dependable old shotgun and pressed the action release. There was not a round in the chamber, so Reece flipped it over and checked to make sure the tube was loaded. He then grabbed the trauma kit and police windbreaker before running back across the street.

"Here, put this on," he said, tossing the windbreaker to Haley, who now had her knee on the wound.

Reece's phone buzzed.

Confirmation: Ali Reza Ansari. BioDine executive. Entered U.S. one month ago. Swiss citizen. Originally from Iran.

Reece shoved the phone in his pocket, then knelt and put the shotgun on the ground. He unzipped the trauma kit and pulled out a North American Rescue Combat Application Tourniquet.

"The wound is too high. That might not do it," Haley said. "We are going to need to clamp it."

An ambulance turned onto the street. Reece could hear additional sirens in the distance that he assumed were fire trucks.

"Haley? Have you ever stolen an ambulance?"

CHAPTER 56

LUCKILY, THE AMBULANCE ARRIVED on scene before any other emergency vehicles. Haley had waved it down in her oversize police windbreaker.

Reece showed the driver and paramedic his U.S. Marshal credentials and gave them a half-truth about needing to save the life of his "suspect." He doubted the first responders would be understanding or supportive of what Reece was prepared to do to their patient to get the information he needed. Together, they loaded the man into the back of the ambulance, and as the fire trucks turned onto the street, Reece was glad he'd grabbed the shotgun. It helps to be armed when stealing a government vehicle.

"Haley!" Reece yelled from the back of the ambulance, where he sat with Ali Ansari duct-taped to the gurney. "Can you get us to the interstate and back to the airport?"

"I think so," she said, speeding through the streets with sirens still on.

"The police are too busy dealing with an insurrection to look for a stolen ambulance, but you never know."

"Yeah, on their list of priorities, I agree this is not at the top."

"We need to keep him alive long enough for me to ask him some questions."

"You know I'm a microbiologist, not a trauma surgeon, right?"

"I know; turn off the sirens and park by the overpass up ahead. I'm going to need help with this. He doesn't look good."

Reece cut Ali's right bio-suit leg off with trauma shears as Haley pulled the ambulance to the side of the road under the overpass. She kept the vehicle running and joined Reece in back.

"Okay," she said, pulling on rubber gloves and assessing the wound, noting Reece had used the tape from the trauma kit to tie Ali's hands and legs to the gurney.

Blood pumped from the wound, covering Reece, Haley, the gurney, and the floor of the ambulance.

"The vein runs under the adductor muscle and medial, and the nerve runs lateral exposing the artery," she said to herself, thinking back to her time in the ER during rotations. "V-A-N: vein—artery—nerve. Medial to lateral, three inches below the inguinal ligament."

"What does that mean?" Reece asked, unable to control the urgency in his voice.

"It means the tourniquet is not working. He's going to be dead in minutes if not seconds."

"*Shit!* Let's clamp it."

"Find the clamps and any IV bags. They are in here somewhere," she said, turning to go through the drawers and cabinets behind her.

Reece did the same, rummaging through the unfamiliar space on his side.

Ali's eyes fluttered open and he managed a weak moan.

"Don't you worry, Ali. We are going to save your life, but only so you can answer questions."

"Found the IV bags," Haley said.

"And I think these are the clamps," Reece said, grabbing the longest tool from a drawer labeled HEMOSTAT.

"Those will work," Haley responded.

She looked down at the wound, still spitting blood.

"I can't see or do anything through that hole. Just hold the pressure. It will take me a second to get this set up," she said.

Reece pushed back down on the wound with both hands, looking into Ali's glassy eyes. He was on the verge of unconsciousness.

"We have to stop this bleeding," she said.

Reece removed his hands from the terrorist's leg, blood continuing to pump from the body.

"Damn it," Haley said. "I can't see in there. The puncture wound is too small."

As she finished her sentence, Reece unsheathed his knife and stuck the tip in the hole, slicing up and then down Ali's leg to enlarge the wound.

Ali's eyes opened wide and he gasped in pain.

"*Reece!* What are you doing?" Haley shouted.

"Now you can see. Clamp it," he said, handing her the hemostat.

Haley took a breath to clear her head.

"Haley, this man is responsible for deaths of thousands and is the key to saving millions more. *Clamp it.*"

Haley grabbed the hemostat from Reece and jabbed it into Ali's leg, using her free hand to manipulate the wound to give her better access.

Ali's screams filled the interior of the ambulance.

"*Shit!*" she said. "Probably clamped the nerve."

Haley repositioned herself and steadied her breathing.

"Vein, artery, nerve," she repeated, as she clamped down again, bringing the arterial pump to a stop.

"Yes! Nice work!" Reece said.

"He needs fluids, or we are going to lose him!"

Haley pulled a bag of lactated Ringer's solution from a drawer along with an 18-gauge IV needle, twisting his left arm, taped to the gurney, in an attempt to find a vein.

"Did you have to tape him up? Hard to get a stick like this."

Reece slashed the tape with his fixed blade.

"Better?"

"Better," Haley confirmed.

"Just need the right angle," she said, missing the sticks on her first three attempts.

"Jesus, where did you go to medical school?"

"*Fuck you*, Reece. His veins are collapsing. There is nothing to put it in. I can't get a stick."

"What about the subclavian vein?" Reece asked.

"And where did *you* go to medical school?"

"I saw a PJ do it in Iraq. Saved my friend's life."

"All right. I haven't done one since my third year of med school, but let's try."

Haley switched positions as Reece retaped Ali's hand to the gurney. She assessed the patient's upper chest and neck. Feeling her way around the clavicle, she placed her index finger in the sternal notch and her thumb at an angle to guide the needle.

"Here goes," she said, inserting it just below the clavicle and above the first rib. She was rewarded with an instant return of dark blood.

Ali let out a groan.

With a spurt of venous blood returning to the syringe, she hooked up the IV, wiped sweat from her forehead, and squeezed half the IV bag into the man on the gurney.

Haley leaned back against the drawers in the cramped space of the ambulance. The three of them were covered in blood, but all were alive.

"You drive. I'll take it from here," Reece said.

"What are you going to do?" she asked.

"Whatever I have to."

CHAPTER 57

ALI WATCHED, OBVIOUSLY STILL in intense pain, breathing labored as Reece read the labels on bottles from the narcotics locker. Haley drove in silence, concentrating on getting them to the private side of the airport and back to the CIA Gulfstream, putting up a mental barrier between herself and what was going on in the rear of the ambulance.

"I know you," Ali whispered.

Reece turned his attention from the medical cabinet to the terrorist strapped to the gurney.

"Yeah? I do tend to get around."

"I saw your car in Chicago. And I saw you in Atlanta. You should be dead."

Reece paused, considering his next move.

"I know you, too, Dr. Ali Reza Ansari. BioDine. Originally from Iran."

"You know nothing," Ali said, forcing a confident smile.

"I have a few pieces, but I don't know everything. You are going to fill in some blanks for me."

"It's too late. I know you are not going to let me live. I am just an innocent Muslim targeted by the xenophobic American intelligence community, a victim of a systemically racist government."

"Yeah, well, the ministry of truth might be on your side. Unfortunately for you, I found a bottle of succinylcholine in the fridge here. Do you know what that is?"

Ali's eyes widened. He was familiar with the drug.

"I was just sent a file with your resume. Very impressive. With a background like that, I bet you know all about succinylcholine. I don't even have to tell you what it does," Reece informed his subject.

Reece knew it well. It had been a favorite of the CIA doctors assigned to his covert action unit in Iraq. They had developed techniques that left no physical marks on the body. This was one of them. The American public was familiar with waterboarding. They had never read an article or heard talking heads debate the merits or legalities of this technique. Waterboarding had nothing on what Reece was preparing to do.

"In case you need a refresher course, it's a muscle paralytic, meaning it's going to paralyze every muscle in your body. You will be able to hear, see, and feel everything, but you will not be able to move. Most notably, you will not be able to breathe."

Ali shifted nervously in his restraints.

"You cannot do this to me. I am a Swiss citizen. I demand to see an attorney and a representative at the consulate."

"Unfortunately, I am not with the FBI, the police, or any agency who gives a *shit*. Let's see if this stuff works as well as I remember."

Reece held up a bag valve mask.

"Do you know what this is?" he asked. "Of course, you do. You're a doctor. It's an Ambu bag, an artificial respirator."

Reece extracted 50 mg of succinylcholine from a bottle into a syringe and injected it into the IV port.

Ali's eyes widened again, and he thrashed in an attempt to free his hands of the duct tape.

"It might take a second or two to fully take effect," Reece advised, pulling a strip of silver duct tape from the roll.

Ten seconds later, Ali went limp as the drug paralyzed his body to include the organs that facilitated breathing.

"You won't be able to open your eyes on your own, so this will ensure you can see everything I'm doing," Reece said, taping Ali's eyelids open. "I'd hate for you to miss out.

"When this first dose wears off, I'll have some questions. If you answer them to my satisfaction, I might let you live. If you don't, well, there is plenty of succinylcholine for us to keep this up for hours, maybe even days. I can carve you up, remove fingers, toes, I might even cut your balls and dick off. You won't be able to move, but you will feel and see, that I assure you. Don't worry, though. I don't think that will be necessary. Taking your air will be all I need to do."

As Ali's ability to breathe shut down completely, Reece gave him thirty seconds before leaning over and placing the self-inflating Ambu bag over his nose and mouth, squeezing it to give him a life-sustaining breath.

"Reece, what are you doing back there?" Haley asked nervously from the driver's seat.

"I'm not sure you want to know."

"Jesus, Reece."

"Just drive."

Reece lifted up one of Ali's fingers, confirming there was no muscle tone. The succinylcholine was working exactly as intended.

Reece came off the breathing bag and watched Ali's eyes. The man was alive but had no control of his body. The very breath that sustained life now came from an infidel.

Reece wiped the blood from the face of his Rolex and counted the second hands ticking away.

"On average, it takes four to six minutes for the brain to die of oxygen starvation. With all your blood loss it will probably be a lot less."

At the one-minute mark Reece gave Ali another breath.

"Ali, I already know the virus is Marburg Variant U. Your little helper broke like all you warriors of Allah. Tough when you are blowing up women and children or beheading prisoners but weak little *bitches* when put to the test. When this dose wears off, all you need to do is tell me where it came from, and if or how it transmits from human to human. I also want to know who came up with this plan and why. If we can work our way through that, we will take you to the hospital. If not, you are going to the morgue."

Reece gave Ali another breath as he began to stir, the paralytic diluting enough for him to begin breathing on his own, the resolve in his eyes replaced by fear.

"You are going to talk to me, Ali," Reece said, drawing a second dose from the bottle.

Ali muttered something inaudible.

"That's not clear enough, Ali," he said before injecting another 50 mg into the IV.

Reece looked back at his watch. At the three-minute mark he gave Ali a breath, forcing precious air into the lungs and brain of a man dying in silent terror from suffocation, unable to do a thing about it.

Haley turned in her seat.

"Reece, feel his forehead."

"It's hot. He's burning up."

"*Shit*, malignant hyperthermia."

"What's that?" Reece asked.

"It's a side effect of multiple doses of that drug you are giving him."

Reece gave him another breath.

"*Damn it*, Reece. He's going to hit 107 and seize. You are going to kill him before you get what we need."

"What can I do?"

"Look in the locker for something called Dantrolene."

Reece pulled the breathing bag from Ali's face and frantically searched the locker, reading labels and throwing bottles to the side.

"Could it have another name?" he shouted, as Haley sped down the highway.

"Possibly: Dantrium, Dantamacrin, or Dantrolen."

"Shit, I just tossed Dantrium," Reece said, scrambling to the discarded bottles rolling around on the floor of the moving vehicle until he found what he was looking for.

"Got it."

"Good. Inject twenty milligrams into the line."

Reece pushed the drug into the IV port and gave Ali another breath as the muscle paralytic wore off.

Haley leaned across the seat and jerked a Yeti cooler from the floor of the passenger side onto the seat. Opening the lid, she pulled out a sandwich and dropped it to the seat. She fished around inside with her right hand and removed a Gatorade and two artificial ice packs.

"Put these in his armpits and groin to help cool him down," she said, tossing them back to Reece.

Ali gasped as the ability to breathe on his own slowly returned. He had never been so utterly helpless, at the complete mercy of another. *Who was this American devil?* He thought of his brother hanging from the noose. Had he regretted his decision to take his own life? Had he desperately tried to loosen the rope that constricted the blood and oxygen to his brain? Ali wondered if he would shit and piss himself the way his brother had.

"What are you thinking about, Ali? Ready to go another round?"

"It came from Angola."

"What was that?" Reece asked, hitting the voice recorder on his phone.

"It came from Angola, or it came from a lab here in America, grown by a radicalized U.S. citizen named Sebastian Phillips. I was only here for a job interview. That's the story that this country will believe."

Without hesitation, Reece injected 75 mg of the paralyzing muscle agent into the IV and watched first the seconds and then the minutes tick by on his watch. He imagined the MC-130s taking off from Hurlburt, the pilots vectoring toward their targets, dropping the MOABs on citizens of their own country. He saw Lauren and Lucy playing together at a park in Coronado, looking up at an unfamiliar whistling sound as the bomb vectored in to explode overhead. Lauren became Katie, rushing to Lucy to shield her with her own body, Lucy's curiosity turning to terror, screaming as the fuel-air explosive burned their bodies from existence.

"*Reece!*" screamed Haley, jolting Reece back to the present.

"I'm here. I'm here!"

"He's seizing!" Haley yelled, twisting in her seat.

"Fuck!"

Reece pushed the breathing device onto Ali's face and started squeezing, forcing air in and out of his lungs.

"Come on, *fucker*, I'm not done with you yet," he said, the vison of Lauren, Lucy, and Katie seared into his consciousness.

Reece slipped his fingers to the side of Ali's neck.

"No pulse!"

"Hit him with the AED!" Haley yelled.

"Shit!"

"Wait," Haley ordered. "Give him Valium first."

"Valium? Where?"

Haley turned in her seat.

"Try that drawer," she said, pointing.

"Got it. How much?"

"Ten milligrams. Right into the IV port!"

Reece drew what was close to 10 mg and pushed it into Ali's body through the IV. He then reached for thc automated external defibrillator and attached the AED pads to Ali's chest, one on the right side, just below the collarbone, and the other on the lower left side of his body below the heart. He was thankful that before his last deployment all

SEALs were required to add Automated External Defibrillator training to their predeployment workup checklist. Reece flipped the switch, bringing the machine to life, and followed the audio prompts. He hit the "analyze" button. At the "stand clear" prompt, Reece leaned back as a jolt of electricity surged through Ali's chest.

Nothing.

"Shit!"

"Hit him again!" Haley shouted from the front of the ambulance.

Reece repeated the procedure and brought Ali back from the dead.

"He's got a heartbeat and he's breathing," Reece reported.

"His body can't take much more, Reece."

"Ali, listen to me. I can do this for days. You want to suffocate for days? I'll keep you alive as long as it takes."

Reece extracted another 75 mg of succinylcholine, deliberately so that Ali could process what was about to happen.

The assassin saw his brother hanging from the beam in his home, looking up at him for hours until his mother had returned.

The wailing of his mother.

"It was a brilliant plan," Ali whispered.

"What?" Reece said, hitting his phone's audio recorder.

"*Brilliant.* Even with this *forced confession.* Brilliant."

"Whose plan, Ali?"

"It was *my* plan. Nothing can stop it now. That traitor Monica Witt planted the seed. Destroy your own cities. The Soviets had those plans, too, you know."

"Witt? The Air Force sergeant?"

"There is no stopping this now. I might just be telling you what you want to hear so that your president calls off the bombing, so that the virus spreads and destroys you."

"Is it a respiratory-spread virus?"

Ali paused, considering his answer.

"No. But can you trust my word?"

"How did it get into the United States?"

Ali paused and Reece injected the drug back into his system.

"Almost there, Reece," Haley reported, taking the exit for the airport.

Reece counted three minutes and thirty seconds on his watch, then gave Ali a breath.

"Just give me a name, Ali. Give me a name and I'll end this."

Ali's eyes darted back and forth, pure unadulterated panic gripping his soul as the drug wore off and allowed him to breathe.

"Here's an easy one," Reece said. "What did you mean when you said I should be dead?"

Through the confusion of the fever burning up his brain, the oxygen deprivation, and visions of his brother swinging from the rope, Ali whispered a name: "Hafez Qassem."

Ali's eyes rolled back unto his head and his body contorted against the duct tape.

"Shit. He's seizing again!" Reece shouted.

"Try the AED."

Reece turned on the machine and followed the prompts. This time the jolts did not return Ali from the dead. Reece transitioned to CPR as Haley rocketed toward the airport. After five minutes of chest compressions where Reece felt ribs breaking under the pressure, he tried the AED in a last-ditch effort to revive the terrorist.

"It's done, Reece."

Reece fell back into the side bench seat, completely spent and exhausted.

"It doesn't spread human to human. We can tell the president to call off the strikes," Haley said, turning down a street leading to the private government terminal.

"What if he was lying?"

"He wasn't lying, Reece."

Reece picked up his phone and sent the recording to Vic.

"I don't think it's enough."

"For Christ's sake," Haley said, "what else do we need?"

Reece looked at the dead body still attached to the gurney, covered in the blood, IV attached to his arm, the bottle of succinylcholine.

Drugs. Vaccines. Bioweapons.

Reece's phone buzzed with a message from Vic.

Final option. Noon tomorrow. Director is taking this information to the White House. Will need scientific evidence to back up claims.

Reece texted back:

Hafez Qassem?

His phone buzzed a minute later.

Iranian intelligence. Chief of station in D.C. Works from Pakistani Embassy.

Put a team on him, Reece typed.

Roger. RTB.

"What did he say?" Haley asked.

"RTB."

"RTB?"

"Return to base," Reece said, closing his eyes and processing everything he'd learned.

"Before we do, pass that cooler back," he said.

"It's empty."

"Perfect," Reece said, pulling it into the back of the ambulance. "Park up ahead and get out of the car."

You saw me in Chicago and Atlanta? Iranian hit team in Maryland? Hafez Qassem? Iranian intelligence?

Haley pulled into a parking space in the government terminal, turned off the ambulance, and got out of the vehicle, leaving Reece alone to finish the job.

PART 3

ERADICATION

"The roaring of lions, the howling of wolves, the raging of the stormy sea, and the destructive sword, are portions of eternity too great for the eye of man."

—WILLIAM BLAKE, *PROVERBS OF HELL*

CHAPTER 58

CIA Gulfstream 550

REECE HADN'T SAID MUCH since they'd gone wheels up.

He offered Haley the first shower and sat staring out the window at 45,000 feet as the Rolls-Royce engines pushed them toward the country's capital at Mach 0.85.

They had packed overnight bags, so at least there were clean clothes to put on.

The G550's cabin was separated into three living areas, with lavatories at each end of the aircraft.

When Haley emerged toweling off her wet hair, she noticed that the cooler Reece had brought on board was by the icemaker. It was wrapped with duct tape.

"You want a drink?" Haley asked, sliding in across from Reece at the four-seat conference table.

"Huh?" Reece asked, still deep in thought.

"You know, a drink?" Haley asked, tipping her hand with an imaginary cocktail.

"Uh, yeah, maybe another water."

"I'll join you," she said, leaning across the aisle and grabbing two waters from the fridge.

"I need to apologize to you, Reece."

"What for? I should be the one apologizing to you after what I just put you through."

"First, *you* didn't put me though anything. Secondly, we are here because of my theory, remember?"

"Good point. Apology accepted."

Haley laughed.

She could tell he was spent: the fighting, the fire, the torture, the knowledge that what he did or didn't do determined the fate of the nation.

"As I was saying, on the apology front, I had a preconceived notion of who you were, who my best friend was dating. Katie and I have known each other for a long time, and I can get protective."

"Believe me, I understand," Reece said.

"I had this vision of an ex-SEAL—do you guys not say 'ex'? It's so confusing with Marines. I think you don't say 'ex' with them, maybe former?"

"I agree with you; it's confusing with Marines."

"Anyway, I watched the news three years ago like everyone else. I couldn't figure what Katie saw in you. She's never felt this way about anyone."

"Really?" Reece said, suddenly more alert.

"Really. So, here's my apology. I saw myself as a doctor dedicated to saving lives around the globe, Médecins Sans Frontières and all that, battling infectious diseases on the front lines. I looked down on the military because it seemed our missions were so diametrically opposed. You take lives and I save them. I admit to being a bit of an elitist. Just ask my husband. He's the conservative one and I'm the hippie flower child. Our marriage works, though."

"He's a doctor at Fort Detrick, right?"

"That's right. He does what I do for CDC, but he does it for the Army. Well, not exactly the same thing. We are flip sides of the same coin. He's working on vaccines for soldiers and citizens infected with bioagents. I study naturally occurring infectious diseases, and trace them to their index cases so we can better understand how they start, how they spread, and how we can stop them."

"I have nothing but respect for what you and your husband do," Reece said.

Haley studied the dark green eyes of the man across from her.

"I know why you do what you do, Reece. I saw it today."

"I just don't see another way. We are close but we are on the clock."

"I've been processing the events of the past few hours. Without you, we would not have the information we do. We'd only have my theory."

"Speaking of processing, let's do a hotwash."

"A what?" Haley asked.

"Hotwash, an informal after-action report, to go through what we learned today so we can apply the lessons going forward."

"Like an operative report?"

"I don't know what that is."

"A report that goes in a medical record postsurgery, documenting the procedure."

"Yeah, like that."

"Let's start with my theory: this is not a naturally occurring virus."

"Starting there, we now have two people involved in the plot confirming that you are correct. Downrange I'd verify those reports via two separate and distinct independent networks to ensure we were not getting played."

"What do you mean?"

"In Iraq and Afghanistan, there were those who saw us as a way to settle what were sometimes centuries-old feuds. Could be because someone stole someone else's great-great-grandfather's goat. Anyway, they would tell us that so-and-so was al-Qaeda or Jaysh al-Mahdi so we would go pay them a visit in the middle of the night. We got wise to it pretty quickly, but it was something we always had to take into account when evaluating intelligence. In this case Shahram and Ali were not independent intelligence sources, as they were working together."

"I see."

"So ideally I'd want confirmation via two *unrelated* HUMINT—as in human intelligence—networks and then substantiate it via some technical means like phone calls, text messages, or emails."

"So, you think that Shahram and Ali might have had this story concocted to mix in just enough doubt that we couldn't trust them?"

"I think that's a distinct possibility and one that our intelligence agencies will certainly highlight when briefing the president. He is going to need solid proof that by avoiding this action he's not condemning ninety percent of the country to death."

"How do we verify their admissions?"

"Let's go back a second," Reece said. "First, why disguise it as a naturally occurring virus?"

"To hide the perpetrator."

"So, who has Marburg Variant U in their arsenal?"

"Russia, China, North Korea, and Iran," Haley confirmed.

"All countries that could potentially sell it to a terrorist organization," Reece said, thinking aloud.

"Maybe they didn't sell it to a terrorist organization. Maybe they perpetrated the attack?"

"Then they'd be culpable," Reece said.

"True."

"Which means we could retaliate."

"Also true."

"Haley, do you know what's on the table as a response to an attack on this country using a weapon of mass destruction? WMD is defined as nuclear, chemical and, you guessed it, biological weapons."

"Nuclear response," Haley correctly guessed.

"That's right. By mimicking a respiratory spread of a naturally occurring virus, a country or group could turn us against ourselves."

"*If* they knew about the FAE option," Haley said.

"You saw it yourself in Africa. There are very few secrets left in the world. And, if you created the U.S. or USSR bioweapon programs after World War Two, you would have put protocols in place to stop the spread of one of your own weaponized diseases."

"Protocols that included destroying your own cities," Haley said, completing the thought.

"I think so. We've learned we have plans in place to destroy sections of the country to contain a spread. I'm sure the Russians did, too."

"Knowing that, who is behind this? Maybe a better question is, what would you do if you were planning this attack?"

Reece paused and looked out the window.

"I'd look to the past."

"Meaning?"

"What has the enemy learned by watching us in Iraq and Afghanistan over the past twenty years? What did they learn before that by watching us react to terrorism of the sixties, seventies, eighties, and nineties?"

"Well?"

"They learned that proxies work," Reece said, answering his own question. "Iran has been at war with us for over forty years, longer if you take it back to the CIA coup in 1953. Ali Ansari is from Iran. He mentioned Hafez Qassem before he died. Qassem is the lead Iranian intelligence chief in the United States. I was involved in tracking down what may have been an Iranian terrorist network before the virus hit. I think that's why Katie and I were targeted."

"Slow down, Reece. You are making the case that Iran used a proxy group to release a bio-agent in the U.S. so we would think it was spreading naturally."

"That's right. If we buy that it's from Angola, there are no Iranian fingerprints. If we buy that it's homegrown radicalized citizens, then we still have no one to retaliate against but ourselves. Iran remains clean just like they have for the past forty years using Hezbollah and Quds Force operatives to do their dirty work."

"Reece, we need to prove beyond a shadow of a doubt that this is a bioweapon and that it is not a respiratory-spread virus."

"Can we just look up Marburg Variant U in the gene book or compare a picture or something?" he asked.

"It doesn't work that way. Back when the Soviets weaponized Marburg, gene sampling or electronic microscope documentation didn't exist. We only have samples from more recent outbreaks, and besides, you would have to compare the two physical samples. We need the genome of the sample, not just a photo."

"So, we need a live sample of a weaponized Marburg Variant U virus next to a current sample from an infected patient from today?" Reece asked, wrapping his mind around the problem.

"Exactly. I need a sample of the original virus, the original Marburg variant from Soviet days. We do a side-by-side genomic evaluation. If there is no variance, then we will have established that this is an intentional bioweapon release on U.S. soil. It would also confirm that it had to have been released through aerosolized droplets by a pressure source, like the example of perfume in a mall."

"So, we need the original Soviet strain."

"Was that a statement or a question?" Haley asked. "Regardless, good luck finding it."

"Luck is the residue of preparation," Reece whispered, his eyes focused past the clouds, beyond the windows.

"What?"

"Just something an old commanding officer of mine used to say." He turned back to Haley. "One more time, who do we know has Marburg Variant U in their arsenals?"

"Russia for sure, and we suspect China, North Korea, and Iran."

"And the United States," Reece said, working the problem.

"Never confirmed but, yes, the United States."

"We need that Soviet sample," Reece said, thinking aloud.

"And how do you suggest we get our hands on a top-secret bioweapon that the U.S. may or may not have developed in violation of several international treaties?"

"We are going to steal it."

"Are you sure you are just drinking water?"

"Haley, what *exactly* does your husband do at Fort Detrick?"

"He studies level-four weaponized pathogens."

"Pathogens that the United States *officially* does not weaponize?"

"Reece . . ."

"How do you think he'd feel about committing treason?"

CHAPTER 59

Masada Security Solutions Corporate Office
McLean, Virginia

"WHAT CAN I GET for you, Senator?" Sawyer asked.

They were sitting in Sawyer's office on the top floor of the Masada corporate building, a short drive from both Langley and the Pentagon.

"Something expensive, now that it's finally on your dime."

"Fortunately for you, all the selections are expensive, as you put it. How about a martini?"

"That would be ideal."

"Vodka or gin?"

"Gin, of course. Bombay Sapphire with three olives, if you would be so kind."

Sawyer made the drink in a chilled glass at his private office bar. He then poured himself a Hennessy Paradis Imperial and sat down in a leather chair adjacent to the sofa where Senator Thwaite now made himself comfortable opposite an eighty-six-inch flat screen set to a cable news channel.

"Shouldn't you be in lockdown in the Capitol Building for briefings from the executive branch?" Sawyer asked.

Thwaite rolled his eyes.

"You best be careful, Senator. You know how the media loves catching politicians breaking their own rules. It makes for great content."

"That's why I'm here in this secure building with you and not getting photographed out at the French Laundry or getting my hair done like those jackasses in California."

Sawyer stifled a laugh.

"It's almost on. Where is the un-mute button on this thing?" the senator asked, examining the remote control in his hand as if it were a foreign object.

"Let me," Sawyer said, swiping to his phone's Savant system application, which bypassed the remote on the coffee table.

"You know, you should invest in some less depressing art," Thwaite remarked, looking around the room.

"Oh, and what would you suggest?"

"Something a little less morbid would spruce things up in here," he said, gesturing to the works that dominated the room, one behind the bar and the other between two bookcases on the opposite side of the enormous office. "What are those, anyway?"

"The one behind the bar was done by an old friend in Ranger Regiment. He was with me in Mogadishu," Sawyer said, examining the canvas from afar. "It's called *The Mogadishu Mile*. It is a reminder of how quickly circumstances can change."

"And that one?" Thwaite asked, taking a stiff drink.

"You don't recognize it?"

"Should I?"

"*Remnants of an Army*. Painted by Elizabeth Thompson, Lady Butler, in 1879. It depicts the 1842 British retreat from Kabul to Jalalabad. Have you been there, Senator?"

"Afghanistan? Of course," the senator said, removing the toothpick with three olives and sliding the first one between his yellowing teeth.

"J-Bad? Gardez? Khost? A-Bad?"

"Erik, you know I visited the troops on base in Bagram in 2004. You provided security. I also spent Thanksgiving in Iraq in 2009. I'm no stranger to war zones."

"Fallujah? Ramadi? Najaf?"

"No, the Green Zone," Thwaite said, making Sawyer's point.

"Ah, yes, I remember the photo op now."

"*Fuck you,* Erik. Some of us are soldiers and some of us are statesmen."

"I think you mean politicians."

"Don't say it with such disdain, Erik. Remember who pays for all this," Thwaite said, devouring his last two olives and gesturing to the grand office with his empty glass.

"Let me get you another."

"Thank you. If you weren't a hired gun you would make an excellent bartender."

Sawyer chuckled and set about making his guest a second drink.

"What happened to our lone ranger, anyway?" Thwaite asked, nodding back at the famous oil painting.

"That's Dr. William Brydon. He was a surgeon. It was rumored that of the sixteen thousand who began the seventy-mile retreat, he, and his horse, were the only survivors."

"True?"

"There were, in fact, other survivors; some straggled in after the good doctor, others had been captured and enslaved, but survived. Regardless, the theme and intent of the painting holds true. The poor horse lay down in a stable in the Jalalabad fort and never got up, he too a casualty of the Afghan plains."

"Poetic."

"*When you're wounded and left on Afghanistan's plains . . . Go, go, go like a soldier . . .*" Sawyer recited.

"What's that?"

"No matter. The original painting hangs in Somerset, you know."

"Somerset?"

"Yes, the Somerset Military Museum. England. One day the original will hang here."

"Bloody depressing," the senator observed.

"Just like in Mogadishu, the tide can turn in an instant, Senator, even against an empire. The enemy is always watching, always learning, always adapting."

"Dismal, if you ask me."

"Have you read *The Great Game*, Senator?" Sawyer asked, handing the older man his second cocktail.

"I don't have time to read, Sawyer. I am busy running a country."

"Pity. And, one might argue that the current president is running the country, I'm afraid," Sawyer said, reminding Thwaite of his loss.

"Not for long. Turn it up. It's coming on now," he said, eagerly consuming all three olives that graced his refreshed drink.

The "whore of war" turned up the volume through his app and watched as the network led with the caption: "Presidential Assassin Targets Innocent Muslims."

"Is it 'taping'?" Thwaite asked.

"Yes, the DVR is recording."

"Good."

The newscaster solemnly lectured his audience:

"We've received disturbing video this evening, video that purportedly shows former Navy SEAL James Reece committing murder. These 'alleged' murders are also classified as hate crimes. You will remember Commander Reece from the Capstone Scandal, where, three years ago, he went on a murderous cross-country rampage killing those he believed were responsible for what some say were his own mistakes that led to the ambush of his SEAL Team in the mountains of Afghanistan. Commander Reece was pardoned under dubious circumstances by the previous administration, so he never stood trial for those murders. I want to warn you, this footage may be disturbing to some viewers."

A crisp image of whites, grays, and blacks filled the screen. Like an old black-and-white TV updated with twenty-first-century resolution, what was clearly a van parked just ahead of a smaller sedan on the right side of a road filled the screen. A man was leaning against the smaller car, his face and hands white against his darker clothing.

"White hot," Sawyer said.

"Excuse me?"

"It's a thermal imaging system from one of our surveillance vehicles. The hotter parts glow white. The colder areas are dark."

"Oh, yes, I know."

The conspirators watched as a man swung his feet over the guardrail and paused to look almost directly into the camera, his face taking on the aura of a ghoul with the light and dark portions re-created by the camera in high-resolution pixelated heat. He stared for what seemed like an eternity before turning to move toward the two vehicles.

They watched the figure walk along the side of the road and raise his rifle to his shoulder as he approached the sliding door of the van. The audio recorder picked up the shot and the video caught the smoking man dropping to the ground.

"He indexed off the cigarette," Sawyer said.

"What do you mean?"

"It's dark. The man he killed was not a professional. Reece must have seen the cigarette in the darkness, which indicated head placement. He sighted on the cigarette and then fired a few inches left, hitting his target in the head."

"This is my favorite part," Thwaite said.

They had both watched the video multiple times before emailing it anonymously to multiple friendly news outlets with agendas in line with the senator's. This was the first network to air it.

With his rifle still shouldered, Reece then turned to the front passenger window of the van and shot the driver through the glass, quickly stepping forward to shoot again.

"Security round," Sawyer said, sipping his drink.

Thwaite grunted.

The ghost then walked to his first victim and shot him in the head.

The screen transitioned to video of a man who was clearly James Reece talking to a police officer and firefighter.

"This footage was obtained by Fox Illinois affiliate 32 News and depicts James Reece in Chicago at the home of Kareem Talib. Talib was a Muslim man who died of a heart attack while James Reece was at the scene. It is worth noting that it is common for serial killers to visit the scenes of their crimes and oftentimes keep mementos from their kills."

The screen then switched to local news footage of police tape in a hallway of what looked to be a garden-variety roadside hotel, the correspondent on scene reporting on the tragic death of Sohrab Behzad, a Muslim American man working at a local Atlanta mosque.

"We have new evidence tonight that puts James Reece on-site at the time of the murder along with statements from a woman who has verified that Commander Reece murdered Behzad before kidnapping her at gunpoint. She later escaped as he was driving her to a remote location."

The screen then ran a video of a man pushing a woman down a hotel hallway, a gun clearly visible in his hand. They then displayed a photo of Reece in his dress blues, clean shaven, rows of medals on the chest of his flawless uniform.

"There are still unanswered questions tonight surrounding why Commander Reece would so deliberately target and kill these Muslim American men after meeting privately with the president at Camp David. The only connection between the deceased is that they are all devout Muslims of Middle Eastern descent. Commander Reece's behavior indicates a pattern of violence that fits with his murders following his last deployment. It also perpetuates a cycle of violence against those of Middle Eastern ancestry.

Did post-traumatic stress or traumatic brain injury play a role in these killings? Is Commander Reece on another murderous rampage, this time connected to President Christensen's administration? We will continue to update you on what is still a developing story."

"I couldn't have written that better myself," Thwaite said, clearly pleased with the anchor's performance.

"You did write it yourself, Eddie," Sawyer said, hitting the mute button on his app.

"That's right. I did," the senator said, now even more pleased. "That should give the White House press corps something to pester the president and his press secretary about at Monday's briefing."

"Senator, do you even care what Reece was doing in Chicago and Atlanta, or who this team was that targeted him in Maryland?"

"Those particulars are no longer my concern. That's an FBI issue now. This is politics. We muddy the waters with this tape and the president is forced to do his job, to live up to his responsibilities as commander in chief, to eradicate the virus in Richardson and Aurora before it infects and kills ninety percent of the country. I mean, by God, there are now reported cases in Atlanta. *Atlanta!* They have isolated the patients thus far but we know it's outside the containment zones. Can you imagine if he has to bomb Atlanta?"

Sawyer remained silent and swirled the brown liquid in his glass.

"We insinuate through our contacts in established media that he bombed Texas and Colorado to divert attention away from his association with Commander Reece," Thwaite continued. "Like when President Clinton bombed Afghanistan and Sudan when Monica's blue dress stains were the talk of the town."

"Ah yes, wag the dog. And, what if he doesn't drop?"

"He *has* to drop, Erik. The country is finished if he doesn't, and I mean that literally. I don't envy him that decision, but we have an airborne virus threatening to destroy the country, possibly the world.

Christensen can stop it. In fact, he's the only one who can stop it. It's political suicide but it's his only viable decision. No one in Congress will publicly support him. They know he has to destroy two cities to save the republic. Supporting it only takes them down with him. It simply has to be done. Only the commander in chief can make that call."

"And the people of Richardson and Aurora?"

"It's truly heartbreaking, Erik. I don't know what else to say. Their deaths save the United States. Their deaths save the world. We will erect appropriate monuments and give speeches, *sincere* speeches. We will never forget their sacrifice. Even though it's the only logical decision, Christensen is finished. His party will forever be known as the party that bombed America."

"Yes, bombed America to save it," Sawyer pointed out.

"But bombed it nonetheless. There is no recovering."

"And you benefit politically from these deaths?"

"Saul Alinsky said it best: 'never let a crisis go to waste.' He was right, you know."

"He didn't actually say that. He was much more eloquent," Sawyer corrected.

"Oh, I know. Rahm Emanuel had to dumb it down for the masses, but the point remains."

"Learning from your enemy, Senator?"

"That's not just for you military types, Erik."

Sawyer's secure desk phone rang.

"Excuse me, Senator."

"Can you bring me another drink while you are up?"

"Of course."

Sawyer took a seat behind the massive oak desk and picked up the receiver. He listened intently, then said "stay on them" before hanging up and making the senator his drink.

"Emergency?" Thwaite asked, as Sawyer handed him his third martini.

"As a matter of fact, yes. James Reece and Dr. Haley Garrett just landed at Dulles. Reece placed a secure call to the CIA, which we intercepted. They believe they have evidence to suggest that the virus isn't airborne."

• • •

When the senator finished his tirade and finally left the building to return to his office to call the president, Sawyer bent down to pick up the broken shards of what just moments before was a chilled martini glass.

Thwaite was prone to these outbursts when things did not go his way, but this latest tantrum was worrisome. Thwaite was convinced the virus was real and spreading. All the science suggested this was true. The liberal-minded president was looking for an excuse not to do his duty. The senator believed Christensen was too weak to do what was necessary. The president was going to bring the republic down with him. He was going to destroy almost two hundred and fifty years of freedom and sacrifice; James Reece was handing him the excuse he needed. For Thwaite, this was not a difficult decision. The few would be sacrificed to save the many. The country would survive; the senator's party would ascend to power once again with Thwaite leading the way. He would take his rightful place and finally occupy the most powerful office in the land.

Sawyer dropped the shards of glass in the trash and refreshed his cognac. Heading for his desk, he stopped and turned toward his bookshelf, approaching *Remnants of an Army.* He sipped his drink, examining the wounded doctor portrayed in the classic Victorian painting. Dr. Brydon was clearly in anguish; a section of his scalp had been removed by an Afghan blade in battle, his horse shot and near death.

Sawyer turned to the large television. It was paused on the IR video of James Reece on the side of the Maryland highway, rifle in hand, staring at the camera, the black-and-white image intensifiers giving him the look of a creature from Hell.

The former Army Ranger searched his book titles. There, next to a first edition of T. E. Lawrence's *Revolt in the Desert*, was the Peter Hopkirk classic *The Great Game*. Sawyer pulled it from the shelf and turned to chapter twenty. The book fell open easily at the binding, Sawyer having spent much time with it over his years of sending contractors to Central Asia. He read slowly, respectfully internalizing every word from a section titled "Massacre in the Passes." Almost a hundred miles of terror through snow-covered mountain passes the Army of Indus marched toward the British garrison at Jalalabad, Afghan warriors snatching souls at every turn, the savages tearing apart the sixteen thousand troops and camp followers as they pushed forward through freezing temperatures. Raids. Sniper fire. Horror. Until a week later, one sole survivor was sighted approaching the fort, wounded on a dying horse.

Sawyer looked at the television and then back at the painting. This time he saw something different. He saw himself on the horse, wounded, clinging to life, trying to make it inside the gates before being struck down, the savage Reece putting his finger to the trigger of a precision rifle, Sawyer in the crosshairs. The Navy SEAL sniper wasn't a man in this vision, he was an apparition, a black-and-white specter of death.

He sat down at his desk and placed *The Great Game* to his left. Sawyer had been in the business of killing for most of his adult life. After Somalia he'd learned how to profit from it. As with any enterprise, success in this business meant diversification. The lucrative U.S. military, intelligence, and diplomatic contracts might only last so long. Washington was a machine. The leadership of both political parties was fickle, all part of the same swamp apparatus, cogs in a Deep State machine.

In business, one had to remain on a trajectory of continual growth. Masada had expanded into worldwide mining security operations and training, advising, and assisting entities who could pay. Precious metals, conflict diamonds, and oil all fell under the Masada profile and Sawyer's purview. On occasion, he had used certain men to solve problems. One of these men had a vested interest above and beyond money in seeing James Reece in the grave. Sawyer had used him over the past two years to eliminate problems in the Middle East and Africa. He was connected to the Russians and currently living in Montenegro on the Adriatic Sea.

Sawyer pulled out a pen and paper and began to write a letter to enlist the services of a sniper.

CHAPTER 60

Russell Senate Office Building
Washington, D.C.

THE FEAR AND CHAOS that had gripped the nation had similarly engrossed the capital.

Rumors were spreading that the executive branch was close to bold and devastating action to contain the virus in Richardson and Aurora. A mass exodus was under way in Atlanta while some took to the streets to take advantage of the lawlessness, looting and destroying at will. Speculation, conspiracy theories, and doomsday scenarios flooded the airways and social media channels. If you were against containment and eradication, you were branded as being for the death of the nation. If you were a politician in favor of those measures, you were in the position of supporting the deaths of your own constituents. Elected representatives from Texas and Colorado were in a state of paralysis. Every answer and decision tied to the virus was rooted in death. Ambassadors from countries not yet affected by the pathogen were clamoring for information. Representatives to the United Nations gave speeches calling for the United States to act to protect the global community of nations.

Throughout the turmoil, the White House remained remarkably

quiet, weighing the most momentous decision ever faced by an American president.

Security, press, aides, interns, staff, senators and representatives, caseworkers, legislative correspondents, schedulers, and communications directors crowded the hallways as Senator Edward Thwaite made his way to his office in the Russell Senate Office Building.

Leaving his assistant holding his coat, Thwaite barged past his receptionist and into his office, slamming the door behind him.

He went right for the gin, attempting to make a martini of the same class he'd downed at Sawyer's building. He ended up forgoing the bitters and lemon twist and emptied what was left of his last bottle of Bombay Sapphire in a glass with ice and a dash of dry vermouth. Unable to find any olives, he swatted a cabinet shut and took a seat in his high-backed leather chair behind the same desk his father had used.

It was up to him to save the country, save the world. He took two oversize gulps of his concoction to acquire some liquid courage before hitting the button for his receptionist.

"Caryn, please connect me to the White House switchboard."

It still annoyed the senator that he did not have the president's direct line or cell number.

"Yes, Senator. Right away."

Thwaite tapped his middle finger against his leather desk mat. After five minutes of tapping he emptied his glass and began fidgeting with the Cross pen he thought he'd be using to sign bills as president.

"Senator?"

"Yes."

"The operator informed me that the president is not taking calls right now."

"*What?* In the middle of a national emergency he's hiding in his bunker? Call back and tell the operator to put you through to the chief of staff... wait, tell them to put you through to Greg Farber. Tell them this has national security implications that impact Richardson and Aurora and that I have information on the reports connecting the president to Commander James Reece."

"One moment, Senator."

Thwaite's eyes surveyed his dark office, taking in the artifacts of two generations in the political spotlight: photos of history-making legislative moments, books he hadn't read, a portrait of his father.

This could all be gone if the president doesn't take the necessary steps to save the nation. Delay means more death, inevitably the destruction of more cities. Richardson and Aurora, maybe even Atlanta, must be sacrificed to save the rest of us.

"Senator, please hold for the president," his receptionist said through the speaker.

Thwaite straightened up in his chair, took the phone from its cradle, and cleared his throat.

After fifteen excruciating minutes, a voice from 1600 Pennsylvania Avenue said: "Please hold for President Christensen."

A moment later the leader of the free world's voice cracked across the line.

"Senator Thwaite."

Thwaite loosened the Windsor knot at his throat and pulled the tie to the side.

"Mr. President, thank you for taking my call."

"Of course. We are in the middle of weighing the options regarding the virus, so forgive me if I ask you to get right to the point."

"That is the purpose of my call, Mr. President. It has come to my attention that you may be delaying the inevitable and unenviable decision of eradicating the virus in Aurora and Richardson."

"That is a callous way of referring to the deaths of a half million of our fellow countrymen, Senator."

"I mean no disrespect, Mr. President," Thwaite said, biting his tongue.

"Then you will understand why I remain dedicated to protecting the nation *including* those in Richardson and Aurora."

"Mr. President, if I may be blunt, without the sacrifice of two cities you are putting the rest of the nation at risk. You are signing the death warrants of millions more. This is time for decisive leadership."

"May I ask where you come by your information, Senator?"

"This town talks, Mr. President. If you waver from doing what needs to be done, my party will have no choice but to take our case to the American people. You are neglecting your duties as commander in chief, putting the future of the nation at risk."

"Rest assured, I will do what needs to be done in the interests of the American people *and* I will exhaust every effort to spare those innocent lives in Aurora and Richardson," the president responded, his tone cold and measured.

"Every second you delay, the chances increase of the virus escaping containment."

"Thank you for your counsel, Senator. I will take it under advisement. I was told you have information on tonight's story about Commander James Reece."

"An unfortunate connection, I'm sure, Mr. President. An irresponsible news media running with only the hint of impropriety."

The president remained silent.

"It would be devastating to the nation if the current emergency was compounded with a scandal. Some might say you took the drastic measures of destroying two entire cities to take focus away from your connection to a CIA assassin. The American people and your administration need to stay focused on the crisis at hand: stopping this virus."

"Anything else, Senator?"

Thwaite had not managed to fluster the boy president in the least.

"There is something else, Mr. President. I have sources who tell me that this murderer James Reece is connected to your administration and has concocted a theory that the virus is not airborne. I'd hate to think the president was taking medical advice from a discredited murderer when the fate of the nation, and the world, hangs in the balance. These latest murders I just watched on the news seem to fit a pattern for Commander Reece. Some might call him a serial killer. It would be best for everyone if he was locked up in the supermax prison in Florence."

"Senator, I want to thank you for your call of support. Before I go, I do have a question for you."

"Yes?"

"Have you ever looked James Reece in the eye?"

Thwaite's mind drifted to the black-and-white image from the video, a specter looking straight through him.

"No."

"Well," the president said calmly, "before you threaten James Reece, you might want to do some research. Had you ever looked him in the eye, you'd rethink your approach."

Before he could respond, the line went dead. The president had ended the call and left Edward Thwaite holding an empty phone.

• • •

President Christensen folded his hands and brought them together in quiet contemplation.

Visions of two American cities burning, possibly a third, haunted him. Innocent men, women, and children incinerated; 500,000 killed on his orders to save 280 million others. He thought of Lincoln; over 800,000 dead on his watch. A country divided. A country at war with itself. Christensen would be responsible for almost as many American deaths in seconds as Lincoln was in four years of civil war.

You must save the country.

By killing half a million of your fellow citizens.

How do you live after making that kind of a decision?

If you don't you are responsible for 280 million deaths. Preventable deaths.

The president swiveled in his chair and looked out at the Rose Garden, then closed his eyes.

His predecessor had told him it was lonely at the top. He had been right.

Did Senator Thwaite really know something about James Reece and his connection to the president's personal mission? Or did he just say that to get through the barriers and connect to the president to pressure him to order the virus eradication option? Was Thwaite linked to the video and media spin of Reece's engagement in Maryland? It was no secret that the senator felt Christensen had stolen the election. If Christensen ordered the destruction of Aurora and Richardson, he was finished politically. If he didn't give the order, not only was he finished politically but the entire country was at risk of infection from a disease with a 90 percent mortality rate. Either way, his presidency would be a single term. One decision to save millions of lives at the expense of two cities.

Unless . . .

Unless what?

Unless Reece could prove the theory conjured up by a doctor at the CDC whose idea was not based on science, but upon conjecture and airline manifests.

The president had cut as much red tape as he possibly could, bypassing all established protocols with a direct line of communication to Reece through the CIA's Special Activities Center. As soon as he received word on the possibility the virus was an aerosolized version of Marburg Variant U, he had immediately ordered a briefing. He was still waiting on confirmation that the military had an original sample of Marburg Variant U. In a system of government as top heavy as the United States, even the president had to wait. All his senior medical advisors agreed that the science pointed to a natural hemorrhagic outbreak in Angola that was now spreading rapidly on U.S. soil. The high infection rate of hospital workers caring for the sick and dying seemed to verify that assertion. He did not have time to wait on an inept bureaucracy for answers. If the virus was spreading as the experts believed, he had no choice but to eradicate it before it killed ninety percent of the country. If it wasn't, he needed to know now.

Christensen turned back to his desk and hit the button connecting him to his receptionist, who worked just feet from the Oval Office.

"Alice, connect me to Vic Rodriguez at the CIA."

CHAPTER 61

Fairfax, Virginia

"WELL, HOW DO YOU want to play this?" Reece asked.

They had landed at Dulles, where the Agency also kept a fleet of Tahoes and Suburbans at the ready, and had pulled up to the curb outside of Haley's Fairfax, Virginia, home. The modest split-level house was built on a corner lot surrounded by trees and not overly close to the neighbors. The first level was brick and housed a single-car garage at the end of a short driveway. A row of hedges obscured a screened-in, well-lit front porch. The second level's vinyl siding looked like it had been dropped on as an addition by someone more concerned with functionality than aesthetics.

"Just as we discussed. Let me go in. I'll explain. My husband is more doctor than colonel, if that makes sense to you."

"It does. Let's hope the doctor part is on duty today."

"I'll break it down for him and then I'll open the door and you can come in. But, listen to me: no guns, no jiujitsu, just logical and pragmatic discussion."

"Check."

"What does that mean?"

"Ten-four. Understood."

"Okay, then. Wait here."

Reece watched Haley walk up the drive. Motion-activated lights illuminated the darkness as she passed the garage, stepped up onto the porch, and entered her home.

The street was silent. Even without a mandatory curfew or lockdown orders, citizens were self-isolating in their homes. The uncertainty surrounding the new virus coming so quickly on the heels of the COVID-19 restrictions had beaten a traditionally fiercely independent citizenry into submission.

Maybe it's just an overabundance of caution? Reece thought.

I hope that's all it is.

Reece kept his head on a swivel.

If the president delayed dropping the FAEs on Aurora and Richardson and the virus was in fact a respiratory-spread airborne virus, then almost 300 million Americans would die. The commander in chief couldn't delay while a bureaucracy figured out the ramifications of admitting to the world that the United States had an active biological weapons program in violation of international law. By the time pulling back the curtain was approved, *if* it was approved, the fate of the country would already be sealed. With cases popping up in Atlanta, the countdown timer was almost at zero hour.

Reece looked from shadow to shadow wishing he had a set of NODs and a thermal.

He had the shotgun from Colorado in the backseat of the Tahoe, but contrary to popular belief, CIA operatives didn't typically run around the country with issued weapons. The paramilitary officers and contractors of Ground Branch applied for their concealed-carry permits just like everyone else.

Reece reached back for the Remington and slid it muzzle down on the passenger side floormat with the stock leaning against the seat next to him.

At the first opportunity Reece would get back to his safe and rearm. Being without a pistol was disconcerting.

Reece saw the door open and Haley gestured to him to come up.

Here we go.

Reece looked at the 870.

No guns, no jiujitsu . . .

He exited the car and walked up the driveway to the house.

"Come in, Reece. Tom just went to get a notepad and pen. He's a planner."

The first floor of the house looked like it had been constructed well before open floor plans had become the norm. The wood floor creaked just inside the threshold. Reece noticed a sitting area to his left with a large easy chair in the corner. The wall that was visible to Reece was adorned with shelves full of books.

Reece heard footsteps in the hallway and turned to shake hands with the doctor.

Instead of a handshake, Reece found himself staring into the working end of a .45-caliber 1911 pistol.

CHAPTER 62

"*TOM,* I TOLD YOU Reece is one of the good ones."

Reece slowly moved his hands to what police officers refer to as the interview stance: hands up at about shoulder level, palms out to give the illusion of being nonaggressive and unarmed. In reality it was a fighting stance.

"Easy, Colonel," Reece said, his mind naturally calculating distance to target, type of weapon, and additional threats.

"Tom, put that thing away," Haley said.

"Please listen to her, Dr. Garrett. I'm not here to hurt anyone. We need to talk."

Reece noted that the colonel's finger was on the trigger. Normally that would be an issue, but the thumb safety was still up. Reece was not dealing with a gunman.

"Haley, come over here behind me," the colonel said.

His left hand held a cell phone.

"Mr. Reece, you are all over the news tonight. I have to call the police."

"News?" Reece asked.

"Yeah, video of murders in Maryland, Chicago, and Atlanta."

"Tom," Haley said, jumping in, "I was with Reece and Katie after they were attacked in Maryland. It certainly wasn't murder."

"I don't know what it is, but I'm calling the police."

"Please don't do that, Doctor," Reece said in an even-measured tone.

"And, why not?"

"Because if you do, you are sealing the fate of half a million Americans, citizens of the country you serve. Let's put down the pistol and talk. If, by the time we finish, you still want to call the police, then there is nothing I can do. You are the last hope the people of Aurora and Richardson have."

Colonel Garrett's eyes went from Reece to Haley and back to Reece.

"Haley explained what you want me to do," Garrett said, keeping the pistol pointed at Reece. "A sample of the Marburg Variant U? Are you *insane*? *If* we had a sample, and I am not saying we do, it would be classified and for research purposes only."

"Tom, if there is a sample at Fort Detrick, I need it to do a genomic sequence analysis and an EM comparison," Haley said. "Imagine what would happen with an official request. How long it would take to get what would be a denial of even having it when a sample is stored fifty miles from here and can prove that what's happening in Aurora and Richardson is an aerosolized Marburg Variant U bioweapon and not a respiratory-spread airborne virus?"

"I didn't say we have a sample."

"But, if you did, how could we get it?" Reece asked.

"You are talking about stealing a bioweapon that the United States denies having, a weapon that would put us in violation of several international treaties of which the country is a signatory."

"That's right," Reece confirmed. "Think about your oath as a doctor."

"Over my oath to country?" Garrett countered.

"Doctor," Reece said, intentionally not using Garrett's rank to frame his position. "This is about saving lives. Your oaths to your profession and to the nation support this action. Imagine, a bioweapon developed in the Soviet Union to destroy this country can now be used for the exact opposite of its intended purpose. It can save two American cities and prevent a disaster unprecedented in American history. It's up to us. No one else is coming. No one else can stop this."

"Tom, please," Haley said.

"Do you realize that *assuming* this virus from the Cold War was weaponized into aerosolized bacteria and was capable of targeted deployment, and *assuming* a Fort Detrick lab contained a potential sample of Marburg Variant U, you are asking me to commit treason, be court-martialed, and to spend the remainder of my life in Leavenworth? *Treason*, Haley."

"Dr. Garrett, I'm going to slowly reach in my pocket, okay?" Reece stated. "I'm going to take out a phone and make a call."

"I don't understand," Garrett said, raising the 1911.

"I think this will help," Reece said, taking out a small flip phone.

"Who are you calling, Reece?" Haley asked.

Reece deliberately opened the phone with his left hand, keeping the right one up to signify that he was not a physical threat. He pressed in a memorized ten-digit number and held it up to his ear.

On the second ring the phone connected.

"Sir, it's Reece. We are close. I need you to verify and condone."

To Garrett's questioning look, Reece held out the phone.

"Colonel Garrett, the president of the United States would like a word."

CHAPTER 63

COLONEL GARRETT'S FIRST CALL after his conversation with the president was to his research partner Major Courtney Burke. The second was to the lab security supervisor at Fort Detrick. The third was to John Culpepper, the lab's lead animal technician. It was out of the ordinary to plan an unscheduled experiment in a level-four bio-containment facility on a weekend. Stranger still when that facility housed the Bat Cave.

Garrett dialed Major Burke.

They were seated around a small round kitchen table. Reece hadn't noticed any pictures of children or the toys that go along with them. They were alone.

"Courtney, it's Tom. I just received a call from General Keating. He's concerned about the results from the last trial. Inconclusive. And with everything going on in Texas and Colorado, he's getting pressure to do an Ebola Zaire respiratory spread test to compare to past results. Yep. Tomorrow morning, 0600. Thanks, Courtney. Have a good night. See you in the morning."

"Think she bought it?" Reece asked.

"Let's hope so," Garrett replied. "These are unprecedented times so it's conceivable. This isn't a request coming completely out of the blue. I think we are good. It's still the military, after all: general to colonel to major. Even in the medical corps we remain rigidly flexible."

"Colonel, in the SEAL Teams we would 'red cell' different bases and facilities."

"I think you can call me Tom now. We are about to steal a bioweapon together, after all. And, what does 'red cell' mean?"

"All right. Tom. 'Red cell' was originally a team of SEALs that tested security on military installations."

"I think I remember reading a book about it."

"You probably did. They did their job a little too well."

"Got in a bit of trouble, if I recall."

"That they did. The term is now used to reference thinking about a problem from the enemy's point of view. If you were a terrorist, how would you strike?"

"Ah, I see," Dr. Garrett said.

"So, in this case, you have been going into these secure level-four bio-containment facilities for years. Have you ever thought through how you, or how an adversary would gain access?"

Garrett nodded his head.

"Okay, let's start there," Reece said. "And remember, it's important to think like a terrorist."

CHAPTER 64

National Biodefense Analysis and Countermeasures Center
Fort Detrick, Maryland

AT 0530 TOM GARRETT pulled his Jeep Cherokee up to the front gate of Fort Detrick. He rolled down his window and handed the contracted security officer his military identification.

The guard force was an assortment of military police and private security contractors. The portly guard was dressed in a blue shirt and dark pants to give him the illusion of being a police officer, replete with a gold badge on the front of his black plate carrier.

"Morning, Colonel," he said, scanning Dr. Garrett's ID with an RFID scanner.

"Morning," Garrett responded.

Reece and Haley held up their military IDs. The guard nodded. Haley had a military ID as a dependent and Reece had one as part of his CIA alias credentials package. Despite being the site of the National Biodefense Analysis and Countermeasures Center and the United States Army Medical Research Institute of Infectious Diseases, Fort Detrick was a military base like any other. It had a gym, fire department, PX, commissary, barracks, and housing. Those with the proper identification could come and go as they would on any other military base. Things took a decidedly different turn in the facilities that the United States government denied even existed. Accomplishing their mission in those secure areas would require some ingenuity.

The colonel dropped Reece and Haley off at the base gym. They were dressed in workout clothes and looked like anyone else out for a run to start the day. Garrett had loaned Reece some ill-fitting and brightly colored workout attire. Fort Detrick had recently amended its reflective belt policy; soldiers were now free to go for a run without the belts if they were wearing bright-colored clothing. Garrett didn't have reflective belts, so Reece and Haley were dressed in a way that would pass inspection from an overzealous first sergeant looking to bolster his ego on an early Saturday morning.

"You ready?" Reece asked.

"Yes. Just don't hurt anyone."

"Let's go."

They made their way to a grassy area for a pre-run stretch, keeping their eyes on Porter Street for a red lifted Ram 2500 truck belonging to Fort Detrick's lead animal handler.

Traffic was light on a Saturday morning, even lighter with most people at home glued to their televisions watching the unrest in and around the containment zones.

At just before 6:30 a.m., a large four-by-four lumbered down the main road in front of the gym and turned left onto Freedman Drive.

"That's him," Reece said. "Give him a minute to get settled and then it's go time."

• • •

Colonel Garrett and Major Burke passed the four air locks within the bio-containment level-four area, going through what to them was a routine process of preparing their bodies and minds for their experiment. Their naked skin was first washed in a warm soapy spray, then in UV light. They donned their disposable "bunny suits," and finally zipped themselves into the impervious rubber of their bio-protective suits and attached the power cords and oxygen hoses that served as their lifelines.

They moved to their assigned alphanumeric keypads against the false wall and entered their seven-digit access codes.

Colonel Garrett half-expected the green light to instead blink red, but it recognized the code and permitted the doctor to move to the next phase of the access sequence. He looked into a small keyhole camera as Major Burke did the same, a laser biometrically scanning their faces. With identities confirmed and access granted, their clearances were reviewed by a guard at a remote site who then hit a button to allow them into the inner sanctum of bioweapons research. The guard watched as he had thousands of times before as the two researchers passed into the Bat Cave and beyond the reach of video cameras. What happened behind those doors was known only to those who entered.

• • •

Compartmentalization was used to prevent the right hand from knowing what the left hand was doing. "Need to know" and various levels of classification were part of the protections that safeguarded America's best-kept secrets. Those walls and barriers also prevented assorted agencies of the federal government from communicating in the lead-up to 9/11. Unable to share intelligence and information, those protective barriers allowed terrorists from abroad to enter the country and take flying lessons. Now Reece was going to use that same compartmentalization to steal one of the deadliest pathogens in existence.

He and Haley jogged on the sidewalk not far from the gym, looking like any normal couple getting in some exercise before the commissary opened for business. Beneath a fluorescent zip-up windbreaker to ward off the cold, Reece wore a fanny pack they had pulled from the back of a closet at the Garretts' home. Inside were his Marshal credentials, zip ties, duct tape, and the 1911 that Colonel Garrett had held on him the night before. It turned out to be a gift from his father. Colonel Garrett had shot it once with his dad and then packed it away in a box. Reece had given it a quick clean and done a function check. It was loaded with 230-grain, full-metal-jacket .45 ACP. When Reece shook it, it had rattled. That was part of the beauty of the old-school .45s. The parts were interchangeable on a battlefield far from home. Reece trusted that the one he carried would work. He just hoped he wouldn't have to take any long shots.

Colonel Garrett had sketched out a detailed diagram of the animal research facility that was separate but attached to the National Biodefense Analysis and Countermeasures Center. Its security cameras were a closed-circuit network to prevent animal rights activists from somehow hacking the system to show the world what was taking place on the grounds of Fort Detrick. On a Saturday there would be five people assigned to the one experiment. Two security guards would monitor the closed-circuit cameras while three animal technicians would sedate the primate and load it onto the stainless-steel tray for delivery into the level-four laboratory.

As Reece and Haley approached the parking area that Tom Garrett had sketched out, Reece looked at his watch.

"They should be inside. Let's do this."

They veered off the sidewalk and over a grassy mound, dropping down onto the parking lot of an unmarked building that was a nonhuman primate housing and quarantine facility. Five cars were in the parking lot near a loading dock of what looked like a warehouse. Reece and Haley bounded up the steps to a back entrance and stopped by a steel door with a camera attached above.

Reece removed his Marshals creds and held them up to the camera. He took a last look at Haley and knocked on the door.

CHAPTER 65

JOHN CULPEPPER HAD BEEN an animal handler for almost thirty years. His wife and kids thought he was a veterinarian assistant attached to a benign animal research institute run by the U.S. Army. None of them knew that he cared for primates that were part of a top-secret bioweapons development program. Culpepper didn't exactly know that himself but after all these years, he had his suspicions. He had signed nondisclosures and had to submit to a periodic background investigation but that was the extent of it. He knew that once a month, trucks arrived in the middle of the night with primates from a facility in Texas. He would supervise the transfer to their new facility, where he would care for them until he was given instructions to prepare one for delivery to the National Biodefense Analysis and Countermeasures Center next door. He liked to believe the research was vital to national security. Even so, knowing what would happen to them, it was never easy to sedate one of the strong animals and load it onto the tray. After that, the system was automated. He knew the body would be incinerated after the experiment. Once loaded onto the tray, he'd never see the primate again.

Coming in on a Saturday was not normal but these were anything but normal times. He'd been expecting it. Though he didn't know what went on at the end of the incineration tunnel, he knew it had to do with infectious diseases. He had read enough online over the years to know that the Army was probably developing vaccines to protect soldiers from contagious viruses in the more tropical parts of the world.

He said hello to Carl and Scott, who watched the cameras to make sure the primates were all in their cages. Someone monitored the cameras 24/7. If they noticed a problem, they had a flowchart to follow with an associated phone tree. More often than not, those calls went to John and the veterinarian. Most of the time it was because an animal got sick and had to be either treated or euthanized so as not to infect the entire population.

Carl was engrossed in the latest Brad Thor thriller and would glance up from time to time to observe the screens. Scott hit pause on his iPhone long enough to say hello. He was listening to a Joe Rogan podcast where the podcaster was somehow discussing psychedelic drugs and bow hunting with Cam Hanes in the same episode.

A small locker room was attached to the security station. Here John and his two subordinate animal technicians changed into the PPE they were required to wear when handling the primates: a white lab coat over a tan flight suit, steel-toed shoes, a surgical mask with clear plastic goggles, and arm-length bite-resistant gloves of Kevlar and stainless-steel mesh to prevent an animal from breaking the skin if they attacked. His PPE was designed to protect from the physical threat of animals whose strength was four times that of a human. Even when the animals were sedated, the National Research Council mandated that technicians be protected, just in case.

When they were ready and had buddy-checked one another to ensure they were all following the proper safety protocols, he let Carl know he was going in. Carl looked up from his book and gave a little wave before turning his attention back to the page.

John unlocked a nearby door and descended the metal grated staircase. The next step was to prepare the sedative and tranquilizer guns for their mission.

The baboons were housed in single stainless-steel cages to help prevent the spread of disease. Referred to as NHPs, or nonhuman primates, in the scientific community, the facility received ten of them a month, which was far fewer than most of the research facilities around the country. It was John's job to care for the animals before they were sent to their deaths. It gave him no pleasure; instead he took pride in keeping the facility clean, the animals healthy, and being skilled in administering the anesthesia to sedate them for transport. As he prepared the long stick that would allow him to inject the animal through the bars of its cage, Walter and Chris removed the tranquilizer guns that acted as backup in case the animal somehow awoke from the sedation and attacked. Carl had seen it early in his career. A baboon had been given an ineffective dose of ketamine and sprung to life on the way to the incinerator, almost killing a female animal handler and disfiguring her face for life. He thought about that day every time he approached a cage to do his job.

"You guys all set?" he asked.

"Ready," Chris said.

"Good to go," Walter confirmed. "Let's do this and get home. It's my three-year-old's birthday today. My wife put together a little playdate for this afternoon. If I know what's good for me, I better be there."

"Ha! Smart man," John agreed. "One sedation and transport and we will get you out of here. Keep those tranq guns out of sight. You know how the other animals hate seeing them."

"We know. You tell us that every time we do this," Chris reminded the senior technician.

"Just habit."

John visually inspected his technicians before exiting the prep station and approaching specimen 8462 to begin the process that would end its life.

• • •

"Tom, what are you doing?" Major Burke asked, her digitized voice cutting through the silence of the Bat Cave.

Colonel Garrett was manipulating the controls of the mechanical arm that allowed him to access the pathogens behind the thick Plexiglas barrier. He had opened a plastic composite freezer and extracted a vial labled MVU874.

"Colonel, that's Marburg," Courtney said, her pen hovering over the stainless-steel clipboard.

"I know, Major. There was a slight change today. General Keating wants this done."

"Colonel, today's experiment was for Ebola."

"We need a comparison to the inconclusive Ebola results. I've got a hunch about this."

"A hunch? Colonel, what's going on?" his confused partner asked.

"We will get the paperwork sorted out," he said, trying to buy time as he extracted the Marburg Variant U and maneuvered the mechanical arm toward the sedated baboon.

"*Sir,* we can't do this."

Perspiring profusely inside his suit, Garrett wished he could wipe the sweat from his brow. He hadn't felt claustrophobic in a suit in years. His hand shook as he tried to focus on the injection.

"Tom, come on. This is not right. What are you doing?"

With no cameras or recording devices in the Bat Cave, Major Burke's options were limited. The protocols and security measures were based around two-person integrity, clearances, and background checks. They were specifically designed to get an extremely limited number of people into a small space to conduct experiments not officially condoned by the U.S. government, experiments that were in direct violation of the 1972 Biological Weapons Convention.

"*Sir!*" Courtney said more forcefully.

Colonel Garrett's next action caused Courtney to drop the clipboard and pen and step toward the exit.

Instead of using the arm to move the baboon to the observation cage, Colonel Garrett left him lying on the delivery tray. He moved to a separate control panel and hit a series of override switches designed for testing the incinerator. Major Burke watched in horror as her superior officer returned their test subject to the anteroom without initiating the cremation cycle.

"What in God's name have you done?"

• • •

John confirmed that the primate had successfully been transported to its destination. The only communication John's facility had with the lab was through the machine that delivered and then incinerated the test subjects. This experiment was scheduled to take two hours. John and his two subordinates would clean areas around the other cages and then wait in the break room until the tray returned. They would then visually confirm that it was disinfected and ready for experiments next week, before signing the paperwork confirming that NHP subject 8462 had been successfully incinerated.

As John and his crew turned to tend to the cages a red light began to blink on the wall next to the incinerator.

"What the hell?" John said.

"What's goin' on?" Walter asked. "They done already?"

John studied the display on the terminal in front of him.

This can't be.

"We're not scheduled to do an incineration test inspection, are we?" Chris asked from over his boss's shoulder.

"No," John said, looking down at his paperwork in confusion.

"Then what's happening?"

"The tray is coming back, but it shouldn't for another two hours."

"Maybe the paperwork got messed up," Walter offered.

"No, we don't do override tests with an animal in the lab."

"Could they have hit the wrong button on the other side?" Chris asked.

"I guess it's possible. The animal will be on the other side for a couple hours. Let's get back to the control room and figure this out."

As they turned to go, the control room door opened. A man and a woman in workout gear rushed down the short flight of stairs.

John looked at them in disbelief. This was a first.

The ramifications of what was happening didn't become clear until the bearded man hit the landing and approached, a 1911 pistol in his outstretched hand.

When Reece and Haley exited the building less than ten minutes later, five men were zip tied and duct taped in the facility break room, the infected baboon had been sent back into the crematorium for incineration, and Haley had a capped, triple-bagged syringe filled with five milliliters of blood, blood that was infected with the original Soviet strain of Marburg Variant U.

CHAPTER 66

Centers for Disease Control Laboratory
Washington, D.C.

"REECE, WE ARE ON the clock."

"I know, let's do this."

"There is no way you can come in with me," Haley responded. "I'm going into a biohazard level-four containment lab. You need badges, clearances, and approvals, which you obviously don't have. I am going in with this sample of Marburg Variant U and will compare it with our samples from Richardson and Aurora. If the virus samples match Variant U, then we know it's not a respiratory-spread infection."

"And if it doesn't match?"

"If it doesn't match, the president only has one option."

"Be careful."

"I will. Reece, to my knowledge, no one has ever stolen a bioweapon from Fort Detrick," Haley said. "My husband is probably in an interrogation room right now. Someone is going to start putting the pieces together. If we are wrong, we are going to jail for a long time."

"And if we are right, two cities will still be standing this afternoon."

"We will know soon, *if* I can get in there and pull this off."

"So, I just wait in the car?"

"Yes. I will do this as fast as I can. If the weaponized Marburg Variant U is a genomic match to the samples from Texas and Colorado, we can get that information to the president and he can rescind the eradication order."

As Haley exited the vehicle, Reece leaned across the seat.

"Haley?"

"Yes?"

"Good luck."

"I thought you had a thing about luck," she said, smiling to break the tension.

"I do. But in this case, I'll take it."

• • •

"What the hell were they doing at Fort Detrick?" Thwaite yelled into the phone.

"We don't know, Senator. My surveillance team did not have access to the base."

"And where are they now?"

"The CDC offices in Virginia."

"Have they made any calls?"

"Not since this morning."

"*Fuck!* Sawyer, you find out what they are up to. For all we know they are terrorists and have released the virus themselves."

"That seems unlikely, Senator."

"Listen to me. Reece meets with the president, is at the site of a suspicious death in Chicago, murders a Muslim man in Atlanta and kidnaps his girlfriend, where now, by the way, we have infected patients. He then executes two Muslim men on the side of the road in Maryland, flies to Denver, where your team is unable to follow him, flies back to D.C., and is now sneaking around at Fort Detrick and the CDC labs? He's involved somehow."

"What if this disease is not airborne?"

"It *is* airborne, Sawyer! All the experts agree. The deadline is upon us. The only chance to save the country, possibly the world, is here. It might be too late already. If the patients in Atlanta were not locked down in time, we are done for; it's all over. Think of your family, Erik! *Dead, all dead!*"

"And, if the virus is eradicated, no one will ever know if it was airborne. Your path is paved into the White House."

"This is not about that, Erik, and you know it. This is about saving the republic!"

"How patriotic."

"Something is not adding up here, Erik. Find out what Reece and his doctor friend are up to and find out now!"

• • •

Two excruciating hours later, Haley emerged from the CDC building. Reece half-expected her to be in handcuffs, escorted by federal agents in dark blue windbreakers. He looked around the parking lot for signs that he was being set up. He scanned the windows in the floors above that would give snipers a clear shot, looking for anything that might indicate a hastily established urban hide site.

Nothing. But, if they are good, you'll never see them coming. An HRT sniper could have you in his sights right now.

Haley rounded the front of the vehicle and slid in across from Reece. Even though it was cool, he saw the beads of sweat on her temples. She clasped her hands together to steady her nerves.

"Are you all right?" Reece asked.

"It's Marburg. It's Variant U."

"*Jesus,*" Reece whispered. "Where is it now?"

"It's in the lab. It's locked in a safe. I sent all the documentation to Vic via email. I want this sample destroyed but, for now, we need to keep it as evidence."

"Just so I have it straight: this confirms that the virus in Colorado and Texas is a weapon. We have that weapon in our arsenal and can prove that it spreads only through direct aerosol droplets from a pressure source."

"That's right, Reece. It only spreads via an aerosolized cloud—a man-made cloud. After the intentional release it spreads the same way as any standard hemorrhagic virus."

"Through direct blood-to-mucous-membrane contact, correct?"

"Correct. It's incapable of human aerosolization like COVID-19. That's why it's the perfect bioweapon under lock and key at Fort Detrick. It strikes with incredible efficiency but only against a targeted population center. That way it doesn't infect the planet."

"And you sent everything to Vic?"

"I did. I followed up with a call from my desk. He said the director is assembling a team for an emergency meeting at the White House and he wants me there to brief the president."

"Well, let's go."

"He also said something else."

"Oh?" Reece asked.

"He said we have a problem. That secure phone you've been using—it's compromised."

CHAPTER 67

"I CAN'T BELIEVE YOU agreed to this."

"It was actually my idea," Haley said, as Reece drove toward the off-site CIA building in Chantilly, Virginia. "It wouldn't work if you left the CDC without me. I just asked myself: *What would James Reece do?*"

"That's a dangerous question. I think we've been spending too much time together," Reece said with a smile.

"Look, we pull into the parking lot. They are expecting us. I'm going to sprint inside. Vic will have a team ready to pounce. He said it was the same team I met at the Annapolis house plus some guy named 'beast' or something."

"Ox."

"That's it: Ox," Haley confirmed.

"I still don't like it. They could hit us between here and Chantilly," Reece said, his eyes in constant motion.

"Just a few more minutes, Reece. Almost there and we are home free."

"You know, Haley. You would have made a good Team guy."

Haley couldn't help but laugh.

• • •

"Senator, we intercepted a call between our subject, James Reece, and the director of the CIA's Special Activities Center, Vic Rodriguez."

"Well, what did they say?" Thwaite asked, through his KryptAll phone.

"Reece said they have proof that this outbreak is a bio-attack, something that infects via an aerosolized spray that can not be secondarily spread," Sawyer reported.

"What kind of idiocy is that? It's in three different cities. People who never came into physical contact are dying of it. That means it is airborne! We are getting cases in Atlanta, for Christ's sake."

"I can only report what we've heard."

"Where are they going now?" the clearly agitated senator asked.

"They are bringing their evidence to an office park in Chantilly, Virginia."

"Sawyer, they are obviously involved in this plot. They are terrorists themselves. *Hell*, James Reece was labeled a domestic terrorist by the FBI. He's clearly finishing what he started all those years ago. He wants to bring down the country he blames for the deaths of his family and his SEAL Troop. It is your job to prevent that from happening."

"He's in a new vehicle, so we don't have him under electronic surveillance, but we know where he's going."

"Well, take him out. Save the country!"

"The office park is a CIA processing facility."

"Fucking CIA is involved, too, then. Sawyer, you take them out. Save the country. I will not let two hundred years of blood, sweat, and tears be destroyed by a domestic terrorist. Kill Reece and the doctor. Help me save the world!"

• • •

"*Holy shit!* Did I hear that right? We get to kill James *Fucking* Reece?" Woody asked.

"That's the order. And the doctor," Crimmins confirmed.

"Well, *fuck me*. How illegal is this?"

"It's a national emergency. Apparently they are involved with the shit in Texas and Colorado."

"The virus?"

"Yeah."

"We are going to take down a terrorist SEAL. *Oh shit.* Think they'll put me on the cover of *Recoil*?"

"Probably, if you pay them enough. You ready to finally be a hero, Worthless?"

"I'm already a fuckin' hero, brah. Now I get to add killer of James Reece to my resume," Woody said, press-checking the AR from the back of the minivan.

"Just be ready. And don't *fucking* miss."

"I don't miss, bro."

"I hope not."

• • •

"It's just up ahead," Reece said, looking in his rearview mirror and noting the dark minivan that changed lanes a few cars back. "Are you ready?"

"I'm ready," Haley said.

"Okay then. Vic has cleared the parking lot except for a few vehicles to make it look occupied. The building is locked down, so no one is coming in or out. Your path to the front door is clear."

Haley shifted nervously in her seat.

"Seat belt on?" Reece asked.

"It's on."

• • •

"We are going to turn in behind them and pull right next to them as they park," Crimmins said.

"Fuck yeah, then I pop the door and take them out."

"Just remember to take the safety off," Crimmins advised.

"Fuck you, Charlie. I know what I'm doing. We did low-vis vehicle interdiction black ops in the 'Stan."

"Sure you did. Just remember the safety."

• • •

Reece slowed the Cherokee and turned into the office park that operated as the processing center for the CIA's Clandestine Service, watching closely as the minivan pulled in behind them.

"Hold on, Haley."

Just inside the parking area, Reece paused as if he was looking for a place to park. Then he slammed the vehicle in reverse and stepped on the gas.

• • •

"What the *fuck*?" Crimmins exclaimed, seeing the target vehicle's reverse lights come on and quickly accelerate toward him.

By the time Crimmins's brain registered the fact that the hunters had become the hunted, it was too late.

His hand put the van in reverse just as Reece's vehicle made impact with the front bumper.

The impact sent Woody, who was already kneeling by the one sliding door, to the floor. Hitting the gas to reverse out, Crimmins felt a second impact and looked at the screen on the dash, seeing that a security barricade had risen behind them. The van was jammed between Reece's vehicle and the barrier.

Reaching for the door handle, he abruptly stopped when a black Suburban slid to a stop, cutting off another avenue of escape. Ignoring

Woody in the back of the van, yelling about a broken arm, he looked up in time to see a second Suburban skid into place in front of Reece and the doctor, trapping the minivan in a textbook L ambush. He barely registered that the passenger-side door of the car had flung open. A female was sprinting from the vehicle, three men in tactical gear falling in with her to escort her to the building in front of them.

Hard-looking operators emerged from the SUVs. Crimmins noticed a man in each element held a MK 48 7.62x51 machine gun. The others had M4 carbines with suppressors.

Maybe I can still push this thing out of the way and get us out of here.

As he put the minivan back in drive and stepped on the gas, he heard the unmistakable sound of a suppressed automatic weapon erupt to his left. Steam exploded from the engine as the open-bolt machine gun tore through the hood and front quarter panel of the vehicle.

Crimmins took his foot from the gas pedal and put the van in park. His hands slowly went to the wheel.

Don't give them an excuse.

"Woody, put down the AR," he said.

"What the fuck just happened? My *fucking* arm's broken!"

As Worthless Woody attempted to prop himself up with his one good arm, the side door opened and he found himself face-to-face with James Reece.

CHAPTER 68

Russell Senate Office Building
Washington, D.C.

SENATOR THWAITE WATCHED THE president's address from the Oval Office in disbelief.

He looked so presidential and reassuring, so sure of himself.

How could this be?

"I want to assure the American people that the end of the crisis is near. We have confirmed through exhaustive international investigations by the world's leading infectious disease specialists that this new virus is indeed a hemorrhagic fever. It originated in Angola but has burned itself out on the African continent. It has done the same here in the United States. We have studied the Angolan virus closely and determined that it will not spread via respiratory pathways as we saw with COVID-19. Once again, to be perfectly clear, this is not spread like the flu or COVID-19 or the common cold. We had early spikes in Aurora, Colorado, and Richardson, Texas, with one-off cases in Atlanta. Since those early spikes the curve has flattened naturally, and current infection rates are almost at zero."

I don't believe it, Thwaite thought.

Even though it was just after noon, the senator held a drink in his quaking, clammy palms.

"I can now assure you that this terrible disease has taken the worst of its toll. It has impacted our society and tested us to our core. But, we are Americans. We will rise above the fray. The scientific community is working on a vaccine so that if we ever face this enemy again, we will be ready."

Thwaite leaned back in his desk chair.

He's actually turning this into political capital. The son of a bitch.

"There have been reports that the virus was a bioweapon delivered by a foreign enemy. These reports are false. There have also been reports that the virus escaped from a lab here in the United States. Those reports are false."

"What are you up to, Mr. President?" Thwaite whispered.

"I want to address the rumors that there are strategies in place to eradicate viruses on home soil with incendiary bombs. I want to address those rumors honestly. I recently became aware of plans put in place during the Cold War, plans that remained in place until today.

"Effective immediately, I have signed an executive order placing what are known as 'eradication measures' on hold. A bipartisan commission will submit a report to me within ninety days concerning these legacy policies, with recommendations on how to proceed so that in the face of a future virus we have other options at our disposal. I commit to you tonight, there will be full transparency in these proceedings. We will harness the power, ingenuity, and brilliance of our scientific community, technology sector, and pharmaceutical industry to develop the most effective means of combatting emerging hemorrhagic viruses. You have my pledge that you, the people, will be heard and we will move forward together, stronger and united."

This is unbelievable. He can't do this.

"Our thoughts and prayers are with all of those affected by the virus, and with the frontline workers who care for them. We are with you. No effort or expense will be spared to provide you with the resources you need to see

this through. May God bless you and may God continue to bless the United States of America."

The video feed switched to a panel of very relieved-looking news contributors. Thwaite continued to stare at the television, not hearing a word.

The phone buzzed on his desk. Slowly he hit the intercom button to connect with his receptionist.

"Isn't this wonderful news, Senator?"

"Uh, what?"

"The president's address. The virus is no longer spreading. We are going to be okay!"

"Uh, yes, Caryn, that's, uh, incredible news."

"Yes, sir. Well, I have a call waiting for you from the FBI. It sounds important."

"The FBI?"

"Yes, Senator. A Special Agent Andrew Kline would like to speak with you."

"Please take a message. If he requests a meeting, please schedule it out as far as possible."

"Uh, yes, Senator."

Thwaite terminated the connection.

Deliberately he opened a desk drawer and removed his secure phone, looking at it skeptically.

Without another viable option, he called Sawyer.

"Did you see it?"

"I did," Sawyer responded. "And I was just about to call you."

"Really?"

"Yes, a source at the FBI has informed me that you and I are both under investigation for the attempted murder of James Reece and Haley Garrett in Virginia, along with a host of other less serious offenses."

"I'm thinking now would be a good time to vacate the premises."

"I'd agree with you."

"Out of the country."

"I'm way ahead of you. Meet me at Signature Aviation at Dulles. If you aren't there in forty minutes, I leave without you."

Thwaite dropped his KryptAll and BlackBerry into the drawer. He took one last look at the portrait of his father and then departed for the airport.

CHAPTER 69

Embassy of Pakistan
Washington, D.C.

HAFEZ QASSEM SAT AT the conference table in the secure room in the basement of the Pakistani embassy in Washington, D.C. Without taking his eyes from the box, he made a slight motion with his right hand. An administrative assistant sliced through the packaging tape and looked to the intelligence chief for further instructions. With another wave the underling was dismissed, relieved to be out of the presence of the Iranian intelligence chief.

It had been labeled a diplomatic pouch but clearly it was not.

The box had been addressed to Qassem personally, which was an anomaly. The Americans knew he operated out of the embassy and even surveilled him occasionally, as they did with all members of the Iranian staff. It was expected for adversaries and even allies to spy on one another. It was all part of the game.

Qassem's job was strategy. He was no longer a tactical player. He hadn't been for a long time.

The box had the return address of a UPS Store in Annapolis. He observed it for any suspicious signs, signs that should have been warnings to some of his brethren in Hezbollah and the Quds Force when mailing death had become a popular tactic of the Israeli intelligence services. It wasn't leaking. It didn't smell. There were no protruding wires. It had been swiped for chemical residue and the Pakistani embassy had the dogs sniff it for explosives; a company provided the service off embassy grounds so as not to offend with the filthy animals. All those tests had returned negative.

It had also been x-rayed.

The electromagnetic radiation had revealed the contents.

Qassem knew *what* it was. He needed to confirm *who* it was.

Qassem was confident it would not explode. It contained a message meant for the lead Iranian spy in the United States.

Qassem stood and pushed away the cardboard to reveal the next layer. Whatever was inside had been wrapped in aluminum foil and plastic wrap. It reminded Qassem of a wrapped present the Americans were so fond of giving one another on the bastardization of the prophet Jesus's day of birth, when *Isa ibn Maryam* was sent with the *injil* to foretell the coming of the prophet Muhammad.

ruh min Allah

The spirit of God.

The Iranian spymaster carefully sliced through the foil with a *jambiya,* the traditional curved blade of his ancestors.

Nizari Ismailis.

Carefully he parted the shiny plastic and aluminum barrier to reveal the tan plastic top of a cooler. He worked his fingers down the front and lifted the rubber latches, continuing to inspect for wires just in case something had been missed in its prior security inspection. It was also never beyond the realm of possibility that someone in the ISI, Pakistan's intelligence service, wanted him dead. One could not be too careful in the world of espionage.

All clear.

Then, slowly, he opened the lid.

Looking up at him was the severed head of Ali Reza Ansari.

Instead of horror, Qassem studied the upturned eyes of the man he'd passed the Marburg virus to just weeks earlier.

Dried ice had been packed around the head to keep it fresh so that Qassem would have no trouble with identification.

There was something peculiar about the mouth. A piece of plastic was protruding from between purple lips.

Qassem pinched it between his thumb and forefinger, extracting a Ziploc bag with a single piece of paper inside. He turned it over.

It read simply: "Sept 10th."

They know.

Hafez Qassem reached for the phone on the table to his right.

"Ready the plane. I will be returning to Iran tonight."

CHAPTER 70

REECE SAT IN THE back of the smallest version of Mercedes's venerable Sprinter van. This one was painted white with a floral business moniker on each side. If someone googled the business to find the website and called the listed number, they would hear a recording in which a pleasant woman's voice would explain that they were busy arranging flowers and would return the call as soon as possible. The call, of course, would never be returned.

Inside it was anything but a flower delivery van. The walls, floor, and ceiling were lined in black sound-dampening material and there was no access to the driver's compartment. Shackles were attached to the floor and wall. A bench seat was built into the right side and one chair was bolted into the floor.

"Okay, he's departing the embassy on foot. No variation from his daily profile other than the time and the fact that his phone is still inside."

"Good copy," came Ox's voice over the encrypted radio.

"You get that, White Knight?"

"White Knight copies," Reece said into his radio. "Just need to know if he is going home or to the airport."

"He's taking route three," a voice informed them.

The voice belonged to the UAV operator whose ISR platform had electronically tagged their target.

They had been tailing Qassem for six days and had identified three routes he used to walk from his office in the Pakistani embassy to the house the Iranians rented for him through their Pakistani surrogates in the North Cleveland Park area of the city.

Hitting him at the embassy was a no-go and security at the rented apartment was run through the Pakistanis.

He varied his daily routine, but one could only take so many routes home. There would always be an identifiable choke point. Choke points presented a problem when dealing with a trained intelligence operative; they knew the choke points as well as those who hunted them. That's why Reece wasn't going to hit him at a choke point.

• • •

Qassem noted that pedestrians were on the streets as they emerged from self-imposed isolation and returned to businesses in the aftermath of the virus scare. Some 5,872 Americans had died from the virus, most of those in Aurora and Richardson, with a few isolated cases in Atlanta; Ali having to use the remote dispersal device had hurt their numbers. Releasing the virus in high-traffic areas before hitting the hospitals had been a stroke of genius. It had been Ali's idea and reinforced to the scientific community that medical staffs were getting it from patients just by breathing the same air.

Another 257 people had died in clashes with the military and law enforcement. In Qassem's estimation, American confidence in government, elected politicians, and the military had hit rock bottom, but unfortunately there were glimmers of recovery. The new president was leading the country out of the pits of despair and working with Congress on an economic stimulus package focused on Colorado and Texas.

Americans were a resilient lot. President Christensen had flown immediately to Texas following his address to the nation. In a video that had since gone viral, a camera crew caught Marine One making an unscheduled landing on University Park Field near the hospital in Richardson that had first reported the virus. A body bag had been removed from a refrigerated truck. It was on a gurney and was draped with an American flag. The president had placed his hand on the flag, taken a knee, and bowed his head in prayer. He had then stood, saluted, and walked back to the waiting aircraft. The media suggested the president was paying his respects to an Air Force doctor who had led the hospital through its darkest hours.

The president had then walked the halls of medical centers, first in Richardson and then in Aurora. He wore no PPE. He shook hands, gave hugs, and offered hope. Hope was something that Hafez Qassem knew was a course of action reserved for those without viable alternatives.

Would the Americans grab him in broad daylight? The FBI would. They would come screaming in, driving black Suburbans with their badges out and guns drawn for a very public arrest. What the FBI would not do was send him a severed head in the mail. This was something else. A different type of animal was hunting him.

He'd exited the embassy and passed the Malaysian and Egyptian embassies on International Court North West. He walked north to avoid the Israeli embassy. He moved onto a wooded path near the Austrian embassy to cut through to Thirty-Sixth Street. From there it was a short walk to his residence.

At first Qassem thought he was having a heart attack. When he felt the second impact he knew it was something else. His neurological system shut down as his brain lost the ability to communicate with his muscles and he toppled to the ground face-first.

He rolled to his side and grabbed at the impact area. That was exactly what the designers of the weapon had intended. Qassem's hand connected with the exposed wire attached to the four barbs of the 12-gauge projectile. His hand convulsed. He was unable to pull it away and another 500 volts surged through his system.

• • •

Logan cycled his Taser X12 Mossberg and emerged from his hide site, forty feet off the path. He was joined by a second operator who did the same, both quickly approaching the Iranian spy and ready to hit him again with the 500 volts of the specially designed less-than-lethal shotgun rounds. A third man approached with an Axon Taser 7 in the low ready. When he was ten feet away, he pressed the trigger and sent the attached barbs into the downed man, shooting 3,500 volts through his body. His two partners slung their Taser X12 XREP shotguns and quickly zip-tied the man's hands and feet. He would be dead weight for at least twenty seconds.

They carried him thirty yards to Thirty-Sixth Street NW, where a flower delivery truck had backed over the curb, its rear doors already open. They loaded him inside and attached him to a chair with restraints before exiting into the street, securing the doors behind them.

CHAPTER 71

QASSEM OPENED HIS EYES and attempted to raise his arms to the areas on his chest and stomach that burned, but was unable to move. As his eyes adjusted to the dim light, he became aware that he was in a moving vehicle and that his legs, arms, and head were strapped to some sort of a chair.

He was not alone.

A figure was sitting on a bench seat across from him, a figure dressed in a fully encapsulating orange biohazard suit. Strapped to the face of the man wearing it was a black rubber mask attached to a self-contained breathing apparatus beneath the suit. Even in the dim light Qassem recognized the man behind mask.

"I know you, don't I?" Qassem asked.

"I think you do. I take it you make it a point to know the target when you send a hit team to assassinate him," Reece said though the internal microphone.

"James Reece, you killed eleven of my men."

"I did."

"I should have sent more."

"You should have sent professionals."

"Ah yes, fortunately for you, professionals are hard to come by in this country."

"You've used amateurs before."

Qassem paused and attempted to tilt his head but it remained clasped to the chair.

"I am a diplomat, Mr. Reece. As I am sure you know, you are in violation of international law, specifically the Vienna Convention. I have diplomatic immunity."

"You are a spy. We have a separate set of rules for spies."

"Usually, one would need proof of some sort. You wouldn't want to create an international incident. Even with evidence you can only expel me."

"*Usually* that would be true, but this is far from a usual case."

"Do you plan to torture me, Mr. Reece?"

"Your fate is in your hands, Qassem. I know you planned the Marburg attack, that you passed Variant U to Dr. Ali Reza Ansari of Biodine Medical Systems, that you wanted us to think it was a respiratory-spread virus that would kill ninety percent of the country in an attempt to get us to trigger an eradication protocol that has been in place since the beginning of the Cold War."

Qassem remained silent.

"And there is something else," Reece said, picking up a photograph next to him. "It's grainy and it might be difficult to see in this light, but I think you will recognize the man in the photo. He's aged twenty years but I'm confident you know him."

Reece held up the photo in his left hand, illuminating it with a small Streamlight Stylus penlight. The photo was indeed grainy: black and white and in low resolution.

"That could be anyone, Mr. Reece."

"But it isn't anyone, Qassem. It was taken in Portland, Maine, on September tenth, 2001, at the same restaurant that also captured photos of two men who would be dead the next day."

"Oh? What happened to them?"

"They flew a plane into the North Tower of the World Trade Center."

"I was in Iran in September 2001," Qassem said, in a voice devoid of emotion.

"Just prior to midnight that same day, this man crossed the border into Canada," Reece continued, holding up another picture. It was still black and white, but the resolution was better. "Facial recognition technology was still in its infancy when these were taken, but it has improved significantly over the years."

"He does not look familiar."

"Look closer, Qassem. I'm sure you will recognize him," Reece said. "Here he is checking into the Montreal airport Marriott hotel a few hours later. He had a flight scheduled for the following day but of course flights were grounded for three days, so he stayed in the hotel and took an evening flight to Frankfurt on September fourteenth."

"A couple of blurry photographs of a Middle Eastern–looking man you say are from September 2001, mean nothing."

"Oh, to the contrary, it means everything when that man reenters the United States as a diplomat of a foreign nation and has access to the diplomatic pouch, and is on U.S. soil at the same time a virus is unleased on the twentieth anniversary of the most devastating terrorist attack in the nation's history."

"It wasn't released," Qassem countered. "I heard your president tell the world it was from Angola and that it burned itself out after an early spike when it was at its most potent."

"I heard that, too, Qassem. Did you believe it?"

"Why would I question it?"

"Because you brought Marburg Variant U into the United States in a diplomatic pouch. You passed it to Dr. Ansari, who then replicated it in a lab in Denver and unleashed it through surrogates to simulate a naturally occurring respiratory-spread virus."

"That seems far-fetched, Mr. Reece."

"It does, which is why I want just a little more information from you."

Reece set the photographs to the side and opened a nylon case.

"I know nothing about this, and I will not be coerced into taking responsibility for 9/11. Everyone knows it was the work of al-Qaeda and bin Laden."

Reece made a production of taking out an IV bag and hanging it just behind Qassem on a hook on the wall of the van. He removed medical scissors and cut the left sleeve off Qassem's shirt to expose the arm.

"What are you doing?" the Iranian intelligence officer asked, trying in vain to pull his arms and legs from the restraints.

"Do you know who you killed that day, Qassem?"

"I killed no one."

"You certainly did. You may not have flown the planes, but you met with Mohamed Atta that night in Portland. No one was able to figure out why Atta and al-Omari drove to Maine the night before their mission of death. But I know," Reece said, as he attached a thin rubber band tourniquet to Qassem's upper arm.

"I killed no one," Qassem repeated.

"I heard you the first time. You won't mind if I forgo cleaning the site, do you?"

Reece anchored the area by grabbing Qassem's upper forearm and pulling the skin tight with this thumb to prevent the vein from rolling. He then flipped the cap off the end of the needle and inserted it into Qassem's vein. Reece watched the flash chamber fill with blood. Keeping the needle in place he advanced the catheter into the arm with his forefinger, exerting pressure on the inserted portion to keep it in place. He removed the rubber band on the upper arm with his right hand and attached the IV tubing to the catheter.

"Do you know why I'm wearing this suit?" Reece asked through his respirator.

Once again, the aging spy chief remained silent.

Reece opened a small aluminum case and extracted a vial from the foam.

"Recognize this?" he said, holding the small, clear bottle up to the man strapped to the chair. "It's Marburg Variant U."

Reece inserted a needle and extracted a milliliter of its contents. He attached it to the injection post on the side of the drip container that fed saline solution into Qassem's arm.

"I know you are familiar with what this will do to you, Qassem. Unlike the innocent people you killed on 9/11 and those you killed in Aurora and Richardson, you get a choice today."

Qassem's eyes darted from the IV to his arm to his captor.

"You answer my questions and I drop you off at Dulles and you fly home to Iran. You don't, I hit this plunger and then I drop you at Fort Detrick. The doctors there are very anxious to study the effects of Marburg Variant U on the man who brought it into the country. They've only performed experiments on baboons and read the reports from the Soviet days of Dr. Ustinov slowly liquefying from the inside. That was over thirty years ago. You will add to the body of classified bioweapons research. Who knows, maybe something we learn from watching your body decompose from within will help develop an even more formidable weapon that we unleash on Iran."

Qassem felt the perspiration soaking his clothing and his bowels begin to loosen.

"Your choice, Qassem. And, just so you are aware, there is nothing I want to do more than hit this plunger and avenge everyone you've killed. Please give me an excuse."

"What do you want to know?"

"I want you to confirm for me that it is you in these photos."

Qassem's eyes went to the pictures and back to Reece.

"Give me an excuse, Qassem," Reece encouraged.

Qassem squeezed his eyes shut.

A'oothu billaahi minash-Shaytaanir-rajeem

I seek refuge with Allah against the Satan, the outcast.

"Qassem, answer me now or become a biomedical test subject. Those doctors at Fort Detrick, they won't take you out of your misery. They will keep you alive as long as possible to prolong your misery and extract as much research data as they can."

Qassem attempted to nod his head but the restraint kept it in place.

"Enjoy your stay at Fort Detrick," Reece said, raising the plunger to Qassem's face and applying pressure.

"It was me," Qassem said.

"Say that again," Reece ordered.

"It was me, but I only delivered a message. I didn't make the decision about 9/11. I passed along a word."

"What word? A word that triggered 9/11?"

"yd alshaytan."

"Arabic?"

"Yes, those al-Qaeda Sunnis did not understand Farsi. I swear I didn't know what it was."

"Somebody knew, Qassem. Somebody knew, because the next day three thousand of my countrymen would be dead."

"I thought it was for an attack on the White House. A car bomb maybe. My job was just to pass along a word and then drive to Canada. I found out about it on the news with everyone else."

"But then you made the connection, didn't you, Qassem?"

Qassem tried to nod.

"So, you waited until flights resumed and then you flew to Germany and back to Iran?"

"Yes."

"Who ordered you to deliver the message?"

Qassem's eyes darted to the syringe filled with liquid death. Not just death but weeks of misery or bleeding through skin pores, through eye sockets, through his penis and anus, a pain no one but Allah could stop.

"Ja'far al-Sadiq," Qassem whispered.

"Louder," Reece said.

"General Ja'far al-Sadiq."

"Who is that?"

"He is now the minister of intelligence."

"Did he plan it?"

"No."

"But he facilitated it, didn't he? He gave the green light. You delivered the message."

"Yes."

"And you planned this Marburg attack?"

"Your country is on its knees, Commander. Your response to COVID surprised even our brightest minds. Close down your schools and businesses and destroy your economy for a virus with less than a 0.3 percent mortality rate? With that kind of a response, what would you do with a respiratory virus with a ninety percent mortality rate? I wanted to call the operation off; you were already doing such a good job destroying yourselves from within. All we needed to do was sit back and watch as COVID, race riots, and identity politics further divided an already weak nation; it's just a matter of time."

"Why didn't you?"

"I am not the minister of intelligence. General al-Sadiq wanted to capitalize on the conditions set through your response to the coronavirus and riots. He has been on the front lines all his life but he is getting old. Rumor has it that he was with Imad Mughniyeh on the hill overlooking Beirut in '83. He's killed more Americans than al-Qaeda or those ISIS fools could ever hope. He should have been more patient, but I believe he wanted to see the Great Satan in ruins before he passes through the gates to Paradise." Qassem smiled. "Now, drop me at the airport and go fuck yourself."

Reece's thumb lingered over the plunger. He looked into Qassem's eyes as he began to increase downward pressure, the Iranian agent struggling in horror against the restraints.

Reece pulled his thumb away and detached the syringe, carefully capping it and locking it back into its padded case.

He then toggled a switch next to him on the wall and said, "Dulles."

They both felt the van turn to the left.

Reece looked into the eyes of the man still strapped to the chair across from him.

"You never answered my question about 9/11, Qassem."

"Which question?"

"When I asked you if you knew who else was killed that day."

To his unknowing expression Reece answered, "President Christensen's fiancée. Her name was Jennifer."

"So that's what you were doing in Chicago and Atlanta?" Qassem deduced.

"And it's what I'll continue to do once you are on that plane."

"You Americans . . ." Qassem said, attempting to shake his head. "You should kill me, you know."

"Don't think I won't one day, Qassem. Right now, the president wants you to send the regime a message."

The van pulled to a stop, but Reece didn't move. He continued to stare into his adversary's eyes as the doors opened and three men jumped inside, releasing Qassem from his restraints and roughly escorting him out the door and into a Goodwill store parking lot.

"You can find your way from here," one of the men said, before moving back toward a trail vehicle and getting inside.

Reece moved to the back of the van to close the doors.

"Hey, Qassem, I'll see you again. In this life or the next."

With that, Reece shut the doors and the van accelerated to the exit and onto Sunrise Valley Drive, leaving the man who delivered the order for 9/11 standing alone in the parking lot.

• • •

Vic Rodriguez joined Reece on the roof of the CIA annex at Dulles.

Reece stood behind a thick waist-high wall that encircled the roof.

"Think he bought it?" Vic asked.

"Not sure. I think he bought that I wanted to kill him. That wasn't a hard sell."

"I imagine not," Vic said. "Do you think he believed you had Marburg in that vial?"

"We'll never know."

"Which one is it?" Vic asked, changing subjects.

"That one there," Reece said, pointing to an aircraft on the tarmac.

Vic raised the binoculars around his neck and observed the twin-engine Beechcraft King Air prepare for takeoff.

"He's on board?" Vic asked.

"He is. I watched him board with a few others."

"Good. We've confirmed that it's a chartered flight making a short hop to JFK. The Iranian ambassador to the UN is staying in New York but his plane just filed a flight plan to Tehran via Madrid."

"What type of aircraft?" Reece asked.

"A Dassault Falcon 50: French long-range business jet flown by Iranian Air Force pilots."

Reece watched the small commuter plane taxi to the end of the runway, turn, pause, and then accelerate, gathering lift under its wings until it took to the sky.

"Good riddance, you son of a bitch."

CHAPTER 72

1st Fighter Wing, 27th Fighter Squadron
Langley Air Force Base, Virginia

THE PILOTS FROM THE F-22 Squadron had been scrambled before. Each time had been a false alarm. This alert was different.

Operation Noble Eagle consisted mainly of F-15 Eagles and F-16 Fighting Falcons flying Combat Air Patrols over the nation's capital, critical infrastructure, and high-profile public events. Authorized four days after September 11, 2001, the program was designed to shoot down hijacked aircraft to avert another 9/11-style attack. The 1st Fighter Wing with its 27th Fighter Squadron of F-22 Raptors trained for a different mission.

While the Noble Eagle aircraft patrolled the skies in and around Washington, D.C., the F-22s were tasked with intercepting incoming planes deemed a threat to the homeland while they were still in international airspace.

The two $334 million machines rocketed through the clouds at 62,000 feet per minute hitting Mach 2 and closed quickly with their target. Designed by Lockheed Martin with stealth as a primary requirement, their low radar cross section and radar-absorbent material rendered them all but invisible.

At 40,000 feet Langley handed off tactical control to the Eastern Air Defense Sector, headquartered at the Griffiss Business and Technology Park outside of Rome, New York.

Targeting Single on the nose, eighty nautical miles, Angels 37, Elvis communicated to his wingman using the fifth-generation fighter's Intra-Flight Data Link, a low probability of detection / low probability of interception communication system designed to augment the plane's stealth capabilities. Check pointer.

Painting a single, eighty out, Burbank replied via Data Link.

Their mission was not simply to engage and confirm destruction; their mission was to first conduct a flyby to ensure the target aircraft identified them as Americans and then to blow it out of the sky.

"Switching from data to voice," the lead pilot said over the MIDS-J, the multifunction distribution system that allowed F-22s to communicate in VHF when stealth was not a primary concern. In this case, U.S. attribution was a mission requirement.

"Target aircraft is leaving U.S. airspace, not incoming," Burbank said.

"Charlie Mike," Elvis replied, using the military jargon for "continue mission" as the two pilots closed the distance.

"Confirming remote ID," Elvis continued. "Confirmed."

"Roger. Remote ID verified," Burbank said.

"Visual confirmation of tail number required."

"Good copy. We don't want to get this one wrong."

The two fighters closed on the Iranian business jet.

"Tally," Elvis said.

"Tally," his dash-two confirmed.

Elvis slowed his aircraft to keep pace with the large passenger jet and approached at its eight o'clock.

"Tail number Echo—Papa—India—Bravo—Alpha, confirm."

Burbank pushed his Raptor to the four o'clock.

"Confirm, Echo—Papa—India—Bravo—Alpha. This is it."

"Roger, Burbank. Let's let them know we are here."

Elvis and Burbank both hit their afterburners, passing the unique trijet-configured aircraft within feet before circling back around to take up positions on the starboard and port sides, close enough that they could see the panicked looks of the pilot and copilot in the cockpit.

Burbank decreased his speed and visually confirmed that the windows were clear of passengers before throttling back up and taking up his position off the starboard fuselage. Elvis did the same on the opposite side of their target.

"Elvis, no passengers starboard side."

"Roger that, Burbank. One passenger port side."

A national intelligence satellite captured the sat-com transmission from the Iranian aircraft to Tehran. As with the targeted assassination of Admiral Yamamoto by American P-38s over Bougainville in 1943, the president didn't want to leave Iran with any questions as to who was responsible. That information was relayed to Eastern Air Defense Sector headquarters, who in turn sent an encrypted message to the F-22s.

`Target aircraft verified. Weapons Red and Free.`

Elvis confirmed receipt.

The two F-22s fell back to two nautical miles and established the airspace was clear. Both aircraft locked on to their target.

"Standing by," Burbank said.

"Roger," Elvis acknowledged. "Cleared Hot. Stand by. On my count: three, two, one, Fox Three."

Two AIM-120C air-to-air missiles dropped from the internal weapons bays of their fighter aircraft, propelled forward by solid-rocket fuel motors at Mach 4.

Unlike Air Force One, this aircraft did not have countermeasures and just like April 18, 1943, there would be no survivors.

The first advanced medium-range air-to-air missile impacted the port wing. A millisecond later the second missile hit mid-fuselage, igniting the fuel necessary for transatlantic flights and turning the Dassault Falcon 50 into a ball of fire over the Atlantic.

CHAPTER 73

Mustique Island, Grenadines, West Indies

"WE NEED TO COME up with a plan, Erik," Senator Thwaite said, cutting into his "lazy" lobster.

They sat at opposite ends of a long rectangular table with a stunning view over the Caribbean east toward Barbados just beyond the infinity pool.

Sawyer offered a condescending smile that bordered on pity. He clamped his hand around the stainless-steel tool and crushed the protective shell of his steamed Caribbean spiny lobster.

"You know you are eating that all wrong, Eddie," Sawyer replied, laying his seafood cracker on the table and using the long crab fork to pierce a section of the creature's succulent meat.

"You are just making a mess," Thwaite countered. "Just like you did with this whole surveillance business."

Thwaite reached for his glass.

"Enjoy that, Senator. It's a 'La Chatenière' Saint-Aubin 1er Cru 2017. Perfect for this meal."

Thwaite took a large enough gulp he hoped would annoy his host.

"Well, we've been here for almost a month. I'm starting to go stir crazy," Thwaite said, dunking a chunk of lobster into warm butter.

"Where would you prefer to go? Here, you are all but invisible. You've seen the news; everyone thinks you left town to avoid questions about illegal campaign contributions and conflict-of-interest issues."

"Those stories are planted. Christensen has the media in his pocket. They'll do anything for him, to include running false stories to ruin me."

"Regardless, it appears to me that the country is getting along quite well without you."

"Fuck you, Erik," Thwaite spat.

"Remember, Senator, it was your ill-advised call to the president that tipped your hand. You were a bit too eager to 'save the country' by dropping bombs on it."

"That *fucking* virus, how could it not be contagious?"

"If you were in your congressional seat, perhaps you'd be privy to classified briefings and might even know the answer to that question."

"Christensen probably orchestrated the whole thing just to give the country something to rally around and then ride in as their savior."

"With talk like that you should probably embrace your new life as a 'retired' expatriate."

"I can't stay here forever."

"You do what you'd like. You are not here free of charge. I'm keeping track."

"Oh, I know you are, Erik."

Mustique was a place one with means went to escape, to disappear. A private island situated between St. Lucia and Grenada, it rose to A-lister prominence in 1960, when the island's owner gifted ten acres to Princess Margaret. Since then, the destination had hosted the likes of Queen Elizabeth, the Duke and Duchess of Cambridge, Mick Jagger, David Bowie, and Tommy Hilfiger, though land once the exclusive domain of royalty, entrepreneurs, and artists was now being encroached upon by financiers and tech oligarchs. With no cruise ships anchored in the harbor, no paparazzi prowling the streets, and a strict no-drone policy, it remained a bastion for those in the jet-set crowd more concerned with privacy than society page stories.

"Lucky for you, my father was not a fan of government-imposed inheritance taxes. He made his money and wanted to keep it. He even made sure he passed away here."

"Lucky for you," Thwaite countered.

"Yes, he was a thoughtful man. Point being, you flew by private jet to Barbados and we used a private charter to get from Barbados to Mustique, as the one runway here is too short for the jet. This plot of land was owned by my father and is now the property of a holding corporation that shelters it from anyone who might want to tie it to me or Masada."

"That may be, but I don't feel safe with only four of your goons onsite for protection."

"Believe me, that is more than enough for Mustique. You are free to leave anytime you desire."

"If I go back, I'll be questioned by the FBI. They probably already know about the FISA warrants; your idea, I remind you. I'll be destroyed."

"Then maybe you just 'retire' down here. You have enough to rent a shack or guest house."

"Fuck off, Erik. I just need time."

"Time for what?"

"Just *time*."

"You are not still spooked by that James Reece character, are you?"

"*No*. Well, yes, aren't you? He's a fucking madman; the president's personal assassin. We were close to proving it. You saw what he did to those men in Maryland. What was it, ten people?"

"Eleven," Sawyer corrected, turning his attention out to sea.

"*Eleven. Jesus.* Eleven against one, Erik, and he killed them all."

"Calm down, Senator. He is not coming to Mustique. He doesn't even know you are here. Trust me. You are safe."

"Safe? I trusted you to eliminate him in D.C."

"Actually, it was Virginia."

"You failed, Erik. It was a simple mission and you failed. Don't think for a second that a man like Reece will let that go."

"You are right, Senator. And that is why I've taken measures to ensure we won't have to deal with James Reece ever again."

"Oh, what are you talking about? Your goons couldn't handle him before; what makes you think they can handle him now?"

"Because I'm not using my *goons*, as you call them. There's a man who solves problems for me, a man whose only job now is to kill James Reece."

"A problem solver? Like an assassin?" Thwaite asked.

"Just like that," Sawyer said.

"Delightful," Thwaite acknowledged. "Where is this man and when will it be done?"

"Patience, Senator. These things can't be rushed when dealing with professionals. Men like this are careful. They don't take chances or make rash decisions. They are calculated and discerning. That's how they stay alive."

"Well, finally some good news," Thwaite said. "In celebration I think I'll pour myself another glass of *your* fine wine."

CHAPTER 74

REECE AND OX STEPPED from the small yacht tender and onto the dock at Basil's Bar. Live music cascaded from the deck where the Wednesday night band provided entertainment to residents, guests, and sailors. No one paid much attention to the two men dressed in the appropriate attire of those who belonged: beige slacks and tropical-colored button-down shirts. Ox wore a light tan jacket to ward off the breeze and Reece had added a navy blue blazer just in case he needed to melt into the shadows. The outerwear also helped conceal the suppressors attached to their subcompact pistols.

The eighty-foot catamaran moored just offshore belonged to a charter company owned by the CIA's Maritime Branch. The seaborne equivalent of Ground Branch, they reported to Vic Rodriguez's Special Activities Center and operated covered maritime assets around the world.

The two operators ascended the steps to the main-level bar and passed among the dancing revelers, free to let loose with the bar's no-camera policy, knowing their pictures would not be plastered all over social media the following day.

"What do you want?" Ox asked, as they approached the bar.

"Whatever you're buying," Reece replied.

Ox waited at the bar while Reece scanned the crowd. He was searching for someone.

"What can I get for you?" a distinguished-looking black man asked. His hair was almost all gray and he was dressed in a long, flowing white robe open to his chest. A beaming smile pushed his round glasses up off his cheeks, the soft lights that illuminated the bar reflecting off the thin lenses.

"What do you suggest, sir?" Ox asked, scanning the selections.

"I recognize a kindred soul when I see one," the old man said. "How about a Hurricane David? Most powerful drink on the menu, blend of rums and vodka. Since I can tell it's your first time here, I'm going mix in a new KōHana rum from a friend in Hawaii."

"Mighty kind. I'll take two," Ox said.

The CIA man turned back to Reece. "See him?"

Reece nodded.

Their target was not hard to find: young, gelled hair, tight polo to show off his chemically enhanced muscles covered with full-sleeve tattoos. He danced with a woman twice his age on the dance floor. Instead of a Patek Philippe or Panerai on his wrist, he sported a Casio G-Shock.

"I've got him," Reece said.

"Here you go," the old man said from behind the bar, sliding the drinks across.

"Thank you, sir," Ox said, putting two twenties and a ten in U.S. dollars on the bar.

"Thank you. Call me Basil. Enjoy your stay."

The former Delta Force sergeant major turned back to Reece and handed him the most expensive cocktail he'd ever purchased.

The two operators moved to a darker corner of the bar, pretending to drink and enjoy a carefree conversation like the rest of the patrons.

When the contractor they'd already nicknamed "Muscles" broke away from his cougar and sauntered across the floor, Ox looked to his partner.

"Ready to ruin his night?" he asked.

Reece set down his untouched drink and moved toward the restroom.

• • •

Fifteen minutes later the three men approached the driveway of Sawyer's villa on the eastern side of the island, just south of Macaroni Bay. Muscles drove the Mule, a side-by-side four-person vehicle used by most island residents to go from the tennis courts to the beach to Basil's.

"Like I said," Ox reminded "Muscles." "You cooperate and you get immunity from whatever comes of this. If not, at the very best you are entering into years of legal trouble where your opponent has government attorneys and you have to pay for yours."

"We are here for your boss," Reece said. "Not you or your friends."

"I understand," Muscles said.

It hadn't taken much: a marshal badge and the recognition that two serious CIA operatives wanted a word with Erik Sawyer and his guest. The suppressed SIG P365 pistol Reece held as Ox explained the situation didn't hurt, either.

"Once again," Reece clarified. "We have no issues with you or your team. We just need you to stand down. If not, we will kill all of you and I'll make sure you take the first bullet."

Muscles swallowed hard and nodded.

• • •

"How about a cigar?" Sawyer asked. "This one's on me. I won't even add it to your bill."

"That's generous of you," Thwaite said, his voice the epitome of contempt.

"The deck then. It's a beautiful night," Sawyer said, rising from his chair and picking up a glossy black and red box from a wood sideboard filled with china.

The doors leading to the balcony that overlooked the pool and ocean were already open.

"I smoked my first cigar out here," Sawyer said, taking in the view. "We'd spend a few weeks here every season."

"You were a lucky *fucking* kid," Thwaite said.

"That is true," Sawyer conceded, opening the box and holding it out for his guest.

"What do we have?" Thwaite asked.

"Cohiba Spectre. Even I had a tough time finding them."

Thwaite picked a thick cigar from the box and ran it under his nose, closing his eyes to inhale the sweet nut and maple flavors of the exquisitely aged leaf.

"A woman is only a woman . . ." he said.

". . . but a good cigar is a smoke," Sawyer added, completing the Rudyard Kipling line from *The Betrothed*.

"Ha! Isn't that the truth," the senator stated. "Pass me your lighter, would you?"

• • •

Reece left Ox holding his weapon on the kneeling four-man contracted guard force and made his way up the stairs and down the hall. The contractors were the modern equivalent of mercenaries. Their loyalty was to the dollar. None of them were ready to die for their CEO. One way or another their boss was going down. They were not about to drown with a sinking ship. Ox's Glock 43 along with zip ties reinforced with rigger's tape ensured they wouldn't have a sudden change of heart.

At the end of the hall, Reece inched a tall door open. Two dirty dinner plates were at opposite ends of a long table. Hearing voices from the balcony, he moved toward his objective.

. . .

A shadow warned them they were no longer alone.

The blood drained from Thwaite's face and his hand fell to the armrest of his wicker lounge chair, the ash from his cigar dropping to the deck.

Sawyer's natural reaction was to go for his pistol, but he recognized the intruder immediately and thought better of it.

"James Reece, what a surprise," the Masada CEO ventured, his voice masking an unease he hadn't felt since the streets of Mogadishu.

Reece moved onto the expansive balcony, weapon extended, a light breeze rustling through the fronds of the imported palm trees below.

The two men sat in high-backed dark wicker chairs. A rattan coffee table was positioned between them, adorned with a massive glass ashtray. Reece redirected the pistol from Sawyer to the senator.

"This ends one of two ways, Senator. You either come back with me or I spill your brains all over your friend's outdoor furniture."

"And what about him?" Thwaite asked, pointing his partially smoked Cohiba at the Whore of War across from him.

"Oh, he's coming, too."

Sawyer took a deep pull of his cigar, exhaling the sweet smoke into the island air.

"How did you find me, Mr. Reece? I'm curious."

"Trade secrets, Sawyer. You aren't quite as smart as you think."

"Fascinating," Sawyer said, making a mental note to fire his attorneys.

"You can't just come in here and threaten me. I'm a sitting United States senator, for God's sake."

Reece raised the pistol and watched Thwaite shrink back into the cushions of his chair.

"You, *Senator*, are much more than that. You leaked a video extremely damaging to the security of the country. You also issued an order to kill me and a doctor trying to save the lives of almost half a million of our fellow countrymen."

"I deny these unfounded accusations!"

"You can deny all you want, Senator. Sawyer's wannabe operators sang like canaries. You can come back with me or you can die here and end up a part of island lore."

Thwaite's mouth opened agape, looking to Sawyer for help.

The former Army Ranger took a drawn-out puff of his Cohiba, weighing his options. When the opportunity arose, he'd go for his Glock and do what his underlings had proven incapable of; he would kill James Reece.

Create your opportunity.

"I think we will stay right here, Commander," Sawyer said, buying time. "The American public will soon forget any good you may have done. They will be much more concerned that a president has a lone-wolf assassin running around in violation of international law and our very own Bill of Rights."

Just create the space you need to go for the Glock. Action is faster than reaction. You've got this.

"That's a distinct possibility, Sawyer, and something we can't control. What you can control is how this night ends."

"My lawyers will have me out of this as soon as I set foot on U.S. soil. It's best for you to let this lie. No good can come from it."

"That's where you're wrong, Sawyer. Something will come from it."

"Oh yeah, and what's that?" Sawyer asked, shifting his weight to give him better access to the modified pistol in his waistband.

"Justice," Reece said.

Three shots tore through the night air in rapid succession, but they didn't come from Reece's gun.

The first two rounds missed completely, sailing off into the night.

The third caught Sawyer just below the heart, his body contorting around the wound. His hands fumbled at his shirt as he grabbed for something in the front of his pants.

Reece spun back to the senator and went to a knee to change his elevation in time to see Thwaite fire another round from a shiny silver small-framed revolver. The fourth round entered Sawyer's forehead, taking most of his skull with it, a large chunk of gray brain matter catching on the wicker seatback. His head dropped to his chest and his lifeless body fell forward in his chair.

Reece slowly stood, his weapon trained on the senator, who still had his pistol pointed at the man who had so tormented and ultimately failed him.

Depending on the model, Reece knew it still had one or two live rounds in the cylinder.

"Senator, you have one chance to put that down."

Unable to take his eyes off his psychological tormentor, Thwaite slowly moved the Smith & Wesson revolver to his lap.

"It's over," he whispered.

"It's over," Reece repeated, his finger taking up slack on the trigger.

"You know," Thwaite said, a knowing smile slowly forming on his lips as he turned his head to Reece. "You won't live through the year."

To Reece's inquisitive look he continued: "I just killed the one person on earth who can call off a hit on you."

The senator's smile broadened.

Then he brought the revolver to the side of his head, closed his eyes, and blew his brains across the veranda.

CHAPTER 75

Catoctin Mountain Park, Maryland

"I GIVE US A one-in-ten chance of making it alive," Katie teased.

It was the inaugural voyage of the 1985 Jeep Grand Wagoneer that had once belonged to Reece's father. It was finally up and running, the 5.9-liter V8 delivering a whopping 140 horsepower. Katie couldn't help but give Reece a hard time about his "classic" as the heavy four-by-four lumbered up Route 15 toward Thurmont.

"Oh, come on," Reece replied. "Sixty percent of the time it works every time."

Katie rolled her eyes at the old movie line.

"I even got the back window to roll up," he said proudly.

"Correction: an army of mechanics attempted to fix the back window, but now it's stuck in the 'up' position."

"You see—progress."

They turned onto Rocky Ridge Road and crossed over Big Hunting Creek.

"This is where she really excels," Reece kidded, stepping on the gas.

"Yeah, this beast corners like it's on rails."

"Nice eighties reference. I'm impressed," Reece said.

Katie turned to the man she loved.

"Thank you, James."

"Thank me? For what?"

"Without you. Without Haley. This . . ." she said, gesturing outside. "This doesn't exist. We'd be driving through a different country."

"Haley put it together. Rumor has it the president wants to honor her with the Presidential Medal of Freedom and the SecDef Medal for Valor. Of course, it would remain classified."

"When I talk with her, she gives you all the credit. I think she's being intentionally vague on a few details."

"Maybe that's best," Reece said.

"Maybe," Katie granted.

"And, Katie, try to go easy on him."

"What do you take me for, Mr. Reece? You think just because this is an exclusive interview at Camp David and that you refer to him the way you would someone you play softball with that I'm going to give him layups?"

"I think you are mixing your sports metaphors. I don't even play bowling."

"You know what I mean, Mr. Reece."

"I know what you mean. Do your interview. Then we'll shoot some skeet and have dinner."

"You say that like it's normal."

"Katie, I don't know what 'normal' is."

Katie tried to hide her fading smile as Reece turned onto Park Central Road and began to wind his way through the white oaks, poplars, maples, birch, and eastern hemlocks toward the presidential retreat.

CHAPTER 76

Camp David, Aspen Cabin

REECE TOOK HIS OFFERED seat on the small couch in Aspen cabin. Following Katie's interview, the three had shot skeet and had dinner at Laurel Lodge. Katie had retired to Hawthorn cabin to go over her notes from the interview and to give Reece and the president some time alone.

"I thought you were going to touch the place up," Reece said as the president set a whiskey in front of his guest and took a seat in the chair across the coffee table.

"I decided against it. I've grown to like it as it is. Simple. Peaceful. Camp David isn't mine. I'm just a guest. This is the presidential retreat, and I am only here for a term, maybe two."

"Looks like two from what I see," Reece said, raising his drink to touch glasses with the president.

"We'll see. If the people trust me with another four years after what we've just been through, I owe it to them."

"How did it go with Katie?"

"Ms. Buranek is quite the journalist. She hit me hard on the revamped plans for eradication in the event of another *naturally* occurring virus."

"She is tenacious. What did you tell her?"

"The truth. That the bipartisan commission has issued me a classified report that I am still digesting."

"Wise answer."

"Reece, less than a handful of people in government know that the virus was Marburg Variant U and that it was an intentional bioweapon attack against the country."

"I know, sir."

"I lied to the American people in my address and I didn't bat an eye."

"You did what you had to in order to prevent a war with Iran. A bioweapon attack means retaliation in kind, which in this case means the nuclear option."

"I'd be the first president since Truman to use the nuclear weapons against an adversary. Ironic that Truman also put the eradication measures in place that almost led to the destruction of Richardson and Aurora."

"Some things are best handled quietly."

"Ah yes, the third option," the president said, taking a sip of whiskey as he recalled the motto of the CIA's Special Activities Center.

"You know why I lied, Reece?"

"To avert a nuclear war."

"Partially, but I really lied for Jen."

"Sir?"

"I thought of that day: September eleventh. Seeing the planes hit. Running through the streets. Digging through the rubble, thinking that I'd find her alive under each slab of debris."

Reece remained silent.

"There was never any hope. I guess deep down I knew it. In weighing my options in response to Iran I thought of all the 'Jens' in Iran, all those young men and women just starting their lives with hope of a better future. I wanted her life to mean more than further deaths. They still have it, you know."

"What's that, sir?"

"Hope."

"We had a saying in the Teams: 'Hope is not a course of action.'"

"Cynical, but true. We also know who gave the final go-ahead in Portland, Maine, on September tenth."

"And he's now at the bottom of the Atlantic," Reece said.

"Yes, that was the shot across the bow to let the Iranians know we are willing to use any means necessary to protect the homeland."

"Just like with Yamamoto," Reece observed.

"Correct, though the downing of his aircraft was the prologue to Hiroshima and Nagasaki. My goal is to avoid that outcome."

"Yes, sir. Iran waited twenty years after 9/11 to hit us again. They used their long-term, deep-penetration agents on a mission that kills them off in the process. Had that facilitation network been killed following September eleventh, we would have pieced it together. But no one would notice when they are among the thousands killed two decades later by a virus or FAE."

"A part of me respects their ingenuity," the president said. "They learn from their successes and failures. We seem to repeat ours."

"They've been studying us since the 1953 coup," Reece confirmed. "Their success using proxies in Lebanon in the eighties got them the results they desired. Up until 9/11 we gave them no indication that we were serious about defeating terrorism at the source. And then we handed them our playbook. They've watched us on the field in Iraq and Afghanistan. They adapted and applied those lessons to their battle plans. Then they watched us take a knee with COVID-19 and the civil unrest that followed in its wake."

"*A house divided against itself cannot stand,*" the president said.

"Lincoln was right," Reece said. "The enemy recognized that and hit us while we were down."

"There is still a lot of work to do, Reece."

"I know, sir. What about the remainder of names on your list?"

The president paused.

"With malice toward none; with charity for all."

"Lincoln's second inaugural," Reece said. *"With firmness in the right."*

"We can all evolve, Commander. FBI has them back under 24/7 surveillance, electronic and physical. If they are contacted, we will know it. Maybe we can use them to prevent more Jens from dying."

"I think that is a prudent move, Mr. President."

"And, not being a compete idealist, the intelligence you and Dr. Haley Garrett provided gave me leverage. We can prove beyond a shadow of a doubt that Iran planned and executed the bio-attack. The Iranian president is scared shitless. He knows that we've confirmed their role in 9/11, assisting al-Qaeda with materials and a support network in the United States, and that if it were ever to go public, I would have no choice but to retaliate in a way that sends them back to the stone age; NATO, the UN, the international community could do nothing to intervene. That leverage has allowed us to send in U.S. and UN inspectors to oversee the dismantling of the Iranian nuclear, bio, and chemical weapons programs. There is nothing they can't access."

"I've been following along. Rumor has it, you might be a candidate for the Nobel Peace Prize."

"So I've heard. I'm no Lincoln, Reece. My heart still has the capacity for malice."

"I'll do what I can to not get caught."

"We can't have an American captured on the ground in Iran."

"Don't worry about that," Reece said, visions of the bullet-ridden bodies of his wife and child imprinted on his mind. Maybe he'd see them sooner than anticipated.

"Do you feel comfortable with the intelligence? With the plan?"

"I do, sir. I was part of a team that studied the target area back in 2004. A DIA analyst had pinpointed Abu Musab al-Zarqawi in the same location. He was in Iran and we had him dead to rights."

"Why didn't we hit him?" the president asked.

"They don't tell you that sort of thing at the tactical level, sir. All we knew was that the insurgency in Iraq was gaining headway and we were losing control. Al-Zarqawi had emerged as the leader of AQI, al-Qaeda in Iraq, and the DIA had cracked the code on the enemy's Thuraya sat phone network. I remember seeing a highway of lights from Baghdad, through Tehran, and up to Chalus on the Iranian coast."

"Lights?"

"Sat-phone pings. The analysts told us it was like a resort town for terrorists, a place where they could get a little R&R on the shores of the Caspian Sea before crossing back over the border to kill more Americans; *respite from killing the infidels and Jews,* we were told."

"What was the plan back then?"

"To drop into the Caspian, go over the beach, and raid the house. We had Kurdish dissidents run by the CIA confirming our technical intel from the sat-phone network. He was there and we were ready to take him off the board."

"But somebody pulled the plug?"

"That's right. Maybe the president or SecDef. Somebody high up the chain didn't want SEALs killing a terrorist eighty miles from Tehran."

"Imagine if you had; the insurgency might have looked a lot different."

"Perhaps," Reece said, thinking of all his friends who had been killed over the intervening years as the United States continued to bog down in the cradle of civilization.

"Okay, then. Get it done, then come home and marry that girl."

"Sir?"

"Katie, your girlfriend who is waiting on you at Hawthorn cabin," the president reminded his guest.

"Ah, well, maybe, sir. I need to figure a few things out," he said, thinking about the note and safe-deposit box key he'd found in the weapons case in the back of the old Wagoneer: his father's message from the grave.

"Well, don't take too long, Reece. She might not wait forever. Trust me, life is about what you two have together."

Reece took another sip of the smooth brown liquid and looked at the president. He'd aged since their first meeting. The gray in his hair was more pronounced, as were the creases around his eyes and across his brow.

"I know," the president said, reading Reece's mind. "This office puts some years on you."

"Sir, before I go, I have a request."

"Oh?"

"I need you to sign an executive notification for the elimination of Nizar Kattan."

Christensen looked into his drink and back to Reece.

"He took a shot at the Russian president in Odessa. And he killed my friend Freddy Strain, the man who saved President Grimes. It's personal for me. I want it to be professional for the rest of the country's intelligence apparatus. I want this to become priority number one until he's dead."

"I see."

"I knew you would," Reece said. "He's a terrorist, which puts it under the purview of the 2001 Authorization for the Use of Military Force. It's legal as long as you deem him a clear and present danger to the United States. He was part of an assassination attempt on your predecessor. That should be enough."

The president considered it for a moment.

"It will be done."

"Something else. I don't want a Hellfire from a UAV to take him out on his way to the mosque and I don't want a Delta or Dam Neck squadron paying him a visit in the middle of the night. I just want him found. Leave the rest to me."

The president studied the man before him. It wasn't long ago that he was asking the same thing of Reece in this very room.

"Since we are in the business of asking for favors tonight," Christensen said, "I have one of my own."

Reece nodded as the president reached behind his neck and removed a necklace with a simple platinum band on it.

"This was Jen's wedding ring," he said solemnly. "We picked them out together before she died. When I got out of the hospital, I put it on this chain. I've worn it every day since. Do me a favor; when you kill him, leave it with the man responsible for her death."

Reece took the burnished gray band and examined it. He remembered sliding a similar ring onto Lauren's finger on their wedding day, lifting the veil and looking into her soft blue eyes.

"It's inscribed with your name," Reece observed.

"It is. Mine had her name inscribed inside the band and hers had mine."

Reece put it in his pocket, stood, and extended his hand.

"It will be done," Reece said, before exiting into the crisp winter night.

CHAPTER 77

Chalus, Iran

JA'FAR AL-SADIQ SAT ON a stool in front of a spigot that protruded from the wall on the second level of a house overlooking the Caspian. He began the ritual cleansing of *wadhu* to prepare for *Salat al-'isha* by washing his right hand and then his left, each one carefully purified in accordance with the second pillar of Islam. It was closing in on midnight. He leaned forward and brought a handful of water to his mouth, spitting it back into the sink to remove any impurities. He remembered going through the same ritual the morning of October 23, 1983. He cupped another handful and inhaled the cold smell before cleaning his face, starting at his forehead and scrubbing down to his chin, making a special effort to clean his ears.

The sleeves of his white robe were pushed up past his elbows and he took time to scrub his forearms, first his right and then his left. He then slicked back what remained of a full head of graying hair. He was sure to once again wipe down inside and around his ears. He then brought his right foot to the spigot and washed it carefully three times before switching to his left.

Finally, he reached down to pick up a toothbrush. One could not be too careful. The prophet Muhammad, peace be upon him, had looked favorably upon him all these years.

The Islamic ritual did more than purify his body; it gave him time to prepare his mind for prayer. He had been thinking of the early days with greater frequency lately, something he attributed to advancing age. Tonight, he remembered the first blow against the invaders, watching the cloud form over the U.S. Marine Corps barracks in Beirut as he stood next to Imad Mughniyeh. They had been young men that October day. It was hard to believe Mughniyeh had been gone for more than a decade, his presence and influence still felt within the ranks of Hezbollah even after the Israeli pigs, with help from their American CIA masters, had killed him in Damascus.

How this latest attack had failed remained a mystery. Still, he had put more than five thousand Americans in the grave. It could have been so many more.

The al-Qaeda martyrs of 2001 had succeeded beyond al-Sadiq's wildest expectations. The Americans had then focused their efforts on hunting down a wealthy Saudi who had taken refuge in Pakistan. *Fools.* Iran had used al-Qaeda as a proxy force to strike at the heart of the West. It was masterful. General Ja'far al-Sadiq was proud of his triumph.

Now bin Laden was dead, shot down by American SEALs. Had he taken refuge in Iran he might still be alive.

The Americans are nothing without their technology.

They are soft.

Yes, they are soft, but now they know the truth.

They have already shifted focus to Iran.

You underestimated them.

Perhaps, but as before, we must adapt.

U.S. and UN inspectors were scouring the country to dismantle the programs designed to defend the Islamic Republic from the infidels. The president had not stood up to the invaders this time. Perhaps a regime change was in order. As director of the Ministry of Intelligence, Ja'far was one of the few with the power to alter Iran's trajectory.

He still had work to do. Sleeper cells remained embedded in the Western world. If they continued to welcome those who wanted to destroy them inside their gates, it would be the death of them. Allah would see to that.

The feeble Americans had never set foot in Iran. Instead they labeled the regime a state sponsor of terror. They applied sanctions. They issued harsh rhetoric, not realizing that their weakness allowed Iran to shape the next generation of Fedayeen, a new generation of holy warriors determined to see the United States in ruins. It might not happen on Ja'far's watch, but it was inevitable.

A space in the beachfront structure had been converted to a *musalla* years ago, a prayer room reserved for those warriors of the prophet Muhammad who would come to Chalus to rest and plan. It had seen considerable use since the Americans invaded Iraq.

Al-Sadiq entered the sacred chamber, faced the al-Ka'bah al-Musharrafah in Mecca, placed his AK at his side, and began to pray.

CHAPTER 78

THEY HAD LAUNCHED OUT of the Iranian fishing town of Jireh Bagh, just east of Dastak on the edge of the Caspian Sea, and trolled the waters off Chalus. No strangers to this southwestern part of the Caspian, the four-man crew had two additional passengers on this run.

They were after beluga caviar, the salt-cured eggs from female sturgeon so sought after by those with means. Classified as a critically endangered species, the sturgeon was nearing extinction. To the fishermen aboard the trawler, it simply meant their catch brought a higher price on illicit markets. Iran was not a country known for adhering to international norms and conventions.

As with most prohibited substances, the prohibitions created even more demand. The same networks that moved people, drugs, and weapons also moved illicit wildlife. In this case, a portion of the income generated from smuggling illegal roe helped fund the PJAK, the Kurdistan Free Life Party, a Kurdish separatist group classified as a terrorist organization by the Iranian regime and the United States. Though the CIA was prohibited from having any official connection to the PJAK, those who worked in the charcoal-gray area of the clandestine service knew the value of maintaining relationships with the enemy of one's enemy.

The caviar smugglers were about to receive a healthy payday to help fund the resistance while at the same time removing an Iranian official involved in what amounted to a genocide against the Kurdish people.

The boat had red paint markings to signify they had paid the appropriate bribes to the right officials to prevent boarding and inspections. The fishermen had their orders: insert their package off the coast of Chalus, 125 miles to the southeast, and continue on their usual path. They were to return to the waters off Chalus two days later, wait until just before dawn, and then continue back to their home port if their package failed to return.

Reece had entered Iran through Iraq by way of Turkey. The Agency maintained a base in Erbil for their Peshmerga fighting force despite the official policy of the United States toward Kurdistan. The CIA-trained direct-action force also ran operations into Iran across borders the Kurds did not recognize, gathering intelligence and atmospherics and distributing cell phones into the black market loaded with spyware from the whiz kids at Langley's Directorate of Science and Technology. Kurdish smugglers moved everything from weapons to cigarettes to alcohol to cars to jeans to illegal drug precursors to walnuts. Two nights ago, they had smuggled in their first American.

The phones the Kurds had been feeding into Iran's economy had penetrated the upper echelons of the Iranian military and intelligence apparatus and had led to the death of Quds Force General Qasem Soleimani at Baghdad International Airport. That same technology had given the CIA access to Ja'far al-Sadiq's travel schedule.

The American hadn't said a word to anyone other than the Iraqi who accompanied him. When they spoke to one another it was only in whispers. A traditional *shemagh* covered his head and face, obscuring his features. They could tell he was bearded, dirt and dust visible around eyes that seemed to change from brown to green depending on the light or his mood. *A chameleon.*

The man sat watching the coast or looking north out to sea. He accepted the offered tea and dates. The intensity radiated by his calm, silent focus made them nervous, but his companion helped put them at ease. They had been instructed to only call him Mohammed, but they heard the American call him by another name: Mo.

When Mohammed wasn't whispering to the infidel, he shared stories and cigarettes with the crew. His easy smile, dark slicked-back hair, and dashing looks made them all feel comfortable with what they were about to do.

Around midnight the American unrolled a dirty rag from his satchel and began to assemble what the fisherman recognized as a Kalashnikov, though this one had a thin metal stock that folded under the weapon. One of the smugglers had seen his share of fighting and recognized the flip-up grenade sights, three cutouts on the hand guard, and Arabic markings identifying it as a "Tabuk," named in honor of the prophet Muhammad's final military expedition. The fisherman watched as their passenger ran his thumb over a symbol of the Lion of Babylon engraved on the left side of the rear sight block. The mariner found himself wondering what, or who, the man was remembering.

They watched as he carefully wiped down the bolt and applied grease to its stem and triangular lug with his finger. He then wiped grease on the bottom of the bolt lugs and across the lower portion of the bolt carrier assembly. When it was finished, he attached what they knew as a silencer to the end of the barrel. He then pointed it out to sea, reached under the weapon, and racked the charging handle with his left thumb. He pushed the selector to its top position and pressed the trigger. Nothing happened, indicating the safety worked as intended. The smugglers watched their passenger move the selector lever to the bottom position and press the trigger. He was rewarded with an audible *click*. He then racked the charging handle again, with his finger still retaining the trigger rearward in the "pulled" position. As he released the trigger, another audible click could be heard as the trigger's disconnector returned the hammer to a ready-to-fire state, confirming that the weapon functioned properly in semiautomatic. He then moved the selector to the middle position and pulled the trigger. *Click.* He racked the charging handle a third time, keeping the trigger depressed. This time he slowly rode the bolt home, hearing the automatic click of the hammer as the bolt seated into battery. He then released the trigger. *Silence.* No *click* permeated the night air, which verified that the hammer had followed the bolt home on the rifle's fully automatic setting, exactly as its inventor had envisioned.

With what the fishermen could tell was practiced efficiency, the American inserted a dark metal magazine and clicked it into place. He then racked the charging handle, returned the selector to the safe position, and pulled the bolt back slightly to ensure a steel casing gleamed back. Americans were strange. He reached into his bag, stood, and lifted a dark green chest rig with what looked to be three magazines over his head, adjusting it before sliding his arm through the sling of his rifle and moving it to his left side.

The fisherman had never seen anyone handle an AK like that before. They'd shot a few themselves and had only put in the magazine and pulled back on the charging handle before letting loose on full auto. The rifles had worked every time. He then did something even more peculiar. The foreigner pulled out what looked like a trash bag and snapped it open to fill with air. He pushed more than half the air from the bag, tied it off, and stuffed it into his satchel. He stood and whispered something to his companion. The two men hugged in the way of old friends. Then the American slipped over the side and disappeared into the Caspian.

CHAPTER 79

REECE PUSHED THE SATCHEL in front of him as his legs worked beneath the surface, propelling him toward shore.

The air-filled garbage bag provided flotation and Reece rested the venerable AK on the leather satchel. He was confident it would work even when filled with sand and salt water; that was the genius of Kalashnikov's iconic design. Even so, Reece did his best to keep it dry, just to be safe.

He could see the lights of Chalus ahead. From the water it appeared no different from any other seaside town or coastal city in which he had trained or operated over his time in Naval Special Warfare. In this case he'd studied the coastline years ago when he and his team had waited for the green light to capture or kill Abu Musab al-Zarqawi, a mission approval that never came. Tonight, that training and those rehearsals would prove valuable.

He didn't come in directly on the urban center of Chalus, choosing instead to come ashore at the far eastern end of the beach, an area devoid of lights.

Fifty yards from shore he paused, holding his homemade flotation device and treading water with his legs as he scanned for threats. He tasted the salt of the Caspian on his lips, its strength diluted by the numerous freshwater inflows to what was essentially the world's largest lake. The water was cold, even this far south of the Volga.

Being immersed in a maritime operating environment was not a new experience for the former frogman. Without a wet suit or dry suit, Reece felt oddly more in tune with his surroundings than he had since he'd ventured across Siberia the year before. He also knew he couldn't scan the shoreline all night. He had someplace he needed to be.

It was imperative he get into position before the sun came up. His local dress and satchel that fit the underfolder-stocked, Iraqi-manufactured AK, and *shemagh* would allow him to pass at first glance. Anything other than a cursory inspection and Reece was going to guns. The PBS-1 suppressor and subsonic ammo would buy him time. How much time? That was an unknown.

Satisfied that this section of the resort town shoreline was clear, Reece alternated between breaststroke kicks and scissor kicks and drove himself toward his target.

I come from the water.

CHAPTER 80

PLACING HIS MIND BELOW his heart in the position of prostration, kneeling to symbolize submission to God, Ja'far al-Sadiq was tranquil and at peace.

He moved from kneeling to sitting for the final verses of *Isah,* which he internalized, eyes closed and focused.

Allaahumma 'innee 'a'oothu bika min 'athaabil-qabri, wa min 'athaabi jahannama, wa min fitnatil-mahyaa walmamaati, wa min sharri fitnatil-maseehid-dajjaal.

O Allah, I take refuge in You from punishment of the grave, from the torment of the Fire, from the trials and tribulations of life and death, and from the evil affliction of the false Messiah.

Allahu Akbar.

Audhu billahi min-ash-shayta-nir-rajeem

Before he could finish the verse, Ja'far al-Sadiq felt the pressure change in the small room as a door opened behind him.

Bismillah-ir-Rahman-ir-raheem, he completed the prayer.

He turned his head to bark at the guard and instead found himself staring down the barrel of a rifle. The candles provided just enough illumination to identify the suppressor protruding from the end of a Kalashnikov held by a tall man, head and face wrapped in a beige and black *shemagh*, a cloth rig of extra magazines strapped to his chest.

"Who are you?" Ja'far demanded in Farsi.

The man moved to Ja'far's left, kicking the AK out of arm's reach.

"Guard!" Ja'far yelled.

"They won't hear you. Not until you join them anyway," the man said in English.

"American? You are American?" Ja'far said, switching to English.

The AK's selector lever was in the down position on semiautomatic and the man's finger was on the trigger.

"You really shouldn't be so afraid of dogs. Had you cleared this place with them you might not have died tonight."

"What do you want?" Ja'far asked, attempting to get to his feet.

"You can stay on your knees, General. This won't take long."

Ja'far settled back on the ground, calculating distances to the door and to his AK in the corner.

"Who are you?"

With the Kalashnikov still trained on the veteran of terror, Reece reached up with his left hand and pulled the *shemagh* around and down to hang loosely at his neck.

Ja'far's eyes widened in recognition.

"I know you."

"You don't *know* me. You may know who I am, but you don't *know* me."

Ja'far's eyes narrowed.

"And you are here to execute an old man on his knees?"

"Not an old man. An enemy. A terrorist."

"Ah yes, a terrorist," Ja'far said thoughtfully, bringing his eyes up to meet his intruder's gaze. "You Americans are so fond of that word. *War on Terror*. Dropping bombs from the sky and killing entire families with drones. The world knows the real terrorists, Mr. Reece."

"And Beirut, 9/11, Marburg?"

"Don't insult me, Mr. Reece. Beirut would be a legitimate military target even by your definition of *terrorism*. I've read your literature: 'car bombs are the poor man's air force.'"

"And 9/11? Marburg?"

"You and the Israelis give us no choice. This is a struggle for the soul of the world. It always has been about religious and economic domination. Bringing the Holy Land under *kafir* control; the objectives of the Crusades are still very much the goals of U.S. foreign policy."

Reece shook his head.

"Where do you think that fool bin Laden got his *fatwā*?" Ja'far asked. "From al-Zawahiri? The brains of *the Base*? He is too smart to tip his hand that way. That al-Qaeda *fatwā* came from *me*."

Ja'far bowed his head again and recited the *fatwā* that had been a declaration of war against the West, a war that only one side recognized when it was issued in 1998.

"To kill the Americans and their allies—civilians and military—is an individual duty for every Muslim who can do it in any country in which it is possible to do it."

"You killed innocent men, women, children, even fellow Muslims," Reece said.

"I think you Americans coined the term *collateral damage*. They are martyrs for the cause and sit at the right hand of Allah."

"Before you join them, I have a message for you to send the regime."

"A message? I think you sent that message when you shot down a diplomatic aircraft over the Atlantic."

"This message is more specific."

"A message? From an assassin? I'm curious, Mr. Reece, the United States does not typically employ assassins. If they do, they are expendable traitors recruited from the lands of Allah, brainwashed, wound up, and sent off to do the West's bidding. You are known for dropping bombs on innocent women and children from above, not sending assassins like this."

"I'm not an assassin."

"Then what are you?"

"I'm a messenger."

Ja'far grunted.

"And what message would you have me pass to the regime?"

"Just this," Reece replied.

He leveled the AK at General Ja'far al-Sadiq's face and depressed the trigger.

The 7.62x39 bullet entered just to the left of the right eye. The round caved in the right side of the general's head, a mass of brain tissue hitting the wall behind him and sliding to the floor of the *musalla,* showering the area in a dark red mist. He collapsed on his right side, blood seeping into the prayer rug.

The man who had collaborated with al-Qaeda and provided them materials, support, and sanction, and who had ultimately approved the plan for September 11, 2001, and the bioweapon attacks on its twentieth anniversary was killed by an American on holy land.

Reece stepped forward and followed up with two more rounds to the head to ensure his target was dead. He then slung the Kalashnikov and removed a chain from around his neck. He held the ring between his fingertips, remembering Lauren and Lucy and wondering what would have happened had Jen survived that Tuesday morning in September. Would two American cities now be smoldering piles of rubble? Did her death inadvertently save half a million lives?

Reece knelt, opened Ja'far's left hand, and placed the ring inside. He pressed the dead man's fingers around it in a fist.

"They'll get the message," Reece whispered.

The messenger then made his way back through the house just

the way he'd practiced in his team's rehearsals when al-Zarqawi was planning the Iraq insurgency from this very compound.

He worked his way through the shadows, past the bodies of Ja'far's four bodyguards. He climbed the back wall and dropped into a dark alley, sinking into the shadows as he listened for any sounds that betrayed his presence. He stood, folded the stock under the AK, and placed it in his satchel. He then adjusted his *shemagh* and walked toward his extract.

He hit the beach and made his way to the water's edge, feeling the sand give way beneath his feet just as it had in Coronado all those years ago. He could see the fishing trawler loitering five hundred yards off the coast, trolling for sturgeon in the early morning darkness.

He knelt behind a cluster of rocks protruding from the sand and scanned the slope that led to the street above. Nothing signified that a foreigner had invaded or that one of the most formidable terrorists in the world had just met his maker.

He had sent the message. It was time to go.

Reece took one last look, then turning, moved through the light shore break, out beyond the waves toward the beckoning sea.

EPILOGUE

"I have a message from God unto thee."

—EHUD THE ASSASSIN, JUDGES 3:20, KING JAMES VERSION

Ulcinj, Montenegro

THE ENVELOPE ARRIVED VIA courier early that morning.

Nizar Kattan tipped the boy a five-euro note and rolled the letter over in his hands. It had traveled a long way.

Although originally developed to transfer money, in the modern world the ancient system of *hawala* persisted as the most secure way to pass information. With the CIA and Mossad collecting electronic communications from almost every keystroke worldwide, sifting it through complex algorithms developed by the tech titans in the private sector, it was becoming increasingly difficult to remain anonymous in a data-driven economy. It amused Nizar that those technology-dependent intelligence organizations could be fooled by a handheld package trading hands and crossing borders with impunity; all one needed was time and patience. Nizar had been given multiple assignments in this fashion. All were profitable when coming from Masada.

The Russian mafia had initially offered him refuge but only because of an arrangement with a banished colonel, a colonel who had been turned into mulch when a PG-32V 105mm anti-armor HEAT round destroyed his armored Mercedes in Switzerland. Intelligence agencies and the media had pointed the finger at a terrorist known as Mohammed Farooq. Nizar wondered if he had really pressed the button that had killed the Russian colonel. It seemed too convenient. What the West liked to call the "free press" was not to be trusted.

After the Odessa operation, Nizar had seen the writing on the wall. He was expendable. True, he'd always been expendable, but without Russian blood in his veins it was only a matter of time before the Bratva separated his head from his body.

He had always scoffed at those who had sacrificed themselves for Allah. Die for the prophet; for the cause? Nizar preferred to live for himself, not for a prophet or ideology. He'd seen too many young, idealistic warriors strap on suicide vests and martyr themselves for a religion they didn't even fully comprehend. That was not Nizar's way. He favored freelance work that benefited his multiple bank accounts.

He'd done a job for the Bratva in Montenegro and never returned to the Russia that had become his base of operations after he sent a bullet at Russian president Zubarev. His partner's bullet had found its mark, eviscerating their target in front of the world. Nizar had adjusted and put his second shot into a man on a rooftop, a man who should have killed President Grimes. Nizar had read the papers. His round had not connected with his intended target. It had killed an American spy. It did not take much digging to associate that death with a funeral in South Carolina of a former Navy SEAL named Fredrick Strain.

The sniper wondered what Strain was doing on the rooftop in exactly the position of Nizar's mark. He should not have been there. Nizar had been hired to kill a member of President Zubarev's FSO security detail, a man with nationalist leanings and ties to Ukraine. Instead, his bullet had killed the American. General Yedid had passed him the details when he'd given him the order that had elevated Nizar to prominence as one of the top guns for hire in the business. He had felt nothing when he pressed the trigger on the suppressed Stechkin and sent the nine-by-eighteen round through the head of his partner, the legendary sniper known as Tasho al-Shishani.

The student had become the master.

Now he worked alone and solved problems. That skill set put him on the radar of a company called Masada. The Masada CEO had told him he was free to work for anyone, as long as they weren't other Americans. Masada wanted sole American rights, a demand to which Nizar readily acquiesced. Masada paid well.

Erik Sawyer had brokered an introduction to Montenegro's president, a man who had previously served as prime minister, a politician who maintained power through connections with the Montenegrin mafia. He had recently been bestowed with the rather dubious honor of "Person of the Year in Organized Crime" by the Organized Crime and Corruption Reporting Project, an organization dedicated to ferreting out corruption through political links to the underworld. That's how things were done in Montenegro.

Nizar was protected by the Montenegrin mafia through the president. He maintained two homes: a flat in the coastal city of Ulcinj and a mountain cottage in Žabljak. He preferred the Mediterranean climate and beaches of the ancient settlement on the Adriatic to the mountains of the Northern Region, but in his line of work it was wise to have options. With the influx of tourists in both areas, he was able to blend in. He was also learning English from the prostitutes run by the mafia in the port town. He'd grown up at war and knew women served a purpose.

The Ukrainian girl still slept. He enjoyed what she did to him in bed and, with her help, his English was improving. He knew she liked it when he was in town because he paid for her services and the mafia did not pimp her out to businessmen or criminals from abroad, many of whom used the powerless as heirs to their violent frustrations. The arrangement worked well for them both.

Nizar did not use a cell phone or own a computer. He had operated without them for long enough to know that their convenience had a distinct and obvious downside. Early on he noted a commonality between those the West took out with their drones and hit teams; they all used cell phones. Sometimes they even found those without the mobile devices. Bin Laden had found that out the hard way.

Montenegro offered access to Europe, the Middle East, and Africa, but as soon as Nizar felt the tides shifting, he would be on his way to his next temporary home. Thailand? Panama? Argentina? There were options for a man with no ties. All one needed was capital.

Nizar had grown to like the ancient seaport, a settlement that had once been the pirate capital of the Adriatic. The mafia ensured it remained connected to its roots. He varied his routine between the flat on the coast and the cottage in the mountains. He traveled enough to keep anyone tracking his movements from being able to discern distinct patterns, though Nizar knew that no matter how many precautions he took, there would always be patterns. A skilled hunter just needed to be able to study him long enough to discern them.

He bought and read newspapers at various shops in the city. There was one cafe by the water that he particularly enjoyed. When he needed to do further research, he would visit one of the Internet cafes that still existed in Montenegro, plug in an external hard drive, and run his search through the installed search engine to minimize his trail.

The Montenegrin government had provided him with passports and identities along with accompanying credit cards. He would miss the Balkans, but that was how one survived; you had to keep moving. There were other Ukrainian girls no matter where he ended up. They were quite popular in the human trafficking trade.

He had read that Erik Sawyer had passed away at an island home in the West Indies. Details were sparse, which was suspicious. Sawyer's death was disappointing. The Masada founder had sent him quite a few lucrative contracts over the past two years. Sawyer's death was also a sign; it was time for Nizar to leave Montenegro behind.

He pulled a book from the shelf, a book he couldn't even read: *The Great Game.* It was written in English, a language he could not yet understand, though he was working on it. The book had been given to him two years earlier when he met with Sawyer in Africa. The American needed him to do a job: to eliminate a problem in Nigeria.

Sawyer had also taught him a code. A note would arrive by courier. Inside were a series of numbers. An intelligence service could attempt to decipher it until the end of time. Its genius was its simplicity: page number, line number, letter number. Even if someone knew how it worked, without the exact edition of the correct book, breaking it was impossible.

Nizar flipped to page 176, ran his finger down to the eighth line, and then moved it across to the twelfth letter: "J."

It took him a while but by the end he had a page full of letters. Nizar had no idea what it said. There were no spaces between them, just a series of letters that only someone who could read and write English could break down into sentences.

He returned to the small bedroom and nudged the naked blond woman awake.

"Translate," he said in Russian.

A destination country for human trafficking, Montenegro was a waypoint for organized crime syndicates that routinely moved young girls and women from Ukraine, Serbia, and Bulgaria to Europe and the United States and into forced prostitution. Despite international pressure, the Balkan nation remained a hotbed for the growing industry.

The young woman slipped from beneath the sheets and moved to the small desk in the main room. It was early and she needed her fix. At least he didn't beat her or put cigarettes out on her skin. Nor did he cut or choke her or invite other men to join. Though she was never permitted to leave the flat, he treated her well. She cooked, cleaned, spread her legs, and taught him English.

She sat naked at the bureau with the sun beginning to break though the thin curtains. It was going to be a beautiful day. After she was done, she'd make them breakfast. She liked the view from the kitchen, out over the city with a slice of the Adriatic Sea in the distance.

Nizar started a kettle of water to make tea, keeping his eye on the lithe young figure at his desk. She circled the words breaking the unending letters into coherent sentences.

She then translated the English into Russian on a separate sheet of paper. By the time her tea was ready, she had finished her work. She handed the document to Nizar.

The assassin held it up to the light and read.

It was a contract.

It was structured in a similar fashion to Nizar's other work for Sawyer. It informed the assassin that two million euros had been laundered through a yacht brokerage service in the British Virgin Islands to a construction company in Montenegro in the form of a fictitious invoice that would be paid to Nizar for consultation on an ongoing commercial development project. The money had already been deposited in the usual account. Unusual to this contract was that Nizar was free to leave it unfulfilled. With Sawyer being dead, that was certainly an incentive. The contract went on to state that another six million euros would be transferred upon completion of the job. Nizar thought of the cost associated with moving his operation from Montenegro to a place like Argentina if the current president was deposed, arrested, or killed, all of which were distinct possibilities.

There was another sentence that stood out.

The mark is actively targeting you.

It would be best if you found him before he finds you.

Additional incentive? That was just like Sawyer. Was it true?

Nizar read on. By the time he finished the document he was certain of its veracity. He had connected the events in Odessa to the death of the SEAL to the news reports of a man who was now in the employ of the United States intelligence services. A man who had proven very hard to kill.

He lit a match and held the papers to the flame. They caught easily, the fire creeping up the parchments until it threatened to burn the assassin's fingers. Moving to the kitchen, he dropped what was left into the sink and turned on the water. The faucet sputtered until it seemed to catch a second wind that was powerful enough to carry the charred remains of the contract into the pipes of the ancient city.

The girl remained sitting at the small desk, sipping her hot tea. She'd learned early on to speak only if spoken to and to simply do exactly as she was instructed. She was a survivor.

Nizar approached her from behind and stroked her hair. It felt good.

She closed her eyes and smiled. Perhaps he would stay for longer this time and she wouldn't have to go back to the house with the other girls. That would be nice. Maybe if she proved worthy, he'd buy her outright? She would be sure to continue giving him nights to remember.

His hand brushed softly down the left side of her head, past her cheek and to the back of her neck.

Maybe there truly was hope.

The terror lasted only a second. Her eyes opened wide as he yanked her hair back, exposing the soft skin of her neck. He inserted the thin blade behind the windpipe, its sharp edge slicing completely through to the other side. Locking her body against the chair, he sawed outward the way the Russian advisors had taught him in the Syria of his youth. She struggled only briefly, scratching at the hand that was taking her life, the blood rushing from her severed carotid artery draining down her breasts and spraying onto the desk in front of her in cadence with the beating of her heart.

Nizar controlled her head as the pumping weakened. When her heart lost the strength to circulate blood through a failing system, the pressure subsided, and her hands fell to her sides.

He looked once more into her dead eyes before letting her head drop to the desk.

He'd have the Montenegrin mafia clean it up. True, he would have to pay for her, but Sawyer's money would take care of that. There were always plenty of girls. With the founder of Masada dead, she was the only other person privy to the contract in the translated note. Only in death could she be trusted to keep the secret. No one would miss or mourn her. No loose ends. That was how Nizar stayed alive.

He walked to the sink and washed the blood from his hands. He then cleaned the blade, wiped it dry with a towel, and returned it to a drawer.

The sun had broken the horizon: an emerging dawn with a new contract for Nizar, his most profitable to date. It was time to study his prey. If what Sawyer had written was accurate, the man was already hunting him. To Nizar, killing Fredrick Strain was business. He did not wish death to the infidels like the true believers who sacrificed themselves for the cause. To his new mark, Strain's death had been personal. Nizar would use that to his advantage. His target's emotion was something he could exploit.

Nizar was a sniper, a hunter of men, an assassin.

He dropped the small thumb drive in his pocket and grabbed his coat. He closed and locked the apartment door behind him and smiled at an old woman who was already awake and sweeping the hall the way she did every morning. He descended the steps to the path that led to a winding road. It was time to buy a newspaper and a tea. It was time to think. He had a problem to solve, a problem to eliminate.

As he walked the narrow stone streets of the port city, the final line of the contract echoed in the recesses of his mind.

It would be best if you found him before he finds you.

When the Internet cafe opened, he would pay his three-euro fee in coins, plug in the external search engine, and begin developing a pattern of life on Lieutenant Commander James Reece.

AUTHOR'S NOTE

THIS IS A WORK of fiction. Fiction with whispers of truth.

On August 7, 2020, al-Qaeda's second in command, Abu Muhammad al-Masari, was assassinated. It is rumored that the gunmen were Israeli operatives acting with tacit or explicit support from the United States. Also killed in the assassination was the widow of Hamza bin Laden, Osama bin Laden's son. The assassination took place in Tehran, Iran.

In the fall of 2017, I had a remarkable conversation with a man in Argentina. He will remain anonymous in this work, though he is mentioned by name in the *9/11 Commission Report*. He asked me how nineteen foreign nationals could pass through security at three separate international airports and one regional airport, some even flagged for additional screening, and not have one report in subsequent investigations of a screener noticing a box cutter or knife.

The regulations pertaining to knives allowed on aircraft prior to September 11, 2001, were confusing. Federal Aviation Administration regulations prohibited "knives with blades four inches long or longer and/or knives illegal under local law." Seemingly in contradiction to that regulation was a nonregulatory *Checkpoint Operations Guide* for screeners interpreting those FAA regulations and prohibiting "box cutting devices." For nineteen terrorists to pass through screening without one security screener at least noticing a blade and ensuring it was of legal length struck him as odd. That conversation provided the basis for *The Devil's Hand.*

The first sentence of the notes to Chapter 1 of the *9/11 Commission Report* reads: "No physical, documentary, or analytical evidence provides a convincing explanation of why Atta and Omari drove to Portland, Maine, from Boston on the morning of September 10. . . ." Twenty years later that question has still not been successfully answered. Mohamed Atta and Abdul Aziz al-Omari took that secret with them to their graves.

On the topic of Iranian involvement in 9/11 the report states: "We have found no evidence that Iran or Hezbollah was aware of the planning for what later became the 9/11 attack. . . . [However] We believe this topic requires further investigation by the U.S. government."

The report also notes that at least eight of the 9/11 terrorists traveled to Iran between October 2000 and February 2001. Tehran is believed to have been a waypoint in travel to and from terrorist training camps in neighboring Afghanistan. There is evidence that suggests senior Hezbollah officials were aware of, and actively tracking, the travel of these al-Qaeda operatives. To what purpose remains unknown.

Al-Qaeda, Iran, and Hezbollah have an incestuous history. The foundations of the relationship were laid in the early 1980s with the founding of Islamic Jihad but were cemented during the 1990s when Osama bin Laden and Ayman al-Zawahiri, then al-Qaeda's second in command, took refuge in Sudan. In the 1990s, Sudan was a breeding ground for terror.

Chapter 2 of the *9/11 Commission Report* notes: "In late 1991 or 1992, discussions in Sudan between al Qaeda and Iranian operatives led to an informal agreement to cooperate in providing support—even if only training—for actions carried out primarily against Israel and the United States. Not long afterward, senior al Qaeda operatives and trainers traveled to Iran to receive training in explosives. In the fall of 1993, another such delegation went to the Bekaa Valley in Lebanon for further training in explosives as well as in intelligence and security."

From Sudan, al-Qaeda sent operatives to train in Iran and Lebanon. In April 1991, Ayman al-Zawahiri traveled to Iran and met with Hezbollah operations chief Imad Mughniyeh. Mughniyeh was responsible for the 1983 bombings of the U.S. embassy and Marine barracks in Beirut, the kidnapping and murder of CIA Lebanon station chief William F. Buckley, the hijacking of TWA Flight 847 in 1985, the 1992 suicide bombing of the Israeli embassy in Buenos Aires, the 1994 attack on a Jewish community center in Argentina, and the 1996 Khobar Towers bombing in Saudi Arabia. Mughniyeh would later meet with bin Laden in Sudan, further bridging the Sunni-Shi'a divide and cementing the al-Qaeda connection with the regime in Tehran.

Two days prior to 9/11, Ahmad Shah Massoud, the leader of the Northern Alliance, was assassinated by two al-Qaeda operatives posing as journalists. A declassified, though heavily redacted, November 2001 Defense Intelligence Agency cable obtained through the Freedom of Information Act by the National Security Archive at George Washington University reads: "Through Northern Alliance intelligence efforts, the late commander Massoud gained limited knowledge regarding the intentions of the Saudi millionaire Usama bin Laden and his terrorist organization al-Qaeda, to perform a terrorist act against the U.S., on a scale larger than the 1998 bombing of the embassies in Kenya and Tanzania." Massoud's al-Qaeda assassins obtained their forged documents via the Iranian Embassy in Brussels.

One of the most damning pieces of evidence on Iran's complicity in

9/11 comes from a classified Iranian document dated May 2001, a transcript of which can be found in Ronen Bergman's *The Secret War with Iran.*

The Islamic Republic of Iran, the Intelligence Apparatus of the Supreme Leader—Top Secret

Date: May 14, 2001

Reference: 4-325-80/s/m

By: Head of the Intelligence Apparatus of the Supreme Leader

To: Head of Operations Unit no. 43 [in the Iranian Intelligence Ministry]

Re: Orders regarding the decision of the Honorable Leader [Khamenei]

[Dear] Hujjat Al-Islam Wal-Muslimin [Mustafa] Pourkanad [director of general Operations Unit no. 43]

We wish your dedicated and courageous team every success. The results [described] in your recent reports have been examined, along with other opinions. After consideration, and in order to remove the existing lack of clarity regarding support for al-Qaeda's future plans, the Honorable Leader has emphasized that the battle against the global arrogance headed by the U.S. and Israel is an integral part of our Islamic government, and constitutes its primary goal. Damaging their economic systems, discrediting all other institutions of these two allied enemies of the Islamic government [in Iran] as part of political confrontation [with them], and undermining the stability and security [of the U.S. and Israel] are obligatory duties that must be carried out.

The Honorable [Leader Khamenei] stressed the need for each of you to be vigilant in his field of activity, and asks you to be particularly attentive. He also stressed [the need] to be alert to the [possible] negative future consequences of this cooperation [between Iran and al-Qaeda].

The Honorable [Khamenei] said that this struggle must be stepped up by tightening the collaboration with other security and intelligence apparatuses in Iran and with supporters outside Iran, thereby hindering the enemy's steadily expanding activities.

[Khamenei further instructed] that in carrying out your duties, you must operate under the direct supervision of the security division of the headquarters of the organization [i.e., the intelligence apparatus of

> the Supreme Leader]. Naturally, identifying [potential] damage is the responsibility of the vigilant and diligent Unit [No. 43].
>
> It has also been decided that, in the upcoming meetings, discussions must be held in order to formulate clear goals and remove the main obstacles and difficulties in achieving these goals and in promoting the issue of expanding the collaboration with the fighters of al-Qaeda and Hizballah [Lebanon].
>
> Finally, I wish to convey [Khamenei's] full satisfaction with Unit [No. 43] and his full support in the implementation of its future plans. The Honorable [Khamenei] is aware of the important and dangerous [nature of] the tasks you perform. [He] emphasizes that with regard to cooperation with al-Qaeda, no traces must be left that might have negative and irreversible consequences, and that [the activity] must be limited to the existing contacts with [Hizballah Operations Officer Imad] Mughniyeh and [bin Laden's deputy Ayman] al-Zawahiri.
>
> May Allah grant you success . . .
>
> [Seal and Signature] Ali Akbar Nateq Nouri

Ali Akbar Nateq Nouri was the chief advisor on intelligence to Ali Khamenei, the Supreme Leader of Iran.

Following the death of Osama bin Laden, Ayman al-Zawahiri ascended to lead al-Qaeda. The United States Department of State has offered a reward of $25 million for information leading to al-Zawahiri's apprehension or conviction. At the time of this writing he remains at large.

• • •

I was well into the research for this novel before the COVID-19 pandemic gripped the world. I was investigating the weaponization of infectious diseases, particularly from the end of World War II through today. It did not escape notice when information began to emerge that a variant of coronavirus had emerged in a market in Wuhan, China. Just three football fields from Wuhan's Huanan Seafood Wholesale Market, where

China tells the world that the COVID -19 outbreak originated, is the Wuhan branch of the Chinese Center for Disease Control and Prevention. That same market is less than ten miles from the Wuhan Institute of Virology, which houses China's only Biosafety Level 4 laboratory, called the Wuhan National Biosafety Laboratory. On February 16, 2020, Senator Tom Cotton said, "We have such laboratories ourselves in the United States run by our military . . . in large part done for preventative purposes, or trying to discover vaccines or protect our own soldiers." The key part of the senator's interview is that "we have such laboratories ourselves."

Unintended release of biological and chemical weapons is not without precedent. In 1979, a Soviet research lab in what was then called Sverdlovsk in the Urals accidentally released anthrax, killing at least one hundred people. The facility was using data from Imperial Japan's bioweapons program captured in Manchuria during World War II. The medical records of those exposed to anthrax were all edited to limit evidence that the Soviets were in violation of the 1972 Biological Weapons Convention, of which they were signatories. The deaths were explained away as coming from contaminated meat.

In 1968, six thousand sheep mysteriously died near Dugway Proving Ground in Utah. Dugway was established during World War II in an effort to counter the Axis biological and chemical weapons programs. It remains in existence today. The U.S. Army had been conducting open-air VX nerve agent testing in the days prior to what is now called the Skull Valley Sheep Kill. An internal Army investigation two years later would find that lethal chemical agents tested at Dugway on March 13, 1968, "may have" contributed to the sheep deaths.

The history of biological weapons is both fascinating and chilling. Bioweapons data from Imperial Japan and Nazi Germany in World War II informed the U.S. and Soviet bioweapons programs of the Cold War years.

In the spring of 2002, I was part of a small group of military personnel assigned to a training mission in Uzbekistan. As the junior member of the team, my job was to train up partner force snipers on the SDV, better known as the Dragunov. It was during this assignment to Uzbekistan that I first heard mention of an island on the Aral Sea, an island synonymous with bioweapon research. My later open-source research would indicate that this was Vozrozhdeniya Island, "rebirth island," a former Soviet biological weapons test site called Aralsk-7. It is clear that the Soviets had not adhered to the United Nations treaty.

The history of Marburg Variant U described in *The Devil's Hand* is true. Dr. Nikolai Ustinov worked at the Vector Bioweapon research center in Koltsovo, Siberia. In April 1988, he accidently injected Marburg into his thumb. He was immediately quarantined. Over the next three weeks, the virus liquefied his organs and drove him insane as it ate away his brain cells. Ever the scientist, he detailed his demise in a journal, its pages stained with blood, vomit, and mucus from his decaying body. Following his death, organ samples were taken. During his autopsy a doctor pricked his skin with a needle that had extracted bone marrow. He was dead a month later. Upon further study, the samples of Marburg taken from Dr. Ustinov's organs appeared different from the original strain. The virus had evolved. It was now more virulent than the original. The Soviets weaponized this new strain and called it Variant U in honor of Dr. Ustinov.

By all indications, the Soviet Union stepped up their bioweapon development and stockpiling programs following the 1972 Biological Weapons Convention. Biopreparat was the lead Soviet agency tasked with weaponizing infectious diseases. What happened to these programs with the collapse of the Soviet Union in 1991? What happened to the scientists who developed these programs? According to Dr. Ken Alibek, the deputy chief of Biopreparat from 1988 to 1992, many of his former colleagues relocated to the United States, Europe, and

Asia as economic conditions in Russia forced scientists to look for work beyond their borders. In Chapter 20 of his book *Biohazard* he writes: "In May of 1997, more than one hundred scientists from Russian laboratories, including Vector and Obolensk, attended a Biotechnology Trade fair in Tehran . . . soon after that Iranians had visited Vector a number of times and were actively promoting scientific exchanges."

How far along is the Iranian bioweapons program and does the success of using proxies over the past four decades mean that Iran could or would use these weapons through nonstate actors as an instrument of terror? It is certainly a possibility and should not be discounted.

Has the United States remained in compliance with the 1972 Biological Weapon Convention? There is no international agency tasked with verification to monitor compliance. It's essentially the honor system. The convention bans bioweapon "agents, toxins, weapons, equipment, and means of delivery." We would be naive to assume that classified bioweapons programs do not still exist. Interestingly, the language of what is officially called the Convention on the Prohibition of the Development, Production and Stockpiling of Bacteriological (Biological) and Toxin Weapons (BTWC) does not ban "biodefense weapons."

Does the United States have protocols in place to eradicate a respiratory-spread virus that threatens to kill 90 percent of the population? I don't know the answer to that question but inferring what I can from the research for this novel, I would be surprised if those plans do not exist. If you were experimenting with the weaponization of viruses, even "biodefense weapons," that had the potential to render the human race extinct, what would you do?

Following the targeted assassination of Quds Force Commander General Qasem Soleimani in January 2020, Iran's Supreme Leader Ayatollah Ali Khamenei said, "With his departure and with God's power, his work and path will not cease, and severe revenge awaits those criminals who have tainted their filthy hands with his blood. . . ."

Iran does not forget.

Of note, the United States signed the Biological Weapons Convention on April 10, 1972, the same day as Iran.

GLOSSARY

160th Special Operations Aviation Regiment: The Army's premier helicopter unit that provides aviation support to special forces. Known as the "Night Stalkers," they are widely regarded as the best helicopter pilots and crews in the world.

.260: .260 Remington; .264"/6.5mm rifle cartridge that is essentially a .308 Winchester necked down to accept a smaller-diameter bullet. The .260 provides superior external ballistics to the .308 with less felt recoil and can often be fired from the same magazines.

.300 Norma: .300 Norma Magnum: a cartridge designed for long-range precision shooting that has been adopted by USSOCOM for sniper use.

.375 CheyTac: Long-range cartridge, adapted from the .408 Chey-Tac, that can fire a 350-grain bullet at 2,970 feet per second. A favorite of extreme long-range match competitors who use it on targets beyond 3,000 yards.

.375 H&H Magnum: An extremely common and versatile big-game rifle cartridge, found throughout Africa. The cartridge was developed by Holland & Holland in 1912 and traditionally fires a 300-grain bullet.

.404 Jeffery: A rifle cartridge designed for large game animals, developed by W. J. Jeffery & Company in 1905.

.408 CheyTac: Long-range cartridge adapted from the .505 Gibbs, capable of firing a 419-grain bullet at 2,850 feet per second.

.500 Nitro: A .510-caliber cartridge designed for use against heavy dangerous game, often chambered in double rifles. The cartridge fires a 570-grain bullet at 2,150 feet per second.

75th Ranger Regiment: A large-scale Army special operations unit that conducts direct-action missions including raids and airfield seizures. These elite troops often work in conjunction with other special operations units.

AC-130 Spectre: A ground-support aircraft used by the U.S. military, based on the ubiquitous C-130 cargo plane. AC-130s are armed with a 105mm howitzer, 40mm cannons, and 7.62mm miniguns, and are considered the premier close-air-support weapon of the U.S. arsenal.

Accuracy International: A British company producing high-quality precision rifles, often used for military sniper applications.

ACOG: Advanced Combat Optical Gunsight. A magnified optical sight designed for use on rifles and carbines, made by Trijicon. The ACOG is popular among U.S. forces as it provides both magnification and an illuminated reticle that provides aiming points for various target ranges.

AFIS: Automated Fingerprint Identification System; electronic fingerprint database maintained by the FBI.

Aimpoint Micro: Aimpoint Micro T-2. A high-quality unmagnified red-dot combat optic produced in Sweden that can be used on a variety of weapons platforms. This durable sight weighs only three ounces and has a five-year battery life.

AISI: The latest name for Italy's domestic intelligence agency. Their motto, *scientia rerum republicae salus*, means "knowledge of issues is the salvation of the Republic."

AK-9: Russian 9x39mm assault rifle favored by Spetsnaz (special purpose) forces.

Al-Jaleel: Iraqi-made 82mm mortar that is a clone of the Yugoslavian-made M69A. This indirect-fire weapon has a maximum range of 6,000 meters.

Alpha Group: More accurately called Spetsgruppa "A," Alpha Group is the FSB's counterterrorist unit. You don't want them to "rescue" you. See Moscow Theater Hostage Crisis and the Beslan School Massacre.

Amphib: Shorthand for Amphibious Assault Ship. A gray ship holding helicopters, Harriers, and hovercraft. Usually home to a large number of pissed-off Marines.

AN/PAS-13G(v)L3/LWTS: Weapon-mounted thermal optic that can be used to identify warm-blooded targets day or night. Can be mounted in front of and used in conjunction with a traditional "day" scope mounted on a sniper weapons system.

AN/PRC-163: Falcon III communications system made by Harris Corporation that integrates voice, text, and video capabilities.

AQ: al-Qaeda. Meaning "the Base" in Arabic. A radical Islamic terrorist organization once led by the late Osama bin Laden.

AQI: al-Qaeda in Iraq. An al-Qaeda–affiliated Sunni insurgent group that was active against U.S. forces. Elements of AQI eventually evolved into ISIS.

AR-10: The 7.62x51mm brainchild of Eugene Stoner that was later adapted to create the M16/M4/AR-15.

Asherman Chest Seal: A specialized emergency medical device used to treat open chest wounds. If you're wearing one, you are having a bad day.

AT-4: Tube-launched 84mm anti-armor rocket produced in Sweden and used by U.S. forces since the 1980s. The AT-4 is a throwaway weapon: after it is fired, the tube is discarded.

ATF/BATFE: Bureau of Alcohol, Tobacco, Firearms and Explosives. A federal law enforcement agency formally part of the U.S. Department of the Treasury, which doesn't seem overly concerned with alcohol or tobacco.

ATPIAL/PEQ-15: Advanced Target Pointer/Illuminator Aiming Laser. A weapon-mounted device that emits both visible and infrared target designators for use with or without night observation devices. Essentially, an advanced military-grade version of the "laser sights" seen in popular culture.

***Avtoritet*:** The highest caste of the incarcerated criminal hierarchy. Today used in association with a new generation of crime bosses.

Azores: Atlantic archipelago consisting of nine major islands that is an independent autonomous region of the European nation of Portugal.

Barrett 250 Lightweight: A lightweight variant of the M240 7.62mm light machine gun, developed by Barrett Firearms.

Barrett M107: .50 BMG caliber semiautomatic rifle designed by Ronnie Barrett in the early 1980s. This thirty-pound rifle can be carried by a single individual and can be used to engage human or vehicular targets at extreme ranges.

BATS: Biometrics Automated Toolset System: a fingerprint database often used to identify insurgent forces.

Bay of Pigs: Site of a failed invasion of Cuba by paramilitary exiles trained and equipped by the CIA.

BDU: Battle-dress uniform: an oxymoron if there ever was one.

Beneteau Oceanis: A forty-eight-foot cruising sailboat, designed and built in France. An ideal craft for eluding international manhunts.

Black Hills Ammunition: High-quality ammunition made for military and civilian use by a family-owned and South Dakota–based company. Their MK 262 MOD 1 5.56mm load saw significant operational use in the GWOT.

***Bratok*:** Member of the Bratva.

Bratva: The Brotherhood. An umbrella term for Russian organized crime, more technically referring to members of the Russian mafia who have served time in prison.

***Brigadir*:** Lieutenant of a Bratva gang boss.

Browning Hi-Power: A single-action 9mm semiautomatic handgun that feeds from a thirteen-round box magazine. Also known as the P-35, this Belgian-designed handgun was the most widely issued military sidearm in the world for much of the twentieth century and was used by both Axis and Allied forces during World War II.

BUD/S: Basic Underwater Demolition/SEAL training. The six-month selection and training course required for entry into the SEAL Teams, held in Coronado, California. Widely considered one of the most brutal military selection courses in the world, with an average 80 percent attrition rate.

C-17: Large military cargo aircraft used to transport troops and supplies. Also used by the Secret Service to transport the president's motorcade vehicles.

C-4: Composition 4. A plastic-explosive compound known for its stability and malleability.

CAG: Combat Applications Group. See redacted portion of glossary in the "D" section.

CAT: Counter-Assault Team; heavily armed ground element of the Secret Service trained to respond to threats such as ambushes.

CCA: According to *Seapower Magazine*, the Combatant Craft, Assault, is a 41-foot high-speed boat used by Naval Special Warfare units. Essentially, an armed "Cigarette" boat.

CDC: Centers for Disease Control and Prevention. An agency of the Department of Health and Human Services, its mission is to protect the United States from health threats to include natural and weaponized infectious diseases.

Cessna 208 Caravan: Single-engine turboprop aircraft that can ferry passengers and cargo, often to remote locations. These workhorses are staples in remote wilderness areas throughout the world.

CIA: Central Intelligence Agency

CIF/CRF: Commanders In-Extremis Force/Crisis Response Force. A United States Army special forces team specifically tasked with conducting direct-action missions. These are the guys who should have been sent to Benghazi.

CISA: Cybersecurity and Infrastructure Security Agency. It's official Web page states: "CISA is the Nation's risk advisor, working with partners to defend against today's threats and collaborating to build more secure and resilient infrastructure for the future." For an agency with such an innocuous Dunder Mifflinesque mission statement, in times of crisis they assume an inordinate amount of control.

CJSOTF: Combined Joint Special Operations Task Force. A regional command that controls special operations forces from various services and friendly nations.

CMC: Command Master Chief, a senior enlisted rating in the United States Navy.

CQC: Close-quarter combat

CrossFit: A fitness-centric worldwide cult that provides a steady stream of cases to orthopedic surgery clinics. No need to identify their members; they will tell you who they are.

CRRC: Combat Rubber Raiding Craft. Inflatable Zodiac-style boats used by SEALs and other maritime troops.

CTC: The CIA's Counterterrorism Center. Established out of the rise of international terrorism in the 1980s, it became the nucleus of the U.S. counterterrorism mission.

CZ-75: 9mm handgun designed in 1975 and produced in the Czech Republic.

DA: District attorney; local prosecutor in many jurisdictions.

Dam Neck: An annex to Naval Air Station Oceana near Virginia Beach, Virginia, where nothing interesting whatsoever happens.

DCIS: Defense Criminal Investigation Service

DEA: Drug Enforcement Administration

***Delta Force*:** A classic 1986 action film starring Chuck Norris, title of the 1983 autobiography by the unit's first commanding officer and, according to thousands of print and online articles, books, and video interviews across new and legacy media, the popular name for the

Army's 1st Special Forces Operational Detachment—Delta. I wouldn't know.

Democratic Federation of Northern Syria: Aka Rojava, an autonomous, polyethnic, and secular region of northern Syria.

Det Cord: Flexible detonation cord used to initiate charges of high explosives. The cord's interior is filled with PETN explosive; you don't want it wrapped around your neck.

DIA: Defense Intelligence Agency

Directorate I: The division of the SVR responsible for electronic information and disinformation.

Directorate S: The division of the SVR responsible for their illegals program. When you read about a Russian dissident or former spy poisoned by Novichok nerve agent or a political rival of the Russian president murdered in a random act of violence, Directorate S is probably responsible.

DO: The CIA's Directorate of Operations, formerly known by the much more appropriate name: the Clandestine Service.

DOD: Department of Defense

DOJ: Department of Justice

DShkM: Russian-made 12.7x108mm heavy machine gun that has been used in virtually every armed conflict since and including World War II.

DST: General Directorate for Territorial Surveillance. Morocco's domestic intelligence and security agency. Probably not afraid to use "enhanced interrogation techniques." DST was originally redacted by government censors for the hardcover edition of *True Believer*. After a five-month appeal process, that decision was withdrawn.

EFP: Explosively Formed Penetrator/Projectile. A shaped explosive charge that forms a molten projectile used to penetrate armor. Such munitions were widely used by insurgents against coalition forces in Iraq.

EKIA: Enemy Killed In Action.

Eland: Africa's largest antelope. A mature male can weigh more than a ton.

EMS: Emergency medical services. Fire, paramedic, and other emergency personnel.

ENDEX: End Exercise. Those outside "the know" will say "INDEX" and have no idea what it means.

EOD: Explosive Ordnance Disposal. The military's explosives experts who are trained to, among other things, disarm or destroy improvised explosive devices or other munitions.

EOTECH: An unmagnified holographic gun sight for use on rifles and carbines, including the M4. The sight is designed for rapid target acquisition, which makes it an excellent choice for close-quarters battle. Can be fitted with a detachable 3x magnifier for use at extended ranges.

FAL: Fusil Automatique Léger: gas-operated, select-fire 7.62x51mm battle rifle developed by FN Herstal in the late 1940s and used by the militaries of more than ninety nations. Sometimes referred to as "the right arm of the free world" due to its use against communist forces in various Cold War–era insurgencies.

FBI: Federal Bureau of Investigation. A federal law enforcement agency that is not known for its sense of humor.

FDA: Food and Drug Administration

FLIR: Forward-Looking InfraRed. An observation device that uses thermographic radiation, that is, heat, to develop an image.

Floppies: Derogatory term used to describe communist insurgents during the Rhodesian Bush War.

FOB: Forward Operating Base. A secured forward military position used to support tactical operations. Can vary from small and remote outposts to sprawling complexes.

Fobbit: A service member serving in a noncombat role who rarely, if ever, leaves the safety of the Forward Operating Base.

FSB: Russia's federal security service responsible for internal state security and headquartered in the same building in Lubyanka Square that once housed the KGB. Its convenient in-house prison is not a place one wants to spend an extended period.

FSO: Federal Protective Service. Russia's version of the Secret Service.

FTX: Field Training Exercise

G550: A business jet manufactured by Gulfstream Aerospace. Prices for a new example start above $40 million but, as they say, it's better to rent.

Game Scout: A wildlife enforcement officer in Africa. These individuals are often paired with hunting outfitters to ensure that regulations are adhered to.

Glock: An Austrian-designed, polymer-framed handgun popular with police forces, militaries, and civilians throughout the world. Glocks are made in various sizes and chambered in several different cartridges.

GPNVG-18: Ground Panoramic Night Vision Goggles. Forty-three-thousand-dollar NODs used by the most highly funded special operations units due to their superior image quality and peripheral vision. *See* Rich Kid Shit.

GPS: Global Positioning System. Satellite-based navigation systems that provide a precise location anywhere on earth.

Great Patriotic War: The Soviets' name for World War II; communists love propaganda.

Green-badger: Central Intelligence Agency contractor

Ground Branch: Land-focused element of the CIA's Special Activities Division, according to Wikipedia.

GRS: Global Response Staff. Protective agents employed by the Central Intelligence Agency to provide security to overseas personnel. See 13 Hours. GRS was originally redacted by government censors for the hardcover edition of *True Believer.* After a five-month appeal process, that decision was withdrawn.

GRU: Russia's main intelligence directorate. The foreign military intelligence agency of the Russian armed forces. The guys who do all the real work while the KGB gets all the credit, or so I'm told. Established by Joseph Stalin in 1942, the GRU was tasked with running human intelligence operations outside the Soviet Union. Think of them as the DIA with balls.

GS: General Schedule. Federal jobs that provide good benefits and lots of free time.

Gukurahundi Massacres: A series of killings carried out against Ndebele tribe members in Matabeleland, Zimbabwe, by the Mugabe government during the 1980s. As many as twenty thousand civilians were killed by the North Korean–trained Fifth Brigade of the Zimbabwean army.

GWOT: Global War on Terror. The seemingly endless pursuit of bad guys, kicked off by the 9/11 attacks.

Gym Jones: Utah-based fitness company founded by alpine climbing legend Mark Twight. Famous for turning soft Hollywood actors into hard bodies, Gym Jones once enjoyed a close relationship with a certain SEAL Team.

Hell Week: The crucible of BUD/S training. Five days of constant physical and mental stress with little or no sleep.

Hilux: Pickup truck manufactured by Toyota that is a staple in the developing world.

HK416: M4 clone engineered by the German firm of Heckler & Koch to operate using a short-stroke gas pistol system instead of the M4's direct-impingement gas system. Used by select special operations units in the U.S. and abroad. May or may not have been the weapon used to kill Osama bin Laden.

HK417: Select-fire 7.62x51mm rifle built by Heckler & Koch as a big brother to the HK416. Often used as Designated Marksman Rifle with a magnified optic.

HUMINT: Human Intelligence. Information gleaned through traditional human-to-human methods.

HVI/HVT: High-Value Individual/High-Value Target. An individual who is important to the enemy's capabilities and is therefore specifically sought out by a military force.

IDC: Independent Duty Corpsman. Essentially a doctor.

IED: Improvised Explosive Device. Homemade bombs, whether crude or complex, often used by insurgent forces overseas.

IR: Infrared. The part of the electromagnetic spectrum with a longer wavelength than light but a shorter wavelength than radio waves. Invisible to the naked eye but visible with night observation devices. Example: an IR laser-aiming device.

Iron Curtain: The physical and ideological border that separated the opposing sides of the Cold War.

ISIS: Islamic State of Iraq and the Levant. Radical Sunni terrorist group based in parts of Iraq and Afghanistan. Also referred to as ISIL. The bad guys.

ISR: Intelligence, Surveillance, and Reconnaissance

ITAR: International Traffic in Arms Regulations. Export control regulations designed to restrict the export of certain items, including weapons and optics. These regulations offer ample opportunity to inadvertently violate federal law.

JAG: Judge Advocate General. Decent television series and the military's legal department.

JMAU: Joint Medical Augmentation Unit. High-speed medicine.

JSOC: Joint Special Operations Command. According to Wikipedia, it is a component command of SOCOM, that commands and controls Special Mission Units and Advanced Force Operations.

Katyn Massacre: Soviet purge of Polish citizens that took place in 1940 subsequent to the Soviet invasion. Twenty-two thousand Poles were killed by members of the NKVD during this event; many of the bodies were discovered in mass graves in the Katyn Forest. Russia denied responsibility for the massacre until 1990.

KGB: The Soviet "Committee for State Security." Excelled at "suppressing internal dissent" during the Cold War. Most often referred to by kids of the eighties as "the bad guys."

KIA: Killed in Action

Kudu: A spiral-horned antelope, roughly the size and build of an elk, that inhabits much of sub-Saharan Africa.

Langley: The Northern Virginia location where the Central Intelligence Agency is headquartered. Often used as shorthand for CIA.

LaRue OBR: Optimized Battle Rifle. Precision variant of the AR-15/AR-10 designed for use as a Designated Marksman or Sniper Rifle. Available in both 5.56x45mm and 7.62x51mm.

Law of Armed Conflict: A segment of public international law that regulates the conduct of armed hostilities.

LAW Rocket: M-72 Light Anti-armor Weapon. A disposable, tube-launched 66mm unguided rocket in use with U.S. forces since before the Vietnam War.

Leica M4: Classic 35mm rangefinder camera produced from 1966 to 1975.

Long-Range Desert Group: A specialized British military unit that operated in the North African and Mediterranean theaters during World War II. The unit was made up of soldiers from Great Britain, New Zealand, and Southern Rhodesia.

M1911/1911A1: .45-caliber pistol used by U.S. forces since before World War I.

M3: World War II submachine gun chambered in .45 ACP. This simple but reliable weapon became a favorite of the frogmen of that time.

M4: The standard assault rifle of the majority of U.S. military forces, including the U.S. Navy SEALs. The M4 is a shortened carbine variant of the M16 rifle that fires a 5.56x45mm cartridge. The M4 is a modular design that can be adapted to numerous configurations, including different barrel lengths.

MACV-SOG: Military Assistance Command, Vietnam—Studies and Observations Group. Deceiving name for a group of brave warriors who conducted highly classified special operations missions during the Vietnam War. These operations were often conducted behind enemy lines in Laos, Cambodia, and North Vietnam.

Mahdi Militia: An insurgent Shia militia loyal to cleric Muqtada al-Sadr that opposed U.S. forces in Iraq during the height of that conflict.

MANPADS: Man-Portable Air-Defense System. Small antiaircraft surface-to-air guided rockets such as the U.S. Stinger and the Russian SA-7.

Marine Raiders: U.S. Marine Corps special operations unit; formerly known as MARSOC.

Maritime Branch: It's best to just google it.

Mazrah Tora: A prison in Cairo, Egypt. You do not want to wake up here.

MBITR: AN/PRC-148 Multiband Inter/Intra Team Radio. A handheld multiband, tactical software–defined radio, commonly used by special operations forces to communicate during operations.

McMillan TAC-50: Bolt-action sniper rifle chambered in .50 BMG used for long-range sniping operations, used by U.S. special operations forces as well as the Canadian army.

MDMA: A psychoactive drug whose clinical name is too long to place here. Known on the street as "ecstasy." Glow sticks not included.

MH-47: Special operations variant of the Army's Chinook helicopter, usually flown by members of the 160th SOAR. This twin-rotor aircraft is used frequently in Afghanistan due to its high service ceiling and large troop- and cargo-carrying capacity. Rumor has it that, if you're careful, you can squeeze a Land Rover Defender 90 inside one.

MH-60: Special operations variant of the Army's Black Hawk helicopter, usually flown by members of the 160th SOAR.

MI5: Military Intelligence, Section 5. Britain's domestic counterintelligence and security agency. Like the FBI but with nicer suits and better accents.

MIL DOT: A reticle-based system used for range estimation and long-range shooting, based on the milliradian unit of measurement.

MIL(s): One-thousandth of a radian; an angular measurement used in rifle scopes. 0.1 MIL equals 1 centimeter at 100 meters or 0.36" at 100 yards. If you find that confusing, don't become a sniper.

MIT: Turkey's national intelligence organization and a school in Boston for smart kids.

Mk 46 MOD 1: Belt-fed 5.56x45mm light machine gun built by FN Herstal. Often used by special operations forces due to its light weight, the Mk 46 is a scaled-down version of the Mk 48 MOD 1.

Mk 48 MOD 1: Belt-fed 7.62x51mm light machine gun designed for use by special operations forces. Weighing eighteen pounds unloaded, the Mk 48 can fire 730 rounds per minute to an effective range of 800 meters and beyond.

MP7: Compact select-fire personal defense weapon built by Heckler & Koch and used by various special operations forces. Its 4.6x30mm cartridge is available in a subsonic load, making the weapon extremely quiet when suppressed. What the MP7 lacks in lethality it makes up for in coolness.

MQ-4C: An advanced unmanned surveillance drone developed by Northrop Grumman for use by the United States Navy.

Robert Mugabe: Chairman of ZANU who led the nation of Zimbabwe from 1980 to 2017 as both prime minister and president. Considered responsible for retaliatory attacks against his rival Ndebele tribe as well as a disastrous land redistribution scheme that was ruled illegal by Zimbabwe's High Court.

MultiCam: A proprietary camouflage pattern developed by Crye Precision. Formerly reserved for special operators and air-softers, MultiCam is now standard issue to much of the U.S. and allied militaries.

NATO: North Atlantic Treaty Organization. An alliance created in 1949 to counter the Soviet threat to the Western Hemisphere. Headquartered in Brussels, Belgium, the alliance is commanded by a four-star U.S. military officer known as the Supreme Allied Commander Europe (SACEUR).

Naval Special Warfare Development Group (DEVGRU): A command that appears on the biographies of numerous admirals on the Navy's website. Joe Biden publicly referred to it by a different name when he was the vice president.

NBACC: National Biodefense Analysis and Countermeasures Center. A facility on Fort Detrick in Maryland that for sure does not weaponize and test infectious diseases in the Bat Cave.

NCIS: Naval Criminal Investigative Service. A federal law enforcement agency whose jurisdiction includes the U.S. Navy and Marine Corps. Also a popular television program with at least two spin-offs.

Niassa Game Reserve: Sixteen thousand square miles of relatively untouched wilderness in northern Mozambique. The reserve is home to a wide variety of wildlife as well as a fair number of poachers looking to commoditize them.

NODs: Night observation devices. Commonly referred to as "night vision goggles," these devices amplify ambient light, allowing the user to see in low-light environments. Special operations forces often operate at night to take full advantage of such technology.

NSA: National Security Agency. U.S. intelligence agency tasked with gathering and analyzing signals intercepts and other communications data. Also known as No Such Agency. These are the government employees who listen to our phone calls and read our emails and texts for reasons of "national security." See *Permanent Record* by Edward Snowden.

NSC: National Security Council. This body advises and assists the president of the United States on matters of national security.

NSW: Naval Special Warfare. The Navy's special operations force; includes SEAL Teams.

Officer Candidate School (OCS): Twelve-week course where civilians and enlisted sailors are taught to properly fold underwear. Upon completion, they are miraculously qualified to command men and women in combat.

OmniSTAR: Satellite-based augmentation system service provider. A really fancy GPS service that provides very precise location information.

Ops-Core Ballistic Helmet: Lightweight high-cut helmet used by special operations forces worldwide.

P226: 9mm handgun made by SIG Sauer, the standard-issue sidearm for SEALs.

P229: A compact handgun made by SIG Sauer, often used by federal law enforcement officers, chambered in 9mm as well as other cartridges.

P320: Striker-fired modular 9mm handgun that has recently been adopted by the U.S. armed forces as the M17/M18.

P365: Subcompact handgun made by SIG Sauer, designed for concealed carry. Despite its size, the P365 holds up to thirteen rounds of 9mm.

***Pakhan*:** The highest-ranked *blatnoy* in prison. Now more synonymous with "senior criminal."

Pakistani Taliban: An Islamic terrorist group composed of various Sunni Islamist militant groups based in the northwestern Federally Administered Tribal Areas along the Afghan border in Pakistan.

Pamwe Chete: "All Together." The motto of the Rhodesian Selous Scouts.

Panga: A machete-like utility blade common in Africa.

Peshmerga: Military forces of Kurdistan. Meaning "the one who faces death," they are regarded by Allied troops as some of the best fighters in the region.

PETN: PentaErythritol TetraNitrate. An explosive compound used in blasting caps to initiate larger explosive charges.

PG-32V: High-explosive antitank rocket that can be fired from the Russian-designed RPG-32 rocket-propelled grenade launcher. Its tandem charge is effective against various types of armor, including reactive armor.

PID: Protective Intelligence and Threat Assessment Division. The division of the Secret Service that monitors potential threats to its protectees.

PKM: Soviet-designed, Russian-made light machine gun chambered in 7.62x54R that can be found in conflicts throughout the globe. This weapon feeds from a non-disintegrating belt and has a rate of fire of 650 rounds per minute. You don't want one shooting at you.

PLF: Parachute Landing Fall. A technique taught to military parachutists to prevent injury when making contact with the earth. Round canopy parachutes used by airborne forces fall at faster velocities than other parachutes, and require a specific landing sequence. More often than not, it ends up as feet-ass-head.

PMC: Private Military Company. Though the profession is as old as war itself, the modern term *PMC* was made infamous in the post-9/11 era by Blackwater, aka Xe Services, and now known as Academi.

POTUS: President of the United States; leader of the free world.

PPD: Presidential Protection Detail. The element of the Secret Service tasked with protecting POTUS.

President's Hundred: A badge awarded by the Civilian Marksmanship Program to the one hundred top-scoring military and civilian shooters in the President's Pistol and President's Rifle matches. Enlisted members of the U.S. military are authorized to wear the tab on their uniform.

Professional Hunter: A licensed hunting guide in Africa, often referred to as a "PH." Zimbabwe-licensed PHs are widely considered the most qualified and highly trained in Africa and make up the majority of the PH community operating in Mozambique.

***The Protocols of the Elders of Zion*:** An anti-Semitic conspiracy manifesto first published in the late 1800s by Russian sources. Though quickly established as a fraudulent text, *Protocols* has been widely circulated in numerous languages.

PSO-1: A Russian-made 4x24mm illuminated rifle optic developed for use on the SVD rifle.

PTSD: Post-traumatic stress disorder. A mental condition that develops in association with shocking or traumatic events. Commonly associated with combat veterans.

PVS-15: Binocular-style NODs used by U.S. and allied special operations forces.

QRF: Quick Reaction Force. A contingency ground force on standby to assist operations in progress.

Ranger Panties: Polyester PT shorts favored by members of the 75th Ranger Regiment that leave very little to the imagination, sometimes referred to as "silkies."

REMF: Rear-Echelon Motherfucker. Describes most officers taking credit for what the E-5 mafia and a few senior enlisted do on the ground if the mission goes right. These same "people" will be the first to hang you out to dry if things go south. Now that they are home safe and sound, they will let you believe that when they were "downrange" they actually left the wire.

RFID: Radio Frequency Identification. Technology commonly used to tag objects that can be scanned electronically.

RHIB/RIB: Rigid Hull Inflatable Boat/Rigid Inflatable Boat. A lightweight but high-performance boat constructed with a solid fiberglass or composite hull and flexible tubes at the gunwale (sides).

Rhodesia: A former British colony that declared its independence in 1965. After a long and brutal civil war, the nation became Zimbabwe in 1979.

Rhodesian Bush War: An insurgency battle between the Rhodesian Security Forces and Soviet-, East German–, Cuban-, and Chinese-backed guerrillas that lasted from 1964 to 1979. The war ended when the

December 1979 Lancaster House Agreement put an end to white minority rule.

Rhodesian SAS: A special operations unit formed as part of the famed British Special Air Service in 1951. When Rhodesia sought independence, the unit ceased to exist as part of the British military but fought as part of the Rhodesian Security Forces until 1980. Many members of the Selous Scouts were recruited from the SAS.

Rich Kid Shit: Expensive equipment items reserved for use by the most highly funded special operations units. Google JSOC.

RLI: Rhodesian Light Infantry. An airborne and airmobile unit used to conduct "fireforce" operations during the Bush War. These missions were often launched in response to intelligence provided by Selous Scouts on the ground.

ROE: Rules of engagement. Rules or directives that determine what level of force can be applied against an enemy in a particular situation or area.

RPG-32: 105mm rocket-propelled grenade launcher that is made in both Russia and, under license, in Jordan.

SAD: The CIA's Special Activities Division. Though it is now called the Special Activities Center, it's still responsible for covert action, aka the really cool stuff.

SAP: Special Access Program. Security protocols that provide highly classified information with safeguards and access restrictions that exceed those for regular classified information. Really secret stuff.

SCAR-17: 7.62x51mm battle rifle produced by FN. Its gas mechanism can be traced to that of the FAL.

Schmidt & Bender: Privately held German optics manufacturer known for its precision rifle scopes.

SCI: Special Compartmentalized Information. Classified information concerning or derived from sensitive intelligence sources, methods, or analytical processes. Often found on private basement servers in upstate New York or bathroom closet servers in Denver.

SCIF: Sensitive Compartmented Information Facility. A secure and restricted room or structure where classified information is discussed or viewed.

SEAL: Acronym of SEa, Air, and Land. The three mediums in which SEALs operate. The U.S. Navy's special operations force.

Secret Service: The federal law enforcement agency responsible for protecting the POTUS.

Selous Scouts: An elite, if scantily clad, mixed-race unit of the Rhodesian army responsible for counterinsurgency operations. These "pseudoterrorists" led some of the most successful special operations missions in modern history.

SERE: Survival, Evasion, Resistance, Escape. A military training program that includes realistic role-playing as a prisoner of war. SERE students are subjected to highly stressful procedures, sometimes including waterboarding, as part of the course curriculum. More commonly referred to as "camp slappy."

Shishani: Arabic term for Chechen fighters in Syria, probably due to "Shishani" being a common Chechen surname.

SIGINT: Signals Intelligence. Intelligence derived from electronic signals and systems used by foreign targets, such as communications systems, radars, and weapons systems.

SIPR: Secret Internet Protocol Router network. A secure version of the internet used by DOD and the State Department to transmit classified information.

SISDE: Italy's Intelligence and Democratic Security Service. Their suits are probably even nicer than MI5's.

SOCOM: United States Special Operations Command. The Unified Combatant Command charged with overseeing the various Special Operations Component Commands of the Army, Marine Corps, Navy, and Air Force of the United States armed forces. Headquartered at MacDill Air Force Base in Tampa, Florida.

Special Boat Team-12: The West Coast unit that provides maritime mobility to SEALs using a variety of vessels. Fast boats with machine guns.

Special Reconnaissance (SR) Team: NSW Teams that conduct special activities, ISR, and provide intelligence support to the SEAL Teams.

SR-16: An AR-15 variant developed and manufactured by Knight Armament Corporation.

SRT: Surgical Resuscitation Team. You want these guys close by if you take a bullet.

StrongFirst: Kettle-bell-focused fitness program founded by Russian fitness guru Pavel Tsatsouline that is popular with special operations forces.

S-Vest: Suicide vest. An explosives-laden garment favored by suicide bombers. Traditionally worn only once.

SVR: The Foreign Intelligence Service of the Russian Federation, or as John le Carré describes them, "the KGB in drag."

Taliban: An Islamic fundamentalist political movement and terrorist group in Afghanistan. U.S. and coalition forces have been at war with members of the Taliban since late 2001.

Targeting Officer: The CIA's website says that as a targeting officer you will "identify new opportunities for DO operational activity and enhance ongoing operations." Translation—they tell us whom to kill.

TDFD: Time-delay firing device. An explosive initiator that allows for detonation at a determined period of time. A fancy version of a really long fuse.

TIC: Troops in contact. A firefight involving U.S. or friendly forces.

TOC: Tactical Operations Center. A command post for military operations. A TOC usually includes a small group of personnel who guide members of an active tactical element during a mission from the safety of a secured area.

TOR Network: A computer network designed to conceal a user's identity and location. TOR allows for anonymous communication.

TQ: Politically correct term for the timely questioning of individuals on-site once a target is secure. May involve the raising of voices.

Troop Chief: Senior enlisted SEAL on a forty-man troop, usually a master chief petty officer. The guy who makes shit happen.

TS: Top Secret. Information, the unauthorized disclosure of which reasonably could be expected to cause exceptionally grave damage to national security and that the original classification authority is able to identify or describe. Can also describe an individual's level of security clearance.

TST: Time-sensitive target. A target requiring immediate response because it is highly lucrative, is a fleeting target of opportunity, or poses (or will soon pose) a danger to friendly forces.

UAV: Unmanned Aerial Vehicle. A drone.

UCMJ: Uniform Code of Military Justice. Disciplinary and criminal code that applies to members of the U.S. military.

UDI: Unilateral Declaration of Independence. The 1965 document that established Rhodesia as an independent sovereign state. The UDI resulted in an international embargo and made Rhodesia a pariah.

V-22: Tilt-rotor aircraft that can fly like a plane and take off/land like a helicopter. Numerous examples were crashed during its extremely expensive development.

VBIED: Vehicle-Borne Improvised Explosive Device. A rolling car bomb driven by a suicidal terrorist.

VC: National Liberation Front of South Vietnam, better known as the Viet Cong. A communist insurgent group that fought against the government of South Vietnam and its allies during the Vietnam War. In the movies, these are the guys wearing the black pajamas carrying AKs.

VI: Vehicle Interdiction. Good fun, unless you are on the receiving end.

***Vor v Zakone*:** An individual at the top of the incarcerated criminal underground. Think godfather. Top authority for the Bratva. Today, each region of Russia has a *Vor v Zakone.*

***Vory*:** A hierarchy within the Bratva. Career criminals. More directly translated as "thief."

VPN: Virtual Private Network. A private network that enables users to send and receive data across shared or public networks as if their computing devices were directly connected to the private network. Considered more secure than a traditional internet network.

VSK-94: Russian-made Sniper/Designated Marksman rifle chambered in the subsonic 9x39mm cartridge. This suppressed weapon is popular with Russian special operations and law enforcement units due to its minimal sound signature and muzzle flash.

Wagner Group: A Russian private military company with close ties to the Russian government.

War Vets: Loosely organized groups of Zimbabweans who carried out many of the land seizures during the 1990s. Often armed, these individuals used threats and intimidation to remove white farmers from their homes. Despite the name, most of these individuals were too young to have participated in the Bush War. Not to be confused with ZNLWVA, a group that represents ZANU-affiliated veterans of the Bush War.

WARCOM/NAVSPECWARCOM: United States Naval Special Warfare Command. The Navy's special operations force and the maritime component of United States Special Operations Command. Headquartered in Coronado, California, WARCOM is the administrative command for subordinate NSW Groups composed of eight SEAL Teams, one SEAL Delivery Vehicle (SDV) Team, three Special Boat Teams, and two Special Reconnaissance Teams.

Westley Richards Droplock: A rifle or shotgun built by the famed Birmingham, England, gunmakers that allows the user to remove the locking mechanisms for repair or replacement in the field. Widely considered one of the finest and most iconic actions of all time.

Whiskey Tango: Military speak for "white trash."

WIA: Wounded In Action.

Yazidis: An insular Kurdish-speaking ethnic and religious group that primarily resides in Iraq. Effectively a subminority among the Kurds, Yazidis were heavily persecuted by ISIS.

YPG: Kurdish militia forces operating in the Democratic Federation of Northern Syria. The Turks are not fans.

ZANLA: Zimbabwe African National Liberation Army. The armed wing of the Maoist Zimbabwe African National Union and one of the major combatants of the Rhodesian Bush War. ZANLA forces often staged out of training camps located in Mozambique and were led by Robert Mugabe.

Zimbabwe: Sub-Saharan African nation that formerly existed as Southern Rhodesia and later Rhodesia. Led for three decades by Robert Mugabe, Zimbabwe ranks as one of the world's most corrupt nations on Transparency International's Corruption Perceptions Index.

ZIRPA: Zimbabwe People's Revolutionary Army. The Soviet-equipped armed wing of ZAPU and one of the two major insurgency forces that fought in the Rhodesian Bush War. ZIRPA forces fell under the leadership of Josh Nkomo, who spent much of the war in Zambia. ZIRPA members were responsible for shooting down two civilian airliners using Soviet SA-7 surface-to-air missiles in the late 1970s.

Zodiac Mk 2 GR: A 4.2-meter inflatable rubber boat capable of carrying up to six individuals. These craft are often used as dinghies for larger vessels.

ACKNOWLEDGMENTS

I DIDN'T REALIZE AT the outset just how research intensive *The Devil's Hand* was going to be. I am indebted to a number of works whose influence will be evident to those who have turned their pages: *The Secret War with Iran* and *Rise First and Kill* by Ronen Bergman, *The Dragons and the Snakes* by David Kilcullen, *Beirut Rules* by Fred Burton and Samuel M. Katz, *Biohazard* by Ken Alibek and Stephen Handelman, *The Persian Puzzle* by Kenneth M. Pollack, *A History of Islamic Societies* by Ira M. Lapidus, *The Great Game* by Peter Hopkirk, *The Art of War* by Sun Tzu, *Corporate Warriors* by P. W. Singer, *Blackwater* and *The Assassination Complex* by Jeremy Scahill, *Rules for Radicals* by Saul D. Alinsky, *The Hot Zone* by Richard Preston, *Surprise, Kill, Vanish* by Annie Jacobsen, and *The 9/11 Commission Report*.

To the doctors and intelligence officials who spent time with me, reviewed the manuscript and added context, insight, and wisdom, thank you. Any errors are mine and mine alone. Some may be intentional. This is a work of fiction, after all.

Thank you to my mom and dad, who instilled a love of reading and writing in me at a very early age. That reading provided the foundation for everything that has followed.

To those authors whose works were, and remain, essential influences in my life: Joseph Campbell, Frederick Forsyth, Jack Higgins, Ken

Follett, Robert Ludlum, John le Carré, James Grady, Ian Fleming, John Edmund Gardner, David Morrell, Nelson DeMille, Clive Cussler, J. C. Pollock, Tom Clancy, Louis L'Amour, Marc Olden, A. J. Quinnell, Lee Child, Daniel Silva, Stephen Hunter, Brad Thor, Steven Pressfield, Vince Flynn, Kyle Mills, and Mark Greaney.

To the "Master of the High-Action Thriller" and the "Father of the Modern Action Novel," the incomparable David Morrell for providing inspiration to follow my two complementary callings: the professions of writing and arms. For writers looking for insight into the craft from a true master, read *The Successful Novelist* and visit the writing section of David's website at davidmorrell.net.

To Stephen Hunter for your friendship and inspiration. We started our book tours together with a joint event in 2019; it was one of the greatest honors of my life. When asked to give his advice to aspiring writers at Thrillerfest in 2019 he replied, "Sleep late, drink early, and shoot in between." Legendary. Whoever said to never meet your heroes never met Stephen Hunter.

To Brad Thor for making all this possible.

To Vince Flynn for setting the bar and to Kyle Mills for continuing the legacy. #MitchRappLives

To Mark Greaney for your friendship and support and for giving us *The Gray Man.*

To Steven Pressfield for capturing the essence of the warrior archetype in your work and for sharing your wisdom in *The War of Art.*

To Ray Porter for bringing the series to life through your narration of the audiobooks. Ray agreed to narrate the novels when I was a complete unknown. Thank you for lending your voice and talent to the James Reece universe.

If you are looking for a recommended reading list, I highlight six books a month that have been impactful to me on my journey. You can find them on my website blog at OfficialJackCarr.com and on my book-specific Instagram page @JackCarrBookClub.

To trusted friends and confidants David Lehman, James Rupley, Dan Gelston, and Kevin O'Malley for taking time out of your extremely busy schedules to apply keen eyes and sharp intellects to early drafts of the manuscript. This book would not be what it is without you. I am worried that one day I'll have to start paying you . . .

To Chris Pratt for the dedication you bring to your craft. To see this project starting to come full circle after I envisioned you as the right person to bring James Reece to screens well before *Guardians of the Galaxy*, *Jurassic World*, and *Avengers* and well before I'd even finished that first novel continues to astonish me. You are going to CRUSH IT!

To Antoine Fuqua, the one person I always imagined directing *The Terminal List*. I am so excited to get to work!

To Kat Samick for being so supportive of *The Terminal List* project.

To David DiGilio, showrunner for *The Terminal List*, for teaching me so much about screenwriting and being such a pleasure to work with.

To Jared Shaw for your time in the SEAL Teams and for being the driving force behind bringing *The Terminal List* Amazon series to where it is today.

To Michael Broderick for bringing together such a talented team to produce the short film *Fathers and Sons—A Terminal List Story*. Written by Navy veteran Vernon Mortensen, directed by Army veteran Ryan Curtis and starring Marine veteran Michael Broderick and Army Ranger veteran Tim Abell with Tyne Stecklein, this short film simply blew me away. You can find it in the blog section of my website.

To Joe Rogan for inviting me on the podcast and for being such a strong voice for freedom and independent thought. Looking forward to getting back out after elk and axis with you soon.

To Dylan Murphy for the work you do with operators at the tip of the spear and for all the time you take to work through the combative portions of the novels. The close-quarters-combat chapters are not just imagined in my head. They start there, but then Dylan gears up and choreographs the fights to make them as primal and visceral as possible. Thank you, brother.

To George Kollitides and Wally McLallen for talking me through the world of 2001 New York finance and Silicon Valley tech start-ups. It is sincerely appreciated.

To Clint Smith, Larry Vickers, James Rupley, Jason Swarr, Jim Fuller, James Rose, and Gary Hughes for taking the time to help me with the Kalashnikov description. You have all forgotten more about that rifle than I will ever know.

To Chip King and Christopher Ellender at Gulfstream for all your help on the aviation side of the house.

To Frank Argenbright for the idea.

To Ryan Steck, aka The Real Book Spy, for all you do for authors and readers of the genre.

To Sean Cameron, author of *Amateur Hour*; Mike Houtz, author of *Dark Spiral Down*; and C. E. Albanese of *The Crew Reviews Podcast*. Aspiring authors—listen to this podcast, take notes, and most important, apply what you learn to your craft.

To C. E. Albanese for his time in the Secret Service and for answering my federal law enforcement questions. I can't wait to see *Drone Kings* on the bookshelf!

To Eric Bishop for your early support of *The Terminal List*. Looking forward to my signed copy of *The Body Man*.

To James Rose, Jamie Swanson, and the entire crew at the Park City Gun Club. If you swing through Park City, Utah, stop in and give the fully automatic AK a run. I might see you there!

To Larry Vickers and James Rupley for the incredible Vickers Guide series of books. There is nothing else like them and they are always my first stop when researching the weapons-centric chapters of my novels.

If you are a student of the gun, these should without a doubt be in your collection. Find them at vickersguide.com.

To Clint and Heidi Smith of Thunder Ranch. If you have not made the pilgrimage to train at Thunder Ranch, make this your year!

To Jack Daniels for holding the line in law enforcement and for your patience with me when I need help ordering and attaching all the different rifle accessory components . . .

To James Yeager of Tactical Response for being *all in* on the James Reece series well before I was a *New York Times* bestselling author or had a social media account. Thank you for being the catalyst for what became a word-of-mouth campaign that got all this started.

To Ironclad Media for filming and producing the most epic book trailer videos of all time and for jumping on board to produce my new podcast, *Danger Close: Beyond the Books with Jack Carr.*

To Katie Pavlich for the years of friendship and support. Pick up and read Katie's books, *Fast and Furious* and *Assault & Flattery,* today!

Daniel Winkler and Karen Shook of Winkler Knives for all you have done and continue to do for those at the tip of the special operations spear and for forging the tomahawks for James Reece.

To Jim Shockey for all your enthusiastic support! I can't wait to help introduce the world to your outstanding novel when the time is right.

To Kyle Lamb of Viking Tactics for your leadership and your time in uniform in service to this great nation.

To Dom Raso of Dynamis Alliance for always being there for me and my family.

To Bill Rapier of AMTAC Shooting for the killer blade that James Reece uses in this novel. Hope we can get on the range together soon. I need a tune-up!

To Biss for a wild ride in the Teams and out. Thank you for all your support, brother.

To Tom Flanagan of Eagles & Angels for all you've done for the nation and all you continue to do for veterans in the private sector.

To Ron Cohen, Tom Taylor, Jason Wright, Samantha Piatt, Olivia Gallivan, Aisling Meechan, Bobby Cox, Max Michel, Phil Strader, Lena Miculek, Daniel Horner, and Hana Bilodeau at SIG Sauer. I'm forever a fan.

To Teddy Novin for your early and enthusiastic support of the novels.

To Elias Kfoury for all you did and continue to do for our brothers.

To Dave Rogers for the spark.

To David Bolls for your energy and for connecting the dots.

To Craig, Heather, Savanna, Zachary, and Cadan Flynn. Thank you for all your support. You are going to make great neighbors.

To Tucker Carlson for inviting me on the show and for holding our elected officials—our employees—accountable.

To Lexi Ciccone for standing strong and for all your support.

To Frank LeCrone for your friendship and for always going above and beyond in all that you do. It's an honor, my friend.

To Brendan O'Malley for being so thoughtful. I'm looking forward to my next delivery of whiskey.

To Andrew Arrabito and Kelsie Bieser at Half Face Blades for your friendship and for such a cool limited edition *Savage Son* Hunter-Skinner blade. Let's do another soon!

To John Devine of Devine K9 and Sara (@thesupercilliesmom) for all your work training Scout as a service dog for my son. And, thank you for all you do at Rescue 22 for veterans suffering the physical and emotional trauma of the battlefield. To help in their mission to provide fully trained service and support dogs to veterans in need, please visit rescue22 foundation.org.

To Jon Sanchez for your time in the SEAL Teams, your example in the private sector at Team Performance Institute, and for putting my post-military life in motion. I'll never forget it.

To Jon Dubin for answering my questions about the FBI, for inviting me to be a part of Pineapple Brothers Lanai, and for all our past adventures and those still to come! If you are in Lanai, you might catch us poolside drinking lava flows with rum shooters to hydrate after a morning afield. If you see us, stop by to say hello and talk weapons, hunts, drinks, and books.

To Evan Hafer of Black Rifle Coffee Company for bringing together a community of coffee-loving patriots and for being an inspiration not just to veterans but to all citizens as to what is possible.

To Logan Stark of Black Rifle Coffee Company for sharing your knowledge of the new media and for being so supportive in launching the novels.

To Tyr S., U.S. Army Special Forces, "doer of things," thank you for use of what is one of the most powerful sentences I've ever read. It is woven into the pages of this novel. Keep writing, my friend.

To Tom Davin for your friendship and guidance, and for always making time for me. Semper Fi!

To Richard Ryan for a great time on *Veterans React*.

To Trevor Thompson for your epic photos and insights.

To Jonathan Hart, founder of Sitka Gear, for over thirty years friendship.

To Mike Schoby for your friendship and for such an awesome shoot for the cover of *Wheels Afield* magazine.

To Dory Schoby for being so awesome and for everything you do at Aimpoint.

To Andrew Kline for your ideas, energy, loyalty, and friendship. We are all better for knowing you.

To Jimmy Klein for all your support for my family. Looking forward to another adventure soon!

To Chris Cox for your advice, counsel, and all the years of friendship. Keep an eye out for the Amazon series . . . you might recognize a certain name.

To Graham Hill for always being there. Don't worry, you will be a character in a book soon . . .

To Nick Seifert at Athlon Outdoors for an incredible cover shoot for *Ballistic Magazine*.

To Len Waldron for your writing and passion for the outdoors.

To Bill Crider for being an outstanding human being. It's an honor to know you.

To the crew at Dead Air Silencers for all you do to preserve my hearing.

To Mato for your example as my Command Master Chief at SEAL Team Two and for setting the standard.

To John Dudley at Nock On Archery for all you do for those who pick up a bow.

To all the authors I miss seeing at Thrillerfest and Bouchercon: K. J. Howe, Gregg Hurwitz, Chris Hauty, Lee Child, Brad Taylor, Steve Berry, Christine Carbo, Nick Petrie, Mindy Mejia, William Kent Krueger, A. J. Tata, Marc Cameron, Josh Hood, Simon Gervais, L. A. Chandler, Matt Coyle, Desiree Holt, Matthew Betley, Tom Abrahams, Don Bently, Rob Olive, Kevin Maurer, Sean Parnell, Brian Andrews, and Jeffrey Wilson.

To everyone who supported my dream of becoming an author as I made the transition from military service: Trig and Annette French, Christian Sommer, Jimmy Spithill, Terry Flynn, Scott Grimes, Jason Salata, Garry and Victoria Peters, Shane Reilly, Jim and Nancy Demetriades, Larry and Rhonda Sheakley, Martin and Kelly Katz, Razor and Sylvia Dobbs, Lacey Biles, Michael Davidson, Paul Makarechian, Natalie Alverez, Ben Bosanac, Tuck Beckstoffer, Mike Atkinson, Mike Port, Alec Wolf, Mike Comacho, and Damien and Jen Patton.

To all those who shared my story with their audiences: Adam Janke at the *Journal of Mountain Hunting*, Tami Louris, Andy Stumpf at Cleared Hot, Chad Prather of *The Chad Prather Show*, Matt Locke at *The Matt Lock Show*, Marcus Torgerson at IKMF Krav Maga, Fred Burton, Cole Kramer, Amy Robbins at Alexo Athletica, Mike Ritland at Mike Drop Podcast, Rob

Bianchin at Cabot Guns, Kurt Schlichter at Townhall, Ryan Michler at Order of Man, Jocko Willink, Jason Swarr and Ben Tirpak at *Skillset Magazine*, Mike Glover at Fieldcraft Survival, Herman Achteruis at Achter Knives, Maddie Taylor, Ross Kaminsky at the *Ross Kaminsky Show*, Brian Call of the Gritty Podcast, Direct Action USA, Dana Loesch of *The Dana Show*, Tim Brent, Eva Shockey Brent, Christian Schauf of Uncharted Supply Company, Gavy Friedson at Israel Rescue, Rick Stewart at American Zealot Productions, Joe and Charlotte Betar of the Houston Safari Club, Jeff Crane and P. J. Carleton of the Congressional Sportsman's Foundation, Larry Keane at NSSF, John Nores of the Thin Green Line podcast, Mat Best, Jared Taylor, and Mike at Last Line of Defense.

To those who live by the gun: Ken Hackathorn, Jeff Houston at TAC 7, Sean Haberburger at BluCore, Pat McNamara at TMACS, Johnny Primo at Courses of Action, Tim Clemit, Keith Walawender at Tomahawk Strategic Solutions, Mickey Schuch at Carry Trainer, Monty LeClair at Centurion Arms, Clay Hergert at ATX Precision, Joe Collins, and Chip Beaman.

I love to see my former Teammates out there crushing it in the private sector: Eric Frohardt, Chris Osman at Rhuged, Jeff Reid at Frozen Trident, Brent Gleeson at Taking Point Leadership, Clint Emerson of 100 Deadly Skills, Eli Crane at Bottle Breacher, Mike Sauers and Samantha Bonilla at Forged, Sean Evangelista at 30 Seconds Out, Jared Ogden of Triumph Systems, Cory Zillig at ZF Technical, Sergio Lopez, Damian Clapper at Lead Nav Systems, and Eddie Penny at Contingent Group. Keep crushing!

To Tim Fallon, and my former SEAL Teammates Doug Prichard and Dave Knesek at FTW Ranch for your expertise behind the glass.

To the cast and crew of *SEAL Team* CBS for all the effort you put in to such an outstanding show.

To Dr. Robert Bray at DISC Sports and Spine Center for always being in our corner personally and professionally. Without you and Tracey this military-to-private-sector transition would not be happening. Thank you for everything.

To Garrett Bray, what can I say? Thank you for putting so much time, energy, and effort into building the foundation of all that is to come. I would not be where I am without you.

To Chris Hunt at Black Rifle Coffee for the amazing artwork.

To Lucas O'Hara of Grizzly Forge Knives. Welcome to Utah!

To Eric and Sarah Cylvick for sharing the Salmon River with us and to Cash and Tor for showing us the ropes.

To Mike Stoner for the incredible photos and for getting me back on the dirt bike.

To Eli Katz of Cahill Gorden & Reindell for sharing your knowledge on the legalities of Israel's targeted assassination program. You will recognize your fingerprints on this novel.

To Billy Birdzell for your time in the USMC and for always being up for an adventure.

To Dr. Harry O'Halloran for your sharp eyes.

Shahram Moosavi of the Phoenix JKD Institute of Mixed Martial Arts for the years of training in MMA before it went by that name. I thought back to our Brazilian jiujitsu rolling sessions many times during Hell Week in BUD/S; if I could make it through your training sessions, I could certainly run around for a week without sleep carrying a boat on my head on the beach in Coronado.

To Erik Snyder for always being so generous with your Defender 100, the vehicle Raife Hastings drives in *Savage Son*. If you ever want to sell it . . .

To Hoby Darling for leading and inspiring a top-tier morning workout crew. If you worked out around noon, I'd join you.

To Stacey Wenger for making the most incredible book-inspired cakes. Our Reagan Library signing for *Savage Son* was sabotaged by COVID-19, but one day we will make it happen!

To Josh Waldron for exemplifying tenacity and determination.

To Mark Bollman of Ball and Buck for starting such a cool company.

To Rick and Esther Rosenfield for your love and support.

To Nick and Tina Cousoulis for making us part of your family.

To Jeff Kimbell, at least we didn't almost get mauled by a bear this year.

To my mentor in the art and science of warfare, James Jarrett. If you have not read his short story "Death in the Ashau," it is available through Old Mountain Press in *De Oppresso Liber: A Poetry & Prose Anthology by Special Forces Soldiers.*

To Brock Bosson, Joel Kurtzeberg, Jason Yeoun, Alexander Kim, Shaun Altshuller, George Harris, and the entire team at Cahill Gorden & Reindell for always exceeding expectations on the legal front.

To Norm Brownstein and Steve Demby at Brownstein Hyatt Farber Schreck for the solid counsel. It is appreciated more than I can express.

To Mitch Langberg at Brownstein Hyatt Farber Schreck for always having my back.

To John Barklow for your time in uniform and for all you do at Sitka Gear for those of us who venture into the mountains. Check out John's knowledge bombs on Instagram @jbarklow.

To Brendan Carr for helping me get organized in the midst of a pandemic. I can't wait to see what you do next!

To Michaela Smith and everyone at Dolly's Bookstore in Park City, Utah. If you are in town be sure and pay them a visit. You might find me browsing the shelves . . .

To Barbara Peters of Poisoned Pen in Scottsdale, Arizona, for your early and continued support. It was an honor to start my first ever book tour at Poisoned Pen.

To Mystery Mike Bursaw for scouring the world for all those hard-to-find signed first editions I'm always searching for.

To Lucky Ones Coffee in Park City, Utah, for keeping me caffeinated as I write the James Reece series. Lucky Ones Coffee is located in the

Park City Public Library. Stop on in next time you pass through town. If you see me in a corner with my laptop and a coffee, be sure to say hello.

To all the readers, veterans, hunters, and tactical shooters who took a chance on an unknown author and then told a friend—I appreciate it more than I can possibly express.

Just like in special operations, the world of publishing is not a one-person endeavor. It takes a team, and I am fortunate to be surrounded by a Tier 1 unit.

To my agent, Alexandra Machinist at ICM, for maneuvering through terrain that remains completely foreign to me. Thank you for all you do.

To my agent at ICM in Los Angeles, Josie Freedman, for all your work on the Hollywood front.

To Emily Bestler, for seeing the potential, taking a risk, and mentoring me through the past four years. We sat down for coffee in New York not quite six months after I left the Navy. It's been a full-on sprint ever since. Thank you for making all of this a reality. I am fired up for what's ahead! And, thank you to the entire team at Emily Bestler Books for adapting to the changing environment brought on by COVID. There is no other group I'd rather have with me in the publishing trenches.

To Lara Jones for your patience and for keeping everything moving forward.

To my dear friend and publicist David Brown, I wake up each day so thankful that you are at the wheel of the Atria Mystery Bus. Thank you for the enthusiasm you bring to everything you do. It is a true pleasure to brainstorm, innovate, and collaborate together on ways to introduce more readers to James Reece.

My heartfelt thanks to production editor Al Madocs for turning my Word document into the book you are reading now.

To James Iacobelli for knocking it out of the park on another cover. I'm already looking forward to what you are going to do with book five! Title classified.

To Jen Long at Pocket Books for outdoing herself on the paperback edition of *Savage Son*. What will *The Devil's Hand* paperback cover look like? I can't wait to find out!

To Jon Karp, CEO of Simon & Schuster, for leading us all through an unprecedented time.

To Libby McGuire, publisher of Atria Books, for being such a champion of these books. I simply can't thank you enough.

To Suzanne Donahue for being such a strong advocate of the novels.

To the amazing Simon & Schuster Audio team, what a blast it has been to get the audio book out there. Thank you to Sarah Lieberman, Gabrielle Audet, Chris Lynch, and Tom Spain for all your efforts!

To Alice Rodgers at Simon & Schuster UK, it has been so cool seeing the James Reece readership grow in the United Kingdom.

Thank you to the marketing team: Liz Perl, Sue Fleming, Sienna Farris, Dana Trocker, and Milena Brown. Without your efforts, no one would know the novels exist.

Thank you to the incredible team in accounts and sales. To Gary Urda, Colin Shields, Chrissy Festa, Paula Amendolara, Janice Fryer, Lesley Collins, Gregory Hruska, and Lexi Dumas for getting the books on shelves.

It is with a heavy heart that I thank Simon & Schuster president and CEO, Carolyn Reidy, for always making time for me on my trips to New York. I'll forever treasure the memories I have of walking by the photos of authors I'd been reading my entire life on my way to your office for a visit to talk about books, reading, and publishing. Carolyn, thank you for believing in me and for giving me my shot. You are deeply missed. Carolyn Reidy, May 2, 1949–May 12, 2020.

To all the booksellers who have recommended my novels to readers across the country and now internationally, I thank you. I can't wait for a day when we can all once again link up in person to discuss the art of storytelling.

Looking for more information on my time in the SEAL Teams, the weapons and gear I used then and now, and a behind-the-scenes look at the writing process? Sign up for my newsletter at OfficialJack Carr.com and follow along on Instagram, Twitter, and Facebook at @JackCarrUSA.

And finally, to my beautiful wife, Faith, thank you for marrying me. There is no one else I can imagine taking this crazy ride with. Thank you for your love, strength, and understanding. And to our three amazing children, thank you for making me feel like the luckiest dad on earth.

Turn the page for an exclusive look at Jack Carr's next thriller,

IN THE BLOOD

For the wages of sin is death.

—ROMANS 6:23

PROLOGUE

Ouagadougou, Burkina Faso, Africa

SHE HAD BEEN STRIKINGLY beautiful once. At just over forty she still turned heads, a trait she often worked to her advantage both personally and professionally, but even as confident and, more importantly, competent as she was, it was not lost on her that fewer heads were turning these days. She was well aware that her looks had a limited shelf life. She accepted it. She had enjoyed them in her youth but now she had other, more valuable skills—skills she had put into practice hours earlier. As she waited her turn in line at the check-in counter at the Air France section of Thomas Sankara International Airport Ouagadougou in Burkina Faso, no one would have guessed that earlier she had shot a man three times in the head with a Makarov 9x18mm pistol.

The Makarov would not have been her first choice but on assignments like this you used what was available. It had worked. The man was dead. The message had been sent.

Aliya Galin brushed her raven-black hair to the side and glanced at her smartphone, not because she wanted to know the time or scroll through a newsfeed or social media app, but because she did not want to stand out to local security forces as what she was, an assassin for the state of Israel. She needed to blend in with the masses, which meant suppressing her natural predatory instincts. It was time to act like a sheep, nonattentive and relatively relaxed. She needed to look normal.

Had she been stopped and questioned, her backstory as a sales representative for a French financial firm would have checked out, as would her employment history, contacts, and references developed by the technical office just off the Glilot Ma'arav Interchange in Tel Aviv, home to the headquarters of the Mossad, the Israeli spy agency tasked with safeguarding the Jewish state. The laptop in her carry-on contained nothing that would betray her, no secret backdoor files storing incriminating information, no Internet searches for anything to do with Israel, terrorism, or her target. The computer was clean.

It was getting more difficult to travel internationally with the web of interconnected facial recognition cameras that continued to proliferate around the globe. Had it not been for the Mossad's Technology Department she would have been arrested many times over. The Israeli intelligence services had learned the lessons of facial recognition and passport forgery in the age of information the hard way on the international stage twelve years earlier, when twenty-six of their agents had been identified and implicated in the assassination of Mahmoud al-Mabhouh in a Dubai hotel room. Al-Mabhouh was the chief weapons procurement and logistics officer for the al-Qassam Brigades, the military wing of the Hamas terrorist organization. The Mossad would not repeat the mistakes of Dubai.

Her French passport identified her as Mélanie Cotillard and if someone were to check her apartment in Batignolles-Monceau, they would find a flat commensurate with the income of a midlevel banker in the financial services industry. No disguises, weapons, or false walls would betray her true profession.

The man she had come to kill was responsible for the bombing of a Jewish day care center in Rabat, Morocco. Not all in the Arab world were supportive of Morocco recognizing Israel and establishing official diplomatic relations. If retribution was not swift, it emboldened the enemy, an enemy that wanted to see Israel wiped from the face of the earth. When Iranian-backed terrorists targeted Israeli children, justice was handled not by the courts but by Caesarea, an elite and secretive branch of the Mossad.

More and more, drones were becoming a viable option for targeted assassinations. They were getting smaller and easier to conceal. But, even with the options that came with the increasingly lethal UAV technology, the Mossad still preferred to keep some kills personal. Israel was a country built on the foundation of a targeted killing program, one that had continued to evolve, as did the threats to the nation. There was nothing that put as much fear in the hearts and minds of her enemies as an Israeli assassin.

Though Aliya maintained her dual U.S.-Israeli citizenship, she had not set foot in the United States in almost fifteen years. Israel was now home. Her parents had been born there and had been killed there, a suicide bomber from Hamas taking them from her just as they began to enjoy their retirement years. She had been in the Israel Defense Forces then, doing her duty with no intention of devoting her life to her adopted homeland. She would be back soon. She would quietly resign from her job in Paris, which had been set up for her by a *Sayan,* and return to Israel. *Sayanim* made up a global network of non-Israeli, though usually Jewish, assets that provided material and logistical support for Mossad operations, not for financial incentives but out of loyalty. Aliya planned to take time off to see her children and her sister who cared for them. She also planned to talk to the head of the special operations division about moving into management. She was getting tired. Perhaps this would be her final kill.

The assignment had been relatively straightforward. She did in fact have a legitimate meeting with a bank in Ouagadougou, Burkina Faso's capital city. The instability inherent to the African continent also provided opportunity for investment. Her cover for action intact, she had three days to locate and case the residence of Kofi Kouyaté. They called it a "close target reconnaissance" when she had worked with the Americans in Iraq. She reflected on the operational pace of those intense days often; the lessons learned, the relationships fostered.

Her days of seducing men in hotel bars were in the past, at least in this part of the world. Enough of them had ended up shot, stabbed, poisoned, or blown up after thinking with the small head between their legs that others became wary when a beautiful olive-skinned angel offered to buy them a drink.

The Mossad could have used a hit team of locals on this assignment, but her masters in Tel Aviv still preferred to send a message—hurt Israeli citizens and we will find you, no matter where you hide. Aliya's generation of *Kidon,* assassins, had proven worthy inheritors of the legacy of Operation Wrath of God, which targeted those responsible for the 1972 massacre of Israeli athletes in Munich.

She had worked this job alone. No accomplice to turn her in or identify her to the infamous Burkina Faso internal state security service. If you were rolled up in this part of the world, you could look forward to an interrogation and torture worse than what you would experience in the West Bank. Out here, you would be questioned, beaten, burned, and mutilated before being gang raped until you were dead.

Though security was lax by internationally accepted standards, she still had to empty her purse and small suitcase onto a table beyond a metal detector that she had a strong suspicion was not plugged in. As the two security guards went through her bag, they paid a bit too much attention to her bras and underwear. Finding nothing suspicious that gave them an excuse to bring her into a back room for a secondary search, they let her proceed to her gate. Perhaps if she were younger they would have crafted an excuse. Aging in this business did have its benefits.

She was looking forward to leaving the African heat behind and settling into her business-class seat on the air-conditioned Air France flight with service to Paris. She was ready for a drink. Air France still took pride in the French part of their lineage and served tolerable white wine even this early in the morning.

Waiting to board, she allowed her mind to wander to the past six months in France, the children she had left in the care of her younger sister in Israel, and a possible return to, no, not normalcy, as life had never been normal for Aliya, but possibly an evolution, yes, that was it, an evolution in her life. Maybe she would visit the United States, travel with her children, and introduce them to the country where she had lived with her parents until they returned to the Holy Land, when Aliya was ten. She smiled, imagining her son and daughter playing on the white sand beaches in the Florida sun. *Normal.* They were still young enough that she could be a mother to them. What would she do at headquarters? Work as an analyst in collections or as an advisor to the chief or deputy director? More appealing was a transfer out of operations and into training. Her hard-earned skills and experience would be put to good use at the Midrasha, the elite Mossad training academy. Would she be able to adjust after all these years in the field? Killing was all she knew.

As she boarded the flight, distracted by thoughts of the future, she failed to notice the man watching her from across the gate.

When she crossed the tarmac and disappeared into the plane, he placed a call.

• • •

Nizar Kattan studied the two men from neighboring Mali as they removed the Strela-2 missiles from the back of the Jeep.

A Soviet-era, shoulder-fired surface-to-air missile, the 9K32 Strela-2 was almost as common in sub-Saharan Africa as RPGs and AK variants. Nizar knew the Strela had been used to successfully shoot down multiple airliners over the years. It was a reliable missile system that had proven its worth, but it was getting old. During the 2002 Mombasa attacks in Kenya that targeted an Israeli-owned hotel, the al-Qaeda inspired terrorists had fired two Strelas at an Israeli-chartered Boeing 747. Both missiles had missed the target. Having worked with enough indigenous talent over the years, Nizar chalked it up to operator error. Still, he wasn't going to take chances, which is why four of one of the Cold War's most prolific weapons would be used on this mission.

Nizar and his French accomplice had recruited the two patsies from the ranks of Nusrat al-Islam, or Jama'at Nasr al-Islam wal Muslimin to the initiated. The group formed when al-Qaeda in the Islamic Maghreb, Ansar al-Dine, and al-Mourabitoun merged in 2017. With a mandate that called for killing civilians from Western nations, they would be perfect. Still reverberating with the echoes of French colonial rule, insurgent groups in West Africa were ripe for exploitation. Financial incentives cemented the deal. In this case, Nusrat al-Islam thought they were striking a blow against their European oppressors in an operation organized by Nizar, who they believed to be an al-Qaeda facilitator. Their tasks were simple: They were to transport the four surface-to-air missiles from Mali into Burkina Faso, where they would link up with Nizar and the Frenchman and be given their target. Unbeknownst to them, their other task required them to die.

French special forces soldiers had proven extremely proficient in decimating the ranks of Nusrat al-Islam in Africa. Say what you will of the French, their operators were some of the best in the world. The officials meeting weekly in the Élysée Palace turned a blind eye to French military and intelligence actions in Africa. With few war correspondents covering what was essentially a forgotten conflict, French soldiers targeted and killed with impunity. Most of the developed world cared little for what transpired on the Dark Continent. The French government was smart enough to allow their citizens the freedom to travel, train, and join terror groups abroad. What they were loath to do within their own borders even in the wake of the attacks in Nice and Paris, they were more than happy to do in their former colonies and protectorates, perhaps as a psychological fuck-you to those who had thrown them out in the wars of liberation that swept the continent in the mid to late twentieth century. In Europe, France was a liberal bastion of democratic socialism. Overseas they hunted their enemies with ruthless efficiency.

Jean-Pierre Le Drian was capable and resourceful. His former teammates would have described him as merciless. A former French Foreign Legion *maréchal des logis-chef*, he now found employment as a soldier of fortune, a mercenary with an axe to grind. Rather than face charges for an atrocity in Africa that was too much for even those fighting an expeditionary counterinsurgency, the former staff sergeant was on the run. And he was valuable. He knew just where to look to find black-market weapons and regional guns for hire in this forgotten corner of Africa.

Le Drian fancied himself a successor to the Waffen SS commandos who escaped Nazi Germany following World War II and found refuge in the Legion, fighting in Indochina in the Devil's Brigade. Were those stories fact or fiction? It didn't matter. Le Drian was guided by the myth. He was his own Devil's Brigade of the new century. He knew that he had done what was necessary. These savages deserved no respect. What was coming next would be easy for him.

Nizar could not care less about the plight of the locals. Africa was just as shitty as the places he had left behind in the Middle East. His assignments in Syria and Ukraine had not been out of allegiance to Allah but out of a desire to leave that world behind. He had feigned support and devotion to *the cause* time and time again, always wondering how those around him could be so naive. Allah didn't care for Nizar. The prophet and the cult that followed him were no different than adherents to any religion the world over, con artists in a protection racket just like he had witnessed in his time with the Bratva, the Russian mafia. Nizar was clear on where real power lay: in the dollar, the euro, the yuan, gold, diamonds, silver, and now bitcoin. Enough of those and you could be a living, breathing god in the flesh.

What Nizar wanted, Allah could not deliver. Praying five times a day in accordance with the Five Pillars only wasted time. His skill with a rifle had been his ticket out of Syria and then to Russia and Montenegro. When his mentor had outlived his usefulness, Nizar had put him down with a shot from a suppressed Stechkin pistol, just as he'd been instructed by his then handler, General Qusim Yedid, a Syrian general who had been found shot in the knee and then poisoned with a highly toxic substance. Nizar had put enough of the story together to conclude that the general's death was the work of James Reece, the man he currently had in his sights. Nizar had escaped to Moscow and into the waiting hands of the Russian mafia before he struck out on his own, finding a home in Montenegro, a way station of illicit trade over millennia. He enjoyed the protection he received there but sensed it was time to move on. *Trust your instincts.* His next kill would allow him to relocate: Thailand, the Philippines, Argentina. He had not decided yet. This last payday, James Reece's death, would make it possible. It would also be his greatest challenge to date, as his prey might at this very moment be hunting him.

Fortunately for Nizar, James Reece was a man with enemies; enemies at senior levels of governments hostile to the United States, governments with intelligence services that had close ties to proxy terrorist groups. Nizar briefly wondered if the information that had led him to Burkina Faso had originated in Russia or Iran. No matter. It was time to move a pawn on the board. It was time to draw Reece out of the mountains of North America and onto the battlefield.

Nizar closed his eyes and took in the dry morning air. He was ready.

The men were dressed in the uniforms of the Burkina Faso security forces. They had parked off a red dirt road flanked by the long grasses of the savanna. Their position gave them a clear line of sight to aircraft departing Thomas Sankara International Airport.

The retainer money from Eric Sawyer that had been laundered through a construction company in Montenegro was not insignificant, but it was not quite enough. The former Army Ranger and private military company CEO had used Nizar to eliminate problems. He had died under suspicious circumstances on his island property in the West Indies, but not before he had set up a contract to eliminate James Reece. Was the CIA involved in Sawyer's death? Nizar could not be sure, but he had his suspicions. Had the retainer been a few more million, Nizar would have considered taking the money and not fulfilling the contract. With Sawyer dead, there would have been no repercussions. Perhaps if he were not on Reece's radar, Nizar would have walked. But he was. Nizar suspected that Reece had killed two of Nizar's past handlers. The former SEAL was a threat, one that needed to be dealt with. Putting him in the ground solved two problems: It eliminated an exceptionally competent professional targeting him and it unlocked the other half of Sawyer's money, allowing Nizar to disappear and to not have to go for his gun every time he caught movement in the shadows. If he was going to vanish and leave this life behind, he needed to kill James Reece.

The Frenchman had come to him courtesy of his new handler, the man in the wheelchair. They had met in person only once, in Dubrovnik. The coastal Croatian city was close enough to Montenegro that Nizar could make the trip with relatively few complications. His potential handler, on the other hand, had to travel by train and ferry from Turin, in northern Italy, to the Balkan state on the Adriatic. Nizar had watched him over the course of four days, looking for signs of surveillance. The man in the wheelchair was a veteran of the game; he knew Nizar was observing and vetting him. He was a professional and would have expected nothing less. Nizar found himself grudgingly gaining respect for the small man who pushed himself through the streets and hauled himself in and out of taxis and into restaurants and cafés without asking for help or letting a moment's worth of self-pity cross his face. The man wore a different tailored suit every day, a bold silk ascot around his neck. Like Nizar, he stayed off cell phones and computers. He was a student of the old school. How he ended up in the wheelchair was a source of mystery and conjecture to those who lived and worked in the darker side of the clandestine economy. It was rumored he had been put there by a sniper.

Having established that the man was not bait, Nizar sat down with him over coffee, and they worked out their arrangement. Without Sawyer he needed someone else who could navigate the underworld, acquire weapons, and find additional talent. Additional talent would be necessary on this job. His one and only in-person meeting with his new handler had felt like a job interview, the small man confined to the chair studying him with those hawklike eyes, judging, assessing.

Nizar needed a partner on this mission, one with language abilities and a high level of martial prowess; the man in the wheelchair had delivered. If James Reece was as good as his track record would suggest, a second set of eyes and another scoped rifle in the fight would pay dividends.

Le Drian glanced at his watch and barked at the two "soldiers." When operating in this part of the world it helped to have a French citizen on your side who also spoke Arabic and Mòoré. That he boasted a background in the French Foreign Legion, operating almost exclusively in Africa, made him worth the investment. That he had a beef with the French government only helped solidify his allegiance.

"Just a few more minutes," the Frenchman said in flawless Arabic.

"Unless they are delayed," Nizar responded.

"Yes, always a probability in this part of the world. *This is Africa,* after all."

"Are they ready?" Nizar asked.

"Yes. They think they are making a statement, killing the colonial invaders, which, as you know, appeals to me."

Le Drian could never set foot in France again, banned to the outer reaches of what had once been an empire. Even the French Foreign

Legion had standards. Hunting and killing were one thing, torture was another; the memory of Algeria had yet to fade.

"Get ready," Nizar said. "Confirm the tail number and—"

The phone in the Frenchman's pocket chirped. He spoke in Mòoré and hit the End button.

"She's on board. Plane is taxiing."

"Good. It is time."

• • •

Aliya leaned back in her seat and took a sip of wine. It was just after 9:00 a.m.

The plane gained speed and lifted off, clearing the buildings at the east end of the runway and making a slow turn over the capital city.

The mission was *never* over. Not now. Not when she landed in France. Not when she returned to Israel. Not ever. This was a war and she was a combatant, something that was driven home in Iraq when the Mossad had detailed her to the Central Intelligence Agency. Her dual U.S.-Israeli citizenship allowed her to liaise between the Mossad and CIA on matters pertaining to the state of Israel. She missed those days. She missed *that* mission. It was straightforward. She missed the people she had worked with. She missed one in particular.

As the aircraft banked northward and gained altitude, she looked through her window. The buildings turned to huts; the semi-paved road of the capital morphed to red dirt and then to the grasses of the African plains. She wondered how long it would take them to find the man she had killed.

Had she not been a trained intelligence officer she might not have taken note of the green Jeep and faded purple van that stood out in contrast to the light brown grasses that surrounded them. At this low altitude she could still discern the outline of four men looking up at the gigantic plane headed for Europe. Had she not been on the receiving end of RPGs and Katyusha rockets, she might have mistaken the four flashes for the glint off a windshield or perhaps a deformity in the thick plastic window at her shoulder. But she *was* a trained intelligence officer and she *had* been on the receiving end of enemy rockets and missiles.

She thought of her two children. She thought of her husband, who had preceded her in death. She closed her eyes.

Though I walk through a valley of deepest darkness, I fear no harm, for You are with me; Your rod and Your staff—they comfort . . .

For the briefest of moments, she wondered if she was the intended target and just before the first missile impacted the fuselage, she determined that was the only logical conclusion. She was responsible for the innocent lives on the plane: mothers, fathers, brothers, sisters, children, and grandparents, who would never take another breath. She wondered who had betrayed her and she went to her death with the weight of one hundred and twenty-eight additional souls on her already troubled conscience.